YA-YAS IN BLOOM

Also by Rebecca Wells

Little Altars Everywhere
Divine Secrets of the Ya-Ya Sisterhood

YA-YAS IN BLOOM

A NOVEL

REBECCA WELLS

HarperCollins*Publishers*

YA-YAS IN BLOOM. Copyright © 2005 by Rebecca Wells. All rights reserved. Printed in the United States of America. No part of this book may be used or reproduced in any manner whatsoever without written permission except in the case of brief quotations embodied in critical articles and reviews. For information, address HarperCollins Publishers Inc., 10 East 53rd Street, New York, NY 10022.

Grateful acknowledgment is made for permission to quote "Have Yourself a Merry Little Christmas," words and music by Hugh Martin and Ralph Blane; © 1943 (renewed 1971) Metro-Goldwyn-Mayer Inc.; © 1944 (renewed 1972) EMI Feist Catalog Inc. All rights controlled by EMI Feist Catalog Inc. and Warner Bros. Publications U.S. Inc. All rights reserved. Used by permission. Warner Bros. Publications U.S. Inc. Miami, Florida 33014.

Designed by Nancy B. Field

ISBN 0-06-019534-7

Printed in the U.S.A.

To my mother and to the memory of my father,
and
To Thomas, whose love holds me up.

Jeff Walker

Lee Walker

Caitlin Walker

Dorey Walker   Kurt Walker

Baylor Walker + Melissa

Siddalee "Sidda" Walker + Connor McGill

Shepley "Shep" Walker Jr. + Kane   Tallulah "Lulu" Walker

Viviane "Vivi" Joan Abbott + Shepley "Shep" Walker

Peter Abbott   Jezie Abbott

Taylor Charles Abbott + Mary Katherine "Buggy" Abbott

Vivi's Family
+ = Married
⸙ = Children

Illustrated

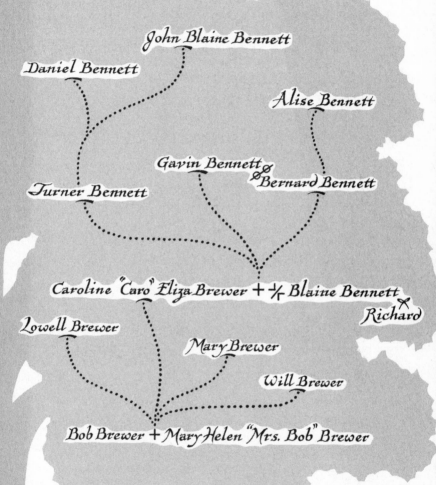

John Blaine Bennett

Daniel Bennett

Alise Bennett

Gavin Bennett ⚭
⚭ Bernard Bennett

Turner Bennett

Caroline "Caro" Eliza Brewer + ⚮ Blaine Bennett
Richard ✕

Lowell Brewer

Mary Brewer

Will Brewer

Bob Brewer + Mary Helen "Mrs. Bob" Brewer

Caro's Family
+ = Married
⚮ = Divorced
✕ = Partners
⊤ = Children
⚭ = Twins

aura Hartman Maestro ©2004

Deep in their roots,
All flowers keep the light.

—THEODORE ROETHKE

CONTENTS

A LITTLE LOVE GIFT

Vivi, January 1994

*M*y name is Viviane Abbott Walker. Age sixty-eight, but I can pass for forty-nine. And I do. I altered my driver's license and kept that gorgeous picture of me when my hair was still thick and I looked like Jessica Lange, and glued it onto every new license I've had since 1975. And not one officer has said a word to me about it. I like to think I am Queen of the Ya-Yas, the sisterhood I've been part of since I was four. But the fact is that *all* of us are queens. The Ya-Yas are not a monarchy. We are a Ya-Ya-cracy. Caro, who is still more alive than anyone I know, even though she is yoked to an oxygen tank most of the time because of her emphysema. Teensy, who is probably the most sophisticated of us, although she doesn't know it, and still cute as a bug. I never know when she'll be home in Thornton—right smack in the heart of Louisiana, where we were all raised—or in Paris or Istanbul. And Necie, our dear, kind Necie, who is still Madame Chairwoman of every charity in the parish, if not the state.

As Ya-Yas, we've grown up, raised our kids—the Petites Ya-Yas—and welcomed our grandchildren, the Très Petites, into this sweet, crazy world. We've helped one another stay glued together through most any life event you can imagine. Except we haven't buried our husbands yet. Well, Caro tried to bury Blaine when she found out he was gay, but decided he and his boyfriend were too much fun and Blaine too good a cook to kill him.

It was the Ya-Yas who brought my oldest child, Sidda, and I back together when we were on the verge of an ugly mother-daughter divorce. They would not stand by and watch it happen, bless their crazy wild hearts. Sidda said it was the three of them and that old scrapbook of mine that I so grandly titled "Divine Secrets" when I was nothing but a kid that helped her understand me. Helped her believe I loved her—even though I was what you might call an "uneven" mother. Sidda has always been melodramatic.

Sidda said she especially loved the snapshots. Snapshots are just snapshots as far as I am concerned. Sidda *analyzes* everything too much, if you ask me. But this morning, I'm the one who wants to study a photograph. And, of all things, it's one with my mother in it.

This morning I woke from the most vivid memory. It was not so much a dream as a completely clear picture of my mother, surrounded by flowers. It triggered an image that I just *knew* I had a photograph of. But I had to have my coffee before beginning the search. Photos in this house are not what you would call organized. You have to be an archaeologist to even form a search team. I've always been too busy *living* to sit around for hours and arrange the photos and snapshots into proper family albums. My life is so full. I might be a card-carrying member of AARP, but I am not retired. Or retiring, for that matter! Hah! I am busy, busy, busy. Work out at the club every single weekday. *Bourrée* with the Ya-Yas. Cruises with Shep. *And* spending time in that garden of his. He's out there so much that in order to see him, I have—for the first time in my life—put on a pair of deerskin gloves and done a very small amount of digging and weeding. He says it will grow on me. I say, What's wrong with being a garden amateur? Mass every Saturday afternoon. Confession twice a month. Reading everything I can get my hands on (except science fiction, too much like my bad dreams). Playing tennis with Teensy and Chick. I am fit as hell. My constitution is amazing. My liver is in fine shape, to the everlasting shock of my doctors. The most trouble I have is a little arthritis in my hands. I'm going to be like one of those women they find in China who live to be one hundred and forty after smoking and drinking all their lives.

Oh, there is pain in my life, but it is harder to put a name to it. Sometimes I lie in bed and wonder if there was a typhoid booster or dental checkup that I forgot to give Sidda, Little Shep, Lulu, or Baylor. Something I missed and should have done. Sometimes I lie in bed and wish I had just *asked* the kids what would have made them feel more loved. But I do not dwell, thank you very much. I follow Necie's words of wisdom: "Just think pretty pink and blue thoughts."

After one strong cup of Dark Roast Community Coffee, I began scrounging through the hutch drawers where I keep most of our family snapshots. I had to pray to Saint Anthony, Patron Saint of Lost Objects, and he finally helped me find the image I wanted. It was stashed in the back of one of the hutch drawers, slightly wrinkled, but there all the same. One of the things I love about Catholicism is that there is a saint for everything. If Sidda can't find a saint for something, that girl just makes one up. Even has one she calls Saint Madge of Menstruation. I don't consider that blasphemous, although there was a time when I would have. Now I just call it creative.

I took the photo and a second cup of coffee out to the window seat in the den, where I can look out on the bayou here at Pecan Grove Plantation. Then I began my meditation.

In the snapshot, my mother wore her wedding ring on her left hand as she held my oldest baby girl's ankle. I snapped the picture with my Brownie myself. There were three generations of us there that day, even though I wasn't in the picture. Even though you can't see me, I'm there. Sidda was barely a year old, and she was being so good. I loved that pink dress. Mother made it for her. I said, "Mother, that fabric must have cost a fortune!" And she said in that martyred tone she always had, "Well, I'd rather spend money on the children than on myself." To say that dress was lovely would be an understatement. It was made of the finest soft pink cotton, with a perfectly stitched Irish linen white collar, and intricate tiny embroidery down the front. The full skirt gave it a bell look, and the hem hit Sidda just above her ankles. A little long, but Mother believed in clothes that children could "grow into." The fact that it was a little long made Sidda look like a little princess, not a regular human little baby girl. She looked like a child who would be painted by one of the Old Masters or the French painters who did portraits of prominent families' children.

Sidda looked like she could not have been born from my body. This was the first time I ever felt that she was not me: that she was someone else. I didn't like that feeling. I'm still not totally comfortable with it. That is one of the reasons Sidda and I will always have to be careful with each other. She explained this to me. But then, she has done a million years of therapy and read scads more books on the subject than I have. I do not obsess like that on things that are not happy.

They say redheads shouldn't wear pink. Ridiculous! My baby girl proved them wrong. Her little curls of red hair made her face glow in that dress.

If I hadn't been so pregnant with the next child already, I might have taken more time to get to know my oldest daughter with the dolphin forehead. She was gorgeous, but she had that big forehead. I called her my "Einstein Baby." I knew she would be a genius. I didn't know in what, but I never doubted for a moment that Siddalee Walker would leave her mark on the world.

Such huge brown eyes that could turn green on you. A perfect little mouth. This was before she fell and scarred her lip slightly, something she expertly disguises with lip liner now that she is grown and beautiful. As a baby, she looked so intense sometimes, that little frown coming across her forehead like stormy weather, like a low front, like a tropical depression. She was definitely my little genius baby, the way she scrutinized everything and everybody. Sometimes I'd say, "Don't look at me like that," even though she wasn't even old enough to speak. I think that child understood what I was saying from the day she was born. When Sidda would look at me like she was trying to figure me out, she would stay so still. It drove me crazy. I couldn't bear it. I would have to scoop her up and shake her a little, get the whole thing moving, just to break up that intensity.

I loved every one of her ten perfect toes, every one of her ten perfect fingers. I loved the color of her skin. She had the coloring of a true redhead, just like I have the coloring of a true blonde. She had that white milky skin. Could never take the sun. I protected her from the sun from the beginning. Even before they knew what horrible things sunlight can do to us. I dressed her in caps with little brims that shielded her from the sun. In fact on the very day that photo was taken, I had only taken off her hat long enough for the photo to be taken, then I put it right back on. Mothers nowadays don't seem to have time for hats. And look at Sidda now: a successful theater director, happily married. She looks ten years younger than she is. Her complexion is simply divine, and it's because of me.

In the photograph Mother was bending over, holding Sidda. She wore her nice starched navy blue linen dress that day. She had actually done something with her hair so she did not look like a maid. The newly opened sycamore leaves were still yellowish and translucent and shimmering with the sun. The spring grass was glowing green, and there must have been a hundred different colored pansy faces staring back at us from the flower beds. It was a perfect April day. Mother had asked me to bring Sidda over, and then she just presented us with the dress. It wasn't a birthday present. It wasn't an Easter dress. It was just something she got in her mind to do. A little love gift. "I saw something like it in a magazine and knew I could make it myself. I did not want any other little girl in the parish to have it but Sidda, so I just changed it slightly. Do you like it?"

"Mother," I said, "it is simply gorgeous. It's pretty as a birthday cake."

We were in Mama's big kitchen with the hearth and the rocking chairs, ten months after Father was killed in a car accident while driving home from his law office. I had the feeling that my mother was coming out of mourning in some way by making that dress for Sidda. If she were a different kind of woman, she might have made herself a beautiful pink dress, but she made it for her first granddaughter.

We put Sidda on the round oak table and carefully pulled that dress over her head. Mother had gotten brand-new dressy socks with ruffles and a pair of the softest white little leather shoes you ever felt. I put them to my cheek just to feel them. I smelled that pure leather and the soft pink satin inside the slipper, and I thought of my mother and how she loved fairy tales, how she believed in fairies. I never listened to her about it, but I said: "Mother, fairies could have made these shoes!"

That made her smile.

"Maybe they did," she said. The happiness in her eyes made my heart hurt.

It was utterly unlike Mother to do this. When I think about it now, I am still touched. Those years are all a blur to me. That's why this image, so clear, is important. While I was having five kids in three years and eight months—including Sidda's twin, the baby I lost—my hormones were doing the craziest tango in town. It has taken me the rest of my life to recover from having those kids so close together. One after the other after the other after the other. No break in between. Dirty diapers, no sleep, and a husband who basically lived at the duck camp.

Mother's yard in early April, with the yellow forsythia and the brilliant magenta azaleas in full bloom, was a beautiful sight. Mother was an excellent gardener, but the gardening genes did not get passed on to me. We walked through Mother's yard with the wild daffodils in clusters everywhere, and after looking at several possible places to take the picture, we decided on that old concrete wall back by the barn. Right at the spot where the crack ran up the side of the wall. There was a Carolina jasmine vine intertwined so completely with a honeysuckle vine that you couldn't tell where one began and the other left off. And the leaves were already so thick that you could hardly see the crack. The three of us had no business being so dressed up—middle of the week, no holiday involved—except for that pink dress that Mother made for Sidda. It gave off magic. The minute I had seen it when I lifted it out of the tissue paper in the box that had been wrapped in pink, I knew I had to change clothes, too. I drove home and put on my best dress, a persimmon-colored linen number with a stylish tunic top over a straight skirt with the belly pegged out. Smartest maternity outfit I had ever seen. I had it copied again and again for all of my pregnancies in different shades of linen and silk. Black, white, beige, and persimmon. You cannot go wrong with those four colors. Especially when the alternative then for pregnant women was these ridiculous sweet-looking things that made you look like a little girl who just happened to have swallowed a basketball. I would die before I'd look like a whale in a muumuu just because I was carrying a baby. These days, pregnant women wear dresses that are stylish and show off their swollen breasts and bellies like they are goddesses. They are sexy! That wasn't the case when I had my babies in the 1950s, but I did my damnedest. I looked good that day.

That picture was about eleven on that fresh morning. Mother and I both wanted to take the photograph to show off that dress, but the day just seemed to call out to be recorded, too. Like the sun and the sky and the trees and the little violets scattered throughout the lawn and the wisteria in bloom were singing out: "Look at me! Remember me!"

And I do remember. April, 1954. I was twenty-eight years old; my mother was fifty-four.

When I took the picture, I thought: Please, Mother, relax and smile. Just for a minute, please don't look like you're working so hard, like it's such a damn strain. For once just relax like you are one of your precious flowers in bloom. Sidda will be okay. She's a good baby. Enjoy yourself, for goodness sakes. But I didn't say anything except, "Smile!"

You can't see that Sidda was a twin in the picture. There's nothing in the picture that even acknowledges it. To look at that picture, you would think that no one died. You would think we were happy all the time: my mother, my baby, and me. The leaves on the trees are full. I'm surprised they are so full. Maybe it was later in the spring, maybe I'm wrong. Just standing there, those trees in the sun seem happy to be a green background for the pink dress and that little bit of red hair on a child who would grow up to become the accomplished, happy woman she is today. Mother's wedding ring is catching some light and the veins in her hands are popping up a little, but she's got her hand in such a way on Sidda's tiny, bitty ankle that it looks graceful. Her hand is so feminine. It's funny; I never thought of my mother as feminine. But there it is in her hand, right there in the picture. So much femininity. Not the kind that comes from frill and fuss, but the kind you notice in a woman's hands who has lived and worked and been betrayed and tried to love in spite of it all. The kind of femininity you notice blooming in your baby girl. The kind that keeps you going—like with the Ya-Yas, my girlfriends of umpteen years. The kind of deep feminine you wish you carried inside all the time.

At that point, Mother had gotten on my nerves a lot. Like for approximately twenty-eight years. But on that day it was good to be with her. It was just the three of us. We were an exclusive little mother-daughter club that no one but Mother, Siddalee, and I could join. We had little cucumber sandwiches afterward, I remember, with coffee and little sugar cookies that Mama had made with pink icing the shape of animals on the front. She could always bake. Her kitchen always smelled like oatmeal, fresh bread, and peanut butter. It was a tonic just to sit in and smell her kitchen. I did it a lot, especially right after I got married. For six months after I got married, Mother cooked every evening meal for Shep and me. Until Shep discovered that I was doing this and trying to pass it off as my own cooking.

He said, "This has got to stop. I'll teach you to cook." And my husband did teach me how to cook. Damn well. How to prepare fish, meat, all kinds of Louisiana wild game, flavors and spices. I learned, and I did it. I had help from Willetta, our maid, I will never say I didn't, but I had food on the table for my four kids no matter what was going on.

Sidda sat in the high chair, and I swear she didn't get a thing on that gorgeous little dress. I thought we should take that dress off before we fed her, but Mother said, "Oh no, let's just put the bib on, everything will be fine."

And it was. Everything was just fine. At any moment things could have gotten ugly between my mother and me. But they didn't. I think it was the flowers. My mother always believed that fairies lived among the flowers. She taught this to Siddalee. These days, when I spend a lot of time in the beautiful garden that Shep has created, I swear I sometimes think she was right. That magical creatures, or at least some kind of *energies*, are coming from flowers and plants and trees, and protecting us from ourselves. Protecting us from the demons inside that want to eat us alive. Fairies, my mother used to say, are small but strong. They don't know the difference between work and play. To them it's all the same. It's all play. My mother knew about seeds and buds and vines and the life of a garden. Maybe she knew other things that I will never learn. But then, miracles do occur.

Sowing Sisterhood Seeds

THE LEGACY OF TEENSY'S PECAN

June 1930

$\mathcal{I}$n the beginning was the word. And the word was *pecan*. Or was it *nostril*?

There are a million stories in Ya-Ya City, but the one the Petites Ya-Yas loved the most was How Vivi Met Teensy. The children would make their mothers tell it over and over, and if the teller forgot one single part, the children would make the raconteur go back and include it. The teller could add in new elements, but she could never leave out the essentials.

That's the way it is with creation stories. You can embroider them, but you must not leave out the fundamental building blocks.

Everything started with Vivi meeting Teensy.

Teensy was four years old, and her Mama loved her and her Daddy spoiled her rotten and her brother Jack would do anything in the world for his baby sister. Nobody could ever tell Teensy Whitman what to do.

One summer day Teensy was bored. She was bored with her jump rope, fed up with her dolls, and irritated by her storybooks. She was irked by every toy she set her eyes on. And so, to keep things exciting, Teensy stuck a pecan—still in its shell—up her nose.

Now, this pecan was not one of the little ones with the tender moist meat. It was one of those big old pecans, hard and dry inside. A fat one, about the size of a fifty-cent piece.

Well, Teensy managed to cram that pecan into her left nostril, but she could not get it out. The nut was wedged in there, and nobody could make it budge. Not Teensy's Mama, Genevieve, who was from the bayou and thought it was funny at first. Not their maid, Shirley, who tried wrapping a hot cloth around Teensy's nose and squeezing. And certainly not Teensy's father in his high-ceilinged office at the bank where Genevieve, in a panic, brought Teensy.

Mr. Whitman was presiding over a very important grown-up businessmen's meeting about a whole lot of money when Genevieve burst in with Teensy and her pecan. Both Genevieve and Teensy explained the dilemma, Teensy's voice sounding a little funny what with one nostril blocked. They thought Mr. Whitman might be able to help because he was such a powerful man. But Teensy's father stood up at his desk and said, "For God's sake, I am a banker, not a doctor! Go right away to Dr. Mott." Then he apologized to the other businessmen, whose mouths were hanging wide open at the sight of a little girl with a whole pecan stuck up her nose.

Genevieve marched her daughter straight over to Dr. Mott's clinic. Teensy wasn't worried. She was having a fine time. She could breathe out of her other nostril, and she adored all the attention. Teensy was a little girl who would rather have attention than food or water. As they walked from the bank to the doctor's office, Teensy called out to each person they passed, "I stuck a pecan up my nose!" She pointed to her nose. "And nobody in town can get it out!"

In Dr. Mott's waiting room, where the seats were hard and there were no magazines like doctor's offices have today, sat Vivi Abbott with her mother, Buggy. Buggy's real name was Mary Katherine, but her mother, Delia, nicknamed her "Buggy" because her little girl claimed she could speak in tongues. If *that* wasn't buggy, that is to say crazy, then Delia didn't know what was.

Vivi had a summer earache, the very worst kind because you can't swim or even get your head wet. Buggy wanted Dr. Mott (who had delivered Vivi) to look inside her daughter's ear with his little instrument with the light on the end and tell them what to do. Vivi, bored and weary of waiting, wished more than anything that something would *happen*.

Teensy Whitman prissed into the doctor's waiting room, leading her mother by the hand, rather than the other way around. Once Teensy was in the room, she walked to the center, put her hands on her hips, and turned in a slow, sassy circle so that everyone could see her. Then she walked over to the couch where her mother was and sat down. Teensy smoothed her dress, the prettiest dress Vivi had ever seen outside of the movies, a crisp blue-and-white-striped frock with the most beautiful hand-smocked pinafore trimmed with handmade lace. Teensy looked like a girl in a storybook. Her hair was jet black and wavy, her eyes so startlingly dark you'd have to call them black. She was a tiny thing, and her feet were clad in soft black leather Mary Janes with little eyelet holes, with a pair of lacy white socks. Dressy shoes were the only thing that Teensy would allow on her feet—something that would continue for the rest of Teensy's life. If she could not wear dressy little shoes, then she would rather go barefoot.

Vivi sat next to Buggy, one hand held up to her sore ear, and studied every move that Teensy made. She could not take her eyes off Teensy. Finally, to Vivi's great excitement, Teensy's eyes met hers. Teensy was on her feet, walking straight over to the chairs where Vivi sat with Buggy. She stopped right in front of them and stood, her hand on one hip, and announced with great pride and a slight Cajun accent: "I stuck a pecan up my nose, and nobody can make it come out! But I can still breathe. Watch!" And she took a deep breath and let it out through her one open nostril, like she was demonstrating an Olympian talent. Then she leaned in closer so that they might view her prize.

"See!" she said, her face three inches from Vivi's. "It won't come out. *Mais jamais!*"

Genevieve stepped to her side. "Are you speaking Bayou again?" she corrected Teensy.

Then to Vivi and Buggy, she explained, "Please do not breathe a word of this to my husband. He forbids us to speak a word of Cajun." Throwing up her arms, she sighed, *"Et bien, ma foi!* What can you do?"

At that, Genevieve gave Vivi and Buggy a big smile and knelt down to her daughter, who was probing the pecan with her delicate little finger just for the sheer pleasure of it. That pecan was power, Teensy decided. If she could get a pecan that big up her nose, just think of all the other things she could do in the world.

"Cher, your father called over, and the doctor is working us right in. Now, please, Teensy, don't touch that pecan again. I don't want you to push it in any farther. *Bien?"*

Teensy's finger did not move from the Louisiana nut. Genevieve looked at Buggy and said, "Please forgive my *fille* for bothering you."

Then, taking Teensy's hand (the one that wasn't up her nose), Genevieve said, *"Cher,* apologize to the *madame."*

But all Teensy did was glare at Buggy. She leaned in toward Buggy as close as she could and wrinkled her nose, pecan and all.

Then Teensy turned to Vivi and asked, "You want to touch it?"

Vivi was dying to touch the pecan. She stretched out her hand, but before her fingers could reach Teensy's nose, Buggy slapped her hand away.

"Don't you dare touch that, Viviane Abbott!" she said. "You're here for an earache, not to touch foreign objects that naughty little girls jam up their noses." Buggy spoke as if touching Teensy's nose pecan would send germs straight into Vivi's ear canal.

Buggy stared at Teensy like she could talk some sense into her. "Child, why did you stick that nut in your nose?" she asked.

"To see," Teensy replied, with a nasty little grin on her face, "if it would fit."

Then the glorious tiny creature began giggling. The sound of her giggles made Vivi feel like she was standing under a waterfall. Vivi started giggling too, and for the first time in two days, she forgot all about her earache.

At that moment, the nurse stepped into the waiting room and announced, "Mrs. Whitman, the doctor will see you and your daughter now."

Genevieve turned to Buggy and said, "So lovely to have chatted with you." Then she reached over and touched her hand lightly to Vivi's sore ear and said, "*Se rétablir, cher.*" Get well, dear one. Vivi felt for a minute like she did when the priest on Saint Blaise's Feast Day crossed the candles and blessed her throat. Only Genevieve was a *lady* blessing Vivi's *ear.*

Vivi watched Teensy and Genevieve walk toward the door that led back to the examining rooms. Teensy turned around and looked at Vivi the whole time. Just as Teensy and Genevieve stepped out of the waiting room, Vivi leapt up and ran after them.

"Get back over here right away, Viviane Joan Abbott," Buggy said in a loud, angry whisper.

Vivi obeyed her mother. She sat back down next to Buggy. She had forgotten all about her earache. She started swinging her legs back and forth, and she knew something good was about to happen in her life. She could feel a happy tingle charging through her whole body.

Buggy reached down and put a hand on Vivi's thigh and said, "Stop that. Stop swinging those legs. Act like a lady."

Buggy took out a handkerchief and dabbed at her nose. "The rudeness of those two. Downright rude behavior. To march right into the doctor's office ahead of us when we have been waiting twenty minutes. Rudeness, that's all it is."

Vivi was not thinking about rudeness. She was thinking about how Teensy had winked at her just as she left the waiting room. It was a magical wink, the kind that not many people can achieve, regardless of their age. Teensy knew how to completely close her right eye without the left one even fluttering. In that moment, Vivi fell in love with Teensy Whitman. That wink was a *promise.* A promise from Teensy's dark gorgeous eyes that said: *You haven't seen the last of me yet. There's more where this came from.*

Vivi began to practice winking the way Teensy did. She began planning—just as soon as she got home—to stick something up her nose. Maybe not a big pecan with the shell still on, but at least a shelled lima bean or a thimble. Or maybe even one of her brother Pete's marbles. In five minutes, Teensy Whitman had made Vivi sure the world was bigger than she had thought it was. Vivi could not wait to see the Pecan Princess again. Vivi was only four years old, but that laughter was something she knew she could not live without.

On a dare from a pediatrician friend in New Orleans some years later, Dr. Mott took certain choice objects he'd removed from children's bodies during his long years as a physician and put them under glass. When the Petites Ya-Yas were growing up, they went with their mothers into the updated waiting room of the clinic, which had been taken over and remodeled by Dr. Mott's son. Unless they were very sick, the children always made a beeline to the glass display case labeled "Foreign Objects Removed from Children's Bodies."

The objects hung like trophies, and Vivi's brood studied them as though seeing them anew each time they set foot in young Dr. Mott's office—which was often, since childhood illnesses ricocheted among them with great frequency. Siddalee especially loved to examine this collection of objects. There was the coin section: a nickel, a quarter, a fifty-cent piece, and an actual silver dollar. There was a thimble, a small metal pencil sharpener, and a top that looked like it came from a tube of Brylcreem. Each item was dated. Above all the other objects was Teensy's pecan. It was starting to crumble a little with age, but it was still intact. The big pecan was displayed in its own small case. The handwritten card underneath it read: "Nut from Teensy Whitman's left nostril. June 18, 1930."

Teensy inspired a legacy of her own among Thornton children. Indeed, so many Thornton kids knew her name from Dr. Mott's office that, when they met her for the first time, their first reaction was: "Are you the Teensy of the nose pecan?"

Once, years later, when Vivi and her four children were in the waiting room, they watched a lady walk up to the receptionist and complain about the trophy case. "You must take that horrid hanging piece away. It only gives children ideas. I insist you remove it. It is tasteless and grotesque."

Finally, Vivi, unable to endure any more of the lady's harping, stood up. "Excuse me," she said to the woman, "I don't mean to interrupt, but listen to me, Dahlin: *life* is *grotesque*. So shut up and stop your whining."

The pecan remained on display in all its glory throughout the

Petites Ya-Yas' whole childhood in Thornton. Not as grotesque, but as a talisman that represented the meeting of Vivi Abbott and Teensy Whitman, members of the Ya-Ya tribe, who made themselves up as they went along and always tried to see what they could hold inside and still keep breathing.

GOPHER GIRLS OF GOD

August 1930

*V*ivi and Teensy had grown thick as thieves, even though they'd only known each other for two months. They played together every single day Buggy would let them, and Vivi spent happy nights at Teensy's house, where she got to know Jack, Teensy's brother, and Shirley, their maid, and the whole rich household, which only grew quiet when Mr. Whitman was home—which was, luckily, a rare event. Genevieve had introduced them to "Coco Robichaux," a character who had been firmly implanted in her own imagination while she was growing up on the bayou. No one knew who Coco was or where she lived or what she looked like. But she was a bad, bad little girl, and she received the blame for everything.

Every time a little girl was naughty, Genevieve would say (as her *Mère* had told her): "Oh, surely *you* didn't do that! Only Coco Robichaux could be so naughty as to do something that bad!"

Coco Robichaux possessed all the faults that any girl could possibly have. Coco Robichaux was the perfect excuse for anything and everything.

This did not set well with Vivi's mother, Buggy, not one bit. She told Vivi, "Stop blaming things on that little devil Coco. That's what Coco is, a devil-girl."

And yet the way Genevieve employed Coco Robichaux seemed to have a corrective effect on Teensy and Vivi. At least sometimes. When Genevieve blamed Coco Robichaux for something naughty, they hung their heads and responded, "Oh, that *bad* little Coco Robichaux. I'm sure glad I'm not her." Of course, they also used Coco to their own advantage, blaming bad things that they had done on her. The one person who Vivi couldn't do this with was her father. She had tried it once and had the belt-whipping marks to prove it. After that, she kept quiet about Coco Robichaux around Mr. Taylor Abbott.

Secretly, the girls chattered constantly about Coco Robichaux. They were always on the lookout for her, girl spies ever searching for the brave, sassy little she-devil "Coco Robichaux." They knew she was mythical, but they also believed she might be real. How they longed to meet a little girl their very age who could do such bad things and just keep on dancing! Once they thought they saw her under an oak tree with the long gray hair of Spanish moss hanging all over it down by the river. Another time they thought they spotted Coco near the storeroom of Miss Beverly's beauty parlor, where Genevieve had her beautiful black hair cared for. But Coco scooted around so smoothly, fast as greased lightning. So they were never sure. Not to mention that Coco could disappear into thin air if she wanted to!

Because Coco Robichaux could be anywhere and take any form, she could be in church, too. Once Vivi and Teensy thought of this, Our Lady of Divine Compassion Catholic Church became another place where they stayed on the lookout for their magical friend. They decided it would be just like Coco Robichaux to disguise herself as the most saintly little girl in church, and then do all sorts of bad things and laugh at people because they thought she was so sweet. Coco would enjoy it all the more because it was in church!

For several Sundays, Vivi and Teensy had their eyes glued on a little girl who sat with her large family on the Lady Altar side of the Our Lady of Divine Compassion Church. The little girl was one of ten children. The size of that family was a sure sign that they were holier than Vivi's and Teensy's smaller families. This girl was just too good to be true. She knelt and prayed and genuflected so perfectly that they were *convinced* that the girl must be Coco Robichaux in her goody-goody disguise! They loved the girl's long dark brown braids of hair that hung down to her waist, and the fact that she carried a little purse where she put her own little prayer book and rosary beads. They decided that if they were right, then all they had to do was yank her pigtail, and she would reveal herself as The One and Only Coco Robichaux. It would be a miracle! For weeks they discussed this pigtailed little girl in the patois unique to their friendship. At age four, they already had code words that nobody else could understand. After much conferring, they came up with a plan, complete with signals and timing. They could get into trouble, especially Vivi, but they decided that revealing Coco Robichaux in all her bad splendor was worth it.

Their target day was Mass on the morning of Friday, August 15, 1930, the holy feast day of the Blessed Virgin Mary's Assumption into heaven. They loved that Mary's whole body had just flown up into the sky! If that could happen, then maybe the Holy Lady would help them reveal Miss Goody Two-shoes as the true Coco bad girl she really was.

At Divine Compassion Catholic Church, each family had its own pew, a tradition that was sacrosanct. If a stranger came in looking for a seat, he had to stand rather than sit in an assigned pew. The Whitmans—Genevieve, her husband, Newton Whitman, their son, Jack Whitman, and Teensy—sat in the third row on the Saint Joseph side of the church, which was the pulpit side. Vivi and her family—Buggy, Taylor Abbott, and her brother Pete—sat in the fifth row back from the Lady Altar.

Oh, how Vivi and Teensy hated to sit still during Mass. It made their bodies *hurt*. Sitting still through a lengthy Catholic Mass in Latin was not made for healthy four-year-old girls. They longed to move and dance and squirm and shimmy. Their plan was to crawl under the pews and do a little traveling.

On most Sundays and holy days, Mr. Abbott did not come to Mass. Claiming he was at his law office, he rode his horses and drank champagne with the horsey crowd out at Mockingbird Park. The previous Sunday, when Mr. Abbott was absent, Vivi tried ducking down underneath the pew and crawling back a few rows. It was a tight fit, but she managed it, even though she got her little hiney spanked when Buggy got her home. On the other side of the aisle, Teensy tried the same trick and was more successful. The space between prayer kneelers and the underside of pews was pretty tight, but at four years old, they were both still quite small. The intrepid unveilers hadn't traveled far, but now they knew the underpew railroad could provide an avenue to Coco Robichaux.

On this holy day, Vivi and Teensy were furious that their mothers had dragged them to Mass even though it wasn't even a Sunday! They had just been to Mass what seemed like yesterday. When Vivi protested, Buggy explained to her, "The Feast of the Assumption of the Blessed Virgin Mary is the greatest of all feast days. Because she was the mother of Baby Jesus and because she didn't have any original sin on her soul, God took her up to heaven with her whole body just like it was. Her body will never rot and have worms crawling all over it like the rest of us who were born with mortal sin on our souls. No, she will live in heaven forever and speak in tongues and understand her daughters like me who know how to speak in tongues, even though nobody around here listens."

Actually, Vivi did listen to her mother speak in tongues, something Buggy did only when Mr. Abbott was out of the house. Buggy explained to Vivi that the Holy Spirit inspired her to speak in tongues. At first Vivi thought it was a game, and would jabber right back at her mother, but when Buggy made her go to bed without dinner for "making fun of the Holy Spirit," Vivi got out of the way when Buggy started making those spooky sounds.

It was hot and sticky on Assumption Day, even with all the windows open at Divine Compassion. Vivi tried to stop thinking of millions of worms crawling all over her body. The priest, Father O'Donohue, was filling in for their regular parish priest, who had been called to visit his sick mother in Donaldsonville. When Father O'Donohue turned to the congregation and spoke in English, he said a lot of words about the Blessed Virgin being lifted up because she was so pure and how she was dressed in the sun with the moon under her feet. Vivi didn't understand most of what he was saying, but she liked the part about Mary having a crown of stars. She wanted one for herself.

When Father started in on how the Lord had brought his enemies to naught, Vivi looked across the aisle and caught Teensy's eye. Teensy gave her famous wink—the signal they'd planned in advance—and in an instant, both girls ducked down and began crawling under the pews. The girls moved so fast and sure that they disappeared before their mothers hardly noticed. Vivi and Teensy slithered through worshippers' feet, crawling over people's shoes and ladies' dress hems, and scooted through Our Lady of Divine Compassion on their hands and knees underneath the pews. They delighted in moving too fast for anyone to grab them. Not that people didn't try. Not that Mr. Gremillion didn't catch the back of Teensy's heel and try to pull her back where everyone could see her. But Teensy was too swift for him. She shook her foot loose and kept on crawling.

You could hear the murmur of the parishioners spreading throughout the church. No one dared speak aloud for fear of seeming disrespectful, but there was a buzz of whispering and grunts and a wave of head-shaking and hard stares at Buggy and Genevieve, as though the mothers were sinning through their teeth to have such behavior in their offspring. The congregation of Divine Compassion had little doubt as to which children were causing the disruption. You could just look at Teensy and Vivi and know they were "high-spirited," to put it mildly. Each of the girls babbled constantly, dropped prayer books on the floor for the fun of it, put their rosary beads on their heads like Cleopatra headdresses, and threw the church bulletin out into the aisle just so they could get up from their seat, priss over, and pick it up. Among the congregation there had been talk about whether these two little girls should even be brought to Mass if they couldn't learn to behave. But both Buggy and Genevieve believed it was important for their daughters to attend Mass, even if the two girls weren't exactly angelic.

On this Assumption Day, both mothers wondered if they'd been wrong. Their girls were bellying their way under the pews, making good time. Fast-moving little girl gophers of God.

Teensy got to the back of the church and scampered from the Saint Joseph Altar side to the Lady Altar side, her white Mary Jane shoes tapping against the tiles of the church floor. Little did people know how much restraint it took her not to break into an all-out tap dance.

Next thing everyone knew, both girls popped up in the pew just behind Denise Kelleher and jerked on her pigtail so hard that she let out a piercing cry. When she turned around, Vivi and Teensy stared at her, waiting for her transformation into Coco Robichaux the Great. After all, if bread and wine could be turned into body and blood, then this little girl could become their heroine. But the surprise, alarm, and hurt in Necie's eyes told them they were wrong. Vivi let out a loud shriek, followed by a squeal from Teensy. They sounded like they were making up their own wild liturgy.

This girl was *not* Coco Robichaux. Coco Robichaux would have laughed out loud like a hyena, then prissed them up the aisle to the front of the main altar, where all the action was. Once there, as Father O'Donohue droned on about the purity of the Virgin Mary, Coco Robichaux would have raised their high little-girl voices in a rousing version of their favorite song:

> "K-K-K-Katy, Beautiful Katy,
> You're the only g-g-g-girl that I could adore!"

Then Coco would have led them in knocking down the altar boys and yanking their red garments up over their ears so the girls could dress up in them. Coco Robichaux would have climbed into the pulpit, shoved the priest aside, and begun singing at the top of her voice. Oh, Coco Robichaux would have been a brave, crazy, short Joan of Arc!

Not so with Denise Rose Kelleher.

This child was a meek and mild Saint Theresa the Little Flower kind of a girl if there ever was one. Seeing the sweet, scared face of Denise Rose Kelleher, the gopher girls of God ducked back down. But by then their mothers were upon them, dragging the little sinners out the side door of the church in humiliation. A collective *tsk-tsk* could be heard throughout the church.

Not one hour after the dinner dishes had been washed and put away, and fresh flowers were placed next to the Blessed Mother's statue in the front hallway, Buggy called Mrs. Kelleher to set up a meeting of the mothers and daughters with Father O'Donohue. Buggy said it was urgent that they seek absolution before Father O'Donohue left Thornton.

Mrs. Kelleher and Buggy knew each other from the Ladies Altar Society. Buggy, a devoted worker bee, donated all her finest flowers to the church, sometimes leaving her own yard with bald spots and her own house empty of color or fragrance. The House of God required—no, *deserved*—flowers. The reason flowers existed was to venerate Our Lady and her Holy Son.

Necie's mother, Rose Kelleher, was head of Our Lady of Divine Compassion Altar Society. Mrs. Kelleher knew how to keep meetings running, and how to give out assignments. She knew enough about each person's garden to know who should contribute to decorate the altar.

The meeting took place at the rectory the following Wednesday. Vivi was scrubbed, dressed, and, after a good swat on her backside, instructed about how to behave. She was to apologize to Mrs. Kelleher and to Mrs. Kelleher's daughter, but first and foremost to Father O'Donohue. Buggy had made that very clear: "There are such things as mortal sins, Viviane. And even though you have not reached the age of reason, you can still burn in hell for the way you hurt the Baby Jesus in church on the very day you should have venerated His Mother on her day of Assumption into heaven. Now you must confess your sin and receive penance and forgiveness, if Father sees fit."

They arrived at the front door of the old brick rectory across the street from the church, and a maid led Buggy and Vivi into the priest's office. There they sat together on a love seat near the window. Soon Mrs. Kelleher and her daughter showed up. Buggy murmured prayers under her breath continuously. Mrs. Kelleher and her daughter sat in two straight-backed chairs against the far wall across from the large desk, which dominated the room. Vivi stared holes at the pigtailed girl and wondered how she ever thought such a little sissy could possibly be the brave and valiant Coco Robichaux.

Soon the last mother and daughter entered the room. Genevieve was wearing a peach-colored frock with a ruffle at the hem. Her hat was in a matching color, and the way it perched on her head told the world that she was not worried about burning in hell.

"*Bonjour*, Madame Abbott," Genevieve said, smiling at Buggy. "*Bonjour*, Mademoiselle Vivi."

What a relief it was for Vivi to see Genevieve's smile. It gave Vivi hope that she would not burn in hell forever after all. It made Vivi love Genevieve all the more.

Teensy looked at Vivi and bared her teeth like a wild animal. Vivi crossed her eyes and stuck out her tongue, then burst out laughing, but stopped the moment her mother pinched her arm.

Genevieve and Teensy sat in two wing-backed chairs that faced the desk.

Soon, Father O'Donohue, a muscular, full-bodied man with bushy eyebrows and clear blue eyes, opened the door and swished by them in his long robe.

"Good afternoon, ladies. Little girls. How are you on this lovely day that the Lord has given us?"

He sat behind his desk and made a steeple with his hands. He looked from girl to girl, waiting for them to speak. No one answered.

Finally, Buggy said, "Father, forgive our daughters, for they know not what they do. Please, I have done my best every moment of the day and night to raise a girl that would please the Baby Jesus and the Holy Lady. I do not know where I have gone wrong. For her to have mocked you and Our Lord so gravely is a horrible thing. I have not been able to eat or sleep since it happened."

The door opened, and the maid brought in a plate of lemon squares and Irish soda bread and sugar cookies and a large pitcher of sweetened iced tea and set them on a table beside the desk. "Well, then," Father said, "I hope you'll allow yourself to break your fast with us.

"Please"—he gestured to all in the room—"enjoy the fruits of our Lord's bounty."

Teensy immediately jumped up and piled three lemon squares on one of the tiny china plates with the Knights of Columbus insignia. She sat back down and began to bite into one, dangling her legs, always happy to put anything sugary in her mouth.

"*Merci, Père*," said Genevieve, standing and crossing to the table. "How *délicieux*." After helping herself to a glass of tea, Genevieve sat back down and took a sip. She wiped her mouth with a small linen napkin, then said, "That was a sermon *très inspirant* you gave on Assumption Day Mass, *Père*."

"Thank you, Mrs. Whitman. I am glad to hear that at least one of the parishioners here thinks so."

"*Oui*," Genevieve said, "all of us did."

Buggy cleared her throat.

"Isn't that right, Mrs. Abbott?" Genevieve said.

"Father, it was as if the Holy Spirit Himself had written it," Buggy enthused. "That is why it is even more shameful that these young daughters of Mary acted so sinfully."

"Indeed," Father said, helping himself to several slices of soda bread and iced tea. He plopped a lemon square in his mouth, washed it down with a gulp of iced tea. Then he said, "Praise God for sweets."

Leaning back in his chair, he looked around the room. Vivi and Teensy gave him big smiles. Buggy bowed her head.

Father's gaze landed on Necie, and he said, "Denise Rose Kelleher, what a fine Irish name. Miss Denise Rose, what is it you wish to say here today?"

A blush rose up and spread all over Necie's face, extending even to her ears. She could not speak.

Mrs. Kelleher gently touched her daughter's shoulder. "Father has asked you a question, Denise."

"Yes ma'am," Necie said. Still she could not speak to the priest.

Father O'Donohue reached over to the table and made up a plate of lemon squares and sugar cookies and poured a glass of tea. He got up from his desk and brought it over and handed it to Necie.

"There you go, girl, have a sweet. And say something. You're Irish, aren't you? The blarney can't have passed you by."

Mrs. Kelleher laughed softly, then got up and poured herself a glass of tea. She watched her daughter and waited.

Father sat back down and took another bite of soda bread.

"Well," Necie said, barely audible, "I would please like to know why they pulled my pigtails. I didn't do anything to them. Is it because they don't like me?"

"No!" Teensy said, almost knocking over her plate of lemon squares.

"No!" Vivi said. She stared at Teensy, then continued. "It's because, well—it's because we thought you were someone we know."

"Really, it's because we want to play with you," Teensy said. "But you're so good you don't even notice us. You don't even look at us after Mass on the front steps of church. You don't even act like we're there when we walk by you at coffee time in the parish hall. You act like a midget saint."

"I am not a midget saint," Necie said. "I see yall."

"Why don't you play with us, then?" Vivi asked.

"You don't ask me."

"We're asking you right now!" Teensy said. *"S'il vous plait."*

Father O'Donohue, who was back in his chair, wiping his mouth with the back of his hand, stared at Vivi and then at Teensy. "So you two think the way to make friends is to pull hair, do you? Is this some rare custom that only exists here in Thornton at Our Lady of Divine Compassion?"

"No, Father," Vivi said.

"No, *Père,*" Teensy said.

"We're sorry," they said in unison.

"Don't be telling me you're sorry," Father said. "It's not my hair—what's left of it—that you pulled. It's Miss Denise Rose Kelleher's lovely long pigtails that you jerked."

Teensy and Vivi looked at each other, and then at Necie. "We're sorry," they said, again in unison.

"Ask her if she'll forgive you," Father said.

"Will you forgive me?" Vivi asked.

"Yes," Necie said.

"How about me?" Teensy asked.

"I forgive you too," said Necie.

"Then," Father said, "if Miss Denise Kelleher forgives you, so do I. But I warn you: if you ever pull such a stunt again in the sanctity of church, you will not be met with such mercy. Do you understand?"

"Yes, Father," Vivi said.

"Oh, yes, Father," Teensy echoed.

Each mother heaved a sigh. But Buggy was not going to let it drop. She was the mother of a guilty daughter, and it was her responsibility. "Father, I heartily beg your forgiveness for the pagan way my daughter behaved during Mass during your most inspiring sermon. I would like to ask you to please give her a punishment. I will leave it in your hands. Thank you, Father."

The priest studied Buggy for a long time. "Mrs. Abbott," he said, speaking slowly, "are you a happy woman?" He reached over to the tray of sugar cookies, popped one into his mouth, and kept looking at Buggy. "Come and talk to me sometime, will you? Not at Holy Confession, just here at the rectory."

"Yes, Father, certainly, Father. When would you like me to come?"

"Sometime soon, before I leave, and before the end of summer demands too much of your time in your garden. I've heard so much about the flowers you grow and grace Our Holy Lady's altar with. Our Lord has given you the gift of the green thumb indeed."

Buggy bowed her head. "Thank you, Father," she said, shyly.

"Now, as far as you two," he said, standing and pointing with large, strong, thick fingers toward Vivi and Teensy. "Stand up and come over here," he said, pointing to a spot before him.

Vivi and Teensy obeyed. He stood before them and stared from one girl to the next.

"Tell me, in the name of all saints, why you two lasses would interrupt my overly long Assumption feast day sermon with such clamoring? Just give me one good answer."

Vivi and Teensy were silent. They wanted to look at each other, but couldn't. Not with Father looming over them.

Vivi gave a false cough, hoping she might make him think she was getting sick. She coughed again. Then again.

"That is one very poor imitation of a sick person," Father said. "I asked you a question."

Vivi was not certain what "clamoring" meant, but she thought she'd give it her best. She thought for a moment, then her eyes lit up. "We were talking in tons, Father. We were trying to get Denise to talk in tons too."

"*Tongs!*" chirped Teensy. "Yes, Father, we were talking in *tongs!*"

"The Holy Ghost *told* us to talk in tons—I mean tongs!" Vivi said.

Buggy dropped her face into her hands.

Father O'Donohue kept staring at them. He rubbed his hand across his face. Vivi and Teensy did not know what he was going to do next. Genevieve gave what sounded like a laugh that turned into a snort because of her attempt to stop it.

Father O'Donohue finally shook his head. He turned his back to them and stared at the books on the tall bookshelves behind the desk. They could hear him laughing, but because he was not facing them, they could pretend they had not heard him.

"Oh, I see. Tongs, it is. Speaking in *tongs?* And because the Holy Spirit told you to?" Father O'Donohue dropped his chin to his chest and let out a small chuckle.

"Something got into you girls, but sure as God made the blue Lakes of Killarney, it was not the Holy Spirit."

"It was Coco Robichaux!" Teensy said, then clasped her hand over her mouth.

"What did you say, child?" Father asked.

Teensy looked at her mother, who almost imperceptibly shook her head no.

Teensy gave Father O'Donohue the biggest smile she had. "I said, *'Merci, Père.'*"

"And how did you girls get away from your parents? Do you really crawl under the pews? You're little gophers, to be sure. Tell me how you manage it—so I can prevent other little heathens from doing it the self-same."

"You have to be smart," Vivi said.

"And real little," Teensy said.

"All right," Father said, standing and shaking his head again. "I have Benediction to say in twenty minutes at the church. I want you mothers and daughters to stay in this office and not leave until every bit of those sweets has been eaten and that good strong iced tea is gone."

He got up to leave, but stopped at the door and turned back to them.

"And try to contemplate that God sent us here to love Him and worship Him and venerate the mother of his Blessed Son. Also keep in mind that He is a generous God who does not expect perfection, but does expect reverence. God needs good little girls. But sometimes He also needs busy little gophers."

With that, Father O'Donohue walked out of the room and closed the door.

"*Chers*," Genevieve said, getting up and crossing to the table with the refreshments. "It seems we got the matter settled, *non?*"

Buggy leaned forward and asked, "But don't you think *some* kind of punishment is in order for Viviane, if not all the girls? I wonder if Father was not too lenient in the matter."

Genevieve smiled. She looked at Buggy and then at Mrs. Kelleher. "What do you think, Mrs. Kelleher?" Genevieve asked.

"Punishment, I think," Rose Kelleher said, "is not a good way for friendships to start."

Buggy was silent for a moment. She looked at the beautiful flower arrangements on the flower stand in Father's office. She looked at her daughter Viviane. For a moment, she forgot about upholding Holy Mother Church and how important it was for her daughter to behave like a good daughter of Mary.

"Now, Madame Abbott," Genevieve said, "will you help us follow Father's orders? We've got plenty of delectable sweets to enjoy here."

At that, Mrs. Rose Kelleher stood to help Genevieve distribute the refreshments. She handed Buggy a glass of iced tea and a plate of lemon bars.

"Thank you, Mrs. Kelleher," Buggy said.

"Won't you please call me 'Rose'? If our daughters are going to be friends, I hope we will, too."

"*Mais oui!*" Genevieve said, raising her glass of tea in a toast.

Necie swallowed almost the entire glass of tea she had been holding, before daintily wiping the sides of her mouth with a napkin. Then she ate two lemon bars one after the other.

"Moms, can I have another lemon bar?"

"Of course, Necie, help yourself."

For the first time since she entered the room, Necie rose and crossed to the table, where she helped herself to another sweet.

"*Necie?!*" Vivi squealed. "Is that your real name?"

"I love that name!" Teensy said. "*C'est bon!*"

Necie smiled. "It's my nickname. I like it better than 'Denise.' My *friends* call me 'Necie.'"

Buggy rose from the love seat and walked over to admire the flowers and chat with Mrs. Kelleher. She thought of telling them *her* real name, too. But she did not.

The three girls took over the love seat, their legs dangling in rhythm.

Necie took another long sip of tea. Then, out of the blue, she let out a burp. A very loud, nonladylike, non-good-girl burp. Vivi and Teensy sat beside her and began to crack up. Necie hid her face in her hands. Each mother was still for a moment, unsure of the situation.

"Necie, Sweetie," Mrs. Kelleher said, reaching for Necie's hands. "Are you all right? You aren't crying, are you?"

Necie removed her hands from her face. She had not been crying. She had been trying to hide how hard she was laughing. Once her hands dropped from her face, little-girl laughter ripped through her body like it had been pushing to get out. She started laughing harder than she ever had in her short life. Laughing at a burp. Something she never thought she would ever do. Burps were to be hidden.

But not from her new friends.

Burps were just one more thing in the wide world to laugh at. And Necie was starting to see how funny it was to be a little girl alive in this life. She had nine brothers and sisters and dozens of cousins. But now she had two friends who turned church into an adventure. Now she had two real friends who had not found Coco Robichaux but would keep looking for her the rest of their lives. That didn't matter now, though. Nothing mattered except that they had found one another. In the whole wide world, they had found true sister-friends. They would crawl on the ground to reach each other. They would not let one another get away. They would create their own original liturgy, if that's what it took to stay together.

HOBNOBBIN' AT THE BOB

December 1930

One Saturday evening in December, Genevieve brought little Vivi Abbott and Necie Kelleher along with Teensy to see a show at The Bob Theater. She'd had her dressmaker, Mrs. Boyette, make them little red velvet frocks, each slightly different, but with matching white lacy collars. In tiny stitching on the collar in the back was a sprig of mistletoe, hand-stitched so that only the most astute eye could even see it. But the girls knew it was there, and they felt like walking Christmas gifts!

There was a magic show on tour: "Master Giovanni and His Miraculous Galaxy of Mystery." In order to ensure the girls' attendance, Genevieve had creatively explained to Buggy that the magician anonymously donated three-quarters of all the money he made to the Catholic Church. In Buggy's mind, that turned Master Giovanni from a devil magician to a man who, sinful though his profession was, paid Mother Church for every magic trick he pulled in front of all those innocent eyes. Buggy then explained this to Mrs. Kelleher, and now all three girls were headed for a night of non-Catholic magic.

Vivi was over the moon at spending this cold December Saturday night with the divine Genevieve and her sassy little daughter Teensy and her new friend, Necie. Genevieve Whitman was the kindest and most beautiful lady Vivi could imagine walking the Louisiana earth. She was beautiful with flashing eyes and jet-black hair, and you got the feeling that life was more exciting when you were with her, that the world was bigger. She sang a lot, and she often suggested that they *dance* instead of walk. She'd say even about the most regular everyday things: *"Faire une danse, filles!"* Throw a dance, girls, throw a dance!

Genevieve had become friendly with Mister and Mrs. Bob Brewer, who owned The Bob in Thornton, along with several other theaters, their flagship theater being The Robert down in New Orleans. The first time the Brewers met her in their theater, they thought Genevieve was part of the touring act that had just arrived from playing in Shreveport. Given her gypsy skirt and huge gold hoop earrings and a bright orange turban on her head, this was understandable. Vaudeville players still came through town occasionally, offering temptation to souls like Genevieve to run away with the circus. Genevieve loved the smell of greasepaint and popcorn; she loved the singers and dancers and piano players; she loved the men who hauled sets and transformed The Bob into another world. She always arrived at the theater early to get the best seats.

"Welcome to our town," Mister Bob had said when Genevieve walked in long before any other customers arrived. "We look forward to your show being a big hit."

"Oh, *non, non, chers,*" she had said, thrilled to be mistaken for a performer. "I wish I were a player! I am a wife and mother. This is my daughter Teensy, and sometime you will soon meet my boy, Jacques. We go to Divine Compassion. You've seen us there."

"Well," said Mister Bob, nodding, "welcome to our theater. We hope you and your family will find a happy home away from home here."

"Oh, yes," Mrs. Bob said. "And your daughter must meet our daughter, Caro. They'll get along gangbusters. Caro loves other little moving picture nuts."

"Well, my Teensy is a nut, I guarantee," Genevieve said, laughing. "She didn't fall far from the tree!"

Not everyone in Thornton thought so highly of Genevieve Aimee St. Clair Whitman. She was married to one of the richest men in town, Newton S. Whitman III, the president of Garnet Savings and Loan. They met when she was going to the Ursulines Academy in New Orleans, compliments of a rich friend of her bayou trapper father. Her patron thought such a smart girl should have a first-rate education. Newton Whitman was confident that he was just the man to tame the wildly beautiful and willful Genevieve. Any woman that ravishing could be turned into a refined southern lady who would make the perfect wife and mother of his children. Or so he thought. It was like wild fillies. You break them, that's all. He was wrong. Mr. Whitman could pinch Genevieve's spirit like a tight girdle to the point of pain. But he could never tame her.

Genevieve did not want to be a "lady" in the same way that Mr. Whitman and most Thorntonians expected. Her language was still peppered with Cajun French, and she dressed in her own distinctive fashion. She wore turbans when she felt like it, and she wore earrings that didn't match because it was fun, and her lipstick was always a little more siren-colored than most good Catholic ladies wore in the little river town of Thornton, Louisiana. Some were offended by Genevieve's hairdos and hats, and claimed that the way she wrapped a scarf around her head made her look more like a Negress in a head rag than the wife of a respectable banker. Genevieve decided to take this as a compliment. When she thought of the other Anglo ladies her age in that town, she said, she'd rather be a Negress than a half-dead proper white woman.

Genevieve loved the vaudeville acts, and she adored the moving pictures. Entering The Bob took her to different worlds, even though it was only a fifteen-minute walk from her house. Genevieve took Teensy, and often Jack, with her to every single function ever held at The Bob, unless one of them was seriously ill. Genevieve always said, "Nothing picks me up quicker than a movie, a Coca-Cola, and a box of popcorn. I could walk in feeling like I didn't want to live anymore, and walk out on cloud nine."

She didn't know the difference between a first-rate show and a third-rate show, and she didn't care. It was all entertainment. It was razzle and dazzle, and that was enough for her. She went to almost every performance of any live act that came to town, and she saw each movie at least three times.

Over time Genevieve had become more than just a regular. The theater and the Bobs themselves became *en famille*. If the ticket taker, Miss Lelia, was sick, Genevieve took her place. If the concessionaire Gerald Giroux's wife was sick—and she was often poorly—Genevieve would sell Mars Bars and Jujubes and Coca-Colas from the soda fountain. This drove Mr. Whitman half-mad with shame and embarrassment. The thought of the wife of the president of Garnet Savings and Loan selling candy in public caused him to threaten her more than once. He forbade her to work at that theater like a common shopgirl. Genevieve would just nod, smile, and say, "*Oui*, yessir." Then when one of the usherettes came down with a bad case of pneumonia, Genevieve donned the usherette uniform, complete with crisp cap and flashlight, and took her place.

Genevieve was an uppity woman, one that her husband did not seem to be able to control. This made her both mysterious and glamorous to the little girls. She looked like an imported exotic visiting Thornton. As for the Brewers, they cherished Genevieve. They became close in the way you only do when you work with someone.

As Genevieve and her three Christmas elves approached the theater, the red light from the huge neon *B*, *O*, and *B* letters (stacked one on top of the other above the marquee) cast a warm rosy glow down on the four of them. It made Vivi, Teensy, and Necie's velvet dresses look even redder and gave them a magical, dreamlike softness as the three little girls twirled around in the cold air. The girls were captivated by the Christmas lights that rimmed The Bob's curved, modern ticket booth. The wide shiny metal trim of the booth wrapped above and below the windows, and the golden light from inside spilled over the woman who talked through the small metal circle set in the glass. For the holidays, Mister and Mrs. Bob had also decorated the booth with swags of pine boughs and red holly berries below the ticket taker's window, and the pine needles smelled so good in the cold air. On the front doors of the theater there were two big wreaths decorated with pinecones. Shimmering through the carefully ironed red ribbon reused from the year before were seedpods from sweet gum trees that had been dipped in white glue and rolled in gold and red glitter—all handmade by the Brewer family in their big kitchen. When glitter fell to the linoleum, Mrs. Bob would say, "Don't yall worry. Glitter on a kitchen floor is the sign of a good life!"

The Bobs greeted Genevieve and the girls warmly as they arrived in the lobby. Few people knew Mrs. Bob's first name. Genevieve did. But she never told. Mrs. Bob hated her first name. "Being called Mrs. Bob suits me swell," she'd say when asked. She would also answer to "Bob" in a pinch. The fact that it was her husband's name didn't bother her a bit.

To Vivi, Teensy, and Necie, the high-vaulted lobby always felt so exotic, with its burgundy and red floral carpeting and rose walls. But it was even more exciting than usual with the garlands of holly strung above the doors. The moldings and trim work were painted to look like bronze, and there was a large bronze and red glass light fixture that surely came from the Orient. In the middle of the lobby stood a Christmas tree strung with popcorn, with lots of little wrapped gifts underneath.

"Cold enough for you?" Mister Bob asked.

"*Temps froid, oui, oui!*" Genevieve said, taking off her hat of red fox fur, bedecked on the side with a rhinestone pin.

The little girls stomped their feet to warm up. "Good evening, Mister Bob," they said.

Mrs. Bob came out from one of the storerooms, wiping her hands on her apron, which she promptly removed. "Good evening," she said, giving Genevieve and the three girls a big smile. Vivi and Teensy and Necie were about to wish her the same when they heard barking from somewhere in the corner of the lobby.

"*Le Joyeaux Noël* decorations are so charming," said Genevieve.

"Thank you," Mrs. Bob said. "The holly is from that big old holly tree in our backyard. We wanted the outside decorations too, so everyone can have a little Christmas cheer, even those who can't afford the price of a movie. Hello, little girls, how pretty you look!"

Vivi, Teensy, and Necie were about to thank her when they heard the barking again.

"Do you have a doggie here?" Necie asked, hiding behind Genevieve. "I'm scared of dogs."

Mrs. Bob rolled her eyes. "Oh, yes, we have a little doggie, don't we, Mister Bob?"

Taking Necie by the hand, Mrs. Bob helped her with her coat and hat. "You don't need to be afraid of this dog, Denise."

"This dog is only half-wild," Mister Bob said. "We know her parents."

"I bet I know who it is!" Teensy said.

"We do have a doggie here," Mrs. Bob said, giving Necie's shoulder a squeeze, and gathering the coats and hats of the others to hang inside the coat-check room. "A doggie we named 'Caroline,' but who is calling herself 'Rin-Tin-Tin' tonight."

At this, Caro crawled out on all fours from behind the concession counter with a Baby Ruth hanging out of her mouth.

"Hi-ho, Teensy," she said. "Hi-ho, Necie Scaredy Cat." Then she glared at Vivi. "Who the foreigner?"

Necie shyly started to speak. "This is our friend, Vivi—"

Putting her fingers at her forehead and wiggling them as though she were trying to hypnotize Necie, Caro said, "I will find out myself."

Caro gave several more barks, then stood straight up and stared down at Vivi, who was three inches shorter than she was. Caro looked Vivi up and down, as if to assess whether Vivi should belong to the gang at The Bob.

"Who sailed the seven seas?" Caro demanded.

"Sinbad?" Vivi said.

"What is the name of the elephant in the Ringling Brothers Circus, the one that leads the parade when they come to town?"

"I don't know," Vivi said.

Caro smiled, evil in her eyes. "What *do* you know?"

Vivi walked over to Caro and rubbed her hands all over Caro's head.

"You're a brave dog, Rinty," Vivi said.

Caro allowed her head to be rubbed, and moved her head around just like a dog does when getting such strokes.

Then Vivi said, "Your hair looks like a Yubangi."

"I am Yubangi!" Caro said, pulling her head away from Vivi's hands. "I am wild. I grew up with Tarzan."

"Me too," Vivi said.

"Then we're sisters," Caro said.

"Sisters of the jungle!" Beating her chest, Vivi gave out what she imagined was the best Tarzan cry at the top of her voice.

"Okay. Jungle sister like Baby Ruth?"

"Yuh, me like Baby Ruth," Vivi said.

Caro put the candy bar back in her mouth and leaned over to Vivi. Vivi, without missing a beat, took a bite out of it straight out of Caro's mouth.

"You good native girl," Caro said, and stuck out her hand.

Vivi stared at her hand for a moment. She had never shook hands with anyone before. But she was not about to be thrown by this barking crazy-haired little girl. She put out her hand.

Caro gave it a shake. Then she gave Vivi the A-OK sign and said, like Spanky in *The Little Rascals,* "Okey-rokey."

Caroline Eliza Brewer, known to all as Caro, made The Bob her own personal playground, and she enjoyed it like Heloise loved the Ritz. Caro was the towheaded terror of The Bob. She knew all of its best hiding places. She slid down the banisters, and barreled down the aisles fast as she could. She became the mascot for every vaudeville troupe that came to town. She bugged everyone who worked there to explain their jobs to her and to tell her stories—the more exotic and scary the better. She watched every movie so many times she could recite the lines along with Myrna Loy or Edward G. Robinson. When she got tired, she flung herself on one of the plush maroon velvet chairs in the mezzanine lounge and read anything she could get her hands on. She was learning to read faster than any of her siblings had, and her mother was quite proud of it. Caro's brother Lowell was three years older than she, and wanted only to play baseball. He was rarely at The Bob. Her big sister, Mary (named for the Blessed Virgin Mary *and* Mary Pickford) was already thirteen, and she had better things to do. Baby Will was still an infant, and he was left at home with Lavonia, their maid, most of the time. Caro was not cute, and she was not "spoilt rotted." She was spoiled just enough to be confident. Her legs were long, and she wore over-alls everywhere she went, except to Mass. She had cut her hair her-self so that it stuck out like a young primate in the wild, which broke her mother's heart. There was something untamed about Caro. Genevieve recognized this in her own daughter and in Vivi and Caro, and it made her fierce for them. She knew that Necie would always find her way in polite society, but she feared for the other three.

Caro and Vivi tried to match their stride as they walked over to Teensy and Necie. Genevieve stepped up to the concession stand. She already knew what the girls wanted, so she made the requests herself. After chatting with Gerald, she called the girls over to the counter and handed them each their favorite candy. Teensy got her Milk Duds, Vivi received her Milky Way bar, Necie got her colorful jelly Chuckles, and Caro, her Bit-O-Honey. When Genevieve handed them each a small Coca-Cola, she also included gobs of nap-kins. "Just do your best," she said to the red-velvet-clad girls, "not to spoil your outfits." Genevieve held a great box of popcorn for herself and to share with her troops.

"Oh, thank you, Mrs. Whitman," Necie said, upon receiving her Chuckles.

"Necie, *ma petite choux*," Genevieve said, "please call me Genevieve, not Mrs. Whitman. Especially here in my palace of escape."

"I'm sorry. But Mama told me to always—"

"I know your Mama means well, *cher*, and you may call me Mrs. Whitman whenever we are in her presence. But the rest of the time, please remember that I am Genevieve. That is my name. I am a free woman."

"Yes ma'am," Necie said, her head hanging down, embarrassed.

Genevieve hugged the girl to her and, as if by magic, produced a Mounds bar from the pocket of her red wool dress lined in fur at the hem.

Necie raised her head and whispered, "*Merci*, Genevieve."

"Caro," Genevieve said, "would you care to join our entourage as we prepare to witness zee Galaxy of Mystery?"

Caro looked at the other three girls, rolled her eyes, then said, "Indeedy-do, free lady!"

"*Très bien!*" Genevieve said, and handed Caro a box of Jujubes. "Now, we have *quatre elfes d' Noël!*"

The four little girls followed Genevieve past the heavy maroon curtain that was held back by a thick gold rope and were led by a uniformed usher to the tenth row, center section—the best seats in the house. Inside the theater, the walls were painted as dark as berry juice. There were bronze wall sconces that cast a soft light up the deep-hued walls. Each sconce had a large red glass jewel in it that glowed like a dragon's eye! The girls' favorite part, though, was the glistening little stars set into the ceiling above.

The presentation was beyond anything they'd seen before! Master Giovanni and his unbelievable magic, how he sawed that lady into not two but *three* pieces, was beyond them. He made soup flow out of a hat, and then doves fly out of a handkerchief. It was sheer heaven. They passed the popcorn box among them and ooohed and aaahed the whole time. It was the first of countless adventures for Genevieve and the four girls together at the glorious exotic Bob—right in their own hometown.

After the magic show, Genevieve and the girls helped the Bobs close up the theater for the night.

"This is fun!" Necie said, thrilled to see behind the scenes.

Then Genevieve invited not only the Bobs, but also Giovanni and his assistants, to join them for ice cream at Labadeaux's Ice Cream Parlor. The sound of bells on the wreath announced their arrival at the ice cream parlor. Not that they needed much announcing. What a sight they were as they opened the glass door with the Christmas wreath! Master Giovanni, still in his tuxedo. His female assistant, clad in a scanty red print dress with a slit on one side. His burly male assistant, who wore his cigarettes rolled up in the sleeves of his T-shirt. And an aged woman who seemed to be Master Giovanni's mother. She spoke halting English, and they could not make out what country she came from or if she just had bad false teeth. The other citizens of Thornton sat sipping their milkshakes and malteds and tried not to stare. But this became impossible. After Genevieve had made sure her entourage had all the ice cream, banana splits, and cherry Cokes they wanted, Master Giovanni produced four different brightly colored scarves. He made the napkin dispenser disappear, and in its place appeared a vase of flowers.

"Yay! Do it again!" Vivi, Caro, Teensy, and Necie squealed.

"But no," Master Giovanni said. "Now it is *your* turn to perform, my lovely ladies!"

With that, he handed each girl a scarf. The four girls jumped up, each of them with a scarf in her hands. Without speaking, they began to swirl the scarves around, and began to turn their little bodies in circles, swirling the scarves high and then low, wrapping the scarves around their faces like One Thousand and One Nights. At first Necie hung back, but soon she gave over to the fever and joined the dancing quartet. The Bobs, Genevieve, and Master Giovanni and his entourage began to applaud, laughing, and calling out suggestions.

"Roll your hips!" called out the female assistant.

"They are *magnifico bambinas,*" said Master Giovanni. "They should consider going on the stage."

"*La danse divine!*" shouted Genevieve.

A local townswoman, who Genevieve recognized from her charity work, approached their table. Genevieve said, "Oh, do sit down with us and enjoy the show!"

"I most certainly will not," the woman said. "I came over to say that you should make those girls behave. How will they ever grow up to be young ladies if you let them behave like this in public?"

Genevieve stared hard at the woman, and for a moment she did not speak. Then she said, "What this town needs, *cher*, is *beaucoup filles* dancing around with scarves in their teeth! This place needs more *joie de vivre!* We need *gaieté! Rejouissance! Laissez les bon temps rouler!*" Let the good times roll!

She gave a wink to Master Giovanni. She smiled at the lady and at the Bobs. The Bobs did not totally agree with her, or even understand everything she'd said, but they thought she was glorious. So long as they did not have to dance with scarves in their mouths.

The girls spun round and round and round the ice cream parlor, scarves in their hands, between their teeth, wrapped around their fingers like scarf rings. They did not dance madly like maenads from some Greek tragedy, but like muses, graceful and ready to inspire. The spark that lived in all of them rejoiced when they turned in circles, little whirling wild spirits. Like junior priestesses of some undomesticated tribe, they went somewhere else as they spun into a trance of dizziness as if they were praying. It looked as if they were bad little girls acting like wild sprites, and some of the folks in the ice cream parlor thought them rude and uncouth. But that is only because these townspeople did not know about whirling dervishes and what happens when they dance and pray, pray and dance. They did not know that dance can become prayer and prayer can become dance. The quartet of little girls knew it, and they were so happy in their bodies on that cold December night that they did indeed seem to glow.

Tending Young Buds

SCENES FROM MY EARLY CAREER

Sidda, February 1994

$\mathcal{M}$ost of all, I remember the Ya-Yas singing. I remember it from the time I was very young. They sang to us when we were toddlers. They did not sing traditional lullabies. They preferred adapting their favorite songs and singing them in a combination between torch and choir. I'm sure that the rest of the Petites Ya-Ya, like me, thought that "Smoke Gets in Your Eyes" was a nursery song. And when Mama sang to us about buttoning up our overcoats when the wind blew free, and to take good care of ourselves because "you belong to me," we thought it was our own special going-outside song, composed by our mother for the special occasion of our leaving the house.

Teensy sang in her spicy Cajun soprano, Caro sang a strong alto, and Mama sang what she called "sopralto," which meant she moved anything to fit into her range. Necie always played the piano. She came to our house and sat down at the baby grand in the living room, and within minutes she'd pick out an accompaniment to whatever they wanted to sing. This well-worn Steinway had been in the family for years; it had been bought by my great-grandmother

Delia for my Mama when she was a little girl. Delia gave her that piano over the objections of my grandmother Buggy, who said that no child should have something so extravagant. According to Mama, Buggy's protests were not the polite demurring of someone receiving a too-elegant gift—they were the jealous raging of a daughter who resented that her own mother, who had refused to get so much as a workmanlike spinet for Buggy, should show such generosity to her granddaughter.

The Ya-Yas had spent many an afternoon when they were girls banging out tunes on this piano. And later we did, too. After so much pounding, the baby grand showed the strain. If you examined closely, the gouges in the wood above the keyboard looked suspiciously like teeth marks. Sometimes frustration would get the better of us when we were practicing. When I was small, I would sink my teeth down into that wooden ledge and grind out the pain of perfectionism. My brother Shep favored sharp blows with whatever object was handy, making dents in the piano that theater prop masters now call "distressed." It is telling that while Mama might go berserk over a broken favorite crystal ashtray, she thought the marks on the piano were hysterical. While she did not encourage beaverlike expressions of angst, she did not punish us either.

When it came to singing, Mama could and would do anything she wanted. What she lacked in pitch, she made up in sheer force of personality. She was the one who did the funny bits—she would work with a cane and top hat, rolling her eyes and making suggestive jokes in between numbers. She didn't have much of a voice, but God, she had stage presence! She *played* with whatever audience was in front of her, like they were her lovers and she couldn't get enough of them. And like she knew they couldn't get enough of her.

When the Ya-Yas sang harmony, they sounded sort of like the Boswell Sisters—if two of the sisters had colds and Connie Boswell was a little tipsy. I imagine that kids who grew up around trained singers might have found the Ya-Yas lacking in talent, or maybe downright scary. But to me they were stars. They were my first inspiration as a theatrical director. I will never, ever forget my first directing experience.

It was at a dressy Ya-Ya Valentine's Day cocktail party in the early

1960s when I was eight. The Ya-Yas could never make it all the way from Ash Wednesday to Easter without a celebration, so they always had a big Valentine's Day party. It punctuated the Lenten season with sweet abandon. It was a big event—almost everybody in town was there, all decked out in their most glamorous party clothes. Mama had it catered, and there were all the fanciest hors d'oeuvres, the names of which I still remember like they were part of a chant: Spiced Crab Canapé, Sherried Shrimp à la Ya-Ya, Mrs. Daniel Doiron's Duck Paté, and Patsy Stafford's Pecan Balls. The dessert table was filled with all kinds of chocolate goodies, along with Brandy Brioche, and my personal favorite, Queen's Tart. Those pastry shells filled with that custard of pecans and Louisiana oranges and butter and cream and—oh, it was just *taste heaven*!

For the Valentine's Day parties, the Ya-Yas made special place cards quoting lines from musicals, and each person was supposed to guess where to sit according to the quote. The four of them were as delighted when guests found the wrong place as when they got the right one. Caro whispered to the others, "You learn so much about a person when they get things wrong!"

For this particular party, Mama hired Willetta's young nephews to park cars, and they showed up wearing their Sunday clothes. Willetta must have planned the outfits, because it was not the kind of thing Mama would have ever asked them to do. The nephews— Carver and Jefferson—took their job seriously. They stood at the edge of the driveway and opened the doors for Mama and Daddy's friends in their Lincolns and Cadillacs. Since the nephews also did yard work for most of the guests, you could hear the ooohs and aaahhs that came from the white people when they saw their Negro yard boys all dressed up in a shirt and tie. At the beginning of the party, my brother Little Shep tried to beat Carver and Jefferson at opening the car doors, and sometimes they got into a little scuffle.

Daddy finally came out and said, "Son, let these boys do their jobs."

Little Shep begged, "But Daddy, why can't I park the cars? They get to do everything around here."

"Son, you're not old enough. When people drive up, you can open car doors and greet them, but that's it."

Jeff and Carver hung their heads. You could tell that they were angry. This was part of their job. They didn't like Little Shep stepping in on their territory.

Little Shep was all excited, until Daddy turned and said: "Now, Shep, don't you be taking any tips from my padnahs here. Jeff and Carver get all the money, you hear me, buddy?"

This wasn't what Little Shep had in mind at all, but Daddy said, "Don't give me any lip. Just let me hear you say 'Yessir.'"

"Yessir," my brother said. But I know that he kept some of those tips. After all the guests had arrived, he came in and emptied his pockets, bragging about how rich he was.

That evening the house was jumping. Moreau, my Daddy's Cajun buddy, came in with big pans of food—duck gumbo, dirty rice, homemade garlic French bread. Daddy always said that Moreau was the best damn cook in the world, and that included anybody at Gallatoire's, Antoine's, and places in Europe, too. Even though it was just a cocktail party, he refused to let Mama serve only finger food. "You got to *feed* people when they come to your house," he said.

Caro, Teensy, and Necie had arrived early with their outfits in blue plastic bags from the cleaners, carrying their train cases filled with makeup. One of the things I loved most about the official Ya-Ya parties—as opposed to just an ordinary dinner party—was that all the women got dressed together. They took over the entire hall and bathroom and Mama's dressing room. It was a glorious thing to watch them getting ready. Some of my friends talk about the romance of watching their mother and father get ready for a party, but I never actually saw much of Daddy before a party. In the long hallway, Mama had moved the coatrack to one side, and all the ladies' outfits were hanging from the rack, like characters they were waiting to become. On that Valentine's Day, it was actually cold outside, a rare occasion in the state of Louisiana. Just the thing to make the Ya-Yas get their furs out of storage and bring them to the party. Mama was the only one who did not own a fur. She said, "I eat enough dead animals. I don't want to *wear* them." Actually, Teensy wore her knee-length mink to parties often, anytime she felt like it. Daddy always said it was because she never knew when she'd end up buck-naked and needing something to keep her warm. Stripping was something Teensy had done since she was a little girl. We had seen her do it since we were born and never thought twice about it.

Back in Mama's dressing room, the small square 45 rpm record player was turned up loud. The Ya-Yas were listening to their "getting-dressed music." Depending on their mood, this was Judy Garland, Sarah Vaughan, Ella Fitzgerald, and later, Dinah Washington. Every once in a while, they would get hooked on a particular song that wasn't by any of their "Tune Ladies." One year they flipped over "The Girl from Ipanema." They played that song so much, it about drove my father batty, but they could not get enough of it.

We kids were supposed to stay back in the indoor playroom with Ruby. She was babysitting us so we wouldn't try and take over the party, like we had been accused of in the past. We had the TV on in there, a bunch of games spread across the floor, and Baylor was playing with his paint set. Only the four of us were in there, since the other Ya-Yas had left their kids at home with their own sitters. Usually they liked to hire one sitter to take care of all of us. But Mama told me that Willetta had refused to let Ruby come back if they dumped all of the Ya-Ya kids on her again. The playroom was a nice enough place. Lord knows, we had just about everything we could have wanted back there, plus an ice chest full of Cokes and a box of petits fours Mama ordered specially for us.

But we knew the real action was happening in the front of the house.

As I sat on the couch with the rest of the kids, watching TV, I heard something that I thought I'd better check out. I was deep into a Nancy Drew phase. Every single thing that occurred—a car on the gravel road, Willetta claiming someone stole her favorite pot for cooking starch, a creak in the floorboards—presented itself as a mystery begging for me, only me, to solve. I tiptoed backward out of the den—girl detective, hoping no one would follow.

I crept toward my bedroom door, and I found them: all four Ya-Yas, spilling out of the dressing room, touching up their makeup. Mama, in her slinky black cocktail dress, was applying bright red lipstick to her lips. Necie wore a very romantic-looking pink chiffon number that I just loved. She was piling her luxurious long brown hair up on her head and spraying it into place. Caro had on black, too, a longer dress with an uneven hemline that looked vaguely 1920s. She had finished primping and leaned against the wall, smoking. Teensy was wearing a flaming red low-cut dress that was by far the shortest dress in Garnet Parish that year. When Mama finished putting on her lipstick, Teensy took that flame-red color from her and put some right on her own lips.

And naturally they were singing, warming up for their "act." At almost every single Ya-Ya party during those years, my mother and her friends provided the after-dinner entertainment. And never, *never* did they rehearse what they were going to do. They waited until the very evening, then ran upstairs, or in the back, or to the cabana, depending on where the party was. Once they got away from the guests, they would start figuring out what to do that evening. They called this "Backstage." It was a huge privilege when they occasionally let me look on.

Mama folded her arms and said, "I feel it, I *feel* it. It's a Judy night."

"Yeah, baby, Judy is talking to me, too," Caro said.

I was so used to the Ya-Yas saying this. At school, sometimes I slipped and said things like, "I hear Joan of Arc calling to me." The nuns would correct me, and later ask Mama if she had had me "tested" yet. The nuns used to regularly ask all four of us if Mama had taken us to be "tested." When we asked Mama about it, she'd laugh. "Oh, for God's sakes. Don't listen to them." I realize now that they were suggesting my mother take each and every one of us to a child psychiatrist. Needless to say, we were not "tested." At least, not then.

"We haven't done young Judy stuff in a while," Necie said, looking a little worried.

"Countess Singing Cloud," Teensy said to Necie, addressing her with her royal Ya-Ya tribal name, "so what? Judy is *in us*."

"Deep within," Mama replied.

"Deep. Very deep," Caro agreed, and they launched into "Somewhere over the Rainbow."

God, they loved Judy Garland. I had heard them sing this song since the day I was born. They'd loved Judy Garland since they—and she—were girls. When they were in high school during the war, they used to go over to each other's houses every day after school to sing and dance and learn the words to all their favorite songs. Judy had been with the Ya-Yas a long time. Maybe they felt the same about Judy as I did about Little Stevie Wonder: I was just so amazed by a little kid with all that raw talent that I could not help but fall in love.

I was sitting there on the hardwood floor in the doorway to my bedroom, watching them get ready. I munched on little candy hearts, biting right into "Dreamboat" and "Be Mine." And that is when I had my big idea.

"Mama," I said softly. Nobody heard me. You had to talk loud around our house to be heard.

"Mama," I said, louder.

She turned and said, "Why, Sidda, Dahlin! What are you doing here?"

"Watching," I replied. Then before she could tell me to get back to the den, I said, "Yall sure are good." Little brownnoser. But I knew it would work, and it did.

"Thank you, Pal," Caro said, and bent down to touch my head. "I swear," she said, "I wish I had your red hair and you had a wart on your nose."

Caro always said that to me. In fact, she'd ask for snippets of my hair to take to different hairdressers, trying to get them to match my color. She called it "Siddalee Red." It made me feel that my hair was beautiful. Sometimes I still feel that way, and I thank Caro whenever I do.

"Sidda has always had impeccable taste," Mama said. "That's why I love her so much." Then Mama tried a vocalization for a moment before she took another drag off her cigarette.

"Filthy habit," she muttered while she French-inhaled.

"Mama," I tried again, "I've got an idea."

"Sidda, you know what I said about interrupting me when I am busy. We're getting our act together—no time to tarry, Dahlin!"

"I know, I know, Mama, but listen to this! Why don't yall sing 'Funny Valentine'? You know, in honor of Saint Valentine's Day."

"My God!" Mama exclaimed, and made a face at the others like she'd just hit the jackpot.

"*Eclatant!*" Teensy said.

"*Magnifique,* Siddalee. Absolutely *magnifique,*" Mama said. She looked at me like she was seeing me for the first time. "You constantly amaze me."

"You think it's a good idea?" I asked her, fishing for more compliments.

"Good?" Caro said. "Good?! It's . . . it's . . ." She waved her arms around in the air like they might accidentally bump into the word she was looking for. "It's *psychological!*" Caro's big word that year was "psychological." Whenever something impressed her, she would say, "Sooo psychological." I don't know if Caro was actually in therapy then, or if she was just reading a lot. Mama read a lot, but nothing like Caro—Caro read things that no one else in the state of Louisiana did.

"No, it's not psychological," Mama corrected her, "it's *directorial.* She inherits it from her mother."

"Whatever it is," Necie said, "I know 'My Funny Valentine' in the key of C. What do yall think?"

"Hunkey-goddamn-dorey," Mama, Caro, and Teensy all said at once.

They began singing right away, with Mama taking up the melody. She started it a little too low, and they were almost lost by the second verse. But they laughed and picked it up again, and sang it through.

Then, like divine inspiration, I had my second big idea of the evening. "Mama, you could play it on your clarinet!" I said. Mama learned to play the clarinet when she was a little girl, and she kept it up in high school. When she went to college, she played with her sorority sisters in a little group. She never advertised this, but I thought it was near genius.

Mama bent down, pulled me up from my cross-legged position, and kissed me right on the lips. "This child is incredible!" she declared. "My oldest offspring. My most stellar, perfect one!"

"*Que le Bon Dieu vous bénit!*" Teensy said.

All the other Ya-Yas chimed in. Mind you, these women had been sipping bourbon or martinis for hours. But they were still sober enough for the show to go on. I could smell liquor on their breaths, mingled with their Chanel, My Sin, Joy, and Mama's signature scent from Hovet Parfum, along with cigarette smoke. For years I thought of that mixture as the essential aroma of womanhood.

"Run!" Mama said. "Go have Little Shep get my clarinet out of the utility room. I stored it up there on the high shelf with the bags of dog food your Daddy doesn't know about." My father forbade storebought dog food in our house. If a dog couldn't live off table scraps, he announced, then it wasn't a real dog and deserved to starve.

I broke into a run down the hall to get Little Shep. "Shep-o!" I announced, "Mama wants you to go get her clarinet out of the utility room. And be careful climbing up to that high shelf to get it, okay?"

Little Shep didn't budge.

"I am talking to you!" I told him, mimicking the way Mama sounded when we didn't mind her.

"I'm busy." He stared at the TV and didn't even look in my direction.

"I know that, you igmo, but I gave you a direction!" I thundered in my most parental tone.

"Go get it yourself," Little Shep said.

Well, that just threw me into a spin. "What did you say?" I yelled at him. I bent over and turned off the TV set. "I told you to do something! Now get up and do it!" And with that, I gave him a little kick in the side with my foot. It didn't hurt him. I wasn't even wearing shoes.

He slammed his fist down on top of my foot. I was about to kick him in the face when Ruby tackled me to the ground.

"Cut out that kickin stuff, Miz Siddy," she told me.

"Who do you think you are?!" Little Shep screamed right into my face. "What do you mean, you gave me a direction? Who do you think you are, the director of the world?! You're outta your tree."

As he reached to turn the TV back on, I grabbed a piece of his hair and twisted it in my hand. Ruby reached out and slapped my hand so hard I had to let go of his hair.

"Ow!" I said. "You hurt me. Colored girls aren't supposed to hit white girls."

"And white girls not supposed to beat up on they bros and call people names. What you tryin to do, Miz Siddy? Mister Little Shep gonna haul off and knock you silly."

"Yeah," Little Shep said, "the only reason I didn't sock you in the stomach is because you're a *girl*. I could knock you flat on your back. You'd be begging for a doctor."

That made me stop and think. He was a year younger, but he was solid muscle.

"Well, you should mind me!" I told him.

"Who said I had to mind you?" he growled.

"Yeah, Miz Siddy, you ain't no boss-lady, you jes another little chile." Ruby got in between us so we could not touch each other.

"Mama *told* me to tell you to go get her goddamn clarinet."

Ruby said, "You better not let your Mama hear you talkin like that, she gonna tan your hide."

"What does Mama need her clarinet for?" Little Shep asked.

"They're gonna use it in their act," I whispered, like I had the inside dope on everything in the world.

Little Shep headed for the door. "Well, why didn't you say so in the first place?" Before he disappeared into the utility room, he stuck his butt out at me and made a big fart sound with the palm of his hand and his mouth.

"Oooh, yall the baddest little white chirren I ever saw," Ruby said, and then opened another Coke. During this whole exchange, Baylor kept playing with his paint box, and Lulu never took her eyes off the TV, her hand digging in and out of a box of Cracker Jacks.

After dinner, when it was time for the performance, we were allowed to sit in the living room and watch. The Ya-Yas sashayed out holding big red heart-shaped boxes of candy in front of their chests. I had put on a little Judy background music. But as soon as Mama and the Ya-Yas were center stage in the middle of the orange carpet, I jerked the needle off the stereo and ran to hand Mama her clarinet.

Mama blew a few notes, and then Necie joined on the piano, and all four of them began to sing "My Funny Valentine." They sang it in their quirky harmony that made any slightly flat notes or incorrect words sound like clever jazz improvisations. After they sang it through once, Mama played a solo. Watching her stand there, blowing on her clarinet, wearing her black satin off-the-shoulder cocktail dress, is something I will never forget. Mama had rhythm, power, and bravado. When she got to certain notes, she was so completely absorbed, her eyes closed, you knew she was flowing in a river of music that she made herself. She loved doing what she was doing so much that I could feel it like heat waves emanating from her body. People gave her a round of applause for her solo, and then the Ya-Yas sang the song again. When they were through, everyone—including my father—whooped and hollered and whistled. Baylor, Little Shep, and Lulu were sitting next to me with their mouths hanging open. They had seen the Ya-Yas sing before, but never with Mama on her clarinet. Once they finished the number, the four of them made deep exaggerated curtsies all the way to the floor, then stood, held hands, and took a bow from the waist in unison.

Mama whistled one of her showstopping whistles that quieted the applause. You could tell she felt *mahvelous*. She said, "Thank you all, Dahlin Hearts. And special thanks to my daughter, Miss Siddalee Walker, who helped direct tonight's special Valentine's Day number." And everyone applauded again.

I had never felt so proud in my life. I felt a surge of power so strong that I could taste it. I had thought up the song, and I had thought up Mama on the clarinet! They all thought it was a good idea! And they did it!

I wonder if Mama ever knew how much that acknowledgment meant to me. I wonder if she knows how it makes up for so many things. That moment stays inside of all the other moments. It's not that it makes the other scary moments go away. But when I am up against the wall, when I am shaking with fear before a show opens, when I am standing in the lobby watching people walk into the theater, the memory of that moment stops me from hiding in the bathroom and throwing up. That was the moment that held me together when I got my first vitriolic review—the one that suggested I run a bowling alley rather than direct plays. It is one of the moments that is helping me stay (barely) glued together now that I'm working in increasingly high-pressure settings. I wonder if Mama knows that. I wonder why I haven't told her.

After everybody finally quit clapping and shouting, Teensy cracked open a bottle of champagne. Champagne was the only thing she drank that year. She drank it alone, drank it with everything. She claimed it was "clean." Teensy poured me a tiny drop in one of the gold-stemmed champagne glasses that had been my great-grandmother Delia's. And then Little Shep, Baylor, Lulu, and I were packed off to bed.

I was so excited that I had not noticed Lulu at all. She was still eating when we got into our twin beds. She had a handful of pecan balls she'd taken off the coffee table clenched in her little round hands.

"Lulu," I told her, "you have got to stop eating. Give me those pecan balls."

She handed them to me.

"You don't even like these," I said.

"I'm hungry."

"Hungry? You have been eating for six hours straight. You are going to be big as a barn. You are going to have huge hips like the ladies on Daddy's side of the family."

"Stop trying to talk like Mama," she said.

"Well, don't come crying to me when they won't let you into a movie theater because they're afraid your big butt will break the seats."

"Okay. I won't," she said.

She was quiet for a minute, then she said, "Sidda, did you really direct their show like Mama said?"

"Yes, I did," I told her. "I directed every single note and every single movement. They did nothing but what I told them to," I lied.

"Golly," she said. I knew she was sucking her thumb by now.

"They are going to start paying me next time," I said.

"Paying you? Like—with money?"

"What do you think people get paid with? Ritz crackers?"

"I wish I could direct something," my little sister said.

"Pray to Saint Jude, Patron Saint of the Impossible," I said, so full of myself I was about to pop. I lay there and tried to sleep, but I was still too keyed up to relax. "Hey, Lulu," I said. "You awake?"

"No," she said. "I'm sleeping."

"Well, do you want to sing?"

"No," she whispered, "I wanna sleep."

"Come on, let's sing 'Side by Side,'" I said.

"You sing it. I don't want to sing, Sidda."

"Aw, come on—" I began to coax when I heard voices in the hallway. These were not usual party voices. These were upset grown-up voices.

I jumped out of my bed and ran to the bedroom door. Yet another mystery for Siddalee Drew. I cracked the door open, and the voices grew louder. I was used to hearing loud voices, that was nothing new. But this had a different sound to it. Higher-pitched or something. I tiptoed down the hall, opened the hall door, and peeked into the living room. In the middle of the room, with a pillow propped under his head, lay Mr. Mitchell Fontenot, my Uncle Pete's law partner. He didn't look drunk. He looked like he was in pain.

Little Shep came out of his bedroom, too. "Hey, what's going on?" he asked, rubbing his eyes.

"I don't know," I told him. "Mr. Fontenot is laying on the floor."

"Is he drunk?" Little Shep asked. We were both used to seeing grown-ups on the floor, but usually that happened at the end of the party. The party was still going on. Everyone still seemed to be there.

Mrs. Fontenot was leaning down, talking to Mr. Fontenot, and then Daddy was kneeling down beside him, saying something.

"Come on," I said to Little Shep, taking his hand. "Let's go out and see what's going on."

"Don't boss me around," Shep said, withdrawing his hand.

"Okay," I said. "Would you pretty please like to come out with me and see what is happening out there on the goddamn floor?"

"You better stop cussing so much, Sidda," he said, but he was laughing. I had just started saying "goddamn" around that time. I only said it around my siblings and black people. Little Shep took my hand again, and hitched up his pajama bottoms with the other.

"Act all innocent, like they woke us up," I whispered to him.

"Don't you tell me what to do," he whispered back.

We approached the large fallen body of Mr. Mitchell Fontenot, who was sipping a Scotch through a straw. I knew how different liquors smelled. When I fixed grown-up drinks, I memorized them. I could smell a certain drink and say Scotch or rye or gin.

"Daddy, what's wrong with Mr. Fontenot?" I asked.

"Honey, Mr. Fontenot was doing the Twist with Chubby Checker, and he threw his back out." Daddy was still by the lawyer's side.

"Does it hurt?" Little Shep asked Mr. Mitchell Fontenot.

"Only when I smile," he said, and winked at Little Shep.

"What's going to happen?" I asked Daddy.

"I don't know," he replied. "Your Mama and them are figuring it out right now. Yall better go back to bed now."

Daddy was slurring his words, but he still had enough balance to kneel on one knee and not fall over.

"Did you like the number?" I asked him, hoping for the big Daddy compliment.

"What number?" he asked.

I was crushed. "The 'My Funny Valentine' number, Daddy! The one I directed."

"Oh, yeah," he said, and dropped it. Just like that. Dropped it right on the floor next to Mr. Mitchell Fontenot.

But if it's one thing I have, it's manners. I took a deep breath and said, "Well, Mr. Fontenot, I hope you feel better soon."

"Me too," said Little Shep, "and I hope you don't sue my Daddy."

Mr. Fontenot began to laugh, but then he groaned.

Daddy was not laughing. "Son, get your butt back to bed before I go bankrupt."

And Little Shep and me padded down the hall and sat looking out the window in his room, trying to see what would happen next.

What happened next is about ten minutes later a big red-and-white ambulance wagon pulled into our driveway. We flew back down the hall and into the living room in time to see the attendants pick up Mr. Mitchell Fontenot and carry him out to the ambulance. Mama and the Ya-Yas and all the others were crowded around him, making over him, telling him jokes.

"You are the bravest dancer of the Twist in all of Garnet Parish!" Mama shouted out the door as the ambulance men carried him away from the house.

At the last minute, just as they were putting him in the ambulance, someone had the great idea of following Mr. Mitchell Fontenot to the hospital. The next thing we knew, all the guests were hopping into their cars, drinks in hand, and pulling out of the field where Jefferson and Carver and my bad brother had parked them.

Little Shep took off out the bedroom, down the hall, and out onto the carport. I followed him, my feet cold against the concrete, goose bumps on my arms from the February air.

"Daddy," Little Shep asked, "are you going to the hospital? Can I go too?"

"Hell, no," Daddy slurred. "Hospital's no place for a bunch of crazy drunks. That's your Mama and her friends, always making fools of themselves." Sure enough, Mama had climbed into one of the cars and taken off with most of the party guests.

Daddy turned to Jefferson and Carver, who looked sleepy, their church clothes rumpled after sitting around waiting to help the guests into their cars. They hadn't had a chance to do that, since the guests had flown off to the hospital. They hadn't been tipped either.

"Boys," Daddy said, reaching into his pocket, "yall go on into the house and get Little Shep to give you something to eat before you go home." Then he handed both of them some folded bills and shook his head. "Yall done good. Tell your daddy I said so."

"Shep," he continued, turning around, "get these boys something substantial, not just that finger food. Get them some duck gumbo and French bread, you hear?"

"Yes sir," Little Shep said. "Come on," he told Carver and Jefferson, and led them back to the kitchen.

Back inside, only Necie and her husband Mister George Ogden (he was the only Ya-Ya husband who *made* all us kids call him "Mister") were still left. Necie was in the kitchen, making a pot of coffee and starting to clean up.

"Don't bother with that, Denise," Daddy told her. "Willetta will do that in the morning."

"Oh, I'm just putting the food away," she said, and kept dripping coffee.

Daddy stood there in the kitchen, staring at Mister Ogden and Necie. I sat at the breakfast table and watched them.

Little Shep opened the door to the icebox.

"What can I help you with?" Necie asked him.

"Daddy told me to feed Carver and Jefferson."

Necie said, "I'll do that, Sweetie," and took over the job.

Carver and Jefferson stood barely inside the kitchen door, not moving.

"I'll have yall something in a minute," Necie told them, and smiled. "Why don't yall sit over there at the kitchen table, and—"

Mister Ogden interrupted her. "Go on out under the carport," he told the black boys, "and we'll bring you something to eat."

Carver and Jefferson stepped outside. Necie tried to hide the look on her face. Sometimes Mama and the other Ya-Yas said they didn't know why she married Mister Ogden.

Little Shep looked at Daddy. He didn't like Mister Ogden talking like he owned the place. But Daddy hardly noticed.

"George," Daddy finally asked, "can Mitchell sue me?" Mister Ogden was a lawyer, too. He was a district attorney. My Daddy has always been a little intimidated by lawyers.

Mister Ogden leaned back against the kitchen counter. "Technically he could, Shepley, but he'd have a hard go of it, since that back of his is always going out. Went out at the Country Club right there on the tennis court not two months ago, and he never tried to sue anyone. I wouldn't worry too much about it."

"You're probably right," Daddy told him. "I worry too goddamn much as it is."

Mister Ogden smiled at him, like Daddy had said something so true he didn't even need to agree.

Daddy looked at Necie. Daddy never knew how to act around the Ya-Yas, not really. Necie especially bothered him. He called her Puffhead.

"Necie, what in the hell are you doing making coffee this time of night?"

"Shep, a little demitasse is all I need to make sure that I never get a hangover."

"I'll be damned," my Daddy said. And then he just sat there at the counter, staring. Sometimes when Daddy got drunk, he just sort of went away. My Daddy looked kind of lost there in his own kitchen. My brother must have sensed it, because he went and sat next to Daddy on one of the kitchen stools.

"Would you care for a demitasse?" Necie asked Daddy.

Daddy looked at her like he could not remember who this woman was, standing in front of him in his own kitchen.

"No, thank you, ma'am," he said. "What I would like is a good, old-fashioned Alka-Seltzer."

Necie went right to the liquor cabinet and took out the Alka-Seltzer box.

"I want one, too, Daddy," Little Shep said.

Daddy stared dumbly at the glass of Alka-Seltzer Necie had set in front of him.

"Can I, Daddy?" Little Shep asked again.

Daddy didn't say anything, he just stared in front of him like Little Shep and the rest of us didn't exist.

Little Shep put his hand on Daddy's arm. I think he wanted Daddy to remember that he was still in the room more than he wanted an Alka-Seltzer.

"Daddy! Can I please have an Alka-Seltzer?" my brother asked again, getting desperate. I hated watching him when he did this. I hated watching any of us kids when we got desperate.

Necie took two big bowls of gumbo and a plate of bread and stepped outside the kitchen door. When she came back in, she asked, "Who is taking those boys home?"

Daddy got up from the stool. He walked out, through the living room and down the hall to his bedroom. We could hear his door shut.

"George," Necie said, "we are taking those boys home."

Mister Ogden looked at his wife and shook his head. "John F. Goddamn Kennedy has gotten to you, hook, line, and sinker," he said.

"This has nothing to do with President Kennedy. It has to do with two little boys sitting on the carport freezing to death and nobody to get them home. We have a car. We can drive them, and we will."

"Just what we need: drive over to Samtown late on a Saturday night."

Necie turned her back to him and said something under her breath that I couldn't hear.

"Shep, you still want that Alka-Seltzer?" Necie asked my brother.

Little Shep stared at the floor and nodded his head. "Yes ma'am, I do. I want an Alka-Seltzer."

Necie made him an Alka-Seltzer and gave it to him in a jelly glass.

He drank some, and then handed it to me. "Here, you can have the rest," Little Shep said. "I don't want it anymore."

"Plop-plop fizz-fizz, oh what a relief it is," I sang, hoping to lighten things up a little. Nobody smiled.

Necie was sipping her demitasse, watching us. "Yall okay, Sidda?"

"Yes ma'am," I lied, "we're just fine."

"Yall going to be all right?" she asked again.

"Yes ma'am," I said.

She looked at her husband, and then she led me and my brother down the hall. When we got to Little Shep's room, I said, "Thank you, Aunt Necie, I can take it from here."

I went into Little Shep's room with him. He got into his bed and lay there with his eyes closed. Then Necie came in with two warm washcloths. She bent and wiped off Little Shep's face, real soft, kind of just patting his face. Then she kissed him on the forehead.

"You going to sleep in here tonight?" Little Shep asked me.

"Yeah, buddy," I said, and I got into the other twin bed with Baylor, who was sound asleep. Necie came over to me and wiped my face, too. When she finished, she kissed me on my eyelid. Then she left.

"You awake?" I asked Little Shep when she was gone.

"Yeah," he said.

"What you thinking?"

"Nothing," he lied.

"I know you're thinking something."

"Okay, I was thinking, would you tickle my back?"

I climbed into bed with Shep and began to tickle his back softly with my fingernails. My brother loved being tickled this way more than anything in the world. It was something he would beg for.

"You know that song?" he whispered.

I couldn't make out exactly what he was saying. "What?"

"You know—the Valentine song?"

"Yeah, kinda."

"Sing it," he whispered.

I kept tickling Little Shep's back, and I started to sing "My Funny Valentine." I sang it quietly while my fingertips were moving across the freckled terrain of my brother's back. I pretended each finger was a different character with a different name, and that they had whole lives filled with secrets and adventures and important roles in the world. As I thought about these characters, I sang the words, and I felt my brother's skin against my fingertips.

I lay awake for a long time. I knew that something big had happened to me that night. I thought about Saint Valentine writing letters of love from prison, how he had so much love in his heart that he had plenty left over to give away, even when he was in jail. On that night, I had plenty of love to spare, too. I didn't know it, but I had just started my career in the theater. I fell asleep hearing a chorus of separate, distinct, and sometimes off-key voices harmonizing into a whole. Not perfect harmony, but harmony nonetheless.

BUCKAROO

January 1963

*T*he day Baylor was supposed to appear on *Buck Lemoine's Junior Buckaroo Show,* he woke up with a headache. Baylor had gotten headaches before. Little Shep always teased him when he got them. So Baylor never said anything about the headaches anymore. He got out of bed and padded down the hall to the bathroom, his cotton-white hair sticking out in front like he was a baby blue jay. Sidda, his oldest sister, was already camped in the bathroom, applying her new false fingernails. She barely acknowledged five-and-a-half-year-old Baylor as he entered the big blue bathroom.

"They came off in my sleep," she told him, and went on sticking the pointed pink plastic nails to her nine-year-old fingers.

Baylor could not understand why a girl as smart as Sidda would glue plastic onto her fingers. But there was a lot he didn't understand. So he just peed and then washed his face in the second sink.

The children's bathroom at the Walkers' house had three sinks. Big Shep claimed that most family fights happened in the bathroom, and he wanted to minimize the possibility of bloodshed among his four kids, who were each a year apart. So when the house was built, he made sure they put in two extra sinks. Now the bathroom had the feeling of some kind of wacky institution. Vivi and Big Shep's cocktail party guests sometimes locked themselves up in the children's bath for hours at a time because they felt protected in the blue-tiled room filled with plants and books. There was an old wicker magazine rack full of *National Geographic* and *Life* magazines in there. A big window at one end looked out on the bayou, so there was plenty of room to stretch out, or sit awhile in the old rocker that belonged to Vivi's father before he passed away.

The bathroom was a big blue haven, and Vivi and Big Shep sometimes forgot about certain friends who tended to drink a little too much bourbon at parties and wander in there. Once Vivi forgot to check, and Lulu woke to find "Uncle" Chick still in the bathroom the next morning, asleep in the long blue bathtub. Vivi did her damnedest to always check after that, no matter how much bourbon *she'd* had to drink. At the end of each party, after she went around emptying ashtrays, she'd peek in the kids' bath just to make sure it was clear for them in the morning. She had asked the rest of the Ya-Yas and their husbands to please not sleep there, but you just never could be sure.

Baylor needed to sit on the toilet, but he did not like to do it with his sisters or brother in the room. It had never felt right, but there had never seemed to be anything he could do about it. All the kids in the Walker family were supposed to share this bathroom. Sidda, Little Shep, and Lulu did it, but he had never been able to. He needed privacy. On an ordinary day, Baylor would never ask that Sidda leave while he used the toilet. Today he asked her, on the off chance that she might oblige him.

But she answered, "I *must* get these fingernails back on, Baylor. And besides, I was in here first."

Baylor sighed and moved to the sink, skipping yet another morning bowel movement.

He brushed his teeth, the third one from the front still growing in. Baylor had almost all his grown-up teeth, but there were those two near the front still waiting to happen.

❦

One night when Vivi and Big Shep came back home from New Orleans, late at night after a long weekend party in the Garden District, they remembered that Willetta had called and left a message at the Monteleone Hotel, saying that Baylor had lost a tooth. Still half tipsy from the weekend, they remembered their Tooth Fairy roles just as they pulled into the driveway, the windows rolled down in the Thunderbird, the sweet April air hitting their faces. Big Shep had nothing but a fifty-dollar bill. So they sneaked into the bedroom that Baylor shared with Little Shep, where the horseshoe-shaped nightlight and the moonlight gave just enough illumination for Vivi to see the side of her youngest child's face. Her breath was taken away by his delicacy, his paleness, his seriousness, even in sleep. Together, the Tooth Fairies bent down, smelling of Vivi's signature perfume, Shep's Old Spice, and bourbon, still dressed to the nines. Vivi wore an off-the-shoulder blue evening gown that looked fabulous, even wrinkled, with her hair mussed from sleeping on the drive home. Under their baby boy's pillow they tucked a crisp fifty-dollar bill, a Monteleone swizzle stick, and three pralines from the French Quarter. When Baylor woke up the next morning, he was astonished to find fifty dollars for one tooth.

"Fifty buckerinos!" he exclaimed upon awakening, using one of his big brother's words. It was like an act of God. He could not imagine what he had done to deserve it. They usually only got a fifty-cent piece.

Even though the other kids complained that they had never got that much for a dumb tooth, Big Shep could never ask Baylor for any of the money back.

Most of the time, Big Shep did not know how to act with Baylor. Baylor seemed like a prince from another world to him; the boy's sense of refinement made Big Shep feel clumsy. Now his oldest son, Little Shep, he knew how to roughhouse with. But Baylor was like a ghost to his father, like a reminder of a dream Shep Walker had once in which, in front of a group of his father's friends, he suddenly discovered he was both a man and a woman at the same time, and had to decide what his real name was.

Baylor studied himself in the mirror with complete concentration. He was four feet tall, skinny as all get-out, with huge brown eyes that looked slightly sad. His complexion was olive, a rare combination with such light hair. His ears didn't yet fit his head, and he feared they never would. There was enough talk about his ears. His older cousins, every time they saw him, said, "Hey Bay-Boy, when you gonna grow into those ears?!" And then they laughed.

He didn't want to look stupid on television. He gently worked his white-blond hair with a touch of Brylcreem like Big Shep showed him to do, but still, there was this tuft that stuck up in front. That was the reason they sometimes called him "Jaybird." He held his ears closer to his head for a moment, just to see what it looked like.

Without seeming to look up, Sidda said, "Bay, your ears are fine. You have fine cowboy ears."

He liked his sister. She was mostly nice to him, took up for him. She once stopped Little Shep from making him drink a glass of Tabasco sauce, after Shep claimed it was "thick strawberry Kool-Aid."

After he finished up in the bathroom, Baylor went back into the room he shared with Little Shep. He had laid out his clothes the night before: the black cowboy outfit and matching boots his daddy had given him for Christmas, and a red cowboy hat. Even if he had a holster, he would not wear it. Holsters are dumb, Baylor thought, and Baylor was not dumb. His head still hurt, and he definitely should use the toilet. This was always the case: the longer he waited to use the toilet, the more his head ached. Maybe Sidda was out of the bathroom by now. Down the hall again. Peeked in. She was still in there, gluing and pressing the false fingernails down over her own short stubby ones. She looked up at him when he lingered there for a minute. "I cannot get the thumb to stick," she complained.

Can't she tell? Doesn't she know? Today is my day. I need the bathroom to myself.

Maybe Mama and Daddy's bathroom, Baylor thought. The Walker children were not allowed to use the adult bathroom except in the most dire emergencies, such as the flu. Maybe this qualified as one. He was, after all, going to be on television. He would, after all, be seen by every single person in Thornton, Louisiana. He was representing his family.

It was very quiet back in his parents' room, Baylor noticed. Maybe they were still asleep. Then he heard giggles from the bathroom. A tiny Vivi squeal. Not still asleep. Playing in the bathroom again. Vivi and Big Shep loved their bathroom. It led out to a small patio out back. There was never any telling what they were doing in there. Baylor knew better than to disturb them.

He must be at K-Dixie-BS-TV at eight-thirty sharp for *Buck Lemoine's Junior Buckaroo Show*. Kids who got there late could not go on television, they made that clear. Baylor looked down at the watch that Uncle Chick gave him for Christmas. It was already ten minutes after eight!

Baylor ran to the kitchen. Fixed Rice Krispies right in the box. Ripped it open at the dotted lines, peeled back the foil, sliced on some banana, and poured on the milk. Baylor loved these little boxes you could eat right out of. They were like something you could take out on the prairie with you to save on pack gear. No time this morning, though, to listen to the *Snap! Crackle! Pop!* He was a cowboy in a hurry. Balancing the small cereal box on his palm, Baylor headed to the den, where Little Shep sprawled, still in his pajamas, watching cartoons. Baylor didn't dare get comfortable because any minute he had to dash off to be a Junior Buckaroo.

"Hey, cowboy," Little Shep said, then ignored Baylor for the rest of *The Road Runner* show. Little Shep loved it when the Road Runner got into fights. He imitated the sounds that the TV made. "RRRRRRRRRRRR—MMMMMMMMM—BEEP-BEEP! KA BLAMMMMMMMMMMM CRASHHHHHHHHHHHHH SPLATTTTTTTTT! BEEP-BEEP!" Little Shep was a Road Runner kind of boy.

The cartoon was too loud for Baylor. It made his head hurt worse. Where was Mama?! Surely she hadn't forgotten his big day! Baylor raced into the kitchen, threw the cereal box away, rinsed the spoon, and put it in the dishwasher like he was trained to do. He went back to his room. It was dark; the curtains were still closed. He sat up on his bed, legs tucked under him, a cowboy in contemplation. He closed his eyes and saw the television cameras closing in on him, saw himself looking into the camera, addressing his hometown like President Kennedy did the whole entire country. *"I have things to tell you, fellow Thorntonians. I want to tell you about the egret behind our house in the bayou. And the new bird's nest in the pecan tree by the playhouse. And there's the huge huge craw-*

fish that none of us can catch and the alligator that Daddy says lives in the bayou although none of us have ever seen it, and—" There were so many things Baylor wanted to tell the world. He daydreamed about the hundreds of stories he had made up, all the tales he could share with the people in TV-land, the countless opinions he wanted to impart to adults and children in living rooms all over town. But most of all, he wanted to sing.

He checked his watch again. It was already twenty minutes after eight! He dashed back to Vivi and Big Shep's room. They were back in the bed, Vivi lighting a Lucky, Big Shep with a relaxed smile on his tanned face. It was Saturday in the Walker household.

"Hi, Angel Boy." Vivi grinned. "Come get in bed with us."

"I can't, Mama, I can't!" Baylor was trying not to shout, but he was getting pretty upset. "I've got to be at *Buck Lemoine's Junior Buckaroos* in exactly *five minutes.*"

"Shit, I completely forgot!" Vivi said, and stubbed out her just-lit cigarette in the silver ashtray on the bedside table.

"Leave your Mama alone, son. Go on in the den and watch it on TV." Big Shep was propped up on one elbow with the sheet pulled up to his bare chest, his hand on the sheet right where it covered Vivi's stomach.

"He can't do that, Shep," Vivi said. She rolled over, then leapt out of bed without a stitch of clothes on. "Babe, can't you see he's already wearing his Junior Buckaroo outfit? This is his big day!"

Vivi didn't waste a minute. Before Baylor knew it, she was flying down the hall in her blue and beige negligee, moaning: "Oh, damn it! I've been telling everybody about this, all week long! I told the Ya-Yas, I told Buggy—" Pausing only for a second to grab her coat and the car keys from the kitchen, she flung open the kitchen door, and in a jiffy, she and Baylor were in the car, pulling out of the driveway. Butterflies going wild inside his stomach, Baylor watched the speedometer and wondered just how the officer's face would look when he stopped Vivi for speeding and saw her negligee under her coat. If he concentrated on the numbers on the dash, he could keep his mind off his headache. Five minutes later, they pulled up right in front of K-Dixie-BS-TV.

The car still running, Vivi reached over and opened the door for

Baylor. "Oh, baby, I'm so sorry I forgot. I'd go in with you, Dahlin, but they don't like mothers in their nightgowns at TV stations. Don't ask me why."

She leaned over and kissed him on the cheek. He could smell her sleeping smell. "You're the finest cowboy I ever saw, Padnah. Go ride the range! I'm speeding home so we can all watch you on television!"

Baylor jumped out of the car and ran fast as he could, the fringe on his cowboy shirt flapping in the morning air. Inside the door of the television station, a chubby lady with black hair piled on top of her head sat behind a desk. She gave him a big grin and said: "Hey there, Junior Buckaroo!"

Baylor was gasping; his head throbbed, and he couldn't think of a single word to say. The lady gave him a smile that he needed, but could hardly take in.

"You better hurry, hon, if you wanna make it onto The Ranch. The rest of them are already in the studio. See that hallway behind you? Just go straight down to the end and then turn left. Can't miss it."

He would die for a bathroom, but he dared not waste a minute. They could lock the studio door on him, and then he would be left outside forever.

They just called it The Ranch, Baylor thought as he turned and ran down a long hallway, the heels of his cowboy boots clicking against the floor. He turned left like the lady said, and saw a door into a studio with a big red light above it. Baylor wondered if the red light had anything to do with the bombs he heard about in Cuba. He pushed open the door, terrified. The lady said to go in, but the red light meant STOP. One foot in the door, he spied a herd of other little kids, mostly boys, dressed in various stages of cowboy costume. They were all already sitting down, and there was a big man standing in front talking to them, telling them how to behave.

For a moment Baylor froze. Should he step forward? Everyone would turn around and look at him, and he would have to slink away and hide. But then everyone at home would ask where he'd been. They'd looked and looked and hadn't seen him on television. He had to go forward. A real cowboy wouldn't just freeze in place. Gene Autry wouldn't stand there paralyzed like he had polio. If only he'd gotten here on time like they told him to!

Finally, the big man glanced over to him and said, "You're late, Buckaroo. Don't like late Buckaroos. But come on in. Sit up there wherever you can find a seat."

Oh, boy. He had planned on sitting up front so Buck could see him, so he could be seen by all of Thornton when he had his big moment.

"Yessir," he whispered, and made himself as small as he could. He tiptoed up a set of bleachers and crawled over endless kids until he finally found a place to sit. Some of the children he knew; some of them he'd never seen before. Still, his outfit held up just fine next to theirs. Thanks to his Daddy, who bought it at the Cowboy Store and gave it to him for Christmas. A lot of the other little boys just had makeshift outfits, tennis shoes instead of boots. No sir, his Daddy would never let him wear a cowboy outfit without real boots to match. His Daddy would laugh at something like that. His Daddy would say, "Look at that country club cowboy, would you?"

There were lights up in the high ceiling, and a big camera mounted on a roller with a guy sitting behind it, with headphones on. The studio was so warm. Baylor felt his headache start to push at his forehead. He thought for sure that everyone could see his forehead pulsing in and out. *They probably think I'm retarded or from outer space. Those outer space aliens always have weird foreheads.*

Why had he insisted on coming by himself? He should have asked Little Shep. But Little Shep had already been on the show twice and thought it was baby stuff. He should have asked Sidda to come, even with those long fingernails. Now he was completely alone. He had wanted to come alone, to make it all his. Everything else in his life was shared with the other three. Everywhere he went, it seemed Sidda, Little Shep, and Lulu were with him. He had wanted to stand out on television by himself. Now he felt an emptiness, a lack of protection that came with being part of the Walker kid pack.

The *Buck Lemoine* theme song began to play, a cowboy song with an up-and-down-in-the-saddle sound to it. Without thinking, Baylor started to whistle along to the tune.

After a moment or so, Buck himself entered the ranch set and greeted the audience. "Morning, Junior Buckaroos! And welcome to Buck Lemoine's Ranch. Fine-lookin' bunch of cowboys we got here today. Yall ready to have some fun?"

Buck was a rangy, almost handsome man, and he wore a silver cowboy outfit. He's not just acting like a cowboy, Baylor thought, he is one. Baylor knew that Lemoine had been a famous rodeo star in the South until he hurt his knee riding bulls. He was a real cowboy, not a fake. Buck got out a small guitar and sang a number about a young cowboy who saved a hundred head of cattle from a terrible storm all by himself. Baylor loved the lights and the camera and all the guys running around doing all the things that get Buck's picture on TV.

But Baylor was not doing so well. He knew he should have gone to the bathroom before he left home. His gut felt like someone was shoving a knife through it.

Baylor told himself to ignore his stomach, and his headache. He had a bigger mission. For weeks he had been practicing a song designed to make him known and loved throughout the town, possibly in all of Garnet Parish. It would give him a new life. This was *the* reason for being on the show—the song he'd written about Andrew Jackson, made up on the bus coming home from school over two months ago. Baylor had been dying to sing it on the air. He had talked Sidda into helping him record it on her treasured, much-repaired tape recorder. When Sidda played that tape back and he heard his voice, he knew he had to sing it on television. He could have appeared instead on K-Dixie-BS-TV's *Nita Marie Jeansonne Thibeaux's Searching for Talent* program. But his daddy always made fun of that show. He always said, "That damn Nita has been searching for talent in this town for years, and she hasn't found any yet."

This was not like Baylor. His siblings were always performing to the hilt, encouraged by Vivi, who claimed to be an ex-Broadway actress. Usually Baylor was the quiet one. This was different, though. This song was all *his*. Not his big brother's or one of his sisters' routines. Nobody knew anything about it except Sidda, and she had no idea he was going to perform his song for the folks in TV-land.

Once he sang his number, Buck would ask him to be a regular on the show, right up there with Buck himself. He'd probably have a silver cowboy outfit custom-made to fit Baylor. Baylor would leave the older Walker kids in the dust. He'd stand out from everybody he knew. His Mama and Daddy would be astounded and treat him like something special, like another little boy, not his own regular self. He wouldn't have to wear Little Shep's hand-me-down shoes anymore that were all bent up at the toe from genuflecting.

Buck started to interview the kids, one at a time. The other children were giggly and shy, holding their hands over their mouths. They were so stupid! If they did say anything worthwhile, you'd never understand them anyway. Baylor knew if he could just hold off going to the bathroom, he would sing his song like a pro.

It took forever for Buck to go down each row, bending over and talking to each dumb kid. Baylor's stomach hurt worse and worse. Time stretched out even longer than a High Mass, after you've been fasting for hours to go to Holy Communion.

Finally Buck stepped in front of Baylor, bent over, and placed his sun-wrinkled face right next to Baylor's. Baylor could see the orangey makeup caked onto the cowboy's face.

"Mornin son," he said, smiling. "How you today?"

Unlike the other little boys, Baylor decided to stand up. Buck was holding a microphone, and Baylor wanted to speak clearly into it. He wanted to do anything to distinguish himself from the other kids. He had never acted like this before. He was possessed. It was his song that was making him do this. He had something to give the world.

"Real fine," Baylor said, proud of himself for adding the word "real." It sounded like a natural-born cowboy.

"What's your name, Buckaroo?" Buck asked, positioning the microphone right in front of Baylor's mouth.

"My name is Baylor Walker. My Daddy is Big Shep Walker."

"Well, sure, I know your Daddy. Darn good hunter, Shep Walker. How many ducks did your Daddy bag last weekend?"

"Oh—" Baylor really had no idea how many ducks his Daddy shot. "Around two hundred. Yeah, my Daddy killed two hundred ducks last weekend."

Buck Lemoine rocked back on his cowboy heels and gave a laugh like a deep-pitched hoot. "You real sure about that, son?" he chuckled.

"Oh, yes sir, I'm sure," Baylor lied.

"Haw-haw-haw! Well, I suspect the game warden is gonna be a tad upset if he's watching the program this morning. I'd say that's a few ducks over the limit." Then Buck turned to the camera and spoke directly: "Shep Walker, if you're watching this morning, you might oughta instruct your son about the power of television." Then he gave a big laugh that made lots of the little kids laugh along with him, even though they didn't get the joke.

"Well, good to talk with you, Baylor. Tell your Daddy I said hey."

Buck was moving down the row toward the next child when Baylor reached out and grabbed his arm.

"Wait, Buck!" Baylor told him. "I've got this song I wrote for your show." Baylor reached down into the pocket of his cowboy pants and pulled up a folded piece of paper with large childlike letters printed across its surface.

"I got to move on here, son," Buck said, tugging on the microphone.

"No! Wait!" Baylor insisted. He reached up and jerked the microphone out of Buck's hand. "Just gimme one minute, please sir!"

Buck Lemoine had never seen such a nervy little kid in all his years on The Ranch. But he couldn't grab back the microphone. Couldn't afford to look mean-spirited when you got a children's television show. He had himself a reputation to consider.

Baylor gripped the microphone tightly in his right hand and held it up to his mouth. He held the piece of paper with the words on it in front of him. He took a big breath, and then he began to sing, to the tune of the *Daniel Boone* television show theme song.

> *"Andrew Jackson was a man,*
> *Yes a big man*
> *He had a fine mind*
> *And he had a fine time*
> *And all along he was one of a kind!"*

Buck reached for the microphone, but Baylor held on to it. He was not finished yet. He was just getting going.

> *"Andrew Jackson had a dream*
> *Yes a big dream*
> *And he worked in the morning*
> *And he worked in the evening*
> *And at night he went to sleep in the pines!"*

When Baylor finished, he handed the microphone back to Buck with just a hint of a flourish. How he wished he had the nerve to whip the microphone cord around like a lasso.

"Thank you, Buck," he said.

Before moving on, Buck looked at him through gritted teeth.

"No, thank *you*, son. Thank *you*."

By this time, Baylor could feel his gut about to explode. After Buck had moved far enough away and Baylor figured he was no longer on camera, he jumped down from his seat on the bleachers, tripping over two little girls who were sitting with their arms around each other, looking frozen in fear. Baylor ran down the bleachers until he got to the studio door, which he pushed open madly. He was mortified at having to leave the set like that, but he knew if he didn't find a bathroom right away, he would have something to be ashamed of the rest of his life.

He flew down the hall to the front of the station, skidding to a halt at the reception desk.

"'Scuse me," he said, his hands held in front of his belly. "Can you tell me where the bathroom is?"

"You okay, baby?" she asked.

Baylor could not look at her. He followed her down the hall, and when he got inside the bathroom, he locked the door and sat for a very long time without turning the light on. It was very dark and still in the room, the darkness providing a tiny respite for his headache. As his stomach began to relax and he released himself, he felt that he was sinking, floating in dark space.

He prayed he hadn't ruined his whole song by running away right after singing it. He prayed all the people wouldn't think he was ashamed of his song, that they wouldn't think he was a chicken.

A fear he could not name, the worst kind, floated up. His body began to contract again, and he feared for a moment that he would stay paralyzed on the toilet in the K-Dixie-BS television station until the end of time. He tried to pray. None of the prayers he had been taught seemed to apply to his situation. They were just words. After a while he started to whistle, then to sing—just anything that came into his mind. He made up words to tunes that were a combination of Sidda's piano music and television theme songs. "My country was a big one," he sang. "Moving on, moving on," he sang again and again, a song he thought he had heard his Daddy whistle along to the radio in the truck. After a while, the small dark stall felt safe after being under the TV lights. Baylor sat and rocked back and forth, and forgot about time. He was pulled out of himself by a knock on the door.

"Hon," he heard the receptionist saying, "you all right in there?"

For a moment he could not speak. "Yes ma'am," he said, finally. "I'm fine."

"You want me to call your Mama to come pick you up? All the other Little Buckaroos have already gone home."

"No ma'am, thank you. I'm on my own," he said.

He waited until she had had time to walk away from the door. Then he wiped himself. He pulled up his cowboy pants and stared at the door of the stall. Open the door and move, he told himself. Open the door and move.

It was a leap of faith for Baylor to unlock and open the door of the stall. Putting one foot in front of the other, he walked to the sink and washed and dried his hands. Then he unlocked the door to the bathroom and left. He walked past the receptionist, who sat reading a paperback at her desk.

He would have preferred not to talk, but he must leave with dignity.

"So long," he said, and gave her a wave like John Wayne before he rode off into the sunset. "Appreciate your help."

Out on Jefferson Street, it was sunny and cold. He'd forgotten his jacket. Baylor was shivering, and a black wave of panic rose in his young body. He walked a few blocks, and he no longer felt like a Buckaroo. He was hungry and little and wanted to be back home at Pecan Grove, where the noise of his siblings insulated him from himself.

He found a phone booth and fished out one of the dimes Vivi made all the Walker kids carry. "You never know when you'll need mad money to phone home," Vivi had said.

The phone rang several times. *What if they're all gone? What if they no longer exist?* He had always known that at any time he could walk straight into *The Twilight Zone*. There was not one episode of that TV show that he had not found completely believable.

He lost count of how many times the phone rang. Finally Vivi answered.

"Mama, this is Baylor. Your son. Would you please come and get me? I'm on the corner by Dr. Mott's office."

"My *Star!*" Vivi squealed. "You were magnificent. I'll be there in a jiffy."

Baylor did not move. He stood in the glassed-in phone booth and watched the cars go by. There were not many on Saturday morning in Thornton, Louisiana. His mind was empty. He could have been anywhere, in some big city where no one knew his name or his family.

It was not until he saw the Thunderbird pull up to the curb that life felt real again. Vivi was blowing the horn, and Sidda, Little Shep, and Lulu were hanging out of the windows, blowing on orange wax Halloween whistles unearthed from the kitchen drawer where Vivi saved such items. His siblings blew the whistles, and Vivi sang at the top of her lungs: "Andrew Jackson was a man! Yes, a big man!"

"Get in here with us where you belong, you little singing Buckaroo!" Vivi said. "We're going to the movies! We already made popcorn to take with us. Imagine! I'm taking a television star with us to the movies!"

Baylor climbed in the car, and he was smothered in the sloppy embraces and slaps on the back of his brother and sisters.

"Hey, you were great!" Sidda said. "I tape-recorded it!"

Lulu started tickling him, and he couldn't help but laugh. Little Shep rubbed the top of Baylor's white head. "Two hundred ducks, huh? Daddy said you better bail him out of jail after the game warden finds him." Sidda hugged and hugged him, trying her best not to disturb her fake fingernails.

The radio was turned up loud, blasting out "It's My Party and I'll Cry If I Want To," and Vivi Abbott Walker and her kids sped up Jefferson Street in the direction of The Bob Theater. "I'm taking my TV star to the movies!" Vivi said, and handed Baylor a peanut-butter-and-jelly sandwich out of a paper bag filled with goodies.

Baylor realized he was starving. He bit down into the sandwich, then took a deep breath. The Thunderbird sped forward, carrying the five of them to lose themselves in front of the big screen. For eight blocks, Baylor Walker was a cotton-top singing Junior Buckaroo, a star in an uncontrollable galaxy.

SNOW IN THE SOUTH

Sidda, December 1961

*T*he first time it snowed in Thornton, my brother Little Shep was more excited than any of us. It was early December. I was in the kitchen with Baylor, and I was making us some hot chocolate. We had all heard of snow and seen pictures of snow, but it had never snowed in our lifetimes. Not in Thornton.

Daddy had told us the story of when it snowed when he was growing up. He said the first day it didn't stick at all. It just melted when it hit the ground. But the second day when he woke up, everything was all white. He ran outside and made snowballs and angel wings in the snow. He had learned how to do this from his cousin's husband from Illinois. He described how you made angel wings. You stretched out on the ground and moved your arms up and down and your legs back and forth. When you got up, there was the imprint of an angel with wings left behind! The way Daddy told it made me want to make angel wings so bad. Daddy said that if we ever saw snow, we better get out and enjoy it, because it might not happen again until we were all grown up.

Lulu was the first one to notice that it was snowing. She was sitting in the den next to the big picture window facing the bayou.

"Hey yall!" she hollered. "Look outside! Snow!"

When Little Shep heard her call out, "It's really *snowing!*" he took off running down the hall, yelling with delight. He flew through the big kitchen, past the armchair by the window, past the long oak table with the picnic table seats.

He ran straight into the sliding glass door leading into the den. He hit the door running at full speed. There was a loud THUNK! and we stood there openmouthed as he bounced off the heavy plate glass like a kickball. He hung in the air for a minute with his feet above his head, then crashed onto the den floor. He didn't move or make a sound. He'd knocked himself out cold. He had gotten carried away with something he'd never seen before.

We all wanted to see the snow, to hold its magic whiteness in our hands, but we couldn't. Not with Shep there on the quarry tile floor with his head tilted over to one side. Baylor got on his knees next to Little Shep's face, Lulu ran on her short fat legs to tell Mama. And I stood there wondering if he was going to die.

I had wanted Little Shep to die about two weeks before because he stole my tape recorder, the one I got for my birthday. He stole it and then broke the rewind button playing with it.

I loved that tape recorder. It was my favorite thing in the world. I spent whole weekends sitting outside with our German shepherd, Lamar, recording songs I made up for him. At night, I used to lie in bed and play back the sound of my own voice to myself. I tried out a hundred different voices and names for myself on that tape recorder. Every time I listened to them, I felt better about things.

Then Shep took it away. And he broke it. I was so mad about that tape recorder, but I didn't really mean for Shep to die. As I stood there watching him stretched out so still on the floor, I wondered if I could be arrested for this.

Next thing we knew, Mama was leaning over him. She turned to me. "Warm up the car right now, Siddalee, the keys are under the seat."

I went out to the car, got in, and reached up under the driver's seat. I could not see over the steering wheel, but Mama had taught me to start the car and let it warm up. She just hated getting into an icy-cold car. I loved doing this. It made me feel grown-up. While the car warmed up, I just sat there and watched the snowflakes coming down on the windshield.

It was more magical than I had ever dreamed. The whole world outside seemed quiet and still. I tried watching just one snowflake fall all the way to the windshield, but I kept losing it in the thousands of whirling flakes. To stare up like that into the falling snow made you feel just a little bit like flying. Then a little gust of wind would move the snow differently and break the spell. The snowflakes would land on the windshield, and for just a little moment you could see their snowflake design. But before you could really study it, the snowflake melted. I could have sat there all day watching the snow. But I didn't. As soon as the heater was going good, I opened the car door and ran back to the house.

Baylor and Lulu were sitting by the door, putting on their shoes and socks and coats. I took their little hands and led them out to the car. Mama picked Little Shep up real gently and came more slowly behind us, holding Little Shep, walking like he would break apart if she bounced him too hard. I closed the kitchen door behind Mama without even being asked and then ran around her and Little Shep to open the car door. Baylor and Lulu and me climbed into the back seat, and Mama carefully put Shep in the front seat, covering him with her coat. Then we were on the way to St. Cecilia's Hospital, where Mama volunteered. Where Little Shep was born. Where we were all born.

It was snowing harder now, and the flakes were bigger. The road was getting a little slushy, and the fields looked like somebody up in heaven had sprinkled confectioner's sugar down on them. Nobody knew how to drive in that stuff. We are warm-weather people down here, Daddy always says.

For once, nobody was talking. I forced myself to look away from the snow and lean over the seat and look at Little Shep. He was huddled up on the front seat with Mama's coat over him, looking like a little puppy who couldn't keep his eyes open. His eyes just kept wanting to close shut.

"Mama," I said, "why can't Little Shep keep his eyes open?"

Mama said, "You have to keep him awake, Sidda. Whatever you do, you keep him awake. If he goes to sleep now, he might die."

Well, it is scary to have to keep your brother awake when you are only eight years old. I carefully climbed over the seat of the Chevy and slid next to him, kneeling on the floorboard. I stuck my face right up to his and started talking to him. I am the oldest daughter. I had to do this.

"Shep," I said, "if you can just stay awake, we'll get one of those big feed bags and tear that thing open, and we'll slide down the hill in the snow right into the bayou. We're going to go flying across the bayou, and that bayou is going to hold us up like it never did before, because that sucker is going to be frozen solid, you hear me? You'll think you are flying, Shep! I'm not kidding, you are going to think you are a *bird*."

I just kept on talking, saying whatever came into my head, things that might make him want to stay awake. Tears started to leak from my eyes, and I had to bite them back. It was my job to keep Shep awake, not to sit there and cry like someone on TV.

"Shep, you can have my tape recorder in your hands and record all of it! Record the sound of the snow falling on your head, record the sound of the feed bag whooshing across the frozen bayou. Record it all, Shep, so when it is hot again in the summer and the blacktop road is melting from the heat, you can play that tape and be right there with the snow! Only, Shep, you have to stay awake now, because we are just little kids and you can't die. Okay?"

His eyes started to close in spite of all my talking. I reached out and started shaking him gently to keep him awake. Mama kept her eyes on the road because she was driving. She had to watch the road even more than usual. I could tell she was nervous behind the wheel. My mother was nervous driving in the best of weather. I looked out the back window, and I could see that we were leaving dark tracks in the slush. There were hardly any other cars out driving on the road. Lulu was holding Baylor's hand, and they were all quiet, just staring out the window at the magic of it. It was awful and confusing, the magic of the snow and the danger that Little Shep was in. No matter how much we fought, we loved our brother. He couldn't really die, could he? Would I think of him dying every time it snowed? If so, I would never live in cold-weather places.

"What are you doing, Siddalee?" Mama asked me while I was shaking Shep.

"Mama, I'm just trying to wake him up. His eyes are closing!"

"Well, you keep him awake, you keep talking. And you go on and shake him *extremely* gently. Don't shake him hard. Don't hurt him."

I would never hurt my brother. I stopped shaking him and started sort of rocking him. For a minute, I imagined I could remember when he was a baby, even though that couldn't be, since I was only a year older than him. I looked at his reddish blond crew cut, at his freckles that stayed all year. I looked at how long his eyelashes were and thought how I had never noticed them before. I thought of all the times we lay in bed next to each other and tickled each other's backs and told stories about flying. Little Shep always dreamed about flying. He dreamed about flying, and he dreamed about animals. Animals were his love. He was the one who took care of all our dogs. He was only seven years old, but he knew every inch of Daddy's land, and he talked about how he was going to farm it when he grew up.

So all the way down Pierce Street and after the right turn onto Sixth Avenue, I kept shaking Shep. I found if I shook him with a steady careful rocking motion, I could get him to stay awake. I never wanted to do anything so right as to keep Little Shep awake in that car. I was doing something very important.

We pulled into the emergency room entrance. Mama carried Little Shep in, with the three of us following right behind her. Some nurses put him on a stretcher and took him away to a room where we couldn't see. We had to sit around in the waiting room for a long time. Mama bought Baylor and Lulu some Cokes and peanut butter crackers from the machine. I didn't want anything. I sat in the chair by the hallway and stared at the door where Little Shep had been rolled in.

I tried to think back and remember how hard I had wished for Shep to die. I tried to feel just what my body was feeling then. And I felt it. I felt it in my stomach and in my head, and when I had the whole feeling back—I wished exactly that hard for him to live. I closed my eyes, and I tried to see Little Shep as a grown-up man. It wasn't easy, but I tried to see him and me as teenagers driving around in cars. And then him farming like Daddy. Driving the tractor like

Daddy, wearing a straw cowboy hat like Daddy, checking the cotton, checking the weather, taking care of the soil. Then I pictured him being a daddy himself. I tried to picture his head full of grown-up kind of hair, his head safe from the sliding glass door, his head full of interesting thoughts that he didn't even know yet. I tried to picture him big, alive, and happy.

I was only one year old when Little Shep was born, but I remember everything about when we were little. I remember wanting to hold him, and then more than once, wanting to kill him when he was lying there so beautiful. I remember these things, and no one can tell me I don't. He was a fast crawler, Shep was, darting all over that house so fast. No one could catch him. Then he'd get himself so tired, he would just fall asleep in the middle of a crawl, under the coffee table, or over by the big chair by the fireplace. And his forehead was a big one that made him look goofy sometimes, but mainly it made him look smart for a kid so young, with brown eyes like the cows staring out at you from Daddy's fields.

It seemed like we sat in that waiting room all day long. Mama tried and tried to reach Daddy. Lulu and Baylor drank their Cokes. I had to go to the bathroom, but I didn't dare move. We sat close together, like refugees from communism on a train or something, like people you saw on the TV but never imagined that you could be. We sat close to each other. If we could have climbed inside each other, we would have done it, just to not be so alone.

The nuns were always talking to us about prayer, but it never meant anything to me until then. Right then I understood: the right way to pray is not to *beg*, but to picture *good* things, to banish all bad things from your mind. To put up a huge wall of prayer so no bad thoughts can get in. To see what you want, and to feel the love that has been hiding there for your little brother, only you were too bossy to feel it before.

This was the first time I knew that someone around me could really die, and it made me different than I'd been before.

When the doctor came out, it wasn't our usual one, but a young one. He walked over in our direction, and Mama jumped up and went to meet him.

"Your son has a mild concussion," the doctor said, smiling with his big beautiful teeth. "He must have lost consciousness a few times, not rare in a child his age. But he's going to be fine. We'd like to keep him here for observation for a day or two. Just to keep an eye on him."

Mama smiled back and said, "Oh, thank you so much, Doctor! I was just worried to death! Yall are just mahvelous." She said this like *he* was particularly mahvelous.

"Well, Mrs. Walker, snow in the South can do weird things to people," he said. Then he bent down and touched Lulu's cheek. He didn't touch my cheek, he touched Lulu's.

"We're moving him up to a room right now," the handsome young doctor said.

We followed a nurse through a bunch of hallways back into the hospital. I would have been totally lost forever, the way one hallway led into another and then branched off into a couple more. But Mama knew her way around. She wasn't lost at all. When we got up to the hospital room, Little Shep was lying in this bed that looked too high and way too big for him. His eyes still looked sleepy. *He shouldn't be here. He should be playing in the snow. This is my fault for thinking the bad thoughts after he broke my tape recorder.*

Daddy finally made it in from the camp by then. Caro went out there and got him. Everybody else was saying little things, but me, I didn't say a word. I looked at Little Shep's temples there at the side of his face. I saw how they moved up and down with his breathing. I had never noticed how those temples moved before, or how they seemed so thin that they could be punctured with the barest of touches. My tough little brother, the one I fought with all the time, wasn't tough at all. He was fragile, and I could see that he was fragile. I said a prayer that I would never forget it.

I went over and whispered into Little Shep's ear: *Your big sister loves you. She is not going to let anything bad happen to you.*

Later that night, Daddy came back again. He brought Shep a wooden train like the one in *The Little Engine That Could.* And the next day I brought my tape recorder and showed Little Shep how to record with it. He interviewed nurses and the cute teenage Candy Stripers and everybody who came into his hospital room.

He started out each interview by saying, "This is Shep Walker Jr.

here reporting from St. Cecilia's Hospital in Thornton, Louisiana, where it snowed yesterday. I am here because I ran so fast and a glass door got in my way."

He came home after two days. All that snow had melted. I was so relieved and thanked God and all the angels that he was home and he was going to be okay. I never told him about wishing he would die. You don't need to flap your arms in the snow to make angel wings. Not when your guardian angels are flying around you and your little brother like all the love in the world.

My tape recorder could record so very many things. I tried more than once to hold the microphone to where my heart was and record its thumping. But all you could hear was the rustling of the shirt I was wearing. It could not record my heart. My heart was a heavy thing. Not as heavy as before my brother came home. But still heavy. I tried to picture the lightness of snow, what little I'd seen. It is hard to picture lightness. It seems to happen only when you stop trying.

Little Shep let me tickle his back the third day he was home. And I sang, "You Are My Sunshine," which Jimmie Davis, a governor of our state, made famous. But I sang it with different words. Words to make him laugh and let him know I loved him. I am the oldest daughter. It is my job to take care of the little ones. I poured all my heart into that song, and when my brother started to giggle, it was the most beautiful sound in the world.

Little Shep and me and my family, we are warm-weather folks. We don't take well to the cold. We like it when we're warm, when it's summer and we dive into warm water. We like it when we're all okay. We don't like to think about dying. We know it's there, but so are hurricanes. Daddy says, "You can't let fear of hurricanes stop you from putting seeds in the ground, even if they're going to grow tall only to be destroyed."

Little Shep just knocked himself out over frozen water, really. I know about water's cycle from science class. Water that melts into the earth. Then all that humidity goes back into the sky, where it turns into clouds. When the clouds become too heavy, they fall back down again as rain. And they do it all over again, and again. No matter what happens to us, water will go on cycling like that.

My family is a family of farmers, and my little brother is the one who will go forward after Daddy is old. If we are lucky and God is good to us, Little Shep and me will grow old together. We'll sit out on the porch and tell stories about how when we were children, about how he was the kind of little boy who'd knock himself out cold for something as beautiful and rare as snow.

SHOW AND TELL

November 1962

THORNTON DAILY MONITOR, NOVEMBER 19, 1962

Our Lady of Divine Compassion Church, at the corner of Oak and 21st streets, suffered a loss of one of its most treasured statues today. The Infant Jesus of Prague statue, donated to the church by Charles Messenger Chauvin, II, in 1928, was evidently hit by a car, causing the glass-framed wooden structure which held it to collapse. It appears that it was a random act of vandalism. Police are asking any potential witnesses to come forth. Monsignor Bergeron, of Our Lady of Divine Compassion, was quoted as saying, "Sad as this is, sacrilegious as this is, we must remember that this is a statue. This is not our God Himself. We must not confuse statues with God the Father or God the Son. We pray for the person or persons who did this." Sister Howard Regina, a first-grade teacher at Divine Compassion Parochial School, was quoted as saying, "Whoever did this will be punished far worse by God than by man." Charles Messenger Chauvin, III, son of Charles Messenger Chauvin, II, has offered a $400 award for anyone who can locate the vandal.

It was one of those damp, rainy, bone-chilling cold November afternoons that sometimes hit in the state of Louisiana and throw everyone's bodies into a tizzy because we are semitropical people. We're not used to the cold and never will be. So when it gets down into the low thirties, that is arctic to the people of Garnet Parish. *Arctic.* It was one of those days when the best thing in the world to do is to fix a nice hot drink of something soothing and lie in front of the fire, reading mysteries. The kind where the killer is caught and punished, where crimes get solved, where wrongs are made right, and you just feel like there is justice in the world even though the weather is crappy.

Vivi asked Caro if her children could play over at Caro's house while she went to Divine Compassion Parochial School for a parent-teacher meeting.

"It's nothing, Caro. Just one of the kids acting up in class, a tiny thing. But you know, one must be the good Catholic parent."

"Hmm," Caro took a long drag off her cigarette. "I've never had one of those meetings. They've pretty much left me and my boys alone."

"Maybe because you have refused to call nuns 'Sister' since you were twelve years old. You just call them 'Howard Regina' or 'Mary George' like they're regular people."

"Well, they most definitely are not regular people." Caro laughed.

"God knows they tried to correct you," Vivi said.

"It's because I say their names with such complete authority that they turn the other ear. Besides, they probably smell that if I were not so flat-out lazy, I would be Anglican. High Anglican. Much better choirs, much better music. Higher aesthetics all around."

"Caro, you kill me."

"I'm a real Phyllis Diller."

"No, Dahlin, you're a real Caro Brewer Bennett."

❧

It took Vivi quite a while to schedule the meeting after she received the note from Sister Howard Regina. Baylor had handed her the note back in mid-September demanding that Vivi visit her immediately about a matter of utmost importance regarding her youngest child, Baylor Walker. The kids had walked home from the bus stop at the end of Pecan Grove Lane and up to the backyard, where Vivi was stretched out on the old pink-checked bedspread with an array of peanut butter sandwiches, raisins, and lemonade. The September light, still warm, but comfortable, shone on Vivi and her brood as well as the 700 acres of cotton that all but surrounded the house. Cotton that was ripe to be picked any day now.

Soon after receiving the note, Vivi quit answering the phone herself. Every time Sister Howard Regina called, Vivi made Sidda take the call and say, "My mother said to tell you she is busy. She is just *swamped.*"

However, Lulu had picked up the phone two days before and handed it to Vivi because she didn't know any better. It was Sister Howard Regina on the phone. At the sound of her voice, Vivi began to feel slightly queasy, like a ten-year-old who has just done something wrong and knows she is going to *get it.*

On this cold evening in November, it is almost dark in the small town of Thornton, Louisiana. Rain is turning to slush, and memories of summer are dim. Vivi Abbott Walker sits in her 1962 Thunderbird in the back parking lot of Pizzo's Market. The turquoise blue two-door T-Bird, with its sleek design, its perfectly round taillights echoing the age of rocket design, the long sleek-lined side panels coming to a point at the front, and the chrome bumper coming up from underneath to meet and reinforce the point, is distinctive and modern. Now it is almost hidden by a large green Dumpster and some bushes behind the grocery.

Caro pulls up next to the T-Bird and blows the horn—*shave-and-a-haircut! Two bits!* Vivi startles so severely that she feels as though she has been electrocuted. Siddalee, Little Shep, Lulu, and Baylor, along with Caro's boys, Turner and the twins Gavin and

Bernard, are riding with Caro in her Renault station wagon, the only one like it in Thornton. Vivi puts her head in her hands and presses her thumbs against her temples.

There is a big dent in the back of the Thunderbird on the passenger side, interrupting its long, low modern lines. The T-Bird has a tight, low-sitting back seat with a hump in the middle that one of the kids always had to deal with. The two-door hardtop featured bucket seats in the front—a car definitely comfortable for the two front-seat passengers only. This is most definitely not a Catholic mom's car.

But now Vivi's little modern roadster is just a mess. It looks like someone took a big concrete bat and bashed it in, then dragged a pipe along the side of it. Caro fears that Vivi has been hurt. Clearly she has been in an accident. "Every one of yall stay in the car," Caro whispers to the seven kids. "I'll go see what's up."

While the children wait, they turn on the colored radio station and listen to Little Stevie Wonder. Every single one of them drums along with "Fingertips, Part 1." They love Little Stevie Wonder. They want to meet him. Vivi's kids try to think about Little Stevie, not about their mother. The world always looks better if you think about Little Stevie Wonder.

A moment later, Caro brings Vivi, shaking and freezing cold, to the station wagon and helps her into the passenger seat. "Vivi, what in the world is going on? Have you been in an accident?"

"Hit and run!" says Little Shep, excited.

Vivi holds a Jax beer can, and the rest of the six-pack is in her other hand. She automatically hands Caro a can of beer. She is all shook up. You can tell by the quiver of her hand and her tight lips and eyes.

"It's too damn cold to be drinking beer," Caro says.

"I can't believe I did it," Vivi says. "I just cannot believe it. It's all her fault."

"What in the world are you talking about?"

"I sideswiped the Infant Jesus," Vivi whispers loudly, terrified.

"Vivi, what in the *hell* are you talking about? Try and make some sense, please."

The Petites Ya-Yas don't know if Vivi is going off her rocker or if she's trying to tell Caro something in Ya-Ya code, something they do when they don't want the children to know what they are saying. The boys are all stirred up in the back seat and way-back of the wagon. They make donkey sounds, like they just discovered how to bray.

"Can it, spooks!" Caro says, "before I knock yall into yesterday."

The boys quiet down a little.

Vivi leans over and whispers into Caro's ear. "We have to leave the Thunderbird parked here. I can't be seen in it anywhere *near* Divine Compassion."

"Oh, all right. Your car doesn't have enough room to fit two midgets, anyway." Caro has long legs, and she always hits her head when she folds her long body into Vivi's T-Bird. Caro backs the Renault out of the parking lot and heads down Alma Street, with Vivi giving directions.

"Drive around to the side of the church where the parking lot is," Vivi directs Caro. "Go up Twenty-first. Whatever you do, do *not* drive by the convent, for God's sake."

Vivi turns to the kids. "Listen to me, Sidda-Shep-Lulu-Baylor. And Turner, and twins," she says. "When we get in the block before the church, every one of yall *duck!* I do not want yall to peek, I don't want your little heads visible at all. Do you hear me? This is serious. We could get in *big trouble*."

Then Vivi slinks way down in the seat so nobody can see her. "The nerve! The sheer unadulterated nerve! I don't care if she is a nun. I don't care if she has taken vows of poverty, chastity, and obedience. I don't care if she has vowed to never have another bowel movement. She does not have the right to talk to me like that!"

They round the corner of Twenty-first and Olive, the block that leads to Divine Compassion. Vivi crouches down on the floorboard of the front seat. "Everybody get down!" she whispers loudly to the kids.

Caro pulls into the church parking lot. As Caro puts the car in park, Vivi, shaking, crawls onto the seat so that her eyes barely reach the passenger seat's window level. This is signal enough for every single child to poke their heads up in unison. At the edge of the parking lot, near the side door of Divine Compassion Church, something isn't quite right. Something looks out of place. It takes them a moment to realize just what. And then they spot it: the Infant Jesus of Prague statue that stood in that same spot for umpteen years suspended in a glass-enclosed altar framed by a wooden structure. The statue is no longer standing. The glass is shattered, and the Infant Jesus of Prague is lying there on the sidewalk! The Infant lies there like, like, well, like someone has backed into it with a Thunderbird and driven off. The statue's hand is broken off, its head is cracked, and its tiara is shattered. The beautiful expensive robes and cloaks are soaked in rain and stained with mud. The only thing left unharmed is the globe that the Infant stands on. It is still intact.

Vivi was involved in a hit-and-run with the Savior of the World! They always knew she didn't drive so good in reverse. But they never thought it would come to this.

Sidda gasps out loud. Little Shep, Turner, Gavin, and Bernard start yelling and shouting. "Wow! Look at that!" Little Shep says over and over. "Way to go, Mama, *way to go!*" Everyone but Baylor and Lulu jump around in the station wagon in excitement. Lulu chews on the ends of her blond hair. Baylor remains silent.

Vivi crawls back down on the floorboard. "Hit the gas, Caro! Get us the hell outta here!"

And so the two mothers and seven kids slink down the street in the Renault away from Divine Compassion. Caro heads in the direction of Lafayette Street. Vivi doesn't sit back up until they're three blocks away from the scene of the crime. When she finally gets back up, she keeps glancing out all the car windows and turning to look behind them to see if anyone is following. Someone could be tailing them. Some kind of Vatican FBI. Like Big Shep the pagan says: You can never tell about those Catholics.

"Well, where to, Viv-o?" Caro asks. "Should we drive you over to the police station and hand you over to the Gestapo?"

When Caro looks at Vivi, she realizes that she shouldn't have said this. Vivi has temporarily lost her sense of humor. She looks more like she has been in a fatal car accident in which human life was lost. When you bump the Prince of Heaven off his stand, it can shake you up.

Caro tries again. "Want to go pick up the T-Bird?"

"No!" Vivi replies. "I don't want to drive. Take me to your house. Please."

∝

Caro lights a fire in the fireplace. Almost everything in Caro and Blaine's living room is white, black, or gray. The floors are all white terrazzo, covered partly by a large zebra-striped rug. The furniture is mostly black leather and chrome, and every piece of furniture is referred to by an architect's name. Caro might say, "Just scooch the Eames over here and have a seat. But don't break it, or my husband will have to sell his office."

When Blaine the architect is home, the boys' toys are never left in the main part of the house. If you didn't know better, you would think they were a childless couple. When Blaine is away, of course, toys are everywhere, and the lives of three young boys compete with an architect's idea of the perfect 1962 living room. One entire wall of the living room consists of windows that go from floor to ceiling. A big black primitive vase and a black African goddess sculpture stand on a pedestal. (The Petites all love the statue because of its bare pointy breasts. Like having a *National Geographic* native right in your own house. When Vivi isn't looking, Little Shep loves to touch the teats on the statue, impure little imp that he is.) And then there is the massive black candle on the large kidney-shaped coffee table in front of the sofa. You can't believe that you are still in Thornton when you are in this room. It always feels cool, and everyone is asked to leave their shoes at the door like they are in China or something.

Caro lights the black candle and hands Vivi a drink. "Drink. Just drink it down."

Vivi takes a big gulp. This is one of Caro's special drinks, with the rum that she discovered when she and Blaine went to that island in the Caribbean. This is all Caro drinks these days. She has Roger at the Abracadabra Liquor Store order the rum special for her. She drinks the dark thick rum with milk, rum on the rocks, rum with Community Coffee Dark Roast. But Vivi isn't calmed down at all. Even though she has finished off her first "Caro," which is what everyone now calls any rum drink that Caro makes with her Puerto Rico rum.

Caro lights two cigarettes and hands one to Vivi. They sit on the black sofa. The couch frame is a chrome grid with a gentle curve and boxy leather cushions. People are always shocked that it is actually so comfortable.

"Tell me about it, Vivi. Just start at the beginning."

"All right," Vivi says, and takes a drag off her cigarette. "That woman—I'm sorry, strike me dead if you want, but I am not going to call her a nun. She is just a mean-ass old hairy mole-faced woman. A while back, that woman sent home a note with Baylor. 'Come in and talk to me,' the note said. It was about the Show and Tell shit, you know."

Caro nods. All the Ya-Yas know about the garter belt. They thought it was hilarious. Well, Necie called it a "tad risqué."

Caro listens as Vivi sinks into the sofa and speaks without stopping.

"Okay, so I made a goddamn appointment. Granted, it took me a little while to get around to it, but I live a busy life. But I put on a skirt and hose and went to Divine Compassion for the face-to-face, okay? Well, I walked into that first-grade classroom, and the woman was sitting at her desk. Did not even stand up to say 'Good afternoon, kiss my ass.' Nothing.

"'Good afternoon, Sister,' I said. 'How are you this afternoon?'

"She did not even look up at me, Caro. Just kept on grading papers. I didn't know whether I should stand up, sit down, genuflect, stick my butt in her face, or what. I mean, there were only these tee-ninecy little desks to sit on.

"She finally gestured for me to sit, with a little wave of her hand like she was the Pope or something. I stared at those baby desks and thought, Oh, what the hell. 'A good thing I watch my weight,' I joked, thinking I might as well *try*. Well, the bitch just frowned.

"'Mrs. Walker—,' the woman started.

"'Please—just call me Vivi.'

"'*Mrs. Walker*. Mrs. Walker, how recently have you received the Sacrament of Confession?'

"I think for a minute. 'Well, Sister, probably a month ago,' I said. 'I'll probably go again this Friday. I don't go every week. I mean, with four little kids, I don't have much time left over for sinning.' I was still trying to get her to crack a smile.

"'So,' the old bat said, 'have you confessed the sin of sending your six-year-old boy to school with an item of your intimate apparel to display to other innocents in a classroom of God?'

"'Sister, are we talking about my garter belt here?'

"'You know precisely what we are talking about here, Mrs. Walker,' she said to me. Like I am one of her first-graders.

"I wanted to scream, I am a thirty-five-year-old woman! Don't talk to me in that tone of voice. But I didn't.

"Anyway, the penguin continued: 'You have gone over a month with that sin on your soul, and still you have not sought the Sacrament of Penance?'

"'Sister, what is your point, exactly?'

"'Do not speak to me in disrespect, Mrs. Walker.'

"I was starting to want a cigarette at this point. In fact, I was dying for a cigarette at this point. 'Sister, you don't mind if I smoke in here, do you?' I asked her. 'I would kill for a Lucky Strike.'

"'I discourage smoking in my classroom.'

"'We can crack a window,' I told her, and I started to get up from the desk.

"'Sit back down!' she said. 'Those windows do not open.'

"'They don't *open?* I was horrified. My baby sits entombed in this room with this woman all day, and the windows do not open. 'Why don't the windows open, Sister?'

"'I do not believe in open windows in my classroom. The noise is too great from the schoolyard, causing distractions. And it is unsafe to have windows that open. The children could crawl up on the ledge and fall out of them.'

"'But we are on the first floor.'

"'If you continue to contradict everything I say, Mrs. Walker, then I will have to ask our principal Sister Mary Paul to come in and help with this discussion.'

"I put my cigarette back in my purse, then decided to take it out again and just hold it between my fingers. If I couldn't smoke it, I could at least hold it. By this point, I wanted that cigarette so bad I could eat it.

"Then she said, 'I hope you know that exposing God's innocents to the near temptations of sin is as grave a sin as one can commit, especially as a Catholic mother.'

"'Sister,' I said, trying to remain calm, 'I handed my son one of my garter belts at the last minute as he was rushing out the door. He didn't have anything else to take to Show and Tell. It was simply the first thing that I picked up in my hand.'

"'Mrs. Walker!' she said sternly. 'That is quite enough!'

"Caro, by this point I wanted to haul off and sock her so hard those moles would fly off her bulldog face. But I was shaking too hard and trying not to cry. She would not let up, Caro. I mean, the woman kept digging, kept turning the knife.

"'This is your fourth child to come through Our Lady of Divine Compassion,' that woman said. 'You have repeatedly exposed your children to impurity. You are married to a non-Catholic. There was the time you allowed your oldest daughter to wear a pair of suede boots with fringe with her school uniform. You show up on school grounds yourself wearing outfits that no Catholic mother should be seen in. Stretch pants. Sweaters that befit a woman of the night more than a Catholic wife and mother. Oh, I have been watching you, Mrs. Walker.'

"I didn't tell her to shut up. But I told her to mind her own business.

"'It is not your mission to give me fashion tips, thank you very much. It is your job to teach my children how to read and write,' I said. 'It is certainly not your job to tell me how to raise them.'

"'Oh, you are wrong, Mrs. Walker,' Sister Howard Regina said to me, like I was some hideous creature from the lower rungs of hell. 'It is indeed my job to tell you how to raise your children. You have entrusted your children to me not just as a teacher of reading, writing, and arithmetic, but also as trainer of their souls, as a shaper of their spiritual lives, so that they will grow up to live as true Catholics in a world too often threatened by the kinds of things that garter belts represent.'"

Vivi starts to laugh. Caro joins in, but Vivi switches from laughing to crying so quick that it is dizzying. She is both crying and laughing at the same time.

Then Vivi stands up and stretches. "Soaring Hawk," she says, using Caro's Indian name bestowed upon her during their Ya-Ya tribal naming ceremony in 1937. "Hit me with a bourbon and branch this time, Caro."

"Absolument!" Caro says, and crosses over to the bar, which is shaped like a boomerang with a little round sink in it. The bar is on the other side of the gravel pit near the stereo console.

Vivi reaches into her purse and pulls out her lipstick. It's a good sign if she's putting on more lipstick, Caro thinks. Vivi never goes long without fresh lipstick unless she is really far gone. Vivi always wears lipstick. When she goes to Communion and the priest puts the host on her tongue, just for an instant you can see the imprint of her lipstick on the white wafer, like she is kissing the body of Jesus.

Vivi looks at Baylor and Sidda, noticing for the first time that they are there in the room. "What are yall doing, spooks?"

Baylor and Sidda smile at her. "Nothing, Mama," Sidda says.

"It's funny, huh, Mama?" Baylor says.

Vivi looks at Baylor for a moment. She puts her lipstick back in her purse, and smiles back. "Yes, it's funny," she says. "It is hysterical."

"Can I sit in your lap, Mama?" Baylor asks.

"Yes, Cotton-top Bay-Boy, you sure can." Baylor crawls into her lap, and she rubs his head. Baylor is always getting his head rubbed. People love to feel his soft white-blond hair against their hands.

Caro hands Vivi her drink, and she puts a plate of maraschino cherries on the coffee table for Baylor and Sidda. Sidda plops a cherry in her mouth. The cherry is so sickly sweet on her empty stomach that it makes her mouth pucker, and she spits it out into her hand. But she likes the way it turns her lips red like Vivi's.

"So!" Caro says to Vivi, "don't stop now! What did you do next?"

Vivi takes a sip of the drink, and when she starts to talk, her whole tone has changed. She acts like she's telling one of her funny stories rather than what really happened. She uses her hands a lot and acts out the different voices.

"I told that Howard Regina woman never to embarrass one of my children again, or she would be sorry. I said, I don't care what you think of me. But you shame my little boy in front of a class again, and I will report you to Monsignor Bergeron so fast that your head will spin out of that headdress and you will be transferred to Timbuktu! And then I got up to walk out, but before I could get out of the door, the bitch says, real soft, like she is praying: 'Holy Mary, Mother of Divine Compassion, please look down upon the innocent

Walker children and protect them from the ways of their evil mother. Lift their eyes unto the purity of thy gaze, and keep them safe under your most chaste protection.'"

Then Vivi begins to cry again. At first she cries without sound, staring down at her hands. She tries to catch her breath, but she can't.

"Why couldn't that nun leave the Holy Mother out of this? Don't drag the Virgin into this! THE VIRGIN IS THE ONE I PRAY TO! SHE IS THE ONLY ONE I TRUST! WHY DO THEY KEEP TRYING TO RUIN HER!"

Vivi becomes so agitated that she knocks her drink on the floor, and the glass breaks. Baylor and Sidda stare at the brown liquid spreading across the zebra-striped carpet.

Caro picks up the broken glass and blots the carpet with a couple of paper napkins. Caro is not upset; she has known Vivi for a long time. At the bar, Caro mixes another drink, holding the bottle of bourbon up to the light to admire its color. Caro does things like that when you least expect it.

"Is that when you climbed into the T-Bird and backed into the Infant Jesus of Prague?" Caro asks.

Vivi is still crying. "Yes, that is when I did it."

"So it was an accident," Caro says.

Vivi hesitates. "Well, yes," she says softly. "It was an accident."

"I give you absolution, Vivi," Caro says, making the sign of the cross over Vivi and handing her the fresh drink.

"Oh, bless you, Dahlin," Vivi says, and takes a sip.

"Did anyone see you?" Caro asks.

"No, they couldn't have. There wasn't anybody there. All the school buses were gone. The lot was empty except for me. The only one who saw was the statue itself."

"And He's not talking," Caro says, and winks at Vivi.

Vivi reaches into her purse for a Kleenex. She blows her nose, and then opens her compact to check her makeup.

"I never did much care for that statue," Caro says. "The kid was snippy-looking. Snotty."

"Me neither," Vivi agrees. "I mean, those fancy robes on a little wooden infant statue! And that tiara! A baby boy wearing a tiara. The way he raised that right hand like he was something hot, like he didn't even need a mother. And standing on a globe. Please. This is the kind of statue that makes people think Catholics are nutcases."

Sidda is afraid to speak but wants to show off how much she knows. She finally says, "Mama, if you think His robes are show-offy, you should hear about his life."

"Oh, my God," says Vivi, "this is what the penguins teach my children: the life of *statues*."

"Tell us about it," Caro says.

"Well, an old Spanish monk got a vision from the Christ child and made the statue. Then it passed into the hands of Saint Teresa of Avila. She gave it to a Bohemian nobleman named Lord Vratislav of Pernstejn when he married Dona Maria Maximiliana Manriguez de Lara. This was all in Spain."

Vivi and Caro are cracking up. The rest of the kids who are still around the fireplace are giggling, not sure whether Sidda is making this up or not.

"Sidda," Vivi says, "you astonish me. Trust me, you will end up in the theater yet."

Sidda is so proud. She has faithfully, compulsively memorized every story the nuns tell her at Divine Compassion. And now she is distracting Vivi from being so upset. She is listening to me like TV or something, Sidda thinks. "Then," she continues, "the statue passed into the hands of their beautiful daughter, Polyxema."

"Jesus," Caro says, "sounds like a name for an acne cream."

Vivi lets out a snort of laughter. "Sidda, you are wonderful! Polyxema! I love it. Caro, do you see what I mean when I tell you that if I have done nothing else, I have raised children with imagination!"

Sidda clears her throat. "Okay, then Madam Polyxema de Lobkowisz, who had been married twice—"

"Aha," Vivi says, "a sinner."

"Unless her husband died," Sidda says. She does not like that they are interrupting her recitation. Once she starts something, she likes to finish it. "May I finish about the Infant Jesus of Prague, please?" she asks.

"Certainly. Absolutely. I had no idea he'd gotten around so god-damn much." Vivi's voice is starting to slur slightly.

"Well, Madam Polyxema de Lobkowisz gave her most precious

possession in the world—the statue—to the Church of Our Lady Victorious, which belonged to the barefooted Carmelites of Prague. Since that time, many miracles have been attributed to praying to the Infant Jesus of Prague. He healed a woman who was paralyzed. And He was always dressed up in aristocratic outfits because he was so royal."

"There you have it," Caro says. "And now the statue is lying on its butt in Garnet Parish, Louisiana, in the rain."

"It's not the *same* statue," Sidda responds. "This is a *replica*."

"Sidd-o," Caro says, "don't take this so seriously. Okay, Pal?"

"Yes ma'am," Sidda says. She waits and watches to see what her mother will do next.

Vivi takes out a cigarette, taps it on the coffee table, and lights it with her monogrammed Zippo. "Who knows how much it'll take to repair the T-Bird? My dream car. Fun, fast, and powerful, that's why I wanted it. Three-ninety engine. God, it was the perfect get-the-hell-out-of-Dodge car. And now it's all hurt." Vivi sighs. "Probably cost eighty-four thousand dollars to repair. I don't know. I don't care. As much as Shep hates the Catholic Church, he might be downright *glad* to spend money since I tore into the fancy statue that one of those old Chauvin farts donated. He can't stand that country club snob clan."

"Well," Caro said, "you have been wanting a paint job on the T-Bird."

Vivi looks at Caro like she's been given a gift. "Fabulosa-osa! I'm sick of that Garden Turquoise! I'll have my baby painted that lickable Monte Carlo Red color. Oh, look out! Whaddaya say?!"

"Red Bird," Caro says, and comes back to the sofa. "Yeah, baby, call her 'Red Bird.'"

"Glorious. Just take it to the body shop, have the damage repaired, and have them slap that coat of red on it that I adore. Oh, I am starting to like this."

"It's a blessing in disguise," Caro says.

Vivi stands up and walks over to Caro's modern fireplace. You can't stand there and warm your backside the way you can with our old-fashioned kind at home, Vivi thinks. It's a black funnel-shaped design that hangs suspended from the ceiling with a gravel pit underneath it. The kids love the way that fireplace just floats above the black gravel. It scares Lulu, though. She says it looks like something Hansel and Gretel might get burned up in.

Vivi tries to warm herself anyway. She has on a wool pleated skirt and a pair of hose with penny loafers. On this cold November evening, she wears a pullover sweater, the kind that she usually doesn't wear because she says they make her itch. She looks like she is trying to figure something out.

"How Catholic do you want to be about this?" Caro asks her.

"Not very," Vivi says. She looks at Sidda and Baylor and says, "Dahlins, yall go in the back and play with the other kids for a while."

"Oh, Mama," Sidda says. "I don't want to go."

"No whining, Siddalee," Vivi says. "Do what I say, and do it *now*." Sidda takes Baylor's hand, and they obey their mother.

Caro goes to the door and peeks down the hall to make sure the kids are gone.

When she comes back, she gazes straight into Vivi's eyes. "Well, then don't pay for repairing that damn statue. *Just don't say one damn word about it.*"

"The thing was too close to the parking lot in the first place," Vivi says.

"Exactly," Caro agrees.

"It's a miracle no one has backed into it before."

"A miracle."

"I've always secretly hated that statue anyway," Vivi says.

"And His face was dirty," Caro says. "God knows what kinds of insects had crawled up in those garments."

"Insects probably crawled up his nose. Not to mention mice. Mice droppings in the folds of those ridiculous garments. When you get right down to it, I did the parish a favor."

"My thoughts precisely," Caro says.

"Nobody but you and I know," Vivi says.

"And the kids, of course," Caro reminds her.

"Of course," Vivi says. "The kids."

"Speaking of the little monsters," Caro says, "they must be starved. I know I am."

Caro heads to the back and calls out: "Any hungry little children back there? 'Chili con Caro' coming up! Come and get it!"

❧

They all gather in the kitchen, where Caro has had chili simmering so long it's ever so slightly burned on the bottom of the big cast iron pot, but the chili is so well seasoned, no one can tell. She ladles out hot steaming chili into bowls for each child, and hands them the bowls on plates with pieces of cornbread that her maid cooked and left after cleaning earlier in the day. Vivi hands them napkins and soup spoons, and pours glasses of orange juice.

Once everyone has their food, they gather back around the fire, say the blessing real fast, and dig in.

"Spooks," Caro says, "just try not to drop chili on the zebra rug, or my husband will think a Mexican tried to shoot it."

For a while, all is quiet except the clink of spoons against the bowls and the happy sounds of hungry children eating good food. About halfway through the meal, Vivi says, "Kids, listen up, okay?"

They all look at her, not knowing what to expect after all they've witnessed today.

"Do yall like *secrets?*" Vivi says in her best Wicked Witch of the West voice.

"Yes ma'am!" they all say, their mouths filled with chili.

"Oh, never mind," Vivi says. "Yall could never keep *this* secret."

"Yes, we could!" all seven kids call out.

"We can keep a secret better than anyone in the world!" Little Shep says. "What is it?"

"Should we trust them?" Vivi asks Caro.

"Naw, I wouldn't," Caro says. "They're a bunch of little sneaks."

"Please tell us!" Lulu begs. "Yall can trust us. I promise. We'll never tell. Hope to die. Stick a needle in my eye."

"If yall really know how to keep a secret, there may be a reward involved," Caro says.

"Yeah? Like what?" Turner asks.

"Like trips to Fred's Hamburger Drive-In for root beer floats. We can bundle up and sip away and pretend it's summertime at Spring Creek," Vivi says.

"Exactly," Caro nods.

"When?" Little Shep asks.

"Soon," Vivi replies.

"I'm not keeping a secret unless yall get us root beer floats tomorrow," Little Shep says.

Vivi throws Caro a look.

"Kid drives a hard bargain," Vivi says.

"Takes after his mother," Caro says, and takes the last piece of garlic bread before Lulu can grab it.

"What's the secret, Mama?" Baylor asks. He has hardly eaten anything. Baylor does not eat when he is upset, and today has upset him.

"The secret is this," Vivi says, like she is originally from Transylvania. "I sideswiped the Infant Jesus of Prague today. *And no one must ever know but us. The Prague Nine.*"

"You didn't sideswipe Him," Little Shep says, "you knocked Him down and called him Shorty."

Caro lets out a laugh. Vivi tries to keep a grown-up face.

"Well, that is the secret. Can yall keep it till the day you die?"

They all gasp. They love this. It is a spicy new ingredient stirred into the thick soup of secrets they already live in.

"You want us to *lie?*" Lulu asks, excited.

"Of course I don't want you to lie!" Vivi protests, laughing like the idea is preposterous. "Lying is a sin against the Ten Commandments. I simply want you to *forget.* Forget we ever drove by Divine Compassion today. Forget you ever laid eyes on that Infant Jesus of Prague."

"Oh. I see," Lulu says, disappointed at not being instructed to lie outright.

"But," Little Shep asks, "what if someone comes up to us and says, 'Hey, did your mother back her car into that statue of Jesus that used to stand by the side door of the church?' *Then* what do we say?"

"No one is ever going to ask you that, Little Shep," Vivi says.

Then Caro's kids chime in, "But what if someone asks us to swear on a stack of Holy Bibles that Aunt Vivi didn't do it? What do we do then?"

These are kids who push things as far as they can.

"Look, spooks, let's don't get dramatic here," Caro chimes in. "All we're saying is: Mum's the word. Got it?"

Little Shep, like a dog with a bone, can't let it go. "But what do you want us to do if someone asks us bald-faced?"

"Just stare at 'em like they're crazy until they walk away," Vivi tells him.

Little Shep thinks for a minute. "Oh, okay," Little Shep says. "I can do that. Easy-greasy."

Then Vivi turns to Sidda. "Any questions, Sidda?" she asks.

"Yes ma'am, why don't you report that woman to Monsignor Bergeron?"

"Don't call her a woman," Vivi says. "Howard is a nun."

"Bride of Christ," Turner says.

"That's right," Vivi agrees.

"Did she wear a garter when she married Christ?" Lulu asks.

Vivi stares at Lulu, then she stares at Caro. "Caro, were there some kind of classes we were supposed to take before we said we'd raise kids?"

"Yeah," Caro replies. "We forgot to go."

"Oh, that's right." Vivi laughs.

"We took the cha-cha classes instead, remember?"

"Let's cha-cha!" the twins demand.

"Absolument!" Caro says, and goes over to the stereo and puts on a stack of records. You can tell she is glad things are starting to lighten up. They all are.

They get up from the table without so much as touching the dirty plates. Caro always leaves her dinner plates for the maid to get the next morning. Instead, she puts a record on the stereo. It's the *Let's Learn to Cha-Cha* record. And it's not the first time they've danced to it.

"One-two-three, cha-cha-cha!" Baylor calls out, and dances with Vivi.

They're all full as ticks, but they're up dancing, counting out the rhythm. It's how they learned their numbers. When they were real little, Vivi and Caro would dance with their kids and teach them: "One-two-three, cha-cha-cha! Four-five-six, cha-cha-cha! Seven-eight-nine, cha-cha-cha!" All the way up to twenty.

At some point Little Shep appears on the dance floor with a garter belt in his hand. He got it out of Vivi's purse! He's dancing with it, shaking it in the air like maracas. After a while, he hands it to Baylor, who ties it to his belt and shakes his little hips with it on.

He shakes it with the cha-cha rhythm so that it bangs against his belt and makes a little chinking sound that becomes an accompaniment to their dancing.

Vivi's kids are so proud of her for getting the garter belt back from Sister Howard Regina. They can't believe she forgot to tell them that part of the story. Sometimes they think their mother doesn't know what a hero she really is.

"Yall just sleep over here tonight," Caro says.

"No, we couldn't do that," Vivi says.

"Why in the hell not?" Caro asks. "Shep is at the duck camp, right? I mean, it is November."

"Of course he's at the duck camp. Do you think there are any men in this town, in this state, who are not at the duck camp?"

"Yes," Caro says. "Blaine. He is in New Orleans, consulting with a client who's remodeling a house in the Garden District, but who wants a 'modern' feel with traditional 'overtones.' Blaine is sashaying around New Orleans like he is the Prince of the French Quarter."

Vivi gives Caro a look. "Sometimes I forget we married such different men."

"Anyway, it's still raining. The kids are exhausted, we have plenty of bunk bed space. Yall are sleeping here, that's all there is to it. Got it?"

"Yes ma'am," Vivi says to Caro.

Caro leads the kids off to wash their faces, pulling out extra toothbrushes for the Walker kids to share. Then Sidda, Little Shep, Lulu, and Baylor climb into Caro's kids' extra pajamas. The pajamas feel so soft and warm on this cold night. In the twins' room, Sidda gives Lulu the bottom bunk, and she takes the top bunk. But soon, Lulu asks to crawl in with Sidda, and Sidda says yes. Little Shep and Baylor sleep in Turner's room, with Little Shep in a sleeping bag on the floor. Drifting off, they can still barely hear Vivi and Caro talking in the living room, but they can't make out the words. Soon they are fast asleep.

Caro puts another log in the fireplace. "Tell me more, Vivi," she says.

Vivi looks at her friend, and thinks, Those three words are as good as the words *I love you.*

Vivi paused for a moment, took out her lipstick, and said, "Okay, I was in the church parking lot, and I was backing up. I was so angry that my peripheral vision just shut down, just completely shut down, do you understand what I am saying?!" Vivi held her lipstick in her hand and stared at it, like it was a foreign object that she had never seen before. "I am sick to death of crap being crammed down my throat. The Mary they shove down my throat is impossibly good. She is blue and pink gowns. She is roses and crowns and stars all around her. She is all sweetness and perfection.

"I want to vomit up all this Catholic shit and choose my own thoughts! Choose a Holy Mother who is strong, who thinks for herself and is brave as hell. I want to blot out all those white-bearded tired-ass old men and pray to a gorgeous woman who crushes snakes with her bare feet. You just watch it: She's the one who'll set us free. One of these days I'm just going to quit praying to God. I'm going to pray only to a strong and sassy Mary. *Only* to her. Am I crazy? Does anyone else think like this?"

Vivi stood and walked to the windows, then suddenly turned back to face Caro. "Don't they realize that the real Mary, the strong Mary, could have said NO to the angel Gabriel?! Did *anybody* ever think of that? She could have said flat-out: 'No, thank you, I will not have an illegitimate child. And I have never heard of Joseph. It is not in my plans to marry a carpenter, especially not one from Nazareth.'

"But she didn't say no. She said yes, at great risk. She was a teenager, for God's sake! And she said yes. And if she hadn't said yes, maybe there would have been no Infant Jesus, period. Let alone any Infant Jesus of the Fancy Little Lord Fauntleroy Outfits of Prague.

"WHAT DO THEY WANT OF ME!! I know I'm not the best mother, but I do the best I can. Which of course is never enough. Every day I wake up and pray, *Mary, please ask God to make me loving and patient and kind all day long. Please help me keep my temper.* And then when I am not perfect, I FEEL LIKE SHIT!"

Caro shifts her position on the sofa. She says nothing for a moment, waiting to make sure that Vivi has finished talking. Then Caro says, "Give up."

"*Give up?* No, you've *got* to keep going. I mean, what I am supposed to do, jump off the Garnet River Bridge? Not that it hasn't crossed my mind."

"Not that it hasn't crossed most everybody's mind, Vivi. But we don't do it."

"Well, you can't just *give up*. Who is supposed to feed my children? Tell me! Who takes care of my children if I don't get out of bed in the morning?"

"I don't mean *give up*. I mean give *it* up. Let it go. Let all that Catholic shit stuff flow past you like water."

"Caro," Vivi said, "I don't know what you mean."

"What if," Caro continues, "just what if God didn't intend for everything to be perfect? What if He knew it was going to be a holy mess, and he loved us anyway? What if Adam and Eve weren't sinning? What if that prenatal original sin stain on our souls is *not even there?*"

"That is exactly the question that came to me with my last child! I looked down at Baylor when Dr. Harrison handed him to me, and I thought, How can this baby have a stain of guilt on him? He is an innocent!"

"Then think it right now," Caro said. "When my boys were born, I looked at each one of them and said NO to that original sin shit. I looked at my babies and thought, You are pure, holy, perfect, complete, and undefiled. And nobody can tell me different, not the Pope his royal self. Believe it now."

"Caro, that contradicts everything we've been taught, everything the church is built on."

"Vivi, if you keep believing that the church is built on the guilt of babies, you will go insane. I was lucky. Mom and Pop never pushed it. Pop just ran the movie theaters with Mom's help, and Mom cooked and watched movies and gardened. They looked at me and accepted me pretty much as I was. When they didn't like something, they talked to me about it. Not like your family."

"Don't talk about my family."

"Why not? Bloodletting takes place in the best of families. Somebody should have called the police to your house when your father took that belt off and stepped toward you and Pete. Or toward your mother, for that matter."

"They say it's a sin to think that."

"They do, huh? Well, I can figure out what's a sin and what's not. If I am deliberately cruel to you for no reason at all, that is a sin. That crap about Turner and the twins being born with the stain of guilt on their souls—oh, no, I don't buy that. That is a story the biggest corporation in the world called the Vatican makes up. So we'll feel like we can never be good enough.

"Why do you buy it, hook, line, and sinker?"

Vivi stares hard at Caro. "Do you at least still believe in Mass every Sunday?" Vivi asks.

"For those who like it, fine. But do I worry if I miss Mass once in a while? Like even for a month? No, Vivi, I don't give it a thought."

"Surely *some* of the times that I don't see yall at Mass, you've gone to St. Rita's instead of Divine Compassion?"

"The times you don't see us at Mass, we are not at Mass—we're not at *any* Catholic church. We're at the Holy Church of Pancakes in my kitchen, with Blaine and me and the three boys laughing and reading the funny papers and staying in our jammies till two in the afternoon. I give my kids Communion with maple syrup on top. And I love up on them and on my far too handsome husband, spook that he is. We just *lounge.*"

"You don't feel a *little* ashamed?"

"Ashamed of what? About flipping pancakes high so the twins squeal with joy? About sitting in my husband's lap and laughing at private jokes that only we understand? About telling the kids to play outside in the yard while Blaine and I make love? No, I don't feel one bit ashamed. *I feel good.* If God doesn't want me to feel good, then He's a Nazi, and I don't care what He thinks anyway.

"But remember, Pal, I didn't have Buggy for a mother."

Vivi is quiet for a moment. "Yeah, there is that," she says finally.

"Yes, there is that," Caro says. "And I didn't get shipped off to Saint Augustine's Penal Academy for Bad Catholic Girls because my mother was jealous of me."

"My mother was not jealous of me!"

"Oh, sorry, I must have you mixed up with some other Viviane Joan Abbott who I have known for thirty-two years."

Vivi begins to sob, softly.

"Your mother fed you the Catholic Guilt Diet whole-hog. You were criticized for everything you did. There was no way you could accept that you were a lovely young girl, because your mother treated you like a *sinner.*"

Vivi is silent for a while. She rearranges herself on the huge pillows that Caro has placed in the living room on the curved black sofa. She hugs a pillow to her. She thinks of her four children, Little Shep in the sleeping bag like he's on a campout, her daughters in the bunk beds. They are bunk beds that Blaine designed and built for his boys out of old pieces of cypress reinforced with rebar. Handmade bunk beds for his boys. Everything in Caro's house is creative. She and Blaine don't do anything like anyone else in Thornton.

Vivi gazes at her friend. The strong jawline, the hazel eyes, the close-cropped hair—a tall, thin, athletic thoroughbred of a woman. Caro stares at the fire. She seems calm. Something in her sees this all, but is unfazed by it. There is something real and comforting about Caro's bluntness, about her defense of the purity of her children.

For a moment Vivi's mind drifts. If she does not work at it constantly, her mind becomes crammed full of sins. Who needs a missal, when she carries the list in her mind at all times?

"Have you murmured against God, at your own adversity, or the prosperity of others? Have you believed in fortune-tellers or consulted them? Gone to places of worship of other denominations? Have you been guilty of immodest dress or impurity? Have you read obscene books, seen immodest films? Been guilty of impure songs, conversations, words, looks, or actions by yourself or with others? Willfully entertained impure thoughts or desires?" Once it starts, it doesn't stop. There are too many sins to list.

Vivi's own body is exhausted. Her adrenal glands have been pumping so hard, her body still feels like it is in an earthquake. A body quake. Her heart is beating fast. Just talking to Caro, hearing the heretical views of a friend she thought she knew everything about—it all makes her want more oxygen. Her face feels flushed at even considering the ideas that Caro has brought up. The very first sin in the inventory before Confession is, "Have you doubted in matters of faith?" If this isn't doubting, she doesn't know what is.

Caro gets up and sits on the sofa next to Vivi. She puts her arm around her and pulls her toward her. "Here's the deal, Viv-o. Stick with your Holy Lady. She's your pal. Think of the strength it takes to be so quiet and calm. She's one strong lady. And she is like a torch in you, Vivi. She keeps on burning, lighting the way, and there is nothing that can put out the light. Not Sister Howard Regina. Not anything. Not anybody." Caro takes Vivi's face in her hands and turns her gently toward her.

"How many years ago did we give ourselves Ya-Ya tribal names, float walnuts with candle stubs down the bayou, and cut our fingers to share our blood? You told the Ya-Ya creation story, and how the Moon Lady saved us from the alligators. I remember it like it was last night: 'You are my darling daughters in whom I am well pleased. I will always keep my divine eyes peeled out for you.' The Holy Lady. The Moon Lady. Don't let them take her away from you. Let her show herself and tell you what to do."

Caro thinks over the evening, and she sighs. I was right: Vivi is hurt. She has been in an accident and has been injured. Then Caro kisses Vivi on the forehead. "That's the end of tonight's sermon by the Reverend Doctor Lady Bishop Caro Brewer Bennett. I'm tired. Let's go to bed."

Vivi, clad in a pair of Caro's pajamas, sinks against her friend's back as they lie next to each other in Blaine and Caro's bed. Vivi thinks about Mary Magdalene, a fallen woman and the first to see Jesus rise from the dead. She thinks of holy things and begins to wonder what is really and truly unholy. She takes three long, deep breaths.

Vivi considers letting it all go. She remembers the twin she lost when Sidda was born. She thinks about all the innocent babies the Catholic Church banished to Limbo forever, because they were not baptized, and how they would never see the face of God. She wonders what kind of cruel mind could devise such a fate for babies. As she falls asleep, she has a hazy picture of Sister Howard Regina as a little girl. She wonders when that girl-child had become the dogma-driven, hard woman she met today.

As exhausted as she is, Vivi cannot sleep without checking on her children. Careful not to wake Caro, who is already deep asleep, Vivi gets out of bed and softly tiptoes into the room where Sidda and Lulu lie sleeping. Lulu is in the top bunk with Sidda, and that makes Vivi smile. She touches their heads gently, then goes to the other bedroom, where Baylor is sleeping with the other boys. She kneels down beside the lower bunk where he sleeps. For a long time, she listens to her youngest child's breathing. She strokes his forehead and holds his hand between hers. He does not stir. She marvels at his beauty, at his completeness. Pure, holy, perfect, complete, and undefiled, she thinks. *Pure. Holy. Perfect. Complete. Undefiled.* She sends a prayer to the Holy Lady, a prayer that she might learn to see this purity in Baylor, and in the rest of her children. She prays that she might see it in all people. She prays that she might surrender all guilt. And let it go.

Back in bed next to Caro, Vivi drifts off into the waiting arms of the Holy Lady, who can wait for Vivi as long as is necessary. She can wait for years, can wait lifetimes for her daughter to know she is loved and that her soul is not stained, but radiant, filled with lunar light, luminous with a star that lives inside her heart, inside her body at all times.

The Holy Lady can wait, she has no clock, no deadlines. Her time is like water, just flowing and flowing and flowing.

CIRCLING THE GLOBE

March 1964

*B*aylor Walker started whistling when he was three. People in Thornton would say they could hear him coming half a mile down the road. Most of the time, he whistled whatever was in his head, little made-up songs about the sun, birds, and Lamar the German shepherd. But if you pressed Baylor to whistle his favorite song, he would blush and go into a fevered version of "Singin' in the Rain." He didn't even know where he first heard the tune, but he loved its jauntiness.

Baylor whistled almost all the time, except when he was eating. He whistled the loudest when Vivi had one of her fits. The afternoon Vivi found out Big Shep went to New Orleans with Sue Ann Morelli, Baylor whistled so loud his face turned blue, and Sidda went over and started to rub his forehead. Vivi threatened to burn the cotton fields that afternoon. With a glass of gin in her hand, she walked out into the rows of green leaves and white cotton bolls and screamed: "Your bolls will be ashes, Shep Walker!" Their maid Willetta managed to get the matches away from her, but not before Baylor had fainted and hit his head on the edge of the marble-topped dresser. Vivi snapped out of it, folded him in her arms, and cried as she sang, "Can't Help Lovin' That Man of Mine." Then she piled them all in the car for hamburgers at Fred's Hamburger Drive-In.

One day when Baylor was in third grade, his mother dropped him off downtown to have lunch with Uncle Pete. Baylor liked riding alone in the car with his mother because he could just stare out the window and take the world in. He loved looking at early spring whizzing past the car. The pussy willows were out, and the dogwoods were in bloom. And the maple trees were brilliant red on the tips of their branches. Uncle Pete was his mama's brother, and he was a lawyer just like his mother's daddy had been. Having lunch with Uncle Pete made Baylor feel like a grown-up, and he admired the way all the other lawyers and businessmen greeted his uncle. Being a lawyer was something neat. And Uncle Pete really talked *to* him, not at him. His uncle had taken him for lunch at Demo's Grill, and they were walking back to the office with the tall bookshelves that smelled like the world. They walked up Third Street, Baylor whistling one of his made-up tunes and Uncle Pete smoking a cigarette. It was one of the first warm, clear days of spring. When they passed the windows of Delta Antiques, Uncle Pete stopped in to chat with Bebe Hanaway.

Bebe Hanaway was a tall lady with straight bangs who attended every estate sale in Central Louisiana. Sometimes Bebe even crossed over to Mississippi. Bebe would travel anywhere for southern antiques. She had installed an antique hotline in her home with a red light, and no one could touch it but her. People called her from all over the state: "I heard from a little bird that the Andy Dubois place cannot make its payments. They're sure to have an estate sale any day now. Keep your eyes out." Bebe was a Southern sleuth of antiques, and she took her work very seriously.

As they stood in Bebe's shop, under the brass ceiling fan and in front of a huge pre–Civil War oak armoire, Baylor caught sight of an enormous brown and beige globe on a heavy bronze stand. He walked over to the globe. It stood about three inches shorter than he was, and it measured about three times as big around. He looked at China and Africa and the seven seas, which were a faded blue like the tile in his grandmother Buggy's bathroom. Baylor ran his hand over the smooth round surface of the globe and pretended he was captain of a small fast ship that traveled regularly and confidently wherever it wanted to go. He pictured the globe in his bedroom next to his bed. He pictured waking up next to the globe. He wanted to hug the globe because it reminded him of the big round world outside Pecan Grove, the plantation his Daddy had inherited from his grandfather. Baylor whistled some unnamed tune that sounded to him like an almost scary pirate song. Someday he would go to all these places he saw on the globe.

"Pete, I think Baylor is in a state of total enchantment with my 1813 globe."

Bebe crossed over to Baylor and put her arm around him. She smelled like Chanel No. 19 and Ammon's Heat Powder, and he stood still under her arm.

"Mrs. Hanaway, how much does that globe cost?" Baylor was trying not to seem too excited.

Bebe Hanaway looked down at him. He hated that look. He knew it meant she was going to talk to him in that kind of flirting voice that some ladies used with little boys like him. "Baylor, sweetheart, that antique orb is worth a lot more, but I'd part with it for one hundred and fifty dollars. Only to the right person, of course. Do I have an interested party?"

She was playing with him. She didn't take him seriously because he was so short. He hated her for a moment, and in his hate he gave the globe a spin. He instantly loathed himself for taking his anger out on the object that he now coveted more than anything in the world.

They left the antique store and went back to Uncle Pete's office, where Baylor had a Coke and drew pictures for a while. He thought about the globe the entire afternoon. He sat on the floor in Uncle Pete's office and drew pictures of it on legal pads. Later Vivi picked Baylor up from Uncle Pete's office in her Thunderbird. For once in his lifetime, he had his mother to himself. Baylor rode up front with Vivi, turning the rearview mirror as she instructed so she could reapply her Rich Girl Red lipstick. How his mother drove and put on lipstick was a source of eternal amazement to Baylor. He wondered how it would be written up in the *Thornton Daily Monitor* when she finally did crash that car. Vivi always said she ought to bring a lawsuit against the lipstick makers because she was always having to reapply it in the car. Baylor pictured handling the lawsuit himself, with a little help from Uncle Pete. He would make thousands of dollars for his Mama, and he would only keep enough to buy the globe and live happily ever after in its light. All the way home, while Vivi told him all about her latest shopping exploits, Baylor smiled.

But Baylor was not one to rush into things. He waited until a week or so had passed. Then one day he walked back into his Daddy's room, crossed over to the wooden valet stand where his Daddy hung his pants, and emptied the pockets. He picked up his Daddy's soft leather wallet that Vivi had bought at Rapps in New Orleans, and he pulled out two hundred-dollar bills. Then he walked out of the room, refused supper that night, and went to sleep early.

The next morning Baylor waited until Big Shep left for the fields and Vivi was heading out the driveway to her *Bourrée* game. He combed his hair again and walked as fast as he could down the long driveway that led up to their house. He reached the blacktop road, turned right, and kept on walking. After a few minutes he saw the Texaco station. He ducked into the pay phone booth in front of the station, trying to stay clear of George Grundy, the black man who ran the place. He used one of the dimes his Mama always made him carry, in case of emergency, and he called himself a taxi.

Five minutes later, he was dropped off at Bebe Hanaway's Delta Antiques Shop. Bebe's door was propped open, and she was inside trying to make a sale to Rosemary McDonald and her mother, Mrs. Boyce. Baylor hung around outside in the warm sun until those ladies finally got out of there. He didn't want to answer questions right now. Finally the two ladies left, and then he could go in.

"Good morning, Mrs. Hanaway." Baylor was always polite, and this was not a time to make an exception. "How are you today?

Bebe looked around for his Uncle Pete or Vivi before she asked, "Honey, where is your Mama?"

"Oh, she's playing *Bourrée* with the Ya-Yas."

"I see. Your Mama does love her *Bourrée*. Well, what can I do for you today?"

"I have come for the globe I looked at last week with my Uncle Pete."

"Come to look at it again?"

"No ma'am," Baylor replied. "I've come to buy it and take it home with me."

"Baylor, honey, that globe costs over one hundred dollars."

"Yes ma'am, I know that. I brought the money."

"You brought the money. Oh, well, that is different." Bebe thought to herself, what a strange crew the Walkers were. Vivi going off to New York to be an actress, coming back and marrying a blue-blooded farm boy like Shep, then having those four kids in about three years. After that, Vivi had cut all her hair off and dressed in men's shirts and zoomed around town in that little sports car that wouldn't even hold her husband and all her four kids at once. Now Vivi and Shep had given their youngest over a hundred dollars to come buy himself a globe. None of my business, she told herself. Besides, I've been trying to get rid of that thing ever since I found it down in Plaquemines Parish at the old Evans place.

Baylor stood next to the globe, staring at the North Pole. He thought he had memorized all its features, but he had forgotten how wonderfully it sat on the bronze axis, how it seemed to hang there like a picture in a coloring book. It was even better than he remembered. He was delighted that it was still here waiting for him.

"Let me just write it up, Baylor." Bebe went over behind the big old desk where she had her cash register. "Uh, will that be cash or check?" She felt kind of funny writing up a bill for that much money and giving it to a little boy who was barely tall enough to reach the top of her desk. But Bebe was a businesswoman. "Tell you what, Baylor, because you are so special, I will give you a break, and we'll call it a hundred twenty-five even."

Bebe wrote up the sale on her Delta Antiques invoice form, which she handed to Baylor. "All right, Mr. Baylor, that'll be one hundred and twenty-five big ones."

Baylor stared at the invoice for a solid minute. On it was a drawing of a woman pulling a wagon full of columns like they'd just been looted from an antebellum home. Then he reached down into the pocket of his seersucker Bermuda shorts and pulled out the two hundred dollars, carefully folded as smoothly as they were in his Daddy's wallet. He handed them to Bebe, who accepted them with a smile. She opened a small antique cash box and handed Baylor his change.

"I hope you will be very happy with your antique globe of the world, Baylor."

"Oh, I will, Mrs. Hanaway, I know I will."

Baylor stood next to his globe for a moment before he realized that he could not pick it up. It was much too big. He had not thought of this before. He looked at the globe for a while, then went back over to Bebe's desk. "May I use your telephone please, Mrs. Bebe?" He felt a little more familiar with her now that the transaction was done, now that he was a real customer. He called himself a cab for the second time that morning. When the cab arrived, Baylor asked the cabdriver to help him with the globe. Then Baylor, the cabdriver, and the globe rode out to Pecan Grove, where Baylor had the cabdriver help him put the globe in the playhouse, which sat on the slope down to the bayou. Then he asked the cabdriver to wait while he went into the house and pulled a dollar out of the recipe drawer, where Vivi always kept a small stash.

Baylor spent the rest of the afternoon in the playhouse with the globe. He imagined going to Nepal and then to Norway and then down to Argentina. He would own a very large house in Argentina. His house would have a study in it, with a fireplace, bookshelves, and a brandy snifter. There would be a Persian rug, and a dog that sat at his feet while he read. He would speak every language and be kind and generous to all people. No one would want for anything as long as Baylor was around. He'd never smoke and only sip little sweet after-dinner drinks. He would be very wise and laugh a deep laugh, and lean his head back whenever someone delighted him, like they did in the movies.

Bebe waited until early evening to call Vivi and ask how they liked the globe. Vivi had not seen Baylor all afternoon; he was still in the playhouse. Vivi took a long, deep breath and told Bebe she'd have to call her back, because she had something cooking on the stove. Then Vivi sat down and made herself a gin and tonic. She drank it down quickly. Then she made herself another and crossed the yard to the playhouse.

❧

Vivi opened the door and stood there for a minute, watching Baylor play. He moved his fingers across the globe, occasionally whispering and gesturing with his right hand. Vivi was furious with him, but in that moment before she spoke, she thought: At least he does know quality and beauty when he sees it. He loves beautiful things. Like I do. Then she cleared her throat. "Baylor."

He jumped and gasped. He had been so involved in his new life that he had not heard her come in.

"Where have you been all afternoon, Baylor? And where did you get that globe?" Vivi said.

"I got it at the antique store."

"Uh-huh, so I heard."

"I didn't steal it!" Baylor said, responding more to the stern tone of her voice than to anything she actually said.

"You paid for it, then?"

"Yes ma'am," Baylor whispered, and he stood and wrapped both his arms around the globe. "Mama, don't make me take it back. Please."

"Where did you get the money?" Vivi said, louder this time.

Baylor tried not to cry. He stood with his arms wrapped around the globe and sobbed with his face against his chubby little blondhaired arms as Vivi's angry words spilled over him: "How could you? What were you thinking, Baylor? Have you lost your mind?! Oh, you just wait till your Daddy gets home!"

Then Vivi paused, took out a cigarette from her engraved sterling silver cigarette case. She lit the cigarette, took a long drag, and said, "Really. What possessed you to do it? Why did you steal that money to buy a damned globe?"

Baylor let go of the globe. He looked up at his mother. "Because I need it."

"I am not even going to spank you," Vivi said. She had yelled herself out. In fact, she was too angry to finish her drink, and it was still there in her hand, or she would have taken a swat at Baylor herself. No need to waste a good bourbon and branch, she told herself. Let Shep handle it. "I am going to let you explain it to your Daddy," she told Baylor. "You tell him how you think it's okay to take money from him. I want to hear you tell him how it was not the same as 'stealing' to do that."

"Don't make me take the globe back, Mama. Don't let Daddy make me take it back."

Damn it, Vivi thought. He is not listening to anything I say. He just keeps yammering on about that damned globe. It occurred to Vivi to wonder if Baylor was right in the head. Well, he sure wouldn't be the first in this family, she said to herself.

"Why, Baylor? What is wrong with you?" Vivi groaned as she sat on one of the children's chairs, her knees splayed out as she perched her bottom on the little square wooden seat.

In his desperation, Baylor did something he never imagined he would do. He told her about his house in Greece, and how he wanted to go all over the world. He told her about riding a camel across the African desert, and climbing the Himalayas. He didn't tell her everything—not the dog or the smoking jacket he'd have—but just some things. The biggest and best things. "I have to know where I'll go when I grow up, Mama. I need to know where I'm going after I leave here," he told her, straight from the heart. Vivi sat on the tiny chair and sipped from her drink.

When he finished, she didn't say anything for a while. Then she sighed. "Let's go back to the house and give Miss Bebe a call. See if she can make us a little deal." Vivi stood and stretched her back, holding the empty glass in one hand. She held out her other hand, and Baylor took it. "Oh, baby. It's so hard to give up dreams. Isn't it?"

Things did not go as Baylor would have hoped. But they didn't go as badly as he'd feared either. After a brief conversation with Bebe on the phone, Vivi hustled Baylor and the globe into her car and zoomed downtown. As they turned onto Third Street, Baylor saw that all the other shops and offices were dark. There was a light in the antique store, and when Vivi knocked on the door, Miss Bebe appeared and unlocked the front door.

For the next twenty minutes or so, Miss Bebe and Vivi impressed each other with their Southern-lady charm. Vivi smiled and kept saying: "Dahlin, I'm just so sorry for this terrible misunderstanding." Miss Bebe smiled graciously back and said it was no problem, not at all. She opened her cash register and handed Vivi one hundred and twenty-five dollars. Then she took Baylor's hand and explained to him about something she called "layaway." Baylor didn't really find it very interesting, but he did cry a little when Miss Bebe took the globe back. Miss Bebe assured him that the globe still belonged to him. She even hand-lettered a big SOLD sign, attached it to the globe, then put the globe in the back of the store.

After that, Vivi gave Miss Bebe a couple of twenty-dollar bills. Miss Bebe brought out another form with the same drawing at the top, a woman pulling a wagon full of columns. This form had lots of small print on it, and Miss Bebe showed Baylor where to sign at the bottom. Then Vivi signed it, too.

They left the shop and drove home. Baylor listened as Vivi explained again about the layaway—they would make payments on the globe, a little at a time. He could take the globe home later, after all the payments were finished.

"Sometimes, Dahlin, we have to wait and put our dreams on hold for a while. We don't get to have them right away. We make little payments on them, and we wait. Later, it is even better than if you got it all at once!"

Baylor said nothing. He knew things could have turned out worse, a lot worse. He knew that Mama and Miss Bebe helped him get out of trouble. But he felt like all the air had been sucked out of him.

"Do you understand what I'm saying, Dahlin?" Vivi said, turning to him, her eyes barely on the road.

"No ma'am. Not really."

As they pulled in the driveway to Pecan Grove, it was dark.

Vivi sighed. "Oh, Dahlin Angel-Boy, I'm not sure I understand either. But trust me, Greece will still be there when your time comes. Brazil too. Some unexplored country will be waiting for you. Even if you stay right here in Thornton."

Baylor stared at his mother as she bit her top lip, as she cried without sound. He put out his hand and laid it on top of hers. Together they sat that way in the long driveway on Pecan Grove Plantation in Thornton, Louisiana, on the edge of the bayou, on the edge of the world.

He tried to whistle for his mother. But no sounds came out. Just little puffs of air.

Vivi opened the car door on the driver's side. "Come on, Buddy, let's look at the stars!"

Baylor climbed out of the car and took his mother's hand.

Together they walked out in front of the house, into the cotton fields. The ground had been tilled and cleaned up, but it was still too early to plant. The March night was clear, no moon, and the stars were luminous above the flat Louisiana farmland.

"Look!" Vivi said, and pointed upward. "There's the Big Dipper. And I think that must be Venus. They say planets don't shine that bright. Don't believe them."

Baylor looked up into the starry night. His mother's hand was warm over his.

"Look up there again, Buddy," she said. "See all those stars? See them? A man named Edgar Cayce says we're made of stars. Every single one of us is made of stars. What do you make of that?"

Baylor was silent while he thought about it, really thought about it. "You mean those stars are in our bodies?"

"Parts of them are, yessir," Vivi said, standing.

Stars in my body, Baylor thought. He pictured them dancing inside his head, shooting through his legs, stars falling out of his mouth.

"I'm made of stars? Mama, are you making this up?"

"No sir, I am not. There are those that might say I am, but do not listen to anything they say."

"*All* of us are made of stars?"

Vivi hesitated.

"Well, I know all of us here on Pecan Grove are. I know all the Ya-Yas and Petites Ya-Yas are. I suspect every single person in the world is."

Baylor stood, still gazing at the sky, letting this soak in.

When Vivi took his hand to lead him up to the house, he felt shiny inside, and he could feel warm little sparks coming from his mother's hand. He thought of his Daddy, Sidda, Little Shep, and Lulu and all their dogs and cows and every animal on the plantation. He thought of them with stars inside. When that thought was strong enough, giving up the globe did not hurt so much. He thought only of shining people all over the world, in Greece, in Peru, and in countries he didn't know the names of yet, continents that hadn't even been discovered.

PILGRIMAGE

Sidda, December 1965

$\mathcal{G}$od, Mama and Daddy can be so cool sometimes. What other parents in the city of Thornton—heck, in the state of Louisiana—would take their four kids all the way to Houston, Texas, to see the Beatles?! The second tour the Fab Four made on American soil, and we were there to see them! We were a part of history! We saw legends! Mama and Daddy knew that, they recognized that. That's why they did it.

It all started on Sunday evening, February 9, 1964. I was eleven years old, and Necie and her husband, Mister Ogden, and the seven Ogden kids were visiting at Pecan Grove. They had come over after noon Mass and had Sunday dinner with us, and we played all afternoon.

It was almost seven o'clock in Louisiana, and Joanie and I were already parked in front of the small black-and-white TV screen, waiting. We had that television set warmed up and ready to go. Every Sunday Daddy and Mama and the four of us always watched *Ed Sullivan* and then *Bonanza,* but this evening was special. Ed Sullivan had announced that he was going to have the Beatles on his "shew," and finally the day was here!

Mainly it was Joanie Ogden and me who were really excited about seeing the Beatles. Joanie was one year older than me, but we were good friends. We had been on pins and needles all day, just counting the minutes for that night's "shew."

There were eleven of us kids in the den. Daddy had a fire going, and Mama and Necie set out leftovers from dinner on the table in the den, along with some of Necie's special knock-your-socks-off brownies. Baylor wore his Superboy costume, left over from Halloween. He changed into it before *Ed Sullivan*. I sat in between Joanie and Lulu on the rug right in front of the television set.

The other kids gathered round, the boys acting all rambunctious until I said, just like Mama, "Quiet! Or I will knock yall upside the head if you don't shut up right now!"

When Ed introduced the Beatles, he was very complimentary. Of course, I didn't care what Mr. Prune Face himself had to say. I just wanted to see the Fab Four. There had been such a buildup in the past week. The Beatles were all we could think about. I had actually prayed at Mass that nothing would happen to make me miss them. I had saved my allowance to buy the 45 rpm of "I Want to Hold Your Hand." In the past month, I had grabbed up every magazine that I could afford or beg Mama to buy. Just to stare at their four faces.

Finally, Ed Sullivan uttered the words, "Ladies and gentlemen: The Beatles!"

How could I ever forget that night?! On our black-and-white TV screen appeared four guys like I had never laid eyes on before! John, George, Paul, and Ringo! I had never seen men with long hair before except in pictures of knights and Sir Galahad and stuff. Their hair came down over their ears, and swung from side to side when they sang. I just loved that! They were all wearing matching suits with no collars and tight, tight pants! And they had on these pointy-toed ankle boots, which were out of this world! The Beatles were just from their own planet. Men like the Beatles did not live in Garnet Parish.

Girls in the television audience were screaming and crying and reaching out for the Beatles. They were fainting and just going crazy.

When the Fab Four started singing "All My Lovin'," Joanie and I just lost it and stood up and started screaming too, flailing our arms, stumbling, knocking over our Cokes. I felt like I was seeing something that was *all mine.* Something new, something different from what my parents and nuns and priests and anything and everybody had ever known. The drumbeat really got me. I couldn't tell why, but my body was just pulsing! Even with all the screaming, the drumbeat came through, and I could feel it in my bones! The Beatles were wild and bad and sweet and clean all at once. Soon Joanie, Malissa, Lulu, and Rose started screaming and jumping up and down, and all us girls were like a pack of dogs that couldn't stop from howling at the moon!

The boys started being stupid and making fun, swinging their heads from side to side and going "Wooooo!" Then Little Shep ran and got a mop out of the cleaning closet and held it up behind his head and acted like it was his hair and acted all crazy. They made fun of us girls for screaming and everything. Baylor had his ukulele and was pretending to play the guitar. He was the only one concentrating real hard on watching the Beatles.

Pretty soon, the grown-ups came into the room with their drinks and cigarettes and stood with their hands on their hips.

Mama said, "Well, what have we here?!"

When Paul began to sing "Till There Was You," that's when I knew that he was the one I loved. I loved everything about him. How big his eyes were, how perfect his skin was, how he was gentle and really meant every single word he sang. He was so, um, *sensitive* compared to all the boys I knew. How there were bells on a hill but he never heard them ringing, how there were birds, but he never heard them singing till there was . . . me. Till there was *me.* He was singing to me. He was singing the right words in the exact way I wanted to be sung to, but I had never known until that very moment!

Then there was bad news about John. They ran the words underneath him while he was singing: "Sorry girls, he's married." Well, at least Paul—my Paul—wasn't married. Oh, I went wild when they showed close-ups of their faces—even Ringo's, which was a goofy face, but in a good way.

Mister Ogden mumbled, "Those no-good beatniks should get a haircut and a decent job."

The Beatles then launched into "She Loves You." By this time even the boys were jumping around singing and yelling, too. The girls on television were tearing their hair out and puckering up their lips, and we saw two girls actually faint!

And that is when Mister Ogden walked over to our television set and turned it off! Just turned it off like he owned the place! He said, "If this isn't a Satan serenade, I don't know what is. I refuse to stand by and watch while innocent babies are sucked in by vipers of vice. I put my foot down."

My father walked right up in front of Mister Ogden and turned the television set right back on. "George, this is my house," Daddy said. "I'll turn off my goddamn Motorola when I see fit. Calm down. Fix yourself another Scotch."

Necie said something, but the grown-ups were nothing but background noise to me. They didn't matter anymore. Not when the Beatles were in front of our eyes.

"Am I the only voice of morality in this room?" Mister Ogden said, raising his voice. "This is the kind of thing that leads to the corruption of culture. Not just our American culture, but, far more important, our *Catholic* culture."

"I didn't realize Catholic was a culture," Daddy said, giving a little laugh. "I thought it was a religion."

Daddy had taken instructions to become a Catholic so he could marry Mama, and swore an oath that he would raise us all in the Catholic faith and pay to send us to Catholic schools. But when it came to Confession, Daddy backed out of the whole thing. He said, "I'm not going to sit in a hot little booth with a priest who has bad breath and tell him what I've done that I'm ashamed of. That's between me and the Old Padnah." That is what my Daddy called God.

"Well, if you can't have respect for all that is holy," Mister Ogden said, "then what about all that our generation fought for? In the trenches, in the air, on the sea? Democracy, decency, respect for the American way of life."

"Dammit, George, you can sure be one sanctimonious SOB,"

Daddy said. "Relax. I'm not too impressed by all this singing or the long hair. It's a craze. The kids love it. The more you shout Satan, the more they're going to love it."

"It's no different than the way we were with Frankie Baby. Old Blue Eyes." Mama sighed. "I remember when Caro and I lived in New York City before we got married. We were modeling designer outfits at Saks. Caro and I—and every other girl in that store—went home sick one afternoon from work because Frank Sinatra was performing and we had the chance to see him. Well, we got caught because the floor lady from Saks decided to check out the line in front of the theater where Frankie was and found all of us there! We were all fired, but then they hired us back. Can you believe it?"

"The Ya-Yas are no strangers to swooning," Necie said. "Even if this music does not quite have the—shall we say, *smoothness*—of Frank Sinatra."

"Besides," Daddy said, "those boys are certainly no worse than Elvis."

"Well, he's the one that started it all," Mister Ogden said. "Playing all that nigger music in front of white children. It's a disgrace."

"George," Necie said, embarrassed. "Please do not use the N word around the children."

"Oh, excuse me for living," Mister Ogden said. *"Colored. Negro. Jungle Bunny."*

He turned away as though he were going to leave. But then he turned back around and said: "This mocks even the laws of basic decency. The Catholic Church does not approve of rock music, sexual promiscuity, or the occult—and that is what this music is all about."

"Well, George," Daddy said, "have you ever considered that this ragtag group of longhairs has more to say to your children than the Catholic Church could ever dream up?"

"Shepley Walker, I hate to say this, but you are a pagan, heathen anti-Christ!"

With that, Mister Ogden stormed out of our house and sat in the Ogdens' Country Squire station wagon until the party broke up.

Which was not until after the Beatles sang five songs. It's a good thing Mister Ogden did leave, or he would have just died if he'd seen

Joanie and me kiss the television screen when they showed close-ups again! We kissed everyone but Ringo. We didn't like his nose.

After *The Ed Sullivan Show*, Joanie and I and all my other girl-friends at school were feverish, just taken completely. Even Lulu and her little friends were starry-eyed over the Beatles. We wanted to go out and get every song the Beatles ever sang! We were afraid we might never hear or see them again, that they were a onetime mirac-ulous thing that came into our house only once and then would be taken away from us forever.

After buying all their singles as soon as they were available, Lulu and I finally bought their first album sold in the U.S., called *Meet the Beatles*. We bought it in March and played it 84,000 times. I loved every single song! There was not one bad song on it. It was definitely worth every penny of the $1.98 that Lulu and I saved to buy it.

The Ogdens weren't allowed to play Beatles music when their father was in the house. In fact, they had to hide the fact that Necie had even let them buy Beatles records. Joanie and I began writing long, fictional stories in which the Beatles and our friends all played major roles. We wrote cratefuls of those stories, which we thought we could turn into a real book called *The Beatles and Us*. We tried to hand them in at school for book reports, but the nuns gave us F's. So we had to stop.

Throughout the year, we learned every word to every Beatle song. Cenla Bop Record Shop downtown became a regular hangout for Lulu and me, with Shep and Baylor sometimes tagging along. We studied everything we could get our little hands on to read about the Fab Four. About how they came from Liverpool and started in that little hole in the wall called the Cavern. We had no idea where Liverpool was. We thought it was a really cool part of London near a pool.

We scoured *Teen Magazine* for pictures of John or Paul or George or Ringo to cut out and tape on the mirror in our bedroom. Lulu even had a photo of John standing next to his mother. She taped it on her side of the bedstand, where it was the first thing she saw when she woke up. His mother was kind of fat and looked like somebody's housekeeper. But just imagine! She brought him into the world. John himself credited her for being the first one to bring an Elvis record into their house. That is what got him hooked on music.

Little Shep, Lulu, Baylor, and I each decided who our favorite individual Beatle was. It was a litmus test for your personality.

I declared, "Mine is Paul because he looks romantic with those eyes."

Lulu said, "Mine is John because he looks bad."

Little Shep said, "George is the only one who looks like a man."

"Ringo," Baylor said. "I like him, even though nobody else does. I want to know why he wears all those rings."

Lulu and Joanie and my friends M'lain and Sissy and I bought every newspaper and magazine that had Beatles pictures. We made scrapbooks and hung the pictures in our rooms.

Mama said, "You can flip over those mop tops, but I do not want to see anything about the Beatles outside of your bedroom. I will not have you redecorate my entire home because of this craze. Do you hear me? No Beatles plates, no knickknacks. Do not even ask for me to order you a Beatles potholder, for God's sake. There is being a fan, and then there is being a nut."

We kept waiting for Mama or Daddy to say, "All right, enough is enough." But they never said anything! We had found something we adored, and they didn't try to take it away! The only rule was that we couldn't play the music as loud as we wanted. Mama took a marker and made a big arrow that pointed to exactly how loud we could turn up the record player. If we obeyed, there wasn't any trouble. That is how wonderful and powerful the Beatles were. When things seemed hopeless, a familiar Beatles song would come on the radio, and everything would be okay. No matter how bad things got, I could go in my room and be with the Beatles, especially my darling Paul.

With all our reading and writing our "Beatles and Us" stories, by the next February I felt I knew and understood each one of the Beatles personally. I fantasized that I could predict what they would say or do in any circumstance. I meditated on their pictures. I believed that they had no secrets from me. And then Ringo came out with "This Boy." Well, you could have knocked me over with a feather! I had no idea that Ringo was so sensitive! He just shocked me. That is the kind of song you would have expected Paul to sing. Not Ringo!!! But he sang it and wrote it, too. That was a real lesson for me: not to always judge a book by its cover. I started looking at boys differently. Like Phil Rabelais in my class, with the big forehead and all the pens in his pockets. Maybe inside he was really a poet, really a Ringo. I started being a lot deeper after that song.

At Our Lady of Divine Compassion Prison, the nuns made us wear uniforms. But when Mama was in a good mood, she would let me wear my John Lennon hat and Beatles boots. This really got the nuns going.

Leave it to the nuns to try and ruin something you like if your parents already haven't. Sister Mary Agatha, who had already separated the fifth-grade boys from the fifth-grade girls into different classrooms, now decided that the Beatles were a mortal sin. Once when I sassed her and she slapped me in the face, she announced to the class, "Siddalee Walker and the Beatles are both mortal sins."

I went to the principal's office and called Mama and told her what happened. She drove up to Our Lady of Divine Compassion with her stretch pants on, smoking a cigarette, and she walked into the office and said, "No one lays a hand on my children but me." Instead of whipping me, she put me in the car and we went to Bordelon's Drugstore for a Coke and some new magazines. She didn't make me go to school for three days after that. We had a ball. It was the miraculous force of the Beatles. For once in her life she admitted that Sister Mary Agatha was an old warthog, and we made fun of the way hairs stuck out of that nun's face moles.

For a whole year and a half, we lived mesmerized by the Beatles and their music. Then our fantasies came true!

In March 1965, over a year after we first saw the Beatles on *Ed Sullivan*, Aunt Jezie called and told us she could get us tickets for their show at the Sam Houston Coliseum in Houston that coming August, part of their second U.S. tour.

"I've got connections," she told Mama.

We hardly ever saw Aunt Jezie. She was Mama's little sister, and she would come home for Christmas, but that was about it. And most of the time she and Mama would get in some kind of argument. I don't think they liked each other much. One Christmas

Aunt Jezie came, and she danced so nasty that my Uncle Pete asked her to stop doing it in front of us kids. She also got in fights with Uncle Pete and Mama over a pool game after Christmas dinner at Uncle Pete's house. Started yelling and screaming and hit Uncle Pete on the shoulder with her pool stick. Finally Uncle Pete, who was always nice to everybody, said, "Jezie, you are pushing it too far. Either behave or leave my house." She roared out of his driveway blowing the horn, and no one saw her again for another two years.

She had been in Houston since she finished college, but none of us knew exactly what she did. We heard she had a job that paid a lot of money, maybe something in real estate, but we were never really sure. One Christmas she brought home a lady with her who was older than her, but very nice and well dressed and classy. Having this lady there made Aunt Jezie act not so crazy as usual. It was this lady, named Louise, who had the connections to the Beatles concert and could get us tickets.

We cornered Daddy when he got home. We thought we would have to sell him on the idea, but he just said, "Yeah, why not? Why the hell not?! Yall spend so much time locked up with those penguins, it's time to see something different. Stop being sheep led to the slaughter. If the Beatles are anti-Catholic, then I think yall should see them. Be sure to tell Saint George Ogden. Drive the man nuts."

Shep and Lulu and Baylor and I danced around, singing. We were going to Houston to see the Beatles! Aunt Jezie would get the tickets and arrange motel rooms, which wouldn't be easy because the entire world would be flocking to Texas to see the Fab Four along with the Walker family.

I called Joanie right away, and she was weeping with excitement. Of course, Mister Ogden went berserk. Necie had to apologize to Mama for the letter he wrote to Daddy and her on his Knights of Columbus stationery.

When Daddy read the letter, he said, "George is jealous of those longhairs. There's nothing he'd love better than hundreds of girls crawling all over him. There are Catholics, and there are nuts. George is a nut."

The fact that Aunt Jezie was getting us tickets to see the four greatest men in the world made me look at her in a whole new light.

I wrote her letters every week, telling her that she was the most wonderful aunt in the world, signing them all with tons of XXXXXs and OOOOOOs.

She wrote me back and said that she remembered when she first saw Elvis on *Ed Sullivan* and then live onstage. She said she cried tears—real ones.

Oh gosh, it seemed like ten years from the time we saw the Beatles on television and the time that August came. It was all we talked about. Lulu, Little Shep, Baylor, and I were celebrities at Divine Compassion that spring, once people heard we were really going!

When the time came, Teensy and Uncle Chick insisted on loaning us Chick's brand-new 1965 Lincoln Continental. It was huge and luxurious, and we felt like movie stars when we rode in it. And there was so much *room* compared to being crammed into Mama's T-Bird.

When Daddy got in it, he said, "Look at this country boy, he is driving dee-luxe!"

We had a blast the whole way from Thornton to Houston, Texas. Mama smoked with her cigarette outside the vent window and would blow the smoke out the window so Daddy wouldn't get asthma. She made faces while she did it, sometimes acting like Lucille Ball getting sucked out the window. It tickled us so much that even Daddy had to laugh. Getting to Houston was a short enough trip that nobody got on each other's nerves too bad. Things don't usually go this good for us. It was the power of the Beatles.

Mama didn't have to reach her hand into the back seat and pinch or slap us one single time. Daddy kept pointing out Massey Ferguson on the road, and finally Mama said, "Shep, that Massey Ferguson must be going to Houston, too. Where do you know him from?" And Daddy cracked up. He had to explain to her that Massey Ferguson was a brand of farm equipment, like John Deere tractors. Mama had thought we were passing a man Daddy knew all the way to Houston, and he was really talking about tractors and combines. Massey Ferguson was high-grade stuff. You couldn't buy it in Thornton.

Lulu and I sat in the back seat, wishing we looked more like we were from London. We had brought every Yardley product we owned with us—mainly little soaps and perfumes, since Daddy refused to let us wear our Mary Quant eyeliner in public. So we busied ourselves with deciding exactly what we'd say to our favorite Beatle when we met him personally. Which we knew in our hearts would definitely happen. Lulu said she would ask John if he'd like to come out to Pecan Grove for gumbo sometime. I tried to explain to her how you just couldn't expect someone famous to come over to your house, and all you feed them is gumbo.

She said, "All right, then what are you going to say to Paul?"

I thought for a long time, and then I replied, "I will simply hand Paul one of the poems I have written about him and let him take it from there."

We stopped at an A&W on the outskirts of Houston and got out and stretched our legs while they were cooking up our order. They had little picnic tables you could sit at, and we did, all of us putting the big frosty mugs of root beer against our faces before the ice melted off.

Daddy said, "Mama, I'm feeling good. This Texas air is good for my sinuses."

The hamburgers came, and Mama made us say grace. After we said "Amen," Daddy did his "Amen/Brother Ben/Shot a goose/And killed a hen," and we all laughed.

Little Shep followed with "Rub-a-dub-dub thanks for the grub."

Mama tried not to laugh, and then Lulu said, "Dear God, thank you for the cheeseburger and for the Beatles."

We were having fun. It was good to be away from Pecan Grove.

You would not have believed the motel that Aunt Jezie booked us into! It had Greek statues all the way around the swimming pool and little twinkly lights in the bushes. Music played outside on the walkways all day and all night. There were thick bathrobes hanging in the rooms for us to wear when we got out of the pool. The robes had the monogram of the motel on them. We never stayed in places with bathrobes. Aunt Jezie said this place was the top of the heap.

Aunt Jezie met us at the motel. Her hair was cut like Barbra Streisand's, the way it hung down on the sides and framed her face. And her hair was a whole lot darker than when we had last seen her, almost black-black. She was so skinny, and wearing a little black linen shift with double spaghetti straps and black sandals with little

French heels. Her sunglasses made Mama jealous, I think. But that is only my opinion. Aunt Jezie had already picked up the keys from the front desk and acted like she owned the motel. When we got to our rooms, there was a basket of fresh fruit waiting for us and a bottle of champagne iced down for Mama and Daddy. It must have cost a fortune!

"Oh, Jezie, you shouldn't have gone to all this trouble," Mama told her.

Aunt Jezie said, "Well, you only come to Houston once in a blue moon, and besides, I charged it all to the room."

Then Aunt Jezie looked at Daddy and gave him a big smile.

Mama looked at Daddy for a minute, and I was afraid people were going to start getting mad like usual.

But Daddy finally said, "What the hell? This is a vacation."

The grown-ups popped the cork on the champagne, and the four of us kids ran down the hall to get ice and Cokes from the machine with the pocketfuls of change Daddy had given us.

God, did we love motel rooms! We had a room all to ourselves. Boys in one bed, girls in the other. Our own television set, and sliding glass doors that opened out onto the pool. Little Shep and Baylor ran into the bathroom to be the first to break the seal on the toilet lid—one of their rituals. Lulu and I grabbed all the little shampoo bottles and hand creams and tiny sewing kits and stuffed them into our suitcases. We always did that, then ran and found the maids and told them we needed more.

Daddy let us take anything we wanted from motel rooms, including sheets and bath mats. He said, "They expect you to take that stuff home with you. That's why the bill is so high."

It was getting kind of late, but we were jacked up. Mama and Daddy let us put on our swimsuits, and we jumped in the pool. It was dark, and the pool lights made everything feel exotic, like we were in a foreign country. Aunt Jezie and Mama and Daddy sat out on their room's patio and drank while they watched us. The water was warm and a little breeze blew on us. We practiced our surface dives and did cannonballs and hollered for Aunt Jezie to come see how good we had learned to swim. Finally she just came over and jumped in with her clothes on! That was just like something Aunt

Jezie would do. She said she'd just wear one of the motel bathrobes home. Mama couldn't stand to be left out, so she ran in and put on her suit and came on in. And then even though Daddy doesn't like swimming—if he gets cold, his asthma flares up—he got in too.

"The temperature is just right," Daddy said, imitating the story of the Three Bears. "Not too hot. Not too cold. Jusssst right."

We had it all to ourselves, a family pool. And we just splashed and laughed and jumped off Daddy's shoulders and laughed at how funny Aunt Jezie looked with all her clothes wet.

Daddy said, "We should travel more often."

And we all agreed.

By the time I got in the bed, I was so sleepy I fell right off, instead of lying awake the way I did at home. It was real quiet in the room with only the sound of the air conditioner humming, blocking out all the other noises. Lulu slept next to me and I was glad to have her there, to smell the slight odor of chlorine on her skin. I liked us all being in the same room like that, all protected. I smiled over at Shep with his white T-shirt on before I turned off the light, and he smiled back and said, "Check, Sidda, this is great."

The next morning we had a huge breakfast in the motel dining room. The waitresses just fell in love with us. Daddy made friends with them and they introduced us to the cook. We got to go on a tour of the kitchen and watched while they took some coconut cream pies they'd just baked out of the oven. They said we could come back and have some later. I had never thought about coconut cream pies actually getting cooked. I thought they just happened.

We walked around every inch of the grounds of the motel.

Daddy said, "You should always get out and know where you are in a new place. That's what the Indians always did."

We went into the lobby and bought some postcards of Houston. Daddy got to talking to the man at the desk, who had some relatives in Lafayette that Daddy thought he knew from the farm co-op. One thing about us when we traveled—we came away with new friends.

Then we went back to the room to rest because it was going to be a long day. Aunt Jezie called to say she was on her way to come get us. She was not about to let us drive to Sam Houston Coliseum where the Beatles were playing. She said we'd get lost forever. Daddy said that was just fine with him. We laid on the bed and watched some Houston, Texas, television shows and just took it easy until Aunt Jezie came.

We were all real excited, wondering if we'd brought the right clothes for a Beatles concert. I was wearing an orange miniskirt with a purple poor-boy short-sleeved pullover. Lulu had on a little lime green shift with huge pink flowers all over it that she looked real cute in. Little Shep wore a paisley shirt with a dickey (for that turtleneck look) even though it was hotter in Houston, Texas, than in Thornton! Mama told him he was going to burn up wearing a dickey in August, but he would not listen. Little Shep didn't say it, but I think he wanted long hair. I think he wanted screaming girls fainting when they saw him.

The best-dressed one in our bunch was Baylor. He had talked Mama into buying him a brown Nehru jacket that he just adored. It had gold buttons and was just a hair too big for him so that his little head floated inside the collar. He looked like a turtle from India. The brown looked great against his skin because Baylor had a gorgeous tan. Mama, Lulu, and I just broiled and had to slather on Noxzema for weeks afterward. Baylor loved that Nehru jacket, and I wonder if he knew how outstanding the whole effect was. He wore it with white pants and brown huaraches with no socks. The kid looked too smooth for words.

But Aunt Jezie! She showed up looking like she'd stepped straight off the pages of Mama's Neiman Marcus catalog. She wore a black-and-white polka-dot linen minidress with black heels and a matching polka-dot scarf in her hair. A wide black bracelet was on her arm, and her eye makeup looked like Jean Shrimpton. Oh, I was so proud! It gave me shivers to be around her, she was so beautiful.

We got into her beige Riviera, and she drove like the city of Houston was hers alone. Daddy used to criticize Aunt Jezie's driving, but now he just sat back and gazed out the front passenger window as she glided through traffic so fast our heads spun. We weren't used to this much traffic or the superhighway ramps that wrap around like macaroni. Aunt Jezie used her horn a lot and cussed at other drivers and laughed and hooted whenever she managed to cut someone off.

"Just call me Aunt Mario Andretti!" she said, blowing the horn.

We got to the Coliseum area early. You had to. Parking wasn't easy, but with Aunt Jezie at the wheel, you didn't have a thing to worry about. She had even thought to bring a bandanna to tie to the antenna so we could spot the Riviera after the concert. I had never seen so many people—not at the Louisiana State Fair, not even at Mardi Gras. Aunt Jezie surveyed the situation, then decided we needed to get out of the sun and have something to drink.

"Not too much—we have to keep our wits about us," she said, "but we need just enough to wet our whistles and take the edge off."

We followed her three or four blocks until we got to a Hawaiian restaurant that was dark and cool inside. We had never been to Hawaii, our fiftieth state. Stepping into this place, we thought we had crossed the Pacific Ocean! There were Hawaiian hostesses and Hawaiian waiters and coconuts on the walls. They put leis on you the minute you set foot in the door! Don Ho's autographed picture was above the cashier's desk, and there were about eighty-four thousand different drinks you could order with little umbrellas in them.

And oh my God! You would not have believed the people in there! These were not regular people from Texas. The men all had long hair. There were women with long straight black hair all the way down to their bottoms and white lipstick smoking long brown cigarettes. They wore leather skirts, and the men they were with wore ruffled blouses and jewelry. Boots, oh, they all had on boots. Tight pants and Beatles boots, zip-up boots, dress boots, suede boots, cowboy boots, and any other sleek pair of boots you could imagine. Ladies with short short miniskirts with boots that laced up to their knees, with eyes so black with makeup they looked like Cleopatra. Daddy said they must be awful hot in the middle of the summer wearing all that leather. But you could tell he was interested. Two women with their arms around each other stood over by the telephones, both of them reading books. A man with a goatee was speaking a foreign language to the hostess.

Little Shep stood next to him and said, "Wow, Maynard G. Krebs!" Mama had to pull him away.

On our way to our table there was a couple tongue-kissing. Right in front of everyone! We had to pull Baylor away from standing at their table and staring at them. Whew!

Oh, it was all just incredible! These people were not just pretending. They were not just dressing up. This is how they really were, and they didn't care who knew it or who gawked at them or what people said. I didn't know where they came from, but they were magnificent. They held all the keys to my future! That's how I wanted to be: different! Just leave it to the power of the Beatles to draw us all here.

For the first time in my life I realized that I could just make myself up! Like these people! Not like when I was a little girl and made everyone call me Madame Voilanska, but for real, for when I grow up. I could be whoever I wanted to be. I could be a different kind of person from Mama and Daddy or the Ya-Yas or anyone in Thornton or the whole state of Louisiana. I could be strange and exotic, like nobody who had ever come before. I could do things and make up things, just like I made up my "Beatles and Us" stories. I could wear flowered pants with legs that flared out. I could do anything. People would see me walking down the street, whip their heads around, and ask: Who is she? How did she get to be such a free bird? It gave me shivers thinking about it. Of course, it was probably a sin to even have such thoughts. But I was in Houston, Texas, so it didn't count.

By the time we sat down, we were just about overwhelmed. I thought Daddy might say something about how trashy it all was. But he just shook his head and said, "I guess it takes all kinds."

My father sure was surprising me on this trip.

We ordered Rob Roys and Shirley Temples with umbrellas. And I vowed I would keep this umbrella forever to remind me of the Beatles. We ordered some little pork appetizers because we were just passing the time more than anything, not really eating. It was so nice and cool in there. You couldn't believe the hot Houston streets were right outside.

Lulu and I went to the ladies' bathroom, which had bamboo everywhere. We stared at the women in there, spraying their hair and smoking handmade cigarettes that smelled like hay or something in the fields. We couldn't take our eyes off them. We wanted to be them so much. We put some of our mad money in one of the machines and got some Tangerine lipstick that kind of stung our lips when we put it on. It didn't look like its name at all but more like if you'd put Quick Tan on your lips. We had to wipe it off before we went back to the table, or we'd be in trouble.

There must have still been a little left at the corner of my lips, though, when I sat back down. Daddy said, "What is that on your lips?"

Uh-oh: here it comes. I was afraid he was going to go into his thing of calling us whores if we wore the slightest smidgen of makeup because he believed we were too young. He could ruin my whole trip to the city of Houston.

But Mama jumped right in and said, "Oh Shep, leave her alone. That is just color from sipping on her Shirley Temple."

Everything stayed fine. The grown-ups had some kind of drinks called mai tais. Mama and Aunt Jezie were both flirting with Daddy, and Daddy said, "Well, I believe one of these days I'm going to take yall to Hawaii, our youngest state. Including you, Miz Jez."

We left the restaurant of Hawaii and headed back out into the hot sunlight again. Aunt Jezie pushed her way through all the lines to get into the hall. She told us to just be quiet and follow her. In that black polka-dot outfit and huge sunglasses, she just elbowed her way through the crowds, and if anyone tried to stop her she said, "VIP coming through! VIP coming through! Out of the way, please, VIP!" Mama's mouth was just hanging open. Daddy doesn't like crowds, and he let Aunt Jezie take over. I was scared I'd get separated from the rest of them. I held on to Baylor's hand. He squeezed mine so tight I could tell he was frightened. The seven of us held hands, Aunt Jezie taking the lead, and we somehow managed to cut through that throng like we were all one person. I could not believe this was happening to me, that I was actually going to see the four greatest men on earth. M'lain Chauvin, my best friend, will be pea-green jealous! I will be the most popular girl in Thornton.

I was so thrilled, and I was proud of my parents for braving that crazy crowd. It took hours for the Fab Four to come on. Act after act performed, and finally it was time!

The stage lit up, and there were two amplifier speakers, microphone stands, and a set of drums. When the Beatles finally ran onto the stage, it was the loudest thing I have ever heard! Everyone in the whole place was on their feet yelling. Jillions of flashbulbs popped all at the same time, giving off a blinding white light that made the huge, dark cavern of the Coliseum turn into instant daylight. We were sitting in the balcony. The speakers were right in front of us, so we heard what they said and heard the songs they sang. As long as I live, I will never forget that moment. It is burned into me.

Not a person was sitting down in those seats they had paid for. So we had to stand up, too. There was a group of girls off to the side who started fainting halfway into the first song. Policemen had to come carry them out.

Daddy had brought the binoculars from the recipe drawer that we always used to stand at the kitchen window and look out at the fields. Boy this was sure a different sight! We passed those binoculars back and forth. When it was my turn, I zeroed right in on Paul's face and just left it there so I could watch his lips move. They were singing "She Loves You." Then Aunt Jezie started hogging the binoculars. I was jumping around so much, maybe she thought that in my state, I'd strangle myself with them!

It was hard trying to decide just where to look. I wanted to see all the people screaming and passing out, but I didn't want to miss anything the Beatles did. It almost made my eyes hurt. Every once in a while I let out a scream, more because I wanted to be like the other girls, not because I really felt like screaming. They went right on into "All My Lovin'." Then they sang some other songs I didn't know the words to because they hadn't made it to Thornton yet. When they got to "My Life," I started crying real tears. I just couldn't help it. It all became a blur. It was so loud and crowded. Out of the corner of my eye I saw Daddy take out his inhaler. Pretty soon he and Mama ducked out. They said they'd find a taxi and meet us back at the motel.

Now everyone was standing on their chairs to see better. We were glad we were in the balcony, not on the ground floor, because you would not see anything there. There were a million screaming girls on the floor seating area, out of their minds, they were so excited. One girl almost climbed up on the stage!

It was funny because Aunt Jezie kept trying to protect us from getting our eyes poked by other people waving Beatles pennants on sticks! If a pennant had stuck me in the eye right then, I wouldn't have even noticed!

I think the Beatles played maybe thirty minutes at the most, but believe it or not, I had to go to the bathroom before they finished their set. I guess I was kind of nervous. Anyway, Aunt Jezie and I left the arena and went to the restroom area. It was actually a good time to go, because nobody else had left their seats. After we finished in the bathroom, we were walking back in the long cement tunnel that led back to the seating area, and to this day, I swear that the Beatles ran right past us! We were the only two people in the tunnel as this big group of policemen came charging past us, and Aunt Jezie grabbed me and pulled me up against the side of the tunnel. I swear that for a millisecond I could see one or two of the Beatles in the middle of them as they rushed past! I even think that for a trillisecond I caught Paul's eye. It was them! It was him! I wanted to call out and say something to Paul, but I was just frozen to the spot where I was standing and could not say a word.

Aunt Jezie said, "Well, I'll be goddamned!"

Then she rushed us back to our seats, and the Beatles were still playing. I don't know how they did it.

I tried to ask Aunt Jezie, but she said, "These celebrities have their ways. Just enjoy the concert."

After the concert, Aunt Jezie got us through all the traffic—once she flashed something that looked like a badge out the window when a policeman stopped her, and then she gunned the Riviera down a blocked-off street.

"Go, Aunt Mario Andretti!" we screamed.

When we finally reached the motel, Mama and Daddy were propped up on pillows in their motel room bed looking real relaxed. Mama was wearing her gold caftan, and Daddy had on his khaki shorts and a sports shirt.

"It was *très* fab!" I screamed.

"Wow!" Little Shep said. "I never saw so many people in my life."

Lulu climbed on the bed with Mama. "Look, Mama," she said, handing her the special Beatles Concert booklet Aunt Jezie bought us with the money Daddy had given her. "This is George. He's my boyfriend," Lulu said.

"Baylor," Mama said. "How about you?"

"It was loud," he said. "Girls fainted."

"They love me, yeah, yeah, yeah!" Little Shep said. "Those girls don't look at little boys, Bay. They like us older ones."

Aunt Jezie laughed. "It was an experience," she said. "An experience I am glad I had. An experience that requires a drink. Got any vodka?"

"Over there on the table," Daddy said. "Brought our own bar."

The boys kept shaking their heads like the Beatles, trying to get their hair to swing from side to side. But their hair was too short, and the shaking just made them look like goofballs.

"Okay, everybody, listen." Then I told them about Aunt Jezie and me seeing the Beatles running through the hall, about them being just inches from us. Aunt Jezie backed me up, said she'd seen it with her own two eyes.

Mama said, "Sidda, darling, that is simply remarkable, simply remarkable." She gave me a hug.

But all the others said, "You liar! You are making that up just because you had to miss part of the show and go to the bathroom!"

But *I* know the truth, and that is what counts.

Mama and Daddy were in a good mood, and we were all just enjoying our own company. Daddy said, "Why don't yall put on your swimsuits?" And so we all got in the pool and Mama ordered a bunch of club sandwiches and we swam and ate under the umbrellas. We had to sit along the edge of the pool for thirty minutes after the sandwiches before we could go back in so we wouldn't get cramps and drown. Once the half hour was up, we dove in and played Marco Polo and sang Beatles songs underwater, trying to get each other to guess which one it was.

The grown-ups went inside after a while. They could see us through the sliding glass doors, even though we couldn't see them.

From time to time, Mama would step out and shout, "Are yall still alive?"

And we'd yell out, "Yes ma'am, we're still alive!"

Then Little Shep got his famous idea of climbing on the Greek statues and diving off. We boosted each other up and just dived right off those Greek gods' and goddesses' heads and shoulders. We sat on their shoulders and pretended we were riding bucking broncos. And we leaned down and kissed the statues all over their faces and called them John or Paul. And then Shep decided to stand on the arm of the naked statue with all the muscles and pose like he was a statue himself. We egged him on like Evel Knievel, and then out of nowhere the whole arm broke off! Shep fell into the water, and we froze in fear. We had been whipped for far less than this!

"Little Shep," we told him, "you're gonna ruin the whole trip, just when it was going so good."

We tried to figure out a way to get that arm back onto the statue. But it just didn't want to stick. We left it lying there and grabbed our towels and ran into our room and went to bed without saying a word, without even turning on the TV.

Mama came in and said, "What is wrong with yall?"

Little Shep said, "We're just tired from all this excitement, Mama."

Wouldn't you know it, the next morning this guy comes knocking on Mama and Daddy's door, right next to ours. We huddled in bed and listened.

"You ruined everything," I told Little Shep. "It's all your fault."

We could hear them in the next room talking, and we thought for sure that Daddy would tear into our room and beat our butts. But nothing happened. We just cowered there, without moving, under the sheets, wondering what was going to happen next. Things can turn from really good to really bad fast in my family. But it quieted down next door, and it sounded like Daddy had gone back to bed.

Then there came a knocking on our door! It was this man wearing a blazer with the motel insignia on it. He told us he was Ken, the day manager.

Ken said, "You kids were the ones roughhousing in the swimming pool last night, weren't you?"

Baylor, who was still in bed, said, "No sir, that wasn't us. That was some other little kids from Arkansas."

Boy, I love a liar with imagination.

Old Ken wasn't buying it, though. Little Shep was hanging his head down, and Ken smelled that something was fishy.

Ken stared into Shep's eyes and said, "It was you, wasn't it, son? You're the one that broke off the statue arm. Do you know what the penalty is in the state of Texas for destruction of property?"

Little Shep started crying, which is not something you can usually get him to do.

I yelled, "You fart motel-man, get out of here." I went over and gave him a push. I don't know what I thought I was doing. I just wanted him gone.

He kind of stepped back and looked at me in shock, and said, "What kind of family are you all from?"

"Catholic," Lulu said, chewing on her hair, which she always does when she gets nervous.

Just then Daddy and Mama stepped through the door that joined our two rooms.

Daddy said, "I beg your pardon. I thought I told you I'd talk to my children and see you at the desk later on."

Then Ken said, "Well, I didn't know whether I could believe you or not. This is serious business here. Those statues cost the owner of this establishment a pretty penny. We sent off for those statues."

Then Mama said, "Well, I'll tell you exactly like it is: you shouldn't have statues out there in the first place. They are hazards to children. What do you expect? There isn't a diving board. Don't you know little kids are bound to climb up on those statues and dive off? Don't you know anything about children here in Texas?"

Old Ken said to Mama, "We cater to an upscale traveler here. We are not children-oriented, madam. We are not a *Holiday Inn.*"

"Well, I don't care who you cater to," Daddy said, "we could slap a lawsuit on you pretty quick for having something as dangerous as those naked statues out there for my kids to get hurt on."

Old Ken changed horses in midstream then. "Well, look here, Mr. Walker, I feel sure we can handle this like adults."

Daddy said, "Well, get the hell out of my children's room if you want to be an adult about it. We haven't even had our breakfast yet."

And old Ken, he just backed out of the door with his tail between his legs.

"Awright Daddy! Awright Daddy!" we yelled.

This was wild. We hadn't even told them about the broken arm, and here they were, standing up for us.

Then Daddy said, "Wait a minute now, just what did yall do?"

And then Shep told him what happened, and we all stepped outside in our pajamas and pointed to the Greek statue with the broken-off arm lying there in the hot Houston sun.

Daddy looked at it, then said, "Close the door, son. You're letting all the air condition out."

Then we ordered some breakfast from room service, and Daddy said, "They don't have any business putting those statues out there anyway. What do they think this place is, a museum? Who do they think stays here? Mummies? Maybe Mister George Ogden and his mummified self could stay here and qualify as upscale, but we are plain American tourists."

After breakfast we packed up our stuff. We took everything we wanted but the bathrobes. They wouldn't fit in our suitcases. Baylor especially loved those shoe-shine cloths. He had a whole collection of them at home.

Aunt Jezie came to tell us good-bye. When she heard about the broken Greek arm, she said, "Shep, you were perfectly right to bring up possible litigation. When you settle your bill, don't you dare pay one red cent for that statue. Just tell them you'll sue the hell out of them if they say one more word about it. Tell them you know Russell Long. Tell them you know Al Hirt."

Daddy paid the bill and then came out and got in the car. He handed us a bunch of after-dinner mints.

"Stick out your tongue," he told Baylor.

Baylor obeyed.

Daddy unwrapped one of the mints and put it on Bay's tongue.

"Now," he said, "yall can go back home and tell everybody that you had a hundred percent Catholic experience here in Houston, compliments of your pagan, heathen-ass father."

Then Daddy laughed, put on his Ray-Bans, and got behind the wheel.

❧

We drove back to Thornton and when we got home we were sort of famous for a while. When school started, we told lies about how we'd gone swimming with the Beatles, who were staying at the same motel with us.

If anyone questioned us, we'd say, "Heck, yeah, it's true, just go ask my brother." And then we'd back up each other's stories. We showed off our Beatles souvenir programs but wouldn't let anyone else hold them. We would not even let people touch them.

Sometime in December, the Dave Clark Five came on TV. Mama and us kids had just come home from Teensy and Chick's house. Daddy was already in the den watching *Ed Sullivan,* and he said, "Kids, come on over here."

And we went over and listened to them sing. After they finished, we all said, "They are just fakes. Copycats!"

Then Mama fixed pancakes and we sat at the breakfast table. We loved pancakes on Sunday night. The Dave Clark Five reminded us of our trip to Houston, and we sat around the table and rehashed it, letting each other add little things that didn't really happen but would have been fun if they had.

When he finished eating, Daddy folded up his napkin and laid it down next to his plate. He looked at us and said, "If there's one thing I have to say to yall, it's don't ever be a copycat. Steal, lie, and cheat— but don't ever try to be something you aren't, you hear me?"

Mama said, "Shep, I couldn't have put it better myself. To thine own self be true, and all else will follow."

Little Shep said, "Yes sir."

I said, "Yes ma'am."

Lulu said, "Please could you pass the syrup, please?"

Baylor said, "I wish we could *live* in a motel. You know what I mean?"

Daddy said, "Yeah, I do, son. Now go on and finish your supper."

I don't think Daddy was really mad, but he said it grufflike. This embarrassed Baylor, and it changed the mood of the evening.

When we got through helping clean up, Mama said, "It's about time for yall to go to bed now."

"Aw, Mama," I whined, "it's still early."

But Daddy said, "Yall heard your Mama. Get on to bed now. This isn't vacation, it's a school night. This is real life."

"Yessir," I said, and gave Daddy a kiss. "Thank you for taking us to see the Beatles."

He gave me a little hug. "You're welcome, babe."

"Thank you for not being like Mister Ogden."

Daddy laughed. Mama tried not to.

"Get your bee-hiny to bed, you little Beatle-girl," my Daddy said.

Back in the bedroom I shared with Lulu, I took out my concert ticket. It had cost five whole dollars. Lulu and I turned out the light on our bedstand. The nightlight by the dresser was glowing. You could slightly make out the shapes of the Beatles' faces on our life-size posters.

"Good night, Lulu," I said.

"'Night, Sidda."

"Good night, Paul," I whispered. *"Sweet dreams."*

Bruised Plantings

TOO MUCH WILD

August 1961

*M*inutes before she ran off the road in her 1961 Bel Air, Myrtis Spevey had been praying. She'd come out of another Heathen Situation, as she always called it, with that horrible Vivi Abbott Walker. Time and time again, Myrtis asked herself what in God's name had possessed poor Shep Walker to marry such a woman as Vivi Abbott. Nothing but trouble, that harlot, and the whole of Central Louisiana knew it.

Myrtis was a pinched-looking lady who wore a size 16, but a "small 16," as she put it. One of the reasons she loved to sew so very much is because she didn't have to pay much attention to the sizes in the stores. Fear coursed through her body like the Garnet River did at the river bottom, but Jesus was her personal savior, very personal. She was shielded by her Jesus cloak, by His shield, His promises, and His protection.

Myrtis knew the Walkers. Myrtis had practically grown up with Shep Walker. The Walkers lived on the plantation next to where she grew up, her daddy leasing land from the Ambroses. She'd watched

Shep Walker every Sunday morning at Calvary Baptist Church, where the Walkers were pillars of the church. Well, at least Mrs. Walker was. Mr. Baylor Walker, big man that he was, came and went as he pleased, dropping into church with a fat wallet on holidays. Other than that, it was Mrs. Walker who represented them both as fine upstanding Baptists. A wife could do that, Myrtis knew. Could carry the moral burden for the whole family, and they would still be saved. The Walkers were just the finest, most upstanding family you'd ever want to meet, as far as Myrtis was concerned. Mrs. Walker was so dependable. You could count on her at every bake sale, and she was known parish-wide for her canning and preserving. Mr. Walker, now, there was a hard worker. He'd taken those old run-down farms he'd inherited from his family and made them into some of the most productive plantations in Louisiana. Myrtis's own mother had told her how Mr. Baylor Walker was a downright hero during the Great Depression. How he trucked potatoes to Texas and far away as Oklahoma to hold on to his land. He even managed to buy up some land that the blue-blood don't-get-your-hands-dirty gentleman farmers let slip away because they couldn't be bothered to get down from their fine front porches and walk among common country people. That was the thing about the Walkers: their blood was blue as it comes in the state of Louisiana, but they were country people and loved the land like a husband loves a wife. You drove by Mr. Baylor Walker's land, with the fences all lined up straight and painted, fields full of cotton as far as you could see, barns full of live-stock, and Negroes all over the place working—well, you just knew that he was the best farmer in all of Garnet Parish. Myrtis's daddy said he just thought the world of Mr. Walker, there wasn't a finer man in the entire state. Not to mention that Mr. Walker was good friends with Huey Long.

Shep had been a chubby, shy little boy with big brown eyes and straw-blond hair. He'd duck hunted with Myrtis's brothers ever since they were kids, since they were barely tall enough to hold their rifles. Myrtis had thought she knew Shep Walker like the back of her hand, like somebody so familiar, so much a part of your life, that you don't even notice them. When he announced his engagement to that Vivi Abbott, Myrtis almost fainted. She was at Wednesday-evening prayer meeting when she heard, and she stumbled to the ladies' room to hide her tears. Vivi, the daughter of Taylor Abbott, hotshot lawyer and breeder of thoroughbred racehorses. Mr. Abbott was part of that set who drank, went to racetracks, gambled, and showed up at fancy parties with beautiful young women they weren't married to. Taylor Abbott hobnobbed with Standard Oil men and had two daughters who both went to college, back when most families couldn't afford to send sons to college, let alone waste good money on sending girls away to school.

Myrtis had watched Shep at Thornton High School, as he grew from a chubby farm boy in overalls to a handsome young man with a black convertible Buick his daddy had bought him. All the girls from Calvary Baptist wanted to go out with Shep. He was such a good-looking, slow-talking boy, and he dated lots of pretty girls. He could have had his pick of any of them, the farm girls, all good steady girls who knew which end of a cow to milk, who knew how to cook and sew and make a home. In fact, Myrtis would not have minded if Shep had asked her out. Oh, she would not have minded one single bit. It was something she dreamed about during most of high school. But it did not happen.

Back in high school, Shep did not date Vivi Abbott. She ran with a group of rich, wild kids. Town kids. Catholics. Vivi Abbott was a cheerleader that year, and already drinking after football games on those sweet Indian-summer nights with those three girlfriends of hers. Vivi was dating Jack Whitman back then, another sweet boy. Myrtis could never understand why these nice boys would get mixed up with a girl like that. Jack Whitman died young in the war in Europe. He enlisted right after he graduated, went off to fight the Nazis, and never came back. Vivi had been gone, too, for a while. But she had come back to town, far too soon as far as Myrtis was concerned. Sometimes the will of God is hard to understand. Sometimes the good die young while the wicked prosper.

Myrtis herself would not have been caught dead running around with Vivi and her girlfriends, who called themselves the "Ya-Yas," for some ungodly reason. Not if they had begged her to come to one of their parties out at Spring Creek. Not if they had gotten down on their fou-fou little rich knees and prayed for Myrtis to become a part of their group. No. If they had even dared to try and include her, Myrtis would have snubbed them big. She had her snubs planned. She had long assorted lists of snubs that she practiced in bed at night. But she never had the chance to use them.

All of this came rushing at Myrtis as she sped out into traffic, leaving behind the Grand Opening of the Southgate Shopping Center. She was driving fast because her maiden visit to the Singer Sewing Center had been ruined by Vivi Abbott Walker.

After two years of demolishing farms and leveling groves of old pecan trees and Live Oaks, hauling out rocks, then grading and laying in dirt—after months of advertisements on K-Dixie-BS-TV and much anticipation—the day of the Grand Opening had finally come.

By the time the shopping center finally opened, downtown Thornton had been simply ruined by the Negroes, as Myrtis well knew. That's what all the ladies whispered on the front steps of Calvary Baptist: "Shopping has just been ruint by the coloreds. You can't even buy a new *girdle* without having them swarm all around you. If the Good Lord would of meant coloreds to shop in the same stores as whites, then He'd of made us all white." Myrtis was alarmed; she imagined trying to fend off Negro men lurking in Whalen's department store as she went to try on her new Maidenform.

All the white people in Central Louisiana had been clamoring for a *real* shopping center like they had down in Baton Rouge so they could get away from the Negroes and not have to drive all the way downtown. Southgate was the first of its kind in Garnet Parish, and the Grand Opening was a major event in the history of the town. There was a Piggly Wiggly supermarket; a Modest Dry Cleaners (run by Pentecostal women, something that Myrtis could never get over); a J.C. Penney's; a Walgreen's; and the new Singer Sewing Center. The Grand Opening was all people could talk about for months. It had even been mentioned by Preacher Becker at Calvary Baptist. He had worked it into a sermon about how holiness could beget prosperity if you were right with Jesus.

The Singer Sewing Center held Myrtis enthralled. After all, wasn't she considered one of the best seamstresses in Garnet Parish? Of course, she did not take in sewing. She had a husband, Mr. Harlan

Spevey, thank you very much, who had a fine job selling life insurance. She did not need to take in other people's sewing. Harlan was a fine provider, even if he was raised a Catholic and had a Catholic mother who acted like she was appointed by the Pope himself to rule over Myrtis and her family. Myrtis did not understand how in God's creation she ended up marrying a Catholic. She sometimes hoped her marriage was a covert missionary calling to bring Harlan into the Baptist faith. The fact that Myrtis herself had been forced by the Catholics, most specifically her Catholic mother-in-law, to take instructions in Catholicism was like sand chafing between her thighs every day and night. She even had to send her perfect children to Catholic schools, where they were forced to put up with the likes of those Catholic snob Walker children. Spoilt rotted brats. Oh, Myrtis loved her Catholic husband. It was not Harlan who did the pushing; it was his mother. And Harlan was not a man to say no to his mother. But in her heart Myrtis would always be a Baptist. Even if they crammed her full of the Body and Blood of Christ, she would remain true. The only thing she and Harlan ever really argued about was when his mother heard that Myrtis continued to sneak off to Calvary for prayer meetings and covered dish potlucks and what-have-you. Myrtis did her best to hide it, but Harlan's mother saw and knew all. You can take the girl out of Calvary, Myrtis told herself, but you can't take Calvary out of the girl.

As for sewing, it was her special God-given talent, something that put her above all other women, Catholic and otherwise. One of her many favorite scripture quotes was: "They which are gorgeously appareled and live delicately are in kings' courts." It was Myrtis's firm belief that the garments she made were gorgeous apparel. She also believed that she lived delicately. Unlike some people she knew.

She made everything she wore, plus all of Harlan's suits. Mind you, a person could count on one hand the number of ladies in Garnet Parish who could make a man's suit. Arguing to the point of red-faced rage, she tried to talk the nuns at Divine Compassion into letting her make her children's school uniforms, but no—the Catholics had a uniform supplier, and she and Harlan were obliged to pay a fortune to them. Each time the children went up a size, this galled her worse and worse. She made up for this by sewing the most special, the most original outfits for each one of her children whenever they were not forced to wear the Vatican's factory-made uniforms. Relatives and friends had been given everything from coats to hats made by Myrtis, and she took no small amount of pride in it. What if Harlan's mother had not worn the garden dress that Myrtis had made for her? What if it was the same as a slap in the face? Myrtis was not going to let that bother her. It was so *Catholic*, is what it was, and Myrtis was not going to let it ruffle her feathers. Even if it had occurred eight and a half years ago.

Hadn't Myrtis won every 4-H blue ribbon from the time she was eight until she was eighteen? Back before Shep fell under Vivi Abbott's spell, he was showing prize heifers at 4-H shows, and the two of them would talk when Myrtis strolled by his stall to admire the livestock. Oh, she could have sewn for Shep Walker. Why, right this very moment, Myrtis was wearing one of her homemade creations. A green and white seersucker shirtwaist dress, with white piping on the short sleeves. She made the belt herself, along with a little bikini scarf to match. She imagined she looked like a Jantzen ad, so jauntily was that scarf placed over her pale brown hair.

This was one of the reasons Divine Compassion made her so nervous. Not one of those Catholics, it seemed to Myrtis, wore anything but storebought clothes. Myrtis always preferred to be with people who wore homemade clothes.

The second Myrtis opened the front door of the Singer Sewing Center and inhaled the scent of all those dyes, all that fabric, she thought she'd died and gone to heaven. Vivi Abbott and her crowd could buy their clothes at Whalen's, but give Myrtis a sewing machine, and she'd mow them down with her talent. Oh, she gloried over the counters filled with bolts of every imaginable fabric. Your plaids and florals; your new synthetic blends and cotton piques! Myrtis worshipped at the altar of notions, the racks of zippers, and the new pattern books—drawers upon drawers of the newest patterns, difficult patterns with fat envelopes of tissue paper, chock full of directions that only the most accomplished seamstresses could follow. And the salesladies, well, they could have gone to *college* in sewing. They probably did, they knew so much. Myrtis had never met ladies who knew more about interfacing.

Now she wouldn't have to be alone anymore in her love for the Zig-Zag stitch. She had found a home. Maybe it would help her not feel so empty inside. Ever since she'd married and given up her full membership at Calvary Baptist, had given up teaching her Sunday school class, she had not felt quite right. And when she snuck out to prayer meetings after promising Harlan she wouldn't, she felt guilty. Like an alcoholic sneaking out to a bar. In fact, one time during a particularly heated argument during Advent, when Harlan's mother had heard about Myrtis's help creating the outdoor crèche at Calvary, Harlan's mother called her a "Baptistaholic." Myrtis would never forgive her for that. She nursed that grievance with a pleasure so deep and private that it resembled how most people feel about their sexual fantasies.

One of the few things that comforted her was that she knew that Shep Walker had married a Catholic too, and had gone through Catholic instruction. But Shep stopped short of letting the Vatican lock him in the Catholic penitentiary. She'd heard Shep Walker had drawn the line when it came to telling his sins to another man, which meant he never made his first Confession, which meant he never got to partake of the Body and Blood of Jesus Christ. Myrtis herself took Communion. Everybody looked at you; you had to. But the most she ever said in Confession to the strange man behind the incense-smelling screen were things like "I spoke rudely to a friend" or "I did not do my best at cooking this week." Myrtis figured that was enough for them.

If only she could talk to Shep Walker, they might find they had still had something in common, like they used to in 4-H. Like when they, along with a small contingent of other Garnet Parish 4-Hers, rode a school bus up to the Louisiana State Fair in Shreveport. Myrtis showed her sewing, and Shep Walker showed the Brahma bull he had raised. But now Vivi Abbott Walker stood between them, and Vivi radiated a force that seemed big as the Catholic Church itself in all its prideful glory.

How jubilant Myrtis was, after three hours in the Singer Sewing Center on Grand Opening day! Who needed pecan trees when you could have a Negro-free shopping center with a shrine to sewing?

That's right: it should have been called the Singer Sewing Shrine. But no, that was too much like something Vivi and her crowd would say, so Myrtis clamped her mouth shut and gave a tight little grin. She would never let anyone know how happy this place made her. It was hers; she would keep it all to herself.

She was in such a good mood, and she was determined that no one would ruin it. She had registered to win the new Touch & Sew Machine they were giving away. She had introduced herself to the manager of the store. She had bought two new patterns for summer swimsuit cover-ups. Such items like she was planning to make would cost twelve to fifteen dollars at J.C. Penney's.

Myrtis walked out onto the expansive blacktop parking lot of the new shopping center, smiling because she was so sensible and thrifty. She smiled because she would soon drive back over to her mother's house and show her mama the new patterns and material. She would sit across from her mother in the cool light green kitchen with the shades partly pulled to block the sun. Her mother would praise her for being such a smart homemaker. They would have an afternoon cup of coffee together as they did every day, and then she would go home and start her own family's supper.

Myrtis raised her hands to her eyes and tried to block out the glare from the sun. The sun was still hot and bright, even though it was late in the afternoon. She looked out over the parking lot at the crowd gathered at the far end of the lot.

"Oh, that's right, they have that *elephant* here for the Grand Opening," she said to herself. The elephant had been advertised for three weeks before the Grand Opening. Pictures of the elephant with her trainer were on the front page of the *Thornton Town Monitor*. The children had been talking about it for weeks. Myrtis had adamantly opposed the elephant rides as soon as she heard about them. "Elephant rides!" she had said to her mama one afternoon over coffee. "Now have you ever heard of such foolishness, I ask you?"

Now she watched as the huge lumbering gray animal bobbed up and down. The heat from the blacktop sent ripples up into the summer air, so the head and trunk of the animal seemed to float back and forth like a hula girl on the back dashboard of a car. The elephant was decorated with a colorful headdress full of beads and little mirrors and ribbons. Myrtis found herself walking over toward the crowd in spite of herself.

As she drew closer, Myrtis could see that it was just as packed and hot and sticky as she'd predicted it would be. Looking over at the elephant, she was convinced that she was right to have forbidden her children to come near the place. The situation was more dangerous than even she had imagined.

Her husband Harlan had said, "Myrtis, I don't know, I think it might be sorta, well—out of the ordinary for the children. When else are they gonna have the chance to ride on an elephant's back?"

But she had told him not to worry about it. She was in charge of the kids, and it was out of the question that her children should so much as consider riding an elephant. Her sons Ronnie and Tim begged and begged. Her only daughter, Edythe, stood by her side and agreed. "We most certainly will not go ride that elephant. Mother is right: this is not *Africa!*"

Myrtis thanked the Good Lord. Hearing Edythe repeat her words let her know she was doing a fine job in raising a young Christian lady. This was especially important because it turned Myrtis's stomach every time she saw her Edythe climb onto a bus that took her to Divine Compassion, tuition paid compliments of Harlan's mother. A Catholic school was where a daughter learned to serve the Pope, not the Lord. But she could not fight Harlan's mother. It was Myrtis's cross to bear.

What Myrtis saw now as she approached the crowd caused her to immediately reach into her sensible brown imitation leather handbag (ordered from the back of the *Delta Sunday Magazine* supplement) and attach a pair of clip-on shades to the front of her pointy blue eyeglasses. She hoped the shades might keep her from being recognized. She did not want anyone from Calvary Baptist to find her here. Not after she had spoken against the elephant ride during a Sunday-school class she snuck into as a guest speaker (something that made her feel like she was a double agent for the Heavenly Father). She could stare from the cover of her clip-on shades, stare—without interruption, without being unladylike—at the scandalous scene before her.

Not far from the stage that had been set up for the Grand

Opening ceremonies, Vivi Abbott Walker had parked her notorious Thunderbird. And there she sat on the hood of the car like the Queen of Sheba, with the car radio blaring. Wearing a pair of pink Catalina short-shorts with a sleeveless cotton shirt tied at the waist and expensive pink sandals dangling from her painted toenails. She leaned back on the hood, a pair of her huge sunglasses covering her eyes, smoking a cigarette and sipping something—Myrtis suspected (correctly) that it was most certainly an alcoholic beverage. Vivi was laughing and talking with several of the teenage boys who always flocked around her. Acting like she thought she was still at Thornton High School with a twenty-inch waist. Oh, it drove Myrtis crazy to see such a sight. If only she had the nerve to take Vivi Abbott Walker aside and give her a piece of advice about how to act now that she was a mother of four. Now that she was the wife of Shep Walker, who was still the most handsome man—other than her husband, Harlan, of course—in Garnet Parish. It would have only been Christian charity to have a talk with this woman who obviously did not know how to behave. Catholics knew nothing of scripture. Still, Myrtis blamed Vivi for not adorning herself in "modest apparel, with shamefacedness and sobriety." It might be Good Samaritanish, Myrtis thought, if she could impart just one smidgen of ladylike, God-fearing behavior into Vivi Abbott Walker. One of these days, she would do it. One of these days.

Vivi's Thunderbird was the kind of car every teenage boy in Louisiana wanted to own. (Probably teenage girls too, but they never approached Vivi about it.) Teenage boys hung around Vivi, offering to pay hundreds of dollars more than that car was worth new. Then they just stood back and adored Vivi while she flat-out refused their every offer, loving every minute of it. On this hot afternoon, Vivi leaned back across her car in splendor, like the Grand Opening was being held especially in her honor, something she accepted as only her due.

"Sweet Lord Jesus," Myrtis muttered to herself. "Basking in sin. That is all that woman is doing, basking in sin. To think that she is the mother of four precious little children." Myrtis's complete Singer Sewing Center joy, her perfect day, was pulverized in a single instant by Vivi Abbott Walker. All her happiness just melted down into the blacktop. That is what Vivi Abbott Walker could do to Myrtis. That is what Myrtis let Vivi Abbott Walker do to her.

Shep Walker had not started dating Vivi until years after high school, after most of the other girls in Thornton had gotten married and had a yowling baby or two on their hips. Myrtis had heard from her mama that Mr. Baylor Walker and his wife were mortified when Shep started dating Vivi Abbott. Before Wednesday-night prayer meeting, when all the ladies stood outside the big double doors in front of the church to gossip, they would ask: Didn't it mean anything to Shep Walker that Vivi and her gang of girlfriends had actually been arrested while they were still in high school? The four of them had climbed up the side of the City Park water tank and jumped in—actually took off their clothes and jumped into the tank that held the entire drinking water supply for all of Thornton. And it was only because Roscoe Jenkins happened to be passing by in his patrol car, cruising real slow, and caught a glimpse of somebody's clothes on the ground that the whole thing was even discovered. Poor Roscoe had to climb all the way up there himself and see that every single girl was buck-naked. He instructed them under penalty of law to get their clothes back on. Then he herded them off to the police station, where their fathers were called. But because of *who they were*, they were only reprimanded and then sent home. Anybody else would've spent time in jail. At least this is how Myrtis heard it, and she was sure she was right.

Roscoe had told Myrtis's Uncle Parnell, who was a bail bondsman, the whole story over coffee at Rotier's. Roscoe said that Vivi Abbott, when he asked her why in the world they jumped into the water tank, had replied that it was a full moon and they were instructed to do it. That alone was enough for Myrtis to know that Vivi Abbott was a witch. Catholics can be witches, Myrtis thought, don't you go doubting it.

Oh, Pastor Dexter Roy Bob Becker had preached about that event! She remembered his sermon title, taken from Job: "How much more abominable and filthy is man, which drinketh iniquity like water." Pastor Becker had the Ya-Yas' number. Even if the rest of Thornton did not.

❦

At the same time that Myrtis stood there appalled by what she saw on that parking lot at the Southgate Center, she began to fear for the safety of the Walker children. Poor little things, with that witch for a mother who was too busy flirting with young boys to notice the peril to her children. Myrtis could just imagine something horrible happening: all four of them, darling even though they were sassy and big-mouthed, lying splattered all over the hot blacktop, their storebought summer outfits covered with blood and elephant dung. After all, Myrtis thought, dark things can happen on even the sunniest day. She played the image across her mind several times. Then Myrtis gathered herself together and walked toward Vivi, who was still lounging on the hood of the Thunderbird, finishing her second thermos full of vodka and lemonade.

Vivi was arguing with one of the teenage boys. "You must think I am some kind of backwater fool, Dahlin. There is absolutely no way in hell I would sell this car for anything less than five thousand dollars. Yes, that is correct, five thousand dollars. Because while it is virtually impossible to put a dollar value on what this vehicle means to me, five thousand dollars would at least fly the *petits monstres* and *moi* to the Riviera for the rest of the summer and set us up in a leased villa. Plus, there might be a little left over for Shep to come visit us when he has the time. I *am* a married lady, yall *must* remember."

Then, flinging her hair back out of her eyes, she turned to an especially virile-looking teenager and said, "James, I have told you a thousand times: take your sweaty hands off my rearview mirror!" At that, she reached down into her purse for another Lucky Strike.

Myrtis could take no more. She marched right to the edge of the shiny chrome bumper and addressed Vivi as though she were an errant schoolgirl instead of a mother of four.

"Vivi Abbott Walker," she said, "you should be ashamed! Get yourself up off the hood of that car and go take care of your precious little children!"

Vivi didn't bat an eyelash. She stared through her Foster Grants at Myrtis, who stood before her wearing the most hideous example of a sewing machine gone mad that she had ever witnessed. There should be a law, Vivi thought. Vivi didn't have to lower her eyes to know that Myrtis would be wearing matching Keds Grasshoppers tennis shoes with white socks turned down in a little weenie roll.

"Why, Myrt, you are Fashion Incarnate," Vivi said, loud enough for the teenage boys to hear and break into loud honking laughs.

Vivi Abbott Walker was the only person in the world who had ever called her "Myrt." *Myrt*. So it rhymed with *dirt*.

Vivi lit her cigarette, French-inhaled, and added: "And Dahlin, those clip-on shades of yours are positively *signature*."

She blew the cigarette smoke out slowly straight into Myrtis's face. Then she leaned back against the windshield.

"Vivi Abbott Walker, those children are going to be killed by that elephant any minute now!" Myrtis said, her mouth opening no wider than was absolutely necessary to get the sounds out.

"No, Myrt dahlin, I believe my boys and girls are still in line. It is almost five o'clock, yes, I can tell by my Indian Guide instincts that the sun is very near the five o'clock mark. My dahlins *must* get on that animal before five, because that is when the elephant and his beloved trainer must pack up and get on down the road. I'd love to stay and chat Myrt but I have to make sure my little dahlins get their elephant ride!" And with that, Vivi slipped down off the hood of her car and dashed off through the crowd.

"Oh," Myrtis muttered under her breath, "Dear Lord, help me keep my temper. Suffer the little children to come unto me." Then Myrtis turned away from the Thunderbird and slowly pushed her way toward the line of children.

She could hardly have been surprised by Vivi's response. It was exactly the sort of thing Myrtis expected. Why had she even bothered? Vivi Abbott had no shame, she never had. Vivi Abbott, who didn't even sew a stitch! Myrtis had seen, all of Thornton had seen, how Vivi actually stapled the hems of her children's pants and then laughed about it when the staples fell out. "They just don't make staple guns like they used to," Vivi would say as her children's pant legs dragged in the mud.

Myrtis never completely got over the fact that Vivi refused to learn to sew, can, or make jam. One time, when Shep and Vivi were newlyweds and seemingly strapped for cash, Myrtis had gone over one Sunday afternoon and offered to help Vivi make drapes for that little rental house they lived in back then.

"Thank you, Dahlin." Vivi had tossed her head and laughed. "My grandmother always told me that *stores* make those things much better than you could at home. But isn't it just too cute for you to offer, Myrt!"

Sure enough, even when the price of cotton was only pennies for a bushel and all the farmers were hurting, including Shep Walker, Vivi Abbott kept on ordering from Neiman Marcus like she was a European heiress. Vivi went four times a year to Dallas or Houston for big shopping trips, instead of taking the trouble to make clothes herself. And at Calvary Baptist, it was whispered that Vivi told her mother-in-law, Mrs. Baylor Walker, that she'd rather starve than spend her days canning tomatoes and corn—and the Walkers with some of the finest farms in the parish!

Vivi seemed to believe that Shep and his family and neighbors were ever so slightly beneath her. They were country people. Granted, they were country people with blue blood, and more acreage than anyone else in Garnet Parish, but still, there was something of the farm about them. They were 4-H people: head, heart, hands, health. But none of it was good enough for Vivi Abbott Walker.

Vivi always laughed at Myrtis, treated her like she was an old joke or something, not the kind of person who the Abbotts and their friends would invite to house parties in the Garden District in New Orleans or what-have-you.

Myrtis reached the roped-off section where the children stepped onto a wooden platform before climbing a rope ladder winding up and over the elephant's enormous belly and onto its huge gray back. She saw Vivi and three of the Walker children about to settle down onto the elephant saddle. The oldest daughter, Siddalee, seemed to be frozen. Maybe, thought Myrtis, just maybe one of those Walker children has more sense than the mother!

Of *course* Vivi would bring those horrid girlfriends of hers, Myrtis thought. There they were, standing farther back in the line with their own poor little children. That ghoul Caro Brewer, wearing black clothes and sunglasses like she always did. That dreadful Teensy, who always looked like a little monkey or something. And Necie Ogden, who was the most normal of all of that bunch. She was the one who Myrtis hated the least, and she could not conceive of how such a nice lady got hooked up with the rest of those Jezebels.

Myrtis was surprised that the oldest Walker child didn't break into a fit. Myrtis had seen these hissy fits before. All the Walker children were famous for occasionally throwing themselves into such frenzies that they eventually became exhausted and had to lie down in a dark room and sleep it off. Vivi said it was good for them, got it out of their little systems.

"Here's what you do," Vivi whispered to Myrtis once, on a Sunday afternoon in winter when Myrtis and her mama had gone over to see Mrs. Baylor Walker and found Shep and Vivi there with their four children. "You give them a little snort of bourbon," Vivi whispered, "lay them down in an air-conditioned room, shut the door, walk out onto the porch, lay down in the swing, and put on a Johnny Mathis record. When they wake up, they are as sweet as angels. That is how you get through being the mother of four."

Myrtis knew this was against scripture. There was no telling how those poor children would turn out. They would probably grow up to become ax murderers. They would end up in the Garnet Parish insane asylum, where Myrtis would have to bring them pecan pies at Christmas.

Myrtis leaned down close to Siddalee to find out what was wrong. But Siddalee would have none of it. She broke away and pushed through the hot crowd. Myrtis tried to follow her, but the crowd was so heavy that she lost sight of the young girl within minutes. She went back to tell the other Walker children: "Wait a minute, don't do it! Get off that beast and go help your sister." But just then she saw Vivi Abbott Walker climb up there on that elephant and heard her call out, "Ride 'em cowgirl!" The elephant began to lumber away with three little Walkers and Vivi perched on top, bobbing up and down precariously.

Myrtis realized that in her zeal to save Shep Walker's wife and children, she had misplaced her new fabric and patterns. And she was getting a headache. In fact, she was well on her way to a migraine. Fine, she thought. Let Miz High-and-Mighty Vivi and those Ya-Ya queens sort it all out. You try and you try to help them, but all they know how to do is to be snooty, ungrateful, and rude. Myrtis was running late now. She'd have to skip that cup of coffee with her mama and hurry right on home to make dinner for Harlan and the children. She got into her car and could hardly work the key into the ignition, her hands were shaking so bad. When Myrtis got angry, she shook because her body could not hold all her anger.

That afternoon, as Myrtis was confronting Vivi Walker, two young men had put away their tools, collected their pay from Shep Walker, and climbed into an ancient green pickup truck. Eddie and Washington Lloyd were proud of this truck that they'd bought with their own money—earned doing long hours of hard and sweaty work for Mr. Shep. Right now, that same sweat shone on their dark skin so heavy that the backs of their shirts were wet and stuck against their skin. Their Uncle Chaney had helped them get hired at the Walker plantation the summer after their Daddy died. Chaney was Mr. Walker's right-hand man, and he'd persuaded Mr. Shep to take them on, even though they'd been real young then. They'd been working at the Walker place for years now. They lived several miles from the Walker place, and it was a long way to walk to work every day, then back at night.

Washington and Eddie had been discussing whether they should go home and change first or head straight over to the new shopping center. They'd just spent ten hours working in the fields under the hot sun, and their shirts were filthy and their overalls were streaked with dirt. Normally, Eddie and Washington didn't like to be seen out looking like this. They liked to look sharp. And their Aunt Willetta always fussed at them about this: "Don't you be going out looking nasty! Won't no girl ever kiss on you, if you all sweaty and smelly. Don't you be acting like a ten-cent self. You good handsome men. Act like it."

But today, Eddie and Washington decided to skip their usual cleanup and head straight out to the Southgate Center before everything closed up. They wanted to see that elephant. They'd joked about how the animal and them both came from Africa, and so maybe the elephant might recognize them somehow.

All of Thornton had been talking about the elephant. The ads had been on the radio for months. When they heard about the Grand Opening, the black kids had been just as amazed as the white ones. Bringing an elephant, all the way from Africa! Like us, they said, all the way from the other side of the ocean! Uncle Chaney had shook his head when Eddie repeated this. "Sure, just like us. Brung to haul the white peoples around," he said. The gossip in the black community was that, of course, blacks would not be allowed to ride the elephant—it was for white children only, as was the shopping center. It had not been lost on folks that the minute downtown Thornton had started to integrate, this shopping center on the outside of town had sprung up. The white people still wanted their own place to shop. But Eddie and Washington had thought about it and talked about it, and they decided that even if they could not ride the elephant, they could at least see it. Surely the white people would not mind if they just looked at the wild animal.

Washington drove out of Pecan Grove and turned on the road that ran along the bayou. He was driving as fast as their old truck could go—he had to keep it at thirty-five, because at about forty, the transmission began a metallic whine. Eddie fidgeted with the door lock on his side and looked over at Washington. "We gonna miss the elephant."

As Myrtis made the turn off the highway onto the two-lane black-topped road that wound along Bayou Latanier toward her home, she was driving fast, replaying the parking lot scene in her head over and over, so furious at Vivi Abbott Walker that she could hardly see. She compulsively counted all the sensible Christian things she should have said, all the scripture she could have quoted at Vivi Walker. Myrtis's body pulsed with anger and humiliation. It was a beautiful twilight, but she did not notice. She came around a curve and was dumbfounded to see another vehicle on the road headed straight for her. In her lane. Or what she thought was her lane.

At the sight of the Bel Air, Washington was stunned. "Sweet Lord, have mercy!" he screamed as he veered to the right, grazing the other car on the front someplace. Hard to tell even color or model, it was over so fast, and the car was gone, almost as though it had never been there. And then Eddie and Washington were screaming: "Tree!

Tree!" as the truck slid to the right toward a big old live oak at the edge of the road. Washington swerved left and slammed on the brakes. The truck went into a skid, and the back end of the pickup boomed as it slammed into the tree. To look at the truck, it was a miracle the two young men escaped with only minor injuries. The bed of the truck was wrapped around the tree, and the rear axle was broken, with one tire rolling off into the neighboring field.

Washington looked around him and realized that their truck was angled into the road, its back end crumpled against the big tree, its front end sticking out into the lane they'd been driving in. He climbed out of the truck, steadied himself, and whispered, "Shit."

Eddie had to work to get his truck door open, and he got out cautiously, not yet sure all his body parts were working correctly. He looked up and down the road and did not see the other car. He wondered if it had just disappeared into thin air. He noticed that his forehead was bleeding some, and his neck and shoulder didn't feel right. Then he walked around the back end of the truck.

There was a deep dent and scrape along the front on the driver's side. And in the back, the right side panel behind the back door was crumpled and twisted and the back bumper was off-kilter. This poor old warhorse of a truck didn't just have a few more scars—it was undrivable, and unlikely to ever be drivable again.

Eddie looked like he'd taken a hard punch to the side of his face. But when he spoke he sounded okay, like he wasn't feeling it yet. "Man, where'd that other car go to?"

Washington, with blood dripping from his nose, looked at Eddie in the road and said, "Who care where that car at? *We alive.* Dear Lord, thank you. One fine-ass miracle done happened in the state of Louisiana today."

They both liked to have cried. Their truck, the thing that made it possible for them to get to work, was demolished. They were still standing, but hoofing it would be their only option now. You didn't get a truck easy if you were a black man in Thornton, Louisiana. Washington hated to remember how he'd had to grovel in front of a fat old white loan shark just to get the money for this truck. No, you didn't get you a truck easy. Nuh-uh. They didn't want to give you the loan they collected on every Friday afternoon. They didn't want you driving your own truck any more than they wanted you to ride an elephant. To them, a nigger on an elephant was a wild animal on a wild animal. Too much wild.

Myrtis's Bel Air had left the road and become airborne. It passed between two of the live oaks that lined both sides of the road, sailing out into a field of sugarcane. For a minute, there was astonishment and terror as Myrtis felt suspended in air, without being completely aware of how any of this had happened. Was this the Rapture? All she could see was blue and green flashing faster than she could even look at it, and a loud swishing sound all around her. Then there was a hard thump when the car landed, and she felt her head hit against something. But it didn't hurt, not yet. In fact, she felt completely numb. The car bumped along now, and all around Myrtis everything was intensely green and swatting at the sides of the car.

Then suddenly everything stopped.

Myrtis took a breath, which she had been holding in ever since the car left the road, and looked up. She saw the rearview mirror, splintered, and her crazily fragmented image stared back at her. She looked away—somehow it was unbearable to look at that mirror. She looked down at the plastic seat cover, still warm from sitting all that time in the afternoon sun. She'd just Windexed those seat covers that very morning. Now there were smears of blood on the front cover. She looked down, and there were drops of blood on her beloved shirtwaist dress. As she looked, a few more drops fell. She began to cry. And then she couldn't stop crying. She couldn't stop. It was like parts of herself were breaking off from her and floating inside the car and then outside into the green surroundings. She was dimly aware of a part of herself detached and watching and saying: *Now Myrtis, here you are, having a hissy fit. No better than those bad little Walker children. Get a hold of yourself!* But for once, she could not get a hold of herself. All she could do was cry. She could not even catch her breath. Whoever Myrtis had been, she was all broken to pieces now.

When she stopped crying, it was getting toward dusk, and she had begun to hurt all over. She moved her arms and her legs. They hurt, but they worked. She carefully opened the car door, since the window on the driver's side had broken, and sat a minute. Then she stepped out of the car. She didn't know where she was, but all around her were stalks of sugarcane taller than she was, as far as she could see. Behind and alongside the car, she saw that the cane was crushed. There was a wide swath of smashed cane stalks that made a crazy, wavering path away from the back of the car. The car listed toward the right—she'd either run the right front tire into a hole, or it had blown out, she couldn't tell which. She did not know what to do next, so she just stood there, feeling like her brain had flown apart during the accident, and some vital pieces had been mislaid.

Suddenly, she became aware of something moving behind the car. There were crunching and swishing sounds that Myrtis recognized as footsteps, and she gasped. It was dangerous for her to be out here alone at night in the middle of some field. Something was coming to get her! She began to sing loudly. She was in a wilderness of her own creation and saw nothing but fear. She prayed not to the Catholic god that the Vivi Abbott Walker crowd sang to, but to her Baptist god, the real true and only Lord.

For a moment she did not recognize her own voice; she turned as though the voice must be coming from some other woman as she heard the words:

> *"Stand up, stand up for Jesus, Ye soldiers of the cross!*
> *Lift high His royal banner*
> *It must not suffer loss*
> *From vict'ry unto vict'ry His army shall He lead.*
> *Till ev'ry foe is vanquished And Christ is Lord indeed."*

During the last line of the hymn, two young black men appeared from a tangle of crushed sugarcane stalks next to her car.

Myrtis screamed with all her might, every cell in her body contributing to that yell reverberating through the green field. Then everything went dark.

"Myrtis? Myrtis, honey?" She heard her name spoken from a long distance. She blinked her eyes open, but was blinded by harsh white light and closed them again immediately. So this is what death is like, she thought. I'm in heaven, and I'm blinded by the light.

"Oh, Lord, Myrtis!" This was Harlan's voice. Myrtis's eyes popped open. Harlan's head came into view as she painfully raised her head. Her neck and back were very sore. She was stretched out on something very hard, under bright fluorescent lights, in what looked like a hospital room.

"Oh, honey, what happened to you? They called me from the hospital. I was home with the children, waiting on dinner."

She was silent for a moment. Then she spoke, haltingly.

"Well, I was driving home . . . and there was this truck, and . . . and then, these black men . . ."

"Oh, Myrtis, no! Honey, no. Did they, you know . . . hurt you?" he whispered.

"Oh, God in Heaven, no!" Myrtis was so alarmed she sat straight up, sore neck and all. Had they raped her? She remembered being terribly afraid they would. But she felt perfectly normal down there. Surely you'd know if something like that happened.

"No, Harlan, all they did was run me off the road." Better nip this in the bud, she thought. I can't have people even wondering if those black boys touched me, I could never live that down. "I was just driving on the bayou road, and this truckload of niggers came barreling around the corner. Driving all over the road. Just wild, like apes behind the wheel. I didn't even have time to react."

"Myrtis," Harlan said, "we were just worried to death when you didn't come, and it was so late. Your mama said she hadn't seen you, and then that Miss Gremillion at the hospital called and said they was bringing you in." This was the most he'd said at once the entire time they had been married, and this time Myrtis just let him keep on talking. She was more worn out than she'd ever felt in her life.

She actually dozed for a little while, and then this young handsome doctor came in and checked her over. He picked shards of glass out of her arms, cleaned and bandaged the right side of her head where she'd whacked it against the rearview mirror. He smiled and told her she had been very lucky. She'd had a concussion, he explained to her, and they were going to keep her overnight for observation, just to make sure she was all right.

Before long, Harlan came back into the room, and with him

were officers from the Louisiana State Patrol. Officer Jimbo Thurman of the State Highway Patrol strutted into the hospital room, and Myrtis could feel her body tighten. Had she done something wrong? Had she caused all this? And if she had, would they ever be able to find out? It was her word against those niggers, that was all there was to it. Officer Thurman walked straight over to Myrtis's bedside.

"Mrs. Harlan Spevey?" he asked, although it was obvious that he knew exactly who she was.

"Yes?" She was so tired and sick of it all, she wanted to tell him to go away and leave her alone. Couldn't he see she had been through enough? "The Lord is a shield unto them that put their trust in him," she prayed.

"I need to talk to you about your car accident. Your car was pretty banged up. Might not be a total loss, though," he said, trying to chew tobacco discreetly at the same time. "And the Vanderhovens' canefield ain't looking so good neither." He looked around like he thought this might be funny, but Harlan and Myrtis didn't smile.

"Officer," Myrtis said hoarsely, "before yall go bothering respectable people, yall need to do something about those niggers who almost took my life today." She was a hospital patient. She was a victim. She got right to the point.

"Well, you'll be glad to hear that they're already in custody. We arrested them at the scene for reckless driving. We've impounded their truck and suspended their driver's licenses. They won't be running any roads for a good while," Officer Thurman said.

Officer Thurman pulled out a form and asked Myrtis questions about the accident. But Myrtis said she could not remember much. She did not remember the truck that hit her, other than the fact that it was big and green. It was upon her before she knew it, she said. When Myrtis was asked by the policeman to tell him what happened, she said the boys had run her off the road, and that was that.

She had walked through the valley of the shadow of death, and now here she was, sitting in St. Cecilia's Hospital, the Catholic hospital, when they certainly should have taken her to the Garnet Parish Hospital, which did not have nuns as nurses, with their ridiculous, scary headgear. She had lots of bruises and cuts, not to mention a concussion. They all agreed that she was lucky not to have been hurt a lot worse.

Finally the state trooper left, and Harlan went down to the cafeteria to get himself a cup of coffee. Myrtis was left alone in the hospital room. The bed opposite hers was empty. The light in the room was strange; she could hear low noises in the hall; she looked at the sterile room: the sink, the plastic chair next to her bed, the window through which all she could see was darkness.

She tried to pray, but all she could think about was that conversation with that heathen Vivi Abbott Walker. She had tried to save Vivi and keep the little Walker children safe. Myrtis's body shook with rage, remembering how Vivi had behaved. If Vivi had not upset Myrtis so bad, none of this would have happened. This was all Vivi Abbott Walker's fault. That woman had ruined everything for Myrtis, all along, ever since high school. If Vivi Walker had been behaving like a normal Christian person, a real wife and mother, none of this would have happened. "Why," Myrtis asked aloud, "does the Lord make to suffer those who love Him the most?"

DAUGHTER OF GOD

Edythe Spevey, November 1994

*F*or too many years I hated children. Then when I realized how bad I wanted one for my own, it was too late for me to bear one. No matter. There is more than one way to skin a cat. I may not be able to carry a child, but if I pray hard and regular to Jesus, He will deliver. He will extend His hand and guide me. Guide me to the right mall, where a bad mother has ignored her precious child for the last time. And I will take the little one. Take her to be with me. The Lord may have taken away my capacity to make the child, but He did not dim my mind.

It makes me sick to the stomach the way the mothers treat their children. It is pitiful. It is a sin. Everywhere you turn, they are too interested in their own lives to care for the child. They do not deserve what they have. They deserve to have the girl child taken from them while they talk with their friends about meetings and jobs. When they drop them at day care and run off to live their lives like they had not been blessed with a holy little child. When they act like they still have control over their lives, which they don't. Because once a baby comes into your life, everything changes, and you lose control, lose your flat stomach and your fine five-year career plan.

Don't think I haven't watched, both people and TV. Don't think I don't read. Don't think I haven't thought about this. Don't think I haven't prayed about this. Don't think I haven't talked to my mother about this at the home. She is the one who first suggested it. All kinds of truths can come out of the minds of Alzheimer patients if you but know how to listen.

My mother, Mrs. Myrtis Spevey, lives at the Harmony Home on the highway outside Thornton. I go see her every single day. She is the one who brought me into this world and carried me those hard nine months. She is the one who has taught me everything I know. I bow down to my mother. It makes me nauseous that people have not realized what a wonderful lady she is and all she has done in her life. How I wish her true wisdom had been recognized before Alzheimer's took her and swirled her mind around.

My brother Ronnie and I share the cost of her care, and he goes to visit her once a month. The other brother has abandoned his responsibilities altogether and no longer deserves to even have the name Spevey. In my book, he should be forced to wander around in the world as just "Tim" and then just see what that brings him one day when he has to go to the Social Security office or the emergency room.

But I am the one who brings Mother her clean clothes every day that I wash in my own machine because she does not want her clothes washed in the machines at the home. My mother has given her life to me. It is nothing to give mine to her. She is one of the reasons I want my baby. To hand it to her as she lays in her bed at the home and let her coo and love my baby the way grandmothers do.

I will find her, the child who is meant for me. I will not force myself upon her. No. When the time is right, she will come to me. She will walk right over. She must give me a sign. That is what Jesus did. He always gives signs. Right and left, the Savior is always giving us signs. And the eyes to see those signs are still intact in His little ones. Oh, I will know when I meet the right one. There will be none of the devil's doubt to cloud my vision when the time of ripeness comes.

Until then, I have my list of places to look. I have the list on my refrigerator door, and I make check marks to be sure I cover each location at least once during the week. This is my basic list:

Magnolia Park
Thornton City Park
All 7-Eleven convenience stores
Piggly-Wiggly Supermarket
Toys-R-Us
John Robert Bolton Recreation Center
The Garnet Parish main library
Jefferson branch library
Hollywood Video
Video Schmideo
Parking lot across from Montessori School
Area around Our Lady of Divine Compassion Kindergarten
The Thornton Mall
The Mall of Cenla
Cenla Cinema

The video stores are especially good. When the working mothers go in there, they show their true colors. Only one mother in ten pays any attention at all to the gifts God has given her. Most of them are too interested in the New Releases and a few of them in the Foreign Film section. Their poor children crawl on the floor or stand and stare at the screen where Satan's trash is playing. The mothers have the right haircuts and the expensive child seats in the brand-new minivans, but not one of them really knows how to love her child.

Now me, I will smile and play with the children while their mother is busy, but I will not so much as touch one of them. I will not do that until the right child gives me a sign. Then I will move fast and sure.

It galls me no end that the Video Depot lady told me to stop coming in her store so frequently. She said, "It makes us a little uncomfortable the way you come in so regularly and never check out a tape. You are making some of our customers nervous."

This made me sick. "This is a free country," I told her. "I can go where I want."

She said, "Do you even own a VCR machine?"

I said, "Mind your own business, please. This is America."

And I know I could go in there any darn time I please, but I am not going to patronize a place that would treat a person like they did me. I deserve more respect than that.

When God closes a door, he opens a window. I found me a larger store, the Blockbuster next to the big Walgreen's with the drive-through window. That is where I get my medication, so it is very convenient. Blockbuster has rows and rows of movies. And a good place for the children to play. They sell popcorn and soft yogurt, so it's a popular place for the ones I am interested in.

Don't think I do this all the time. I am not some kind of freak. Since I quit working Intake at the Veteran's Hospital, I have not just sat on my hands.

I quit Intake because of Larry Reidheimer. Lying scum. I quit because of his lies to me. Lies about giving me a baby. Said he had everything it took.

How it happened was, I went to Dr. Roland to evaluate my female organs. Even though I am not military, I got a discount at that hospital due to my Intake position. But Dr. Roland said to me, "Ms. Spevey, in terms of conceiving, I afraid you are not a good candidate. You are in an early menopause. I don't usually see women your age who are this far into menopause, but you most definitely are. In addition, you are obese. The loss of at least eighty to ninety pounds is essential. You are also borderline diabetic. I suggest you concentrate on your own health rather than the delusion of having a child. I want to make it perfectly clear: the chances of your conceiving are, as we say, slim to none."

I ran into Larry just after that visit. We had known each other from around the hospital, him working lab tech and me in Intake. And I don't know what made me, but I told him everything. I told Larry how it gnawed at me to have a baby, and about the doctor killing me the way he did with his pronouncement on the lateness of my body.

The next day, Larry told me he had looked at my charts, and what the doctor said wasn't true. Larry said he could help me, he might be able to do something for me. He said, "Edythe, if you open your legs just right, I could help you."

But he didn't do a damn thing except make me sin against Jesus Himself. Twenty-seven times I sinned with Larry, nothing blocking his sperm from me, and him saying God would bless us soon. *Twenty-seven times.* It makes me puke to think about it. All the fluid dripping out of me. Sometimes I would lay there and actually picture that a baby was swirling around, trying to take form inside all that stickiness.

But it was all lies. I was dry and old inside. Larry the Satan liar just laughed. He said, "Well, it was fun trying, wasn't it, old girl?"

He will suffer. God will see to it that the man will suffer. And if God should give me a sign to aid in the punishment of Larry Reidheimer driving his silver Corvette, I will not shrink back.

As far as the being overweight goes, I have been a large girl since high school. That is what Mama told me: "Edythe, you are not fat. You are simply a big-boned girl." I would lose this weight if I thought it would help God give me a baby. I could lose one hundred pounds if I knew that is what God wanted. Don't think I couldn't.

Before God let me know that a little one would be mine, hate was high for children in my heart. High hate for their noisemaking for no reason. High hate for the poop and the running and all the questions and disturbing everything you own. All I wanted was to go on with my work and have an orderly day. Come home in the evening and watch the news, like I do. Eat a decent meal, without having someone throw up all over me or get up under my feet like roaches.

Oh, now I hate myself for the years I wasted rejecting the little ones. But it is my cross to bear, and I do not shirk from carrying it. Holy Mother Church is there for me, and I go to Confession every Friday of the week. The priest knows I am a good woman. He knows I try to please God in all I do, think, or say.

One night while I tossed and turned in bed, burning for my baby, Jesus climbed down from the cross and told me I could have a baby girl. So I can be patient. Patience obtains everything. Saint Teresa of Avila said so.

All I want is one little baby girl of my own. I don't want a boy. I don't want the boy with his little tallywhacker hanging between his legs that will grow up with him, and pretty soon he's swinging it all over the place like a king. Like Larry Reidheimer. Like my father got to be after I went to high school. Mama told me.

Once I went to my father and told him what I thought of him. He was not ugly or angry. He said, "Edythe, there are things you do not understand. There are parts of marriage that your mother wants no part of. Those are the only parts I go elsewhere for. I love your mother. I love you."

But he was damned as far as I was concerned. No, I don't want a boy child. As far as I'm concerned, when they clip them at birth, they should just cut the whole damn thing off.

I want a little girl. Like me. One I could love. A little daughter of God.

And I am ready. I got a two-bedroom apartment, which does not come cheap. But I have been paying the extra just so I can be prepared when the sign comes. God will not give me a sign from the little one if I'm living in a one-bedroom. Of course, I will not move my baby into her own room until she is ready to stop sleeping in the same room with me. That could take years, but I need to be ready. God is counting on me being ready.

When I quit at the Veteran's Hospital, Miss Honansson in Personnel, who was from Chicago (you could tell), was the only one asked me why. "Why are you leaving, Edythe?" she said. "You are so effective at your job, why do you want to resign?"

I told her, "The only way I could stay was if Larry Reidheimer was to have his pecker removed. If they would just leave it to me, I would put that thing in between a car door and the car and slam it off. That is what I would do, with no hesitating."

Miss Honansson was the one I had liked, the one who brought me a Valentine card that one year. She's so cute with that smile and those shoes. But then she had to go and say to me, "Edythe, have you ever thought about getting some professional help?"

Getting some help. I do not need help, thank you. God is my help. The Holy Mother Roman Catholic Church is my help. What I need is my child.

My baby girl is revealed to me at Video Schmideo, the little video shop in the Garden District, as they call it. On Wednesday, just before three in the afternoon, I am standing there looking, always looking, acting like I'm reading the back of *The Magnificent Ambersons*. My baby girl toddles in with her mother, who is none other than Joanie Hammond, who insists on being called Joanie *Ogden* Hammond. The nerve and disrespect of that woman to insist on using her maiden name like that after she found a perfectly good husband! I refuse to say it. I have seen Joanie Hammond with her baby girl before. I seem to recall that they call the baby Rosalyn.

She looks about three years old, with blond hair and hazel eyes and a little pair of overalls. Wearing a tiny chubby jacket with her clothes all bunched up underneath at the shoulders so that she almost looks deformed. But that is only an illusion because without the clothes she is perfect. She looks at me, straight at me. I can see in her eyes that she is ready to come to me. She starts flirting with me, rolling her beautiful eyes and playing peekaboo. I give only a tiny smile. Like she is not God's gift to me on earth. I must not draw attention to myself.

Her mother is standing over there jingling the car keys, her hands on her hip. So busy with a friend she ran into, making fun of that actress Melanie Griffith's voice. She is Ms. Joanie Petite Ya-Ya, all dressed to the tee. Like she does not have a child, like she is still free on her own. Oh, Joanie, you're so modern you can't keep your eye on the little precious one. You won't be so modern when you lose your baby. Will you, Joanie, popular girl with Siddalee Walker and the other princesses? Your heartache will be so strong and last so long that all your popularity will be drained dry. The phone will not ring. Your husband will walk out on you. But you will happily remarry. You will have another little baby or two or three, and still you will not know what you have.

I know you and your type: Siddalee and her gang—you included—laughing at me all the way through school, the way the Ya-Yas laughed at Mama when they were in high school. Mama told me. Mama tells me everything. But you will be just fine. You people always are.

And then the little one walks straight to me. Smiling. Without hesitation. I bend down and pick her up like I know her, like I am her aunt or something. She makes a low little sound, not quite talking. I walk straight out the door. I am holding her, no one can stop us now. A straight line to my car, and she is in the seat next to me. I hate it that I don't have time to buckle her into the baby seat I bought and strapped into the back of my car. But it is okay, I will drive so careful with my precious new daughter. My heart is beating fast, I am perspiring. But my head is clear. There is no room for doubt. I am sure-footed. The sign has been given.

I start driving her back to the apartment. But after a few blocks, when we are out of danger, I know I must stop and put her in the baby seat. It is a way of my giving thanks, of not taking for granted the life that has been given to me. I know how to do it, and she is not scared or fussy. I have practiced this with a stuffed bear many times.

I drive safely and slowly the rest of the way home. I take the baby girl inside, and I lock the door. We go into my room. I lie down next to her on the bed, strewn with the stuffed animals I have had ready for her, and I stroke her baby hair, her tender skin. I tell her everything about me, things I have never told anybody. And she listens. She understands. She is the one God has sent to me. She is like me. We lie next to each other, the sheets softly touching our skin. She has waited like I have waited. Outside, they have all been the bosses, but now our time has come. We are in the temple, the doors are closed. I have lived my life to come to this moment. I have been vigilant because I know: *The daughter of God will not come unless you have the eagle eye.*

Laughing, Joanie Ogden glanced down to check on her daughter. But she did not spot Rosalyn. She interrupted her conversation with Anne Gautier by raising her hand slightly, then stepped away to peek around a cardboard video display. She walked back the other direction to look in the next aisle, saying, "Rosalyn," in a happy singsong voice. "Rosalyn, honey? Rosalyn?" As she moved quickly to the next two aisles, she called in a louder voice: "Rosalyn?" A tingling of fear coursed through her body. Joanie tried not to panic, but she broke out in a cold sweat. She walked quickly from aisle to aisle, not realizing that her calls to her daughter were getting louder and more desperate. Her heart and her ears were pounding. Everyone's attention was on her now, although no one was helping. They all looked at her with confused, concerned faces. They stood there dumbly blocking her way as she ran about the store.

Her mind started to race. There was no other place Rosalyn could be. "God, help me, God help me," she murmured without thinking. She felt frantic and faint. Joanie bumped into Anne and clutched the front of her friend's blouse. "Call 911. Someone's taken Rosalyn." People began to move and help. They were looking under displays she had already checked twice. One woman went to check the parking lot.

Joanie started to cry. She cried uncontrollably, and she knew it was true. She ran out the front door and joined other voices in shouting her daughter's name. There was still hope. There was still time. People were trying to take her arm and comfort her or ask questions, but she pulled away—she had to keep moving and calling for her daughter. She could hear a siren now. Everything began to swirl and collapse. She could feel herself being sat in a chair that someone brought out.

A police officer stood in front of her, holding her by the shoulders, trying to get her to focus on his voice, "Ma'am. Ma'am. Ma'am, tell us what happened." She tried to tell them between sobs, but she could not.

Finally someone nearby shouted, "Someone's kidnapped her three-year-old!"

Another police car arrived, and then a Garnet Parish sheriff's car. She heard an officer say, "It's George Ogden's granddaughter who's gone missing."

Immediately George Ogden, the baby's grandfather, and Necie Kelleher Ogden called on every connection they ever had. George was the Garnet Parish Court judge, and his reach was wide. He didn't take no as an answer. Consequently not only did the Thornton Police Department become fully involved, but also the Sheriff's Department and the Garnet County Search and Rescue Division.

The search was hard and fast, with all the stops pulled out. The Sheriff's Department flotilla was deployed to the small bayou behind the video store. Within two hours, officers and volunteers were combing the neighborhood. The parking lot of the video store was a zoo all afternoon. Small-town hysteria set in quickly. Squad cars blocked the street at either end, and detectives and officers did not let anyone leave. They made people go over their stories of what happened again and again. Someone remembered a strange man by himself who disappeared after the mother started screaming. Another person remembered an odd woman with a dog. Most people didn't remember anything at all. "The child was just gone. Just disappeared—," was the most common reply. And it was getting harder to concentrate with Cenla's only news helicopter hovering overhead, and the newspaper and radio reporters who arrived, and the TV van with that blond woman from the local evening news.

The moment she heard, Necie Ogden had started a Novena to the Blessed Virgin to find Rosalyn unharmed. So did Vivi and Teensy. Caro, who didn't go in for Novenas, meditated and cursed.

The Ya-Yas set up camp at Necie's house before nightfall. Joanie went back and forth between her own house and her mother's. She was afraid to stop moving. She felt if she stayed in motion, things would somehow be okay. Her husband, Grove, and three of her sisters kept vigil with her, driving her around, answering the phone, trying to shield her from the growing circus of media, concerned citizens, and nosy parkers. Her brother Frank, who was now called "Francis," flew in from Atlanta.

That first evening, the police kept the child's identity out of the press, referring to Rosalyn only as "the three-year-old child of a prominent Thornton family." But then big news broke, interrupting the scheduled programming later that night. A convicted felon had escaped from a prison roadwork crew twenty-six miles outside Thornton at approximately seven that same morning. While being transported to the work site where fifteen prisoners were clearing ditches because of drainage problems, one Doyle Dubro had made a run for it into the woods nearby. There were only two deputies to supervise fourteen remaining convicts, so the law enforcement officers on hand had not followed Dubro into the woods to try and find him. In fact, the prison had not reported the incident to local authorities until twelve hours later, hoping to find him themselves and avoid bad publicity.

The Ya-Yas, even Caro, spent the night at Necie's, spreading themselves among the numerous second-floor bedrooms kept in gracious condition as guest rooms. Caro slept in the downstairs den, oxygen tank at her side on the sleeper sofa, so she wouldn't have to walk up the stairs.

Vivi and Teensy, who were in the bedrooms upstairs, could hear raised voices coming from Necie and George's bedroom suite. Silently they cheered her on each time they heard Necie speak back to him. She was not satisfied with his approach to the situation, and she let him know it.

When they all woke up the next day, it was still not clear who had won the argument.

On the steps of the Garnet Parish Courthouse at 10:00 A.M., George Ogden held a press conference. To the left of the podium was a blown-up mug shot of Doyle Dubro. To the right was a blown-up photo of Rosalyn on poster board, propped on an easel. George stood at the podium with his wife, Necie Kelleher Ogden, beside him, along with Joanie and her husband, Grove Hammond. Television cameras were taping as George looked directly into the camera and spoke. "As of fifteen hundred hours yesterday, November 5, 1994, a three-year-old girl is believed to have been kidnapped from Video Schmideo, a local business here in Thornton. The prime suspect at this time is an escaped convict, one Doyle Dubro. We have deployed all available law enforcement teams, including the Thornton Police Department—"

At this point, Necie edged herself to the microphone and began to speak. George was so shocked, he did nothing at first.

"The little girl is Rosalyn, my daughter Joanie's child," Necie said, speaking quickly in a wavering voice. "Please, she is a precious child. Even if she were not our own flesh and blood, she would still be precious, still a child of God. Please: become your own deputy. Give us your eyes, ears, and every gift God gave you to help find—"

At this point, George edged Necie aside and commandeered the microphone.

"As I was saying, in addition to the Thornton Police Department, we have also deployed the Garnet Parish Sheriff's Department, the Louisiana State Patrol, the Garnet Parish Search and Rescue Division, and specialized units from surrounding parishes. Dubro is believed to be armed and dangerous. If you see Dubro, do not attempt to approach him, but call 911 immediately. May God bless and keep us all in His protection and care. Thank you."

By this time, both Necie and Joanie were sobbing, leaning on Grove, who had his arms around both of them. Unaware that he could still be heard in the microphone, George said, "Necie and Joanie, I *told* you I would not have any female hysterics! I should have known better than to let you appear in public with me."

The camera moved off the family and onto the lovely, vacuous face of the onsite reporter, a blond woman in her twenties. "Judge Ogden," she asked, "what assurance can you give us that the authorities are doing their job?"

George looked solidly at the young woman. "Police and state patrol, as well as other units, are putting maximum effort into investigating the possible connection with the kidnapping."

"Are you saying that Doyle Dubro is now the prime suspect?" the reporter asked.

"Yes, I'm afraid it looks that way," said George, who then turned and grabbed Necie by the elbow and herded Joanie and her husband back into the courthouse.

The blond reporter faced the camera as she wrapped up the news report: "And so continues the unthinkable odyssey as Thornton struggles to save one of its beloved children. In addition to the hotline set up by the city, we at K-Dixie-BS-TV have our own hotline. We will be flashing Doyle Dubro's photo at the top of every hour, and we ask that you memorize his face. Help bring an end to the suffering of one of Thornton's most prominent families."

Vivi, Teensy, and Caro were watching the press conference in the den, lying in the sofa bed. Caro was still in her pajamas.

Caro flicked off the TV remote in disgust and threw it across the room.

"Idiots!" Vivi spat out.

"Goddammit," Caro began in her raspy, deep voice, "Vivi, why after all these years are we still letting these numb-nutted good old boys run everything?! A felon escapes from a road crew. A felon who once— *once*—robbed a convenience store with a water pistol! No history of sexual abuse, kidnapping, or pedophilia. A onetime loser of an offender. He doesn't disappear into the state forest across the road. Instead, he somehow manages to travel unseen along a state highway for twenty-six miles—wearing a bright orange prison jumpsuit, mind you—and has nothing better to do than walk into a video store in the *center* of Thornton, in the *toniest* part of Thornton, for Christ's sake, and kidnap a three-year-old girl! There were only ten people in the store at the time. Granted, they probably had their heads up their asses, but no one sees the muddy, scraggly convict in his fucking bright orange prison jumpsuit walk through the door in broad daylight—"

Caro began to cough, that deep cough that racked her whole body. One of the things she hated the most about emphysema was how it cut her off from fully speaking her mind.

"Ease up, Dahlin," Vivi said, "take a few slow, deep breaths."

Vivi sat still while she watched Caro steady her breathing.

Finally, Caro added: "I'm so proud of Necie for speaking up. That heinous ape of a husband of hers is worse now than he was when he tried to shut down the black music station in the sixties because it played what he called 'race music.' I should have cold-cocked him back then when he tried to get in between Dinah Washington and the Ya-Yas."

"You are right, of course, Caro," Vivi said. "It's time to take things into our own hands while there is still time."

When Necie got home with Joanie and Grove at her side, the Ya-Yas stationed her by the phone. Teensy, Vivi, and Caro would head out in Teensy's convertible, Teensy at the wheel. Caro would stay in the car, taking notes and marking their city map with the highlighter pen. Vivi would get out and question people. Anyone they saw outside would be questioned about what they had seen the previous afternoon.

"It's a bit improvised," said Vivi. "But we haven't got time for perfection."

Then the Ya-Yas did something they hadn't done in a long time. They put their arms around each other, forming a circle in Necie's living room. Vivi called out the Ya-Ya tribal names they had given each other in their initiation ceremony decades ago.

"Duchess Soaring Hawk?" Vivi asked.

"Check," said Caro.

"Princess Naked-as-a-Jaybird?"

"Check," answered Teensy.

"Countess Singing Cloud?"

"Check," said Necie.

Then Necie softly chimed in, "Queen Dancing Creek?"

"Check," Vivi said in an even voice. "Let's roll."

The Ya-Yas had ridden in countless convertibles during their long friendship, but never had they been as subdued and serious as they were that day. It was a beautiful November afternoon, but other than exchanges about what street should be next and Vivi's reports from her interviews, nothing much was said. This was no Ya-Ya joyride. After about two hours they were getting discouraged. Caro sighed. "The word *futile* comes to mind."

Vivi said, "It also doesn't help that in over two hours, we found only eight people to talk to. And not one lead."

Teensy voiced everyone's frustration when she said, "If this were forty—even thirty—years ago, we would have already talked to fifty people by now. And they wouldn't be acting as if we were walking up to mug them either."

It was Caro who spotted the maintenance man in the shadows next to the First Baptist Church. No one else saw him, and she announced her observation in typical Caro fashion. Without utter-ing a word, she snapped the fingers of her left hand at Teensy and then pointed toward the church. Then she went back to studying the map, wearing her prescription wraparound sunglasses, with the little clear oxygen tube just below her nose.

Teensy pulled to the curb. Vivi got out and marched purposefully across the lawn to talk to the old man clipping the hedge in the shadows. Vivi guessed him to be in his late seventies, but wasn't sure. His gray work shirt and pants looked like they had probably fit him long ago but now just hung loosely on his skinny frame. He wore a red stocking hat, and had a café-au-lait-colored face. His old work clothes were clean and pressed.

Vivi started in with her questioning routine, which she had down pat by this point.

"Excuse me, sir, I hate to bother you, but—"

"That the new Saab convertible I seen on the TV?" he asked.

The old man didn't really look at Vivi, but he scratched his chin slowly for a good long while and looked out toward Teensy's car.

Vivi did not really get the impression he was asking her. She stifled the urge to grab his hedge clippers and snip at his toes, yelling, "Dance! Dance!" She quickly snapped out of her little fantasy and added: "This is really very urgent. It could be a matter of life and death."

He said, "Yeah, I seen something a little unusual yesterday.

"What I seen was a white woman pull over in front of the church. She done got out of her car holding a little girl, then walked around the car to the passenger's side. She hold that baby up high in the sunlight for a long moment and then open the side door. Then she strap that baby in a car seat and done drove off. I ask myself why she stop right here in front of the church like that, all sudden-like."

Vivi's hands were shaking as she wrote down the make of the car and the description of the woman. She asked him about the license plate.

"My eyesight not good enough no more to see no license number."

"Well, can you remember anything, anything at all? A little girl has been kidnapped, and we have to find her."

"Lady, just how many white Mazdas with a dent on the front fender be in this town? The lady be heavy-like, with brown hair, and the baby be fair as can be. My eyesight might be fading, but I tell you that car was a Mazda, musta' been ten, twelve years old. My nephew drive a Mazda. I know my Mazdas. Ain't give him nothing but trouble. I know my Mazdas."

"Thank you, sir," Vivi said.

"God bless you and that baby child," the man said, turning back to his yard work.

Viviane Walker headed back to the car, waving her tablet in the air, running as fast as any sixty-eight-year-old had ever moved across that church lawn.

They drove straight to the police station with the information.

"Thank you, ladies," the detective said, after making them wait for almost an hour, during which they took turns raging. "We appreciate your citizenly behavior, but the professionals have the situation fully under control. And you can trust that Judge Ogden is watch-dogging the investigation carefully. I'll pass this information down the appropriate channels. Why don't yall go on home now, leave it to the trained *professionals?*"

They drove over one more block, and Caro stayed in the car as Teensy and Vivi rushed up the steps of the courthouse toward George's office. A starched young male secretary in the outer office told them that he understood that they were personal friends of Judge Ogden, but the judge could not possibly be disturbed.

Vivi whipped out the Zippo cigarette lighter she had carried in her purse since 1944. "If George Ogden does not come through that door in thirty seconds to have a word with Vivi Abbott Walker, I will light his tasteful reception area on fire." The young man just stood there with his mouth hanging open, so Vivi ignited a few of the silk leaves on the fake ficus tree for dramatic effect.

Vivi was shown into George's office, and she stood in front of Necie's furious, red-faced husband. "George, you and I have not always seen eye to eye on many issues, to say the goddamn least. But I think I can say that we have always acknowledged each other's intelligence."

She then recited the facts as the Ya-Yas knew them. To his credit, George Ogden ran with them.

The SWAT team broke down the door of Edythe Spevey's apartment on the third morning after the child disappeared. They went in with riot gear and Kevlar vests and guns at the ready.

What they found was a clean apartment that smelled like home-made applesauce. The windows had lace curtains, and the kitchen floor had been recently waxed. What they found was an overweight woman with a pale complexion, thick glasses, and a rather large nose playing with a blond-haired baby girl on a blanket on the carpet. The child was spotlessly clean, and she was surrounded by new toys. Rosalyn cried when she was taken away from Edythe by the police-man with the headgear on. He terrified the baby.

Necie Ogden was the one who single-handedly pushed to have Edythe put in Central Louisiana State Mental Hospital for observation, rather than putting her on trial for kidnapping as George had insisted. Necie had defied her husband few times in her life, but they had been important times. "George," she had insisted, "God has been merciful to us. Not a hair on Rosalyn's head was damaged. We should show mercy as well."

The Ya-Yas had been at Necie's side almost the entire time. They had cooked food, prayed, manned the telephones, and organized the flyer distribution. They had loved her the best they could. When the hearing and everything was over, Necie collapsed into the arms of Vivi and Teensy. Caro sat in a chair nearby, holding Necie's hand. Necie began to sob.

"Don't worry, I'm crying from relief," she told her girlfriends of more than half a century. "But it's so sad! That young woman Edythe was in my charge at one time. She was in Troop 55. You remember, Vivi. Edythe Spevey was there when I backed the station wagon into the telephone pole during the Girl Scout campout. Was there something I should have done for her? Were there signs back then that she needed help?"

"Please," Vivi said. "Don't carry that cross, Denise. That child was a weirdo back then, and I knew it. Her mother was a weirdo in high school, and that daughter didn't fall far from the tree. Just thank God and the Holy Lady that we got Rosalyn back. Just be grateful your daughter did not crack up during the three days she waited, not knowing what was happening to her only daughter. Just pray that Edythe doesn't get loose and do it again."

"You did the right thing, Necie," Caro said. "Edythe will spend the rest of her days in the mental health care system. Which, in the state of Louisiana, might as well be like being imprisoned in the Middle East or something. That woman won't see the inside of a video store again."

Teensy sighed. "You're right, Necie. It is sad. It is nothing but sad."

For a while, the entire extended Ya-Ya tribe was paralyzed with fear. With each passing day, though, each of them found a way out of the fear that had been injected into their lives like poison. All except Joanie.

She refused to leave the house, even to go grocery shopping. Necie and Grove brought everything in. Joanie held on to Rosalyn, who was not allowed out of her sight—was barely allowed out of her arms. She grew obsessed with having the most sophisticated surveillance system available installed in their home. Rosalyn was not allowed to go to day care. Lee-Lee Walker was allowed to come over and play, but that was it. Grove stayed home from his law office for almost two weeks, but eventually he had to get back to work. Then Necie came over daily, and when Joanie had to do something within the house, Necie held her granddaughter and crooned old Harry James tunes and saw that the child had a ring of protection around her. When Joanie was out of the room long enough, Necie encouraged the child to romp on her own, although Joanie had forbidden anyone to let Rosalyn even play outside.

Her prayer life stronger than ever, Necie's own terror dissolved far faster than her daughter's. Necie did not feel they were truly safe, however, until she started visiting Edythe at the mental institution. She prayed for a miracle: for the ability to see through Edythe's actions to the innocence within her. When she learned that Myrtis was at Harmony Home with no one to visit her, Necie's volunteer hours increased. She saw not only how lonely Edythe was, but how confined Myrtis was—confined in her scrambled brain, confined in a nursing home where she rarely saw the light of day. She began to visit each of them regularly. Then she forgave. And with forgiveness came peace.

The other Ya-Yas weren't so sure. Necie was too good-hearted, or even "downright naive." Sometimes they agreed with George: the Spevey woman should have been locked up at St. Gabriel Women's Prison in South Louisiana, and never let out.

One day when Necie visited Edythe at the hospital, she decided to bring Edythe a baby doll. "Here's your baby, Edythe," Necie said. "She's been waiting for her mama."

Edythe's entire body changed. The tight, deep wrinkles between her eyebrows relaxed; her whole face opened up and her eyes shone; her chest swelled under her pink flannel nightgown. Tears filled Necie's eyes as she witnessed Edythe's rapture and joyful obsession with the baby doll. She watched as Edythe kissed the doll's forehead and then closed her eyes, pressing the baby doll tenderly to her breast. Necie's heart broke as she watched Edythe slowly open her eyes and begin to stroke the doll's hair. Every finger of Edythe's hand spoke of peace, spoke of completeness.

There are mysteries in this world I will never understand, Necie thought.

After a while, Edythe began to hum. After a moment of humming, she began to sing.

> *"Hush little baby, don't say a word*
> *Mama's gonna buy you a mockingbird*
> *And if that mockingbird don't sing,*
> *Mama's gonna buy you a diamond ring."*

In that moment, Necie saw Edythe as she had been outside the curtains she and Vivi had made from sheets during the Girl Scout campout when Edythe was ten and Joanie a year older. She remembered Edythe wearing an old bathrobe, a hairnet, and those hideous black pointy eyeglasses, like a little old lady. But she also remembered the little girl who loved nature. The little girl who knew the names of plants and butterflies when the other little girls barely even noticed.

Necie's heart grew ripe. "I'm leaving now, Edythe. I know you'll take good care of your baby."

"I'll take good care of my baby, oh yes ma'am I will," Edythe said. "I will place a crown of stars upon her head. She is my little daughter of God."

Necie sat in the parking lot of the mental hospital for a long time before she drove home. She thought of things she had done that no one knew about, not even the Ya-Yas, not as far as she could tell. She thought about how tangled the mind can get. She thought of the Blessed Virgin, who must have held her baby tenderly. Was Mary really aware of what would happen to her Savior Son? If she was, how was it that her heart did not burst from pain in that first moment the Angel Gabriel appeared to her? If we knew the suffering ahead, Necie thought, we would all jump off the Garnet River Bridge.

Necie thought of currents, deep at the bottom of the river. She thought of her husband, the Republican, the racist. Of how she loved him. Of how she forgave him for what he did not yet know. She thought of her life, of the love that she had possessed and let go of.

I am blessed, she thought. *I have seven wonderful children. I did not have to long for a baby girl. I did not have to steal one. I have stolen other things, though. Haven't we all? There are no stones to throw here. I have no stones in my hand.*

A Bountiful Garden

SAFETY

November 1994

The afternoon that little Rosalyn was kidnapped, Baylor Walker had just returned to his law offices after being in depositions all day. He was tired. Didn't even know what time it was, but it felt like time for a nap. When Carlene, his secretary, buzzed him to tell him his mother was on the phone, he hesitated before taking the call. Calls from Vivi could exhaust him. They could sometimes make him laugh, but often even the laughter exhausted him. His mother was half elixir, half poison to his system.

He took a deep breath, and took the call on the speaker phone.

"Hey, Gorgeous," he said. "What's up?"

"Bay, I need to talk fast. There is a crisis. I'm calling you because I don't want to be blamed for upsetting Melissa. Joanie's daughter, Rosalyn, was kidnapped *less than ninety minutes ago.* I wanted you to know. Where are Lee-Lee, Caitlin, and Jeff?"

Baylor picked up the receiver. "Hold on. Did you say Rosalyn has been kidnapped? Have yall been drinking?"

"No, we have *not* been drinking. It happened at Video

Schmideo. Rosalyn simply disappeared. We're terrified that some-thing awful has happened. I'm worried about the children. Do you know where Caitlin and Jeff and Lee-Lee are right now? Are they with Melissa?"

Baylor's voice dropped into its deeper range, his "lawyer" range, the one he'd cultivated in law school, the one he slipped into when-ever he was upset and trying hard not to show it.

"Mama, I'm sure the kids are safe with Melissa. Please just calm down. Rosalyn probably wandered into another store. We live in a small town here; kids don't just get kidnapped like something out of a TV movie. Take a deep breath and say your Rosary. Everything's going to be okay, you hear?"

"I've got to run," Vivi said. "The Ya-Yas and I have to be with Necie. I love you. Bye." With that, his mother hung up.

For a moment, he missed her voice, wished she had stayed on the line a bit longer. A wave of anxiety started to rise, but Baylor kept it down. He had to stay calm. Had to take care of his family. He went into the bathroom that was private to his office. Standing in front of the sink, he splashed water over his face, cold as he could stand it. *Wake up. You thought your day was winding down, but it has just begun.*

Baylor stepped back into his office and grabbed his suit coat off the antique coat stand. Within five minutes he was out the door and in his car, speeding down Jefferson Street. He dared any cop to stop him. There wasn't a ticket he couldn't have fixed. He sped down the old brick streets at fifty miles an hour, took a left onto Olive Street on two wheels, and then a right on Twenty-first before screeching to a halt in front of Our Lady of Divine Compassion parochial school, where he thought Melissa would be picking up the twins, Jeff and Caitlin, who were in fourth grade. He scanned the street for Melissa's white minivan. Jesus! Where was she? He looked at his watch. What was he thinking? It was already 4:45 P.M. His wife would have already picked up the twins and gone home. He reached for the car phone and punched in his home number.

"Walker residence, Jeff Walker speaking," the boy's voice said, like Melissa had taught the children to say. Phone manners were everything to Melissa.

"Jeff," Baylor said, relieved. "You okay?"

"Yessir. I'm doing my history homework. Daddy, did you know that a squirrel used to be able to travel on treetops all the way from Alabama to Maine back in the 1800s? That was before all the trees got—"

"Jeff, where is your sister, Caitlin? Let me speak to Caitlin."

"Uh, I don't know where she is, Daddy."

"What do you mean, you don't know where she is? Go get her. Put her on the phone."

"She and Mama are somewhere else."

"Are they home?" Baylor asked.

"I think so."

"Jeff, listen to me. Put down the phone and go find your mother and Caitlin and Lee-Lee, too. You hear me? Go find them right now. This is important. This is no time to mess around."

"Yessir," Jeff said, sounding scared.

Baylor started the car and pulled out of the parking spot. He automatically crossed himself as he sped by the church he was raised in. He thought of his guardian angel. He thought of his children's guardian angels. The concept of a guardian angel was something that he was taught before he even started school, and it was somehow easier for him to grasp than the existence of God. Each of us has an angel assigned to us alone, to take care of us throughout our whole lives. How Sidda told him in secret that she once thought she saw an angel over by the Divine Compassion cafeteria by the azalea bushes.

> *Angel of God,*
> *my guardian dear,*
> *to whom God's love commits me here,*
> *ever this day,*
> *be at my side*
> *to light and guard,*
> *to rule and guide.*
> *Amen.*

He tried his best to imagine each of his children's guardian angels. How Lee-Lee's angel looked different from Jeff's. Even though they were twins, Jeff and Caitlin had two completely different angels. Was there such a thing as twin angels? Baylor was amazed at the ocean of Catholicity that flooded his mind. Hah. Laugh. Laugh if you want, he thought. I'll take whatever help I can get.

As he drove through town, he made a bargain: God, let my children be okay, and I will do whatever you want. Turn my practice into a Legal Aid for the thousands of poor, uneducated black people in Louisiana. No, he knew he would not convert his entire law practice to that. But he vowed that if the children were kept safe, he would work on a sliding scale for any poor person, black or white, who walked into his office. He would make up the difference by working longer hours for clients who could pay well. He already did this from time to time, but he would step it up, make it an office policy. And he'd give up hard liquor. He'd been meaning to anyway. Now he would do it. Beer only from now on. Maybe a little wine. Hell, they gave you wine at Communion now. Yeah, he could still drink wine. He had not been to Mass since last Christmas; he was no devout Catholic. Yet how quickly it all came back in his hour of need.

As he crossed Alma Street, Melissa finally picked up the phone.

"Baylor!" she said. "You scared Jeff. What's wrong?"

"Are the kids with you? Everything okay?"

"Of course. Lee-Lee is singing into that toy microphone you gave her. She thinks she's Mick Jagger."

"Great. Just wanted to see what was going on. I'm on my way home right now. There's, uh, there's something I need to tell you."

"What?" Melissa asked.

"It can wait till I get home."

"Okay, fine. See you then."

"Hey, are the doors and gate locked?"

"Baylor, what is going on?"

"Nothing. Just lock the doors, that's all. Just a thought. It's only common sense, okay?"

"We're fine. Or we were fine. *You're* the one who's scaring everybody," Melissa said. "What in the world is going on?"

"Tell you when I get there. See you in a few minutes. Love you."

"You've got me nervous, Baylor. Stop acting weird."

"Hey, you knew I was weird when you married me. Baylor the Weird. You used to think it was sexy."

"I didn't think it was sexy; I thought it was weird. You tell me what all this is about."

Baylor slipped deeper into his lawyer's voice, steady and strong.

"Sweetie, Rosalyn has disappeared."

"Rosalyn? Disappeared? What do you mean?"

"We'll talk when I get home. But don't turn on the radio or TV where the kids can hear it, okay?"

Baylor could hear Melissa's breathing change.

"Look, I'm passing Pizzo's Market right now. I'll be there in less than five minutes."

"Don't drive too fast. Drive carefully, okay? We're all here."

"I love you."

"I love you. Even though you are a weirdo."

"That's what I like to hear," Baylor said.

Immediately after switching off the phone, Baylor turned on the local news station. Rosalyn Ogden Hammond, daughter of Joanie and Grove Hammond, had disappeared from a local video shop this afternoon, and law enforcement agents were organizing a search. Anyone with information should call police immediately. Baylor thought he would be sick.

When Baylor entered his home, it was silent. The kitchen was empty. The huge living room with the atrium looking out at the pool and live oaks showed no sign of life. Slowly he walked through the house, whistling. You could not totally lose it when you were whistling. At the master bedroom door, which was shut, he started whistling louder. The tune he whistled was written by one of Louisiana's ex-governors, one Jimmie Davis, the classic, "You Are My Sunshine." He tried the door handle. It was locked, so he knocked hard—*Shave-and-a-haircut! Two bits!* Melissa said, "Who is it?"

"Boo," he answered.

"Who?" she said.

"Boo-hoo, you're standing on my toe."

She opened the door. Her face was drained of color. He saw his three children, all on their parents' king-size master bed, surrounded by toys and watching a Shirley Temple video.

"Hey, kiddos," he said, "what yall doing?"

He tried to hold himself back, but couldn't. He took off his shoes, took a running jump, and landed in the bed in the midst of his three children. He began hugging all three of them, rubbing the tops of their heads, touching their cheeks, breathing in their scents. Screaming with laughter, the children hugged their father back, even though nine-year-old Caitlin echoed her mother and said, "Oh, Daddy, you are so *weird.*"

"And you," he said, "fair Mary Caitlin, twin to Jeff, are Daughter of Weirdo!" He made one of his faces, and she started laughing.

Melissa climbed up on the bed with them and ran her hands through Baylor's hair.

"Count those hairs," he said, "they will soon be a vanishing breed."

She smiled and shook her head.

"We're watching Shirley Temple," Jeff said, crossing his eyes in disgust. "It is too girly-girl for me, Daddy. The girls get to choose every time."

Baylor ruffled Jeff's hair and pulled his son to him. "Ain't that the truth?" he said.

His baby, Lee-Lee, crawled into his lap and said, "Want to see me dance like Shirley?"

He kissed her head and said, "Maybe in a little bit."

Baylor leaned over and gave Caitlin a kiss on the cheek and pulled her toward him.

"What do you think, big girl?"

Caitlin gave him a big hug. He hugged her back. All of his children were deeply affectionate. From the moment each child was born, he had made sure to shower them with as much love as was humanly possible.

"Daddy, why are you home so early?" Caitlin asked. He usually worked at the law office until late, and went in on Saturdays as well.

"I just couldn't wait a minute longer to lay eyes on yall. I threw down the law books and thought: I need to lay up in the bed and watch Shirley Temple with my three kiddos and their beautiful mother."

He kissed each of them again. Then, faking a ridiculous limp and whistling the theme song from *The Simpsons,* he turned and left the bedroom. But not before casually strolling to the French doors that opened on the pool area, pretending to look out, and making sure the door was secure.

☙

Baylor and Melissa sat at the long antique cypress table in the big kitchen. He repeated what little he knew about Rosalyn, and said he was going to make some calls.

Melissa kept nodding her head. A tear rolled down her cheek. Baylor gently wiped it off with his finger. "Hey, Hey, We're the Walkers!" he sang, to the tune of "Hey, Hey, We're the Monkees!" "Nothing can happen to us. Only kryptonite can harm Big Daddy Baylor. Remember that."

Melissa attempted a small smile. "Try to find out as much as you can."

"Let's act normal around the kids, okay?" he said gently.

"Us?" Melissa said, turning to open the refrigerator. "Act normal? No problem. Especially with Big Daddy Wacko to lead the way."

Before Baylor left the kitchen, he turned to Melissa at the same time she turned to him, and they didn't need to speak. He stepped toward her and pulled her into his arms. He did not need to tell her what he was thinking: *Do not leave the kids unwatched.*

In his study, with the door locked, Baylor called Cliff McDaniel, a detective in the Thornton Police Force, who was an old buddy. Cliff gave him the rundown, and assured him that all the stops were being pulled out. He asked Cliff to keep him posted. Then Baylor sat in his study and wondered whether it was too early to call Joanie and her husband, Grove Hammond. He'd known Joanie since he was born. She'd been closer to Sidda while they were growing up, but Baylor and Joanie had become close because Lee-Lee and Rosalyn were born two weeks apart, and the two girls were inseparable. The two couples had dinner together every month or so, and Melissa and Joanie played tennis together. Of course, they all met at Ya-Ya gatherings, which continued as the Petites Ya-Yas had their children, the Très Petites. Grove and he had been in law school together, and Baylor saw him almost daily at the courthouse. While they were not best friends, they were close, and they trusted each other.

Teensy answered the phone at the Hammond house.

"Aunt Teensy," he said. "It's Baylor. How's Joanie?"

"*Cher*, the doctor gave her a sedative and she's napping. Your Mama, Caro, and I are heading over to Necie's as soon as Chick picks us up. George and Necie are going to stay here with Grove for a few hours longer in case Joanie wakes up. Can you imagine? Chick doesn't want us driving ourselves tonight. Like someone is going to abduct the three of us."

"There's no one brave enough to tango with the Ya-Yas," Baylor said.

Teensy was only able to give him a small, tired laugh.

"How about Grove? He around?"

"He is. Hold on. I'll get him."

Grove Hammond took the call standing in his kitchen, his head aching, stomach churning. His voice was rough as he took the phone.

"Hammond?" Baylor said. "Hey, it's Walker. You okay?"

"It's hell, man."

Baylor leaned back in his leather office chair in his perfectly appointed study and closed his eyes. He straightened the legal tablet on the desk in front of him. He stared at the antique globe whose muted colors gave his study an appearance of Old World calm. *There but for the grace of God go I.*

"Tell me what's on your docket, and I'm your man," Baylor said. "My office is your office. I can work out whatever you need. Just say the word."

They discussed Grove's obligations briefly. Baylor took notes on a legal pad, sharpening his pencil in the electric pencil sharpener at least six times during the conversation.

In the middle of describing a particular insurance negotiation, Grove's voice broke. He began to sob.

"Hey, enough of this," Baylor said. "I'm sorry if I jumped the gun by talking business. Carlene will call your office in the morning. Got you taken care of. Just call if you think of anything else. Hell, call me day or night. You or Joanie. Melissa and I are with yall, buddy, you hear?"

"Thank you," Grove said, his voice still shaky. "Hey, your big sister called Joanie just before the doctor gave her the sleeping pill. They must have talked for half an hour. They have their own language."

"The Ya-Ya hotline is like quicksilver. Makes us men seem like chimps," Baylor said. "Try to get some sleep. Everything is going to be all right. I promise you. You hear me? I promise you."

After dinner, the kids put on their jammies, and then Baylor announced: "Okay, troops! This is an Official Pre-Thanksgiving at home campout! We all sleep in the big bed together. Except you, Jeff, 'cause you're too much of a man. You bring your sleeping bag in, and—"

"I've got it ready," Melissa said, standing in the doorway, having fluffed Jeff's flannel sleeping bag with the flying ducks on it. Paw-Paw Shep had given it to Jeff for going to the duck camp, which Baylor had yet to let him do.

She handed it to Jeff.

"Mmm, it's all warm. Thanks, Mom."

Jeff positioned it against the wall next to the antique armoire that held the bedroom television. Melissa knelt down and handed him his pillow and tucked him in.

"You want Henry Clay with you?" she asked him, referring to a ragged stuffed dog he'd had since childhood.

"No ma'am. That's for babies."

Baylor walked out of the bathroom and spoke while brushing his teeth.

"Henry Clay Dog is most definitely not for babies. He's a hunting dog. He protects people. Go get him. We need the whole family here at this campout."

Jeff could not hide his relief as he ran to his room, returning with a stuffed animal that had been loved hard.

Soon Baylor and Melissa were in bed, their two girls between them. They were not a family who normally prayed together. But tonight, Baylor said, "Queen of my heart, would you lead us in a little good-night prayer?"

Melissa looked at him like he was crazy.

"Let's turn off the lights first," she said. Baylor flicked off the light quickly before his children could see that he was about to cry—no, to "tear up," as his father called it.

"Dear God," Melissa said, "thank you for this day. Thank you for our family and our friends. Thank you for—" Then she could not continue. Baylor knew what she was picturing. He picked up the prayer where Melissa left off.

"And thank you for our safe sleep here at our campout. We know you will be looking out for all the other campers all over town. Amen."

"Amen," the children echoed.

Baylor lay still, then reached his hand out for Melissa, trying not to disturb the girls. Their fingers touched. This is my family, without whom I could not bear to live, he thought. In his mind he saw Rosalyn's little face and pictured putting his hands around her chubby cheeks. He thought of the way Lee-Lee and Rosalyn performed "This Little Light of Mine, I'm Gonna Let It Shine," which the Ya-Yas had taught them, and how wild the two little girls were and how much they loved each other. Sometimes they just hugged each other out of the blue, and they held hands when they walked. Baylor did not even try to sleep. He just lay there, listening to the breathing of each child until he could tell they had dropped off into sleep. Until he felt Melissa's hand fall away, until her breathing told him she had fallen back into the arms of sleep. He thought of Sidda, of how she once told him that when she got most panicked, she would picture falling back into a great big pair of loving arms that held her. "You lean back into these loving arms and they hold you up and nothing bad can happen. It works, Baylor. Try it." He hated her psychological talk, but this he remembered. And finally, in the middle of the night, when he thought he would go crazy from frustration at not being able to walk out into the night and find Rosalyn Ogden Hammond, he let himself fall back, if guardedly, into that big pair of arms.

For the next two days, Baylor worked double time. He rescheduled his own court dates to cover for Grove. He boned up on Grove's cases first thing, then started taking his status conferences, depositions, routine matters—hearings, motions, and rules. In the few free minutes he had, he called Sidda to touch base.

"Bay," she said, "I'm lighting candles. I've got Joanie's picture propped up on my ad hoc altar. It kills me that I cannot drop what I am doing and fly home and be by Joanie's side."

"Hey," Baylor replied, "your phone calls to Joanie might be even better. She gets to talk without having to try and 'hold up.' She gets to close her eyes and listen, and to feel you listening."

"You doing okay?" Sidda asked.

"I'm doing my job."

"I asked if you were doing okay, not if you were doing your job."

"I don't know if I'm 'doing okay' or not, all right? When I'm doing my job, it takes my mind off the worst. I'll tell you this, I'll never look at the side of a milk carton the same way again."

"You sleeping?"

"Yeah, I'm fine. You and Connor okay?"

"Yeah," she said, but Baylor thought his big sister's voice sounded strained. Well, whose voice wasn't strained these days?

For the next two nights, Baylor came home from work as early as he could, although never as early as he wished. Baylor, Melissa, and the kids watched old movies. Old comforting movies where children were safe, where people could count on what would happen in their world. They watched nothing made after 1944, sticking to the old classics like *National Velvet* or episodes of *The Little Rascals*.

Although they both wanted to keep the twins home from school, they didn't. They tried to keep things as normal as possible. Sister Brenda Vanderhoven, the principal of Divine Compassion, returned Baylor's call, and agreed to the police patrol. He'd owe Detective McDaniel for this favor of assigning a cop to go by the school several times a day.

They decided to keep Lee-Lee at home, at least for the first day, in case anything was said at preschool. She kicked and screamed. The worst was when she started complaining because "Me and Ra'lyn are working on a 'prokect.'"

Baylor went to visit Joanie and Grove, bringing food and feeling like a fool because their kitchen was overflowing with casseroles. A tragedy in a town like Thornton always compelled every female parishioner of Divine Compassion to cook up everything from gumbo to tuna noodle casseroles.

Joanie sat rigid with the portable phone in her hand. Her eyes were red and glazed.

"Hey, Joanie," Baylor said, sitting next to her on the sofa. Gently he put his hand over hers and said, "You got the Ya-Ya Prayer Hotline open. Operators are standing by. It's going to be fine."

He knew better than to utter Rosalyn's name. He knew it would pierce her heart.

෯

Baylor heard the news of Rosalyn's rescue on the police band radio. He'd been driving to the courthouse to take care of some of Grove's business. A blessed relief flooded his body. Baylor rushed through his business in the courthouse on the waves of euphoria, smiling at everybody, stopping to talk with friends, acquaintances, and strangers alike. He had to share his joy.

He called Melissa from the old pay phone in the lobby.

"Sweetie, it's over. They found her. Unharmed. Everything is fine."

"Thank God," Melissa said. "Thank God."

But as he left the courthouse, the wall came crashing down. The wall of keeping it together, the wall of being responsible, the wall of being strong. All rational thought left him for a moment, and then it all became clear: he needed a gun. Now that Rosalyn had been rescued, a primal masculine drive to protect his family overtook his body and mind. *I will buy a gun, and if anybody touches one hair on my children's heads, I will shoot the bastard once in the head and again in his heart. I will even the playing field. I will buy whatever I need to keep my family safe.*

He drove slowly, all the way to Security Sporting Goods. "Sporting goods" in Louisiana does not mean jogging shoes. Sport means hunting. Sport means shooting guns, rifles, firearms.

Once in the parking lot of the sporting goods store, he fully intended to bound out of the car and walk in, greet his old buddy Chuck Couvillion, who had inherited the store from his father, and simply tell him he needed a decent revolver. Not anything fancy, nothing semiautomatic. Just a revolver. Nothing with too long a barrel. Nothing as long as the barrel on his toy Buckaroo revolver.

A three-year-old girl kidnapped with her mother standing not three feet away from her. How long could Joanie's eyes have been off Rosalyn? Two minutes? Three? You can't blink anymore. Not these days. Not if you want your children to remain safe. *Shit*, Baylor thought, *Mama could drop me off in front of K-Dixie-BS-TV station by myself, let me walk into the place, appear on TV, then walk down Jefferson Street to a pay phone. She knew I'd be okay. Didn't have to think twice. That was over thirty years ago,* he told himself. *Get with it. Our children are growing up in a different world. You want to protect them, then get with the program.*

Baylor had been around guns since he could remember. How could he not? To grow up a boy in Thornton, Louisiana, *meant* hunting. It meant being exposed to shotguns and hunting rifles when you were five years old. Boys had BB guns and pellet guns, then finally at seven or eight, they were shooting a real shotgun.

Big Shep gave each of his sons a Winchester as his first gun. When each boy's twelfth birthday arrived, he proudly presented him with a Browning A-5 automatic double-barrel shotgun with his initials on the gun. The presentation took place under the huge live oak tree at Pecan Grove, and was as close to ritual as Big Shep got. He took time to introduce each boy to the gun, and how to handle it. "Guns are real personal," he'd say. "You treat them good, they'll treat you good." Big Shep himself had an L.C. Smith and a 70 Winchester. Not to mention the guns he had inherited from his own father. Baylor knew all about them because they were mentioned in his father's will, for which he was the executor. He'd told his father: "I'm no hunter. Leave all the guns to Shep. Don't do me any favors." Good guns, rare guns, were a staple item in the wills he drew up as an attorney in Thornton. In his family, only the boys hunted, but he knew some families where girls were given guns and taught to hunt—forced to hunt, in some cases. Especially if the father had wanted a son and ended up with only daughters. That was not the case in his family or in the Ya-Ya circle.

When folks talked about Opening Day in Thornton, it wasn't baseball, football, or some new shop at Southgate Shopping Center. Opening Day was the first day of deer season, dove season, duck season. Those in the know didn't need to be told which Opening Day it was. High school girlfriends had to learn to live with it. Married women used to tell young women how Opening Day was as sacred for the men as going to Sunday Mass was for the women.

Weeks before Opening Day, Big Shep would take Baylor and Little Shep to scout The Deer Land, showing them how to look for deer spore, deer tracks, flattened grasses in a thicket where deer may have slept, and tree rubbings where the bucks had rubbed their antlers and scraped bark from the tree. Sometimes they'd leave corn or a salt lick from the feed store out on The Deer Land to attract deer. But only before Opening Day. After the season was open, that was "baiting the field." There was a Code, and baiting was against it. It was illegal, but more importantly, there was no honor in it. "Only low-life trailer trash does that kind of thing," Big Shep told his sons. "Gives hunters a bad name." Same for "shining"—riding through the woods at night with a bright light in the back of the pickup, guns at the ready. On the back roads, hunters could spot deer this way and shoot while the deer's eyes were blinded by the light. Bad form. "Only redneck SOBs pull that kind of shit," Big Shep instructed them. Big Shep never hunted with baiters or shiners. He was devoted to The Code and didn't have any truck with those who broke it. He'd turn those kind of hunters in to the game warden quick as lightning.

Baylor remembered how his daddy taught him that on Opening Day, the deer are most naive and innocent. You have a better chance of killing them. That first day, they aren't as careful. They had been living their deer lives, free of bullets for months. Catch 'em while they're most innocent. Bag your big one on Opening Day. The more points on the antlers, the better the kill.

On every Opening Day, the Ya-Yas delighted in throwing parties for themselves. They had nothing to do with guns, but didn't think twice about their boys handling them. Opening Day was just another reason for them to celebrate with no men in sight. They ate, drank, smoked, played *Bourrée*, and dared their husbands to expect them to clean anything they'd shot. When the men arrived home, dirty and full of tales, the Ya-Yas listened politely for a few moments before suggesting that they bathe immediately.

Baylor had hated hunting from the very beginning. He went because it was expected of him. He didn't mind hiking and being at the camp. And when he sat around a campfire with Big Shep and Little Shep, there was a brotherhood he could feel. Men talked easier around a fire. He liked the stories. But mainly he liked sitting next to his father, watching him stoke the fire, sip his drink, throw his arm around his son, and tell about the time Manny Calvit had actually rolled around in cow manure in his fatigues so he could "get up in there amongst 'em." The belief was that this would get rid of the human scent and bring the deer closer.

Big Shep would end the story by saying: "I told him, 'Manny, I hope to hell it does bring the deer closer to you, because it sure as hell is gonna' keep anything human ten miles *away* from you!'"

Everyone would crack up when Big Shep told that story. The other men loved Shep's stories. He was a good storyteller. The other men looked up to his father. Baylor preferred the funny stories. Some of the other stories made him sick to his stomach. Stories passed down from grandfather to father to son. One was the Baptism in Blood story, where the hunter gets baptized with a bucket of deer blood from his first kill as a rite of passage. Little Shep thought that was cool. For Baylor it was yet another reason to never kill a deer.

For a Louisiana boy, not to hunt was to be an outcast like Necie's son, Frank. Frank would have nothing to do with hunting, and he was labeled "sissy" from the time he was six years old. Frank's real name was Francis, after Saint Francis, and the other boys called him "Francissy." Baylor had watched the "sissy" label color Frank's whole existence. He heard Vivi and Necie talking in the den in the afternoons, Necie upset because of the way George made fun of his own son for being afraid of guns. George had even tried to get Necie to let Joanie hunt, but Necie had refused. Vivi had told Baylor about this one afternoon as though it might be important to him someday. She had said, "Hunting is not everything, Dahlin, even though your father may think it is."

In secret Baylor had admired Frank for doing what he himself was too scared to do: go to movies on the weekend, lie around and read, dress up in costume, and make up plays with the girls.

I have never even killed a deer, Baylor thought. A deer would be the closest I could imagine to killing a human being. I've killed ducks. Didn't like it, but I did it. I've killed doves. That I really hated. Such small, delicate birds. I vomited the first time I ate dove gumbo made from doves I'd shot with my father and brother.

Deer hunting. You wake up early, like three-thirty, four in the morning. To get to the Deer Land. As a very young boy, before he could spell, he thought his daddy and brother meant the "Dear

Land," like when Buggy or Willetta called him "Dear." He thought it meant "sweet land." It wasn't until he was a little older that he began to understand that it was the land where you went to kill deer.

Pecan Grove wasn't deer land. Not the right groupings of trees. Good for dove, some quail, but not deer. The Deer Land was owned by his grandfather's friend, Mr. Andrew Maddox, and it was never referred to by any other name but the Deer Land. His grandfather had hunted there with Mr. Maddox. His daddy had grown up hunting there with his own father. There was a group of men and their sons and their son's sons who knew where it was. Outside of that group, nobody knew. You didn't want other hunters to know where your deer-hunting spot was. It was private. Privacy was part of The Code. There was a small hunting camp on the Deer Land, just a shack in the shape of an L, lined with enough bunks to sleep eight. Rough cooking setup, an outside john. Sometimes on the weekend you might spend the night because you had to be ready and in the tree stand by dawn, that magic time when the Louisiana sun shyly began spreading its pinks at first light.

That's what he loved about deer hunting. The light. That's what he would tell Sidda, but no one else. And being with his daddy, that's what he loved. That's when he could smell his father, see his father for hours at a time, receive his father's attention, all at the camp.

At the camp, with its primitive fireplace, *Playboy* magazines, and stacks of *Field and Stream,* Baylor would look at grown ladies bucknaked. He would read the ads in the back of *Field and Stream* for the mail-order scents of the hunt. You could order doe scent, fox urine, all kinds of scents that were advertised to cover up human scent in the woods. You had to cover up your scent. Deer, his daddy told him, had a stronger sense of smell than even dogs, and he knew that dogs had a sense of smell that was hundreds of times stronger than a human's.

He liked hunting because that was when his father talked to him. Big Shep might be drinking, playing poker with the other men, but Big Shep always checked on Baylor, made sure his gun was ready, made sure he brought something with him to eat early in the morning: biscuits stuffed with venison sausage made from last year's kill; a small thermos of coffee milk. And, of course, some toilet paper. Big Shep would lean over him in the bunk and touch him on the shoulder. "Son, you gonna sleep all day? We got deer just waiting for us out there. Come on, get up, time to put on your fatigues."

When he was too young to be left in a tree stand alone, Baylor pretended to miss the deer he saw. Not that he had to pretend much. The first time he tried shooting, the recoil had gotten him so bad that his shoulder was black and blue and he could hardly move it for two weeks. Vivi had complained to Big Shep about this, but finally deferred to him when he said it was all part of the game.

They'd walk silent as Indians to their different tree stands, and when Baylor was old enough to be left in a tree stand by himself, he'd climb up and will the downwind deer to smell him so they wouldn't come near. Sometimes he'd even urinate down into the brush to give the deer his scent, keep it away. The first time he saw a deer, he'd been staring at a thicket for the longest time before he realized the deer was there. The subtlest flick of the deer's tail tipped him off, and he froze. He concentrated until he could see the deer right in the eyes. He'd will the deer to know that it was safe with him. *Stay close to me, buddy, I won't kill you. This rifle is in my hand, but I don't like it any more than you.*

For the longest time, he watched this deer, a young buck. Beautiful smooth hide. He could see the animal's eyelashes. He could see his head. He could tell how smart the animal was. He didn't know how long it lasted, but he never forgot it. He prayed that the deer would elude the other hunters. He imagined a deer guardian angel and prayed the angel would help keep the animal safe. He sent thoughts to that deer: *Look out, just stay here, and nothing will happen.* Finally he heard shots fired some ways away, and the deer close to him bolted away into the trees.

If you got a deer, you'd fire a certain number of shots and shout to let the others know. Sometimes, the deer kept going after being shot and had to be tracked.

Sometimes Baylor shot at nothing. Didn't do to be up in a tree stand for hours and never fire a shot. But mostly he never told anyone back at the camp that he'd seen a deer. They would've asked too many questions about why he didn't shoot. It was easiest to say, "Didn't see nothing."

❦

A revolver. Yeah, I'll walk in there and buy myself a goddamn revolver. No getting out of it. I'll be like Daddy every Sunday night and clean my gun.

Every single Sunday evening after supper for as long as Baylor could remember, Big Shep had laid out his guns on the kitchen table and cleaned them. Baylor could still see it: the old cotton bedspread laid out underneath the rifles and shotguns. The scent of Hoppe's No. 9 gun cleaner, distinctive and pungent. Little Shep would join him. Just pieces of metal, but they touched them like they were sensuous things. He could remember his father's voice instructing Little Shep: "Just a little Hoppe's, on a little size patch. Now run it up and down the barrel until it's clean. Then a couple of dry patches to get the cleaner out, and a drop of gun oil on a patch and run it through the barrel." Baylor tried it once and got a headache. From then on out, he claimed he had homework. Baylor did his best to avoid watching his big brother and father, who seemed to be relaxed, comforted by cleaning their guns, the two of them forming this tight little unit. It was like they were caressing the damn guns. It made him sick. And jealous. Shit, Baylor thought, maybe it was a weird type of therapy. The smell of Hoppe's could still give him a headache.

Heart. You want to aim for the heart. That's the best way, a shot through the heart and lungs, just behind the deer's shoulder. Or you could aim for the neck. Yeah, that would break the spine. Problem is that the deer could run off to die. It was considered good form to wait ten or fifteen minutes so you weren't running after a dying deer but instead following him and finding him after he's dead.

Baylor remembered the first time he'd seen a deer actually shot. He was twelve. Sharing a tree stand with his father and brother. Little Shep shot a six-point buck straight through the heart.

"Hot dog!" his brother hollered, and fired off a number of shots to let the other hunters know he had bagged one. Then Baylor watched as his father helped his brother drag the once magnificent deer to the nearest road and put it into the bed of Big Shep's old hunting pickup. Little Shep sat in the back with his dead deer. Baylor sat in the cab with his father.

"One of these days, you'll get you one," Big Shep said. They hauled the dead deer back to the camp. Baylor could see the bright red blood on the tan and white hide, could see the wide-open stare of the animal. One moment the buck had been looking for berries. How long a time lapsed between the moment he smelled his killer and the moment the bullet ripped through his heart? He could feel his father's pride as his brother hung the deer from the tree. It was cold, late November.

"Gut him quick," Big Shep said. "With this cold and a quick gut, we'll have some damn fine meat."

Baylor watched as his father supervised Little Shep butchering the deer. His brother tore out the deer's entrails, oblivious to anything but the task at hand. Oblivious to anything but pleasing his father. Baylor stood silently and watched. Until a violent wave of nausea overtook him, and he vomited all over his hunting boots. Little Shep and his father never let him forget it.

His brother said, "You turnin' Francissy on us, bro'?"

Years later, after the twins were born, Baylor had quit pretending and given up hunting for gardening. He had turned his backyard into a gardener's paradise, a bird sanctuary, a place where butterflies convened. He told anyone who asked that he had joined the Church of Gardening. In fact, Baylor did indeed believe that gardening was a salvation. The year before, when most boys were given their first pellet guns, he had given his son Jeff a camera. He gave him binoculars and a book on birding. Still, in order to do "bidness" and keep up professional social ties, Baylor occasionally went on hunts. But he never carried a gun. He didn't care what they thought of him.

Baylor was awakened from his reverie by a feather landing on the windshield of his car. He did not hear it land, but something in its coloring caught his eye. He opened the car door and picked the feather up. He held it up to the November light and turned it one way and then the other, trying to decide what kind of bird it was from. He was usually able to identify feathers. But this one was foreign to him. It was a grayish feather with faint spots and a pale yellow shaft. It was soft and gently curved. A feather from the body, not the wing. He was struck with its subtle beauty. Suddenly a gust of wind picked up the feather from the palm of his hand and took it away. Baylor wanted to run after it. Find it, identify it, or at least keep it with him, a talisman. But the feather was gone.

For the first time Baylor noticed that there were Christmas lights in the display window of Security Sporting Goods. Red, white, and blue lights twinkled among boxes of bullets, small American flags, plastic basketball hoops for toddlers, and various toy guns and rifles. A full-size Santa dressed in hunting fatigues stood with his hand pointing out toward only God knew what. Baylor was struck with the obscenity of it all. He turned away and looked up as though he might still be able to spot the feather. But all he could see were changing cumulus clouds and a kind of soft, overcast light. He stood there in the parking lot, waiting for something he couldn't quite articulate.

Finally he got back in his car. He pulled the car out of the parking lot into traffic. He didn't think; he just drove.

At Our Lady of Divine Compassion Catholic Church, the Saint Joseph Altar is on the side near the stained glass window of the Archangel Michael. One fierce angel. Now Baylor sat in the front row nearest the Saint Joseph Altar and alternated between looking at the fierce angel of the Lord and the image of Saint Joseph, "the earthly father of Jesus." He simply sat and studied the different images. The man the statue depicted wore light brown robes, and he held a sleeping baby in his arms. Baylor thought of the thousands of times he had held his babies in his arms. He thought about their births. How each birth had seemed like the Holy Spirit coming. The birth of his children were the miracles in his life. He stared at the statue. At Jeff's age, he had thought of Joseph as such a wimp. Man married a woman already pregnant, hung around, then nobody heard about him doing much except leading a donkey to a stable and taking the kid to the temple. He'd always been a little embarrassed for Saint Joseph. Now he sat in the pew, with the old familiar scent of years of incense and candles and wooden pews and cracking leather on the prayer kneelers, and he began to see Saint Joseph differently. He thought he saw a fierceness in the statue's eyes. He noticed a muscularity about the arms. Hell, the man was a carpenter, probably strong as an ox. But mainly what he noticed this time was a tenderness, a tenderness that he had once mistaken for weakness. Now he noticed how Joseph held the baby to his heart, how he seemed to press him to his heart, how his head bent down as though he were just about to kiss the baby's fine head. The closer he stared at the statue, the more he saw that here was an image of a father who knew how to protect his baby, holding him close to his heart, but also out there for all the world to see. For the first time, Baylor let himself weep. Not "tear up," like his father said, but weep. Weep at the tenderness he felt in his own heart. Weep at the realization that to the extent any of us could ever protect our children, we could do it only with this kind of heart-fierceness, this kind of loving gaze, this seemingly sissified masculine gentleness.

Kiss the baby for me, Baylor prayed, *go ahead, Saint Joe, lean down and kiss his forehead. Kiss all the children. All the little ones in this crazy Louisiana town and all the ones all over the world, stepping on land mines or starving because their mothers are too malnourished to produce milk, the ones with cancer, the ones with AIDS, kiss the ones who can't walk, Joe, the ones who will never get out of a wheelchair, kiss us all, man. We need it. We need your prayers. We can't do it alone.*

He did not think about his sobbing. He simply let it come. He dropped his head and gave up. *Ain't no gun made can do what love can. How did I go so long without knowing this?*

On the way home, the slogan came to him: "Guns don't save people. *Parties* do!" That's when he decided that he would host the Ya-Ya Tribe Christmas gathering this year. He remembered Vivi leading them in singing "We Need a Little Christmas!" from *Auntie Mame* when he was little. *Boy, that's never been more true.* Then he dialed Melissa on the car phone.

"Hey, you fine-looking mama," he said when she picked up.

"God, I'm relieved, Bay. I feel like I can finally exhale," she said.

"God is good. How about pizza?"

"We're starving."

"Call it in, and I'll pick it up on the way home. Thick crust for me, Baby. Thick with lots of cheese just oozing."

"Got it," Melissa said. "Love you, Crazy."

"Love you, Melissa the Magnificent. Give the kids hugs for me. See you pronto wickie-wickie!"

Baylor clicked off and dialed Sidda. "They found her unharmed."

Sidda let out a huge sigh. "Thank you, thank you, thank you, God."

"Thank you, Saint Joseph, too," Baylor said.

"Thank you, all angels and saints," Sidda responded.

"We sound like Catholic nuts."

"We *are* Catholic nuts," Sidda said. "I wish I were there."

"Me, too. Come home for Christmas. I'm gonna host the party."

"I am up to my ears with this show. There is no way I can leave. It's not healthy to be this busy."

"Are you okay?"

"Who knows if I'm okay?" she replied. "I stay so busy I don't think about it. I'll think about it next year."

"Okay, Scarlett. Love you. Hugs to Connor. Bye."

Baylor waited before calling Grove. He didn't want to rush them. He could only imagine the kind of nesting Joanie and Grove would need with Rosalyn. Finally, the first week of December, he called.

"Hey, it's Baylor."

"Hey," Grove said. "I haven't had a minute to call and thank you. How you doing?"

"No, how *you* doing?"

"We're all right. I'm going into the office half-days. Necie is with Joanie all the time. Joanie won't let Rosalyn out of her sight. Well, actually, she won't hardly let her out of her arms."

"I can imagine."

"Maybe not. It's a little scary. Joanie is petrified. By the way, thanks for giving my secretary all the info about your home security system. We're in the process of building Fort Knox, Louisiana, at the house."

"I put all that shit in my house when I built it. Paranoid since birth, you know me."

"Really, man, thank you for everything."

"Would there be a good time for me to drop by? I have an invitation for yall."

"Sure. Let me talk to Joanie and call you back. She's—uh—a little delicate. And I have to warn you, it doesn't look like we'll be accepting invitations if they mean stepping outside the house. Joanie has pulled up the drawbridge."

"She okay?"

"She's not having a nervous breakdown or anything. She's just—well, overly cautious. Has to know who is coming and going all the time. Hears things outside at night. That kind of thing."

"I gotcha. Just let me know when I can visit."

Joanie agreed to see Baylor a few days later. When he walked into their house, which was in the Garden District of Thornton, on the bayou that ran through town, Joanie was sitting on the sofa with Rosalyn in her lap. She did not get up to greet him.

Rosalyn said, "Unca' Bay!" and started to climb down from her mother's lap. Joanie stopped her.

Baylor sat across from them in a wing chair.

"I got something for you from Lee-Lee," he said to Rosalyn.

"Miss Lee-Lee! Miss Lee-Lee!"

The two girls had spoken on the phone, but had not seen each other since the day before the kidnapping. A long time for the two Très Petites Ya-Yas.

Baylor started to hand Rosalyn a wrapped gift, but Joanie reached out and took it first. "Mama will open it for you," Joanie said.

Oh, shit, Baylor thought.

Turning away from her daughter, Joanie opened the package and pulled out a little red felt hat with reindeer antlers.

"Mine!" Rosalyn said, grabbing it from her mother and putting it on her head. Then she jumped out of her mother's lap and began to do a little dance like Baylor had seen her and Lee-Lee do a million times. The little girls were born prisses.

"Mirror!" Rosalyn said, and took off in the direction of the downstairs guest bathroom. Joanie ran after her.

"I told you to stay by my side, Rosalyn!" Joanie called out.

Grove gave Baylor a look that was worth a thousand words.

"It'll pass," Baylor said.

"Yeah," Grove said. He was quiet for a moment, then offered Baylor a drink.

"Sure," Baylor said.

"The regular?" Grove said, referring to Baylor's usual bourbon and water.

"Uh, no—no thanks. Yall got any beer?"

"Yep. Heineken okay?"

"Fine," Baylor said.

When Joanie and Rosalyn were back in the room, Baylor laid it out.

"I'm hosting the Ya-Ya tribe Christmas party this year, and I want yall to come."

There was silence except for the sound of Rosalyn gibbering to her Barbie doll.

"We're going to stay close to the house for the holidays," Joanie said finally.

Grove lowered his head.

Baylor opened his briefcase. He was prepared for this.

"Look, I know yall are putting in a security system similar to mine, and I just thought I'd show you how my house is protected."

Joanie leaned forward.

Baylor spread a plan of his house and grounds on the large coffee table as Joanie moved books and magazines out of the way. Painstakingly, he pointed out how the electronic gate worked.

"I got the ten-foot one, solid, with grill work and points at the top. It's the most secure."

Then he showed Joanie where each door and window in his house was and how it was protected. He was especially careful to show her where the panic buttons were, and to explain how the motion sensor lights and alarm for outside worked.

She seemed to relax. "That's just the kind of thing we've been putting in. But the damn electronic gate is taking forever."

"Please come?" Baylor asked.

Grove looked at Joanie. Joanie looked at Rosalyn, who looked up.

"Me call Lee-Lee now to say thank you, okay?"

"It'll be a drag without yall. Mama will be disappointed. She and your Mama and Teensy and Caro have gotten this idea in their heads that they are staging a Christmas pageant. Caitlin has been p.o.'ed because the nuns at Divine Compassion haven't cast her as Mary yet. So Mama said, 'How dare them not cast Caitlin? We'll have our *own* g.d. pageant!' I think your Mama is doing the costumes."

"Okay," Joanie said, and dialed Baylor's number, handing the phone to her daughter.

The grown-ups were silent for a moment as they heard Rosalyn singing on the phone. To the tune of "Jingle Bells," she sang:

"Jink Hotel
Jink Hotel
Jink Hotel, OK!"

"Were you that bad as a three-year-old?" Grove asked Joanie.

"I was that *good*," she replied. "And I sang my duets with Sidda."

"So," Baylor said, taking a sip of beer. "Yall will come, right?"

Joanie hugged herself. She leaned closer in to Baylor.

"I don't think so, Bay. I can't. I can't leave the house. I have to keep my eyes open every moment. I need her in my sight. If I blink, she could disappear. I can't handle leaving the house and keeping my eyes on her all the time. It's just too much."

"Joanie," Baylor said softly. "You will have four Ya-Yas, three Ya-Ya husbands, an ex-Ya-Ya husband and his lover, all your sisters, your brother if he can make it from Atlanta, Shep, me, Melissa, the rest of the Petites Ya-Yas, and eighteen other Très Petites with their eyes on Rosalyn. Believe me, there is no place safer. Nobody in that room will let anything happen to her. You know us all. The house will be locked. Hell, I won't let Santa come down the chimney. It'll just be us. We'll be safe. I promise, Joanie. I promise."

Joanie started to cry while Baylor was still talking. Grove sat next to her and took her hand.

"I think it's safe," he said. "You'll be wrapped up in the Ya-Ya cocoon."

"It's just—," Joanie said, wiping tears back, "it's just that I messed up once. How do I know it won't happen again? I looked away, and she was gone."

"Joanie," Baylor said gently. "Trust us. Rosalyn will be secure, and if you blink, there will be so many eyes on that little girl that nothing could happen. I don't think I can handle what Lee-Lee would do if Rosalyn didn't come. The kid thinks she's Mick Jagger.

She thinks she's Supergirl. She'll destroy everything I've worked for if 'Ra'lyn' isn't at her Christmas party."

Joanie was silent for a moment. Then she nodded. "Okay. Okay, we'll give it a try."

Rosalyn let out a peal of laughter at something Lee-Lee had said on the phone, and she began talking so fast and intensely that the three adults were certain she was speaking another language entirely. They listened, fascinated.

"Hey, Joanie," Baylor said, "you think our mothers sounded like that when they were little?"

"Probably," she replied. "I bet Sidda and I did too."

Baylor got up and touched Joanie lightly on the shoulder. "May the sisterhood be unbroken, by and by, Lord, by and by."

A STAR'S A SEED A SEED'S A STAR

December 1994

O n Saturday, December 17, three minivans full of Ya-Yas and
their offspring's offspring pulled up to Baylor's house, blowing their horns to beat the band. Baylor thought he had been ready
to host this party, but at the sight of them he realized he might have
overstepped himself.

"Merry Christmas!" Melissa said as she came out on the porch.
She was dressed smartly and warmly in a pair of navy wool slacks, a
white silk shirt, and a red blazer that set off her dark hair and beautiful complexion.

As Vivi stepped out of the van, Baylor could see that she was wearing a black wig and heavy black eye makeup. She kept her coat pulled
close around her as though she were hiding something. Her eyeglasses
were missing. In fact, his mother now had different-colored eyes.

"Help your mother!" Caro rasped loudly from the third van. "She
can't see a damn thing through those violet-colored contact lenses she
bought so she'd look more like La Liz."

Baylor hurried to take his mother's arm.

"I'm ever so slightly thrown off by the lack of my trifocals. The violet only came in bifocals, so I was forced to cut out my dance number. Lord, it's cold out."

"Mother," Baylor asked, "what in the world are you dressed like that for?"

"What are you talking about? I'm a Wise Woman, dummy. I am Visiting Royalty, a queen from afar traveling to bow before the Baby Jesus. The Baby Jesus loves visitors. By the way, *adore* your red vest. Very English country gentleman."

"Shoulda known you couldn't resist a chance to go full-tilt boogie," Baylor said.

Another pack of kids spilled out of the next van. Then Teensy stepped down, another Wise Woman, more Visiting Royalty. Just how Teensy had managed to attach the long blond wig, which was done up in a ponytail, was testament to her creativity and determination. They had gone all-out.

Baylor went over to help Caro out of the third van. Her oxygen tubes and tank were hooked up as always, but she looked bulky in a long camel coat, which bulged out as though she wore a huge garment underneath. Baylor didn't want to ask. It was cold—cold for Thornton. The morning had started off sunny and frigid, with cornflower-blue skies. A high, even cloud cover had formed over the afternoon, and the light had become pale and washed out. The temperature stood at thirty-three degrees, with a forecast of it dropping even lower.

A wild assortment of eighteen children bundled up in coats, scarves, hats, and gloves continued to scramble out of the vans, the littlest ones being helped by the older ones, and all of them helped by Necie's son. Frank, who was recently divorced, now asked to be called by his given name, Francis. He'd flown home from Atlanta the week before to be with Joanie and to help Necie sew costumes and organize the pageant. Under his gray wool Armani coat, he was dressed swell-elegantly as the Little Drummer Boy, complete with tights and bloomers.

"Brrrr Rabbit, Bay! I'm freezing my balls off out here."

"Well, get in the house and warm up—and make it quick before the neighbors see you. I'm a *professional* in this town, you know."

"A professional *what*, though, that's what inquiring minds are asking."

"Merry Christmas, Frank—I mean Francis—I've been thinking about you. Is that getup what folks are wearing in Atlanta these days?"

"Certain ones of us are thusly attired when it's time to deck the halls."

Baylor was one of the few who had not been surprised in the least when Francis and his wife of two years divorced. He'd known Francis all his life and was happy to see him let his true self out. He wasn't all the way out of the closet, but Baylor figured it would happen any day.

"Come on," Francis said, "I've got to help the Divas and their grandchildren inside and 'backstage.' You did set up a full dressing area for us all, didn't you, babe?"

"The bedroom, bathroom, and hallways of my home are at your disposal. As long as no blood is shed, do anything you want."

"I just want to get the kids back there before they ruin their costumes. Fingers crossed that Joanie will show up. Any sight of her and her Grove and her Rose?"

"Not yet."

"Well, we're all praying."

As Baylor swung open the front door, he cleared his throat and loudly announced in his most magisterial, faux British accent, "Children, ladies, scoundrels, please welcome His Royal Highness, the magnificent, splendiferous Count Viscount with no discount, Uncle Francis, Royalty from the East, and a cast of thousands!"

Everyone (except George, who took one look at his son and then turned the other way) smiled and applauded and yelled, "Here, here!"

Baylor realized now why Big Shep had come over even earlier than usual to put a pork loin on the BBQ pit. "I thought I'd give the pageanteers a little more room out at the house to get the show together," Big Shep had said. What he hadn't said spoke volumes.

The Ya-Yas had been at Pecan Grove, trying to have a run-through of the pageant. They'd managed to hold approximately one rehearsal, if you counted the break for the variety acts that several of the children and three of the Ya-Yas tried to insert into the pageant over Necie's attempt to "keep this thing something sweet and holy."

Once the crowd arrived, Big Shep came inside and took off his barn jacket (with the liner zipped in) to reveal a new red flannel bathrobe over a pair of green pants out of which one could see his best dress-up cowboy boots. "Meet Shep the Shepherd. I've been waiting fifty goddamn years to wear my bathrobe to one of these Ya-Ya shindigs. I figure now was my chance."

Inside the house, a fire was roaring in the fireplace, and Christmas lights and pine boughs greeted the Ya-Ya tribe. The pageant scene had been set up earlier in one corner of the big living room with the high ceilings and tasteful but comfortable furniture. Shep and Baylor had built the set, a small ramshackle lean-to stable, out of wood they'd found down by the old oak tree at Pecan Grove. They'd also built a small manger, and spread hay around everywhere. Melissa had insisted that plastic be laid underneath everything, and they'd done a good job hiding the plastic, but the two brothers had agreed that women could get in the way of verisimilitude. Melissa also insisted that the hay be *clean* hay, which cracked Big Shep up.

"*All* my hay is clean hay. You don't find Shep Walker dealing in any dirty hay. Against The Code."

The dishes cooked by the Ya-Yas had been delivered the day before, and were warming in Melissa's sparkling kitchen. Teensy's "Down on the Bayou Gumbo," chicken and shrimp to be served with rice and lots of homemade filé. Vivi's "Tipsy Sweet Potato Fluff," with lots of marsh-mallows—and laced with bourbon. Caro's ex-husband's boyfriend, Richard, had cooked for her, and the scent of his jambalaya, made with chicken, sausage, and lots of spices, could be smelled from the back burner where it was simmering, to be served later from the buffet table in the dining room from a big crockery bowl he and Blaine had bought in Provence. Necie had to be talked out of cooking because she was handling the pageant. Her daughters Melanie, Rose, Lissa, and Annie more than made up with their own more contemporary cooking.

The sudden rush of energy and noise that flooded the house as all the kids and parents came in made Baylor feel happier and more relaxed than he had been in a long time. This much chaos in his orderly house would normally have put him on edge. But it was all a blessing, and he knew it. Silently he gave thanks.

Chick had also arrived early to set up the bar. He was dressed as an elf, complete with shoes that curled up at the toes. Chick's eggnog (one jigger of bourbon for each egg, then one jigger for the bowl) was necessary to start off any Ya-Ya Christmas gathering. He had plenty of champagne, wine, Cokes, and hot cider with cinnamon and nutmeg for the kids simmering on the burner he'd plugged in at the bar he prided himself on. He'd already doled out plenty of old-fashioneds and whiskey sour punch, and was stocked for the party to last for days. No bar of Chick's ever went dry. To accommodate the Petites Ya-Yas, especially the women, he also had plenty of Perrier and a huge thermos of Dark Roast Community Coffee at the ready.

"Joyeux Noël, Petits Monstres!" he called out. "What little angels want a Shirley Temple? What little shepherds are ready to slug back a Rob Roy?"

Mothers were trying to keep the Très Petites from running around the house. Squeals and shouts and laughter rose and fell over the comforting din of greetings and conversation. The adults who weren't part of the pageant entourage helped with putting out the hors d'oeuvre trays and putting tablecloths over the card tables that had been set up for the children to eat at.

Big Shep came out of the kitchen and put his arm around Baylor's shoulder, taking in the scene. After a bit he patted his son on the back and said to no one in particular, "Life's pretty good."

Francis and Necie corralled the children to the "backstage" area, while Vivi accepted a bottle of Moët from Chick. Teensy waved to the others. They, the stars, hurriedly absented themselves from the room. Blaine and Richard planted kisses on either side of Caro's cheeks, handed her a vodka tonic, and soon she was on her way backstage as well.

Chick and Little Shep's wife, Kane, bustled backstage carrying Cokes and other drinks back to the little ones, along with trays of cashews and cheese and crackers.

"You are amazing, Chick," Kane said. "To have thought of spill-free cups!"

"Well, we don't want our little angels to spill their Shirley Temples down the front of their gowns, do we? It's great to see you and Shep all duded up! And Dorey and Kurt—who knows what's under those coats and hats."

"It's great to see Jacques," Kane said.

"I'm just thankful my son and his family could make it."

"When did they get in from Italy?" Kane asked.

"Ten-thirty last night. And we are pleased as punch. I hardly slept a wink. Did you see those children?"

"Yessir, I did. Eyelashes as long as little Jack's should only be given to girls. Totally lost on a four-year-old boy."

"Who said life was fair?" Chick replied. "And how about Genevieve? Is she not the most gorgeous two-year-old in the world?"

"Chick, I think you're smitten."

"I'm *smote*." Chick winked. "Totally *smote*."

Back in the living room, the room was filled with the smell of sausage, smoked by Big Shep, Shep, and Baylor. They'd brought it in early, cut into slices, and it was served with mustard for dipping. Parched pecans, straight from the oven, smelled delicious with all the garlic, salt, butter, and other seasonings they were dressed with. "Angels on horseback"—oysters wrapped in bacon, breaded, then deep-fried—were on everyone's appetizer plates, and bowls of oyster crackers with dill weed for seasoning were spread about on every table, along with plenty of cheese straws.

The decree had gone out from the Ya-Yas that everyone was to dress like a Christmas character. Some had gone all-out; others had just added touches. Shep wore a hat with reindeer antlers. Necie's daughters all wore hand-knit wool Christmas sweaters with original designs. Each of them except Lissa had learned to knit from their Gramma Rose or Necie, their mother, but they rarely got to wear their woolens in the semitropical Louisiana weather.

Their husbands all wore some Christmasy touch—a pair of Santa slippers, a sprig of mistletoe pinned to a sweater, and the like.

Blaine and Richard had taken the Ya-Ya decree most seriously. They were dressed as toy soldiers from *The Nutcracker Suite*.

"Man," Big Shep said. "You boys went to town. Those boots alone must have cost a fortune."

"To tell you the truth, we already had the costumes from a party two New Year's Eves ago. And we do love boots."

"Just like you, Shep," Richard said.

"Yep, but mine are shit-kickers next to those," Shep said.

"We're all shit-kickers at heart," Blaine said, and raised his glass. "To shit-kickers!" he said. And the three of them raised their glasses.

Baylor caught this scene from the corner of his eye and marveled at how easily his father had accepted Caro's longtime husband's homosexuality. He remembered how Big Shep, upon hearing, had said, "Well, finally Blaine has come out and admitted he liked the boys. I'd known that since we were in our twenties. Doesn't bother me as long as they don't ask me to put on a skirt. That is where I draw the line."

Only George looked out of place at this party. He wore a tailor-made suit more in place in a court of law than at a family gathering, not to mention a Ya-Ya tribal get-together. His only concession to the season was to carry a Wise Man crown in his hand. Baylor eyed George closely when he came in. There was something off about his carriage, something more than just his suit's formality. The man moved differently than the other men, like he was carrying some kind of powerful secret that gave him added confidence, almost a smugness. At the same time, it was if he were hiding something.

Necie's daughters and their husbands mingled with Caro's sons, Turner, Gavin, and Bernard, and their wives. Rumors about the pageant were shared.

"I heard from Mama that Caitlin is quite the little director," Rose said. "Mama said she was giving directions the whole time they tried to pull this thing together. Think she might take after her Aunt Sidda?"

"I don't know which of my daughters takes after their Aunt Sidda more—Caitlin or Lee-Lee," Melissa said, sipping her chardonnay. "Caitlin has the imagination and bossiness—not that Sidda is bossy, but you know what I mean. And Lee-Lee has the flair for drama. Lord knows what they will come up with. I know Necie has had her hands full. My hat's off to her for taking on this pageant."

Turner said, "I cannot imagine Necie pulling all those costumes together. I guess having daughters who know how to sew helps."

"Hah!" Rose said. "Mama said to Vivi just yesterday, in my presence—and I quote—'Francis is a better seamstress than my five girls put together.'"

They all laughed, glad to have Francis in town.

Jacques (or Ruffin, as he was called growing up) and his wife

Sophia were the center of much attention. Jacques was an artist, currently doing a series on the ancient water features in small Tuscan towns and villages. He'd met his wife at the Rhode Island School of Design, and as sophisticated as they both looked and lived, they were easy to get along with, and funny to boot.

"I want to thank you again," Jacques said to Melanie, "for making costumes for the bambinos."

"You'd think," Sophia said, "that I'd be together enough to have brought some exotic Italian clothing for my offspring, but to be perfectly honest, it was all I could do to pack their underwear. International travel with a two-year-old was not something I learned about in art school." With that, she took a deep sip of her red wine, then laughed. "We're lucky *any* of us have underwear."

While the mood was festive and the music good—Baylor had made a special compilation CD of Frank Sinatra singing Christmas carols, mixed in with Motown and holiday jazz renditions—every person there was acutely aware of the clock ticking. The later it got, the more everyone glanced down at their watches, hoping. On their minds was the key question: Would Joanie, Grove, and Rosalyn show up? The Ya-Yas had insisted that the pageant not begin until everyone was there, and already Francis had come out twice, saying, "The tribes are getting restless. Is my sister Joanie here yet?" Each time he'd been told no, and had returned "backstage" to assist with the chaos.

Just as Baylor was thinking about calling Grove, he heard the buzz of the front-gate intercom. They had arrived! He buzzed them in, opening the garage doors so they could drive straight in, as Baylor had promised Joanie. He went to the garage to greet them, making sure the garage doors were shut immediately. He'd promised security for Joanie and her little one, and he would be damned if he didn't deliver.

When Joanie, Grove, and Rosalyn stepped into the room, they were hugged and kissed and made fuss over. Rosalyn wore a green velvet dress with handmade Irish lace around the collar. In her hair was a red bow, and her little legs were clad in warm white leotards and red leather Mary Janes. She kept asking, "Where Lee-Lee? Where Lee-Lee?"

Baylor ran to the back of the house to inform Francis that his sister had indeed arrived.

"Let the show begin!" Francis said. "Got your intro ready?"

"Do I look like a dullard?"

"No, you look terribly handsome in a sort of George Clooney-ish way," Francis said, turning back to the rest of the gang to alert them.

Baylor stood in front of the crèche, with everyone gathered in front of him. Some sat on the sofas, some on dining room chairs, some on stools from the kitchen. Right smack in the front sat Grove and Joanie, who held on to Rosalyn like a precious jewel.

"Ladies and gentlemen, *mesdames et messieurs,* and our special guest of honor, Mademoiselle Rosalyn, I am happy to welcome you to my home and most importantly to the First Annual Ya-Ya Christmas Pageant—and variety show!" With that, he stepped aside and leaned against a side table next to where Melissa sat.

A hush descended over the room as Necie slowly emerged from the door that led back to the bedrooms. She wore the costume of a Bethlehem village woman. The only exception was the tiara that the other Ya-Yas had forced her to wear: they refused to let her be a Plain Jane townswoman. "You *must* acknowledge your royalty somehow!" Vivi had insisted. Her robes flowing, she crossed to a tall brass antique church candleholder that Melissa had found at her favorite shop in New Orleans. She lit the candle that stood atop the holder and then crossed over to the baby grand that Baylor's kids practiced piano lessons on.

Softly and reverently, Necie played an intro to "O Little Town of Bethlehem." Then she began to read the ancient words from Luke: "And it came to pass in those days . . ."

The sound of singing from the back of the house could be heard, a pure if raggedy chorus of children's voices singing "O Little Town of Bethlehem," helped along by the voices of Francis and the Ya-Yas.

Nine angels ranging in age from two to seven stumbled in, all wearing homemade wings strapped onto their backs with elastic. There were six angel girls and three boy angels. Two of the kids' wings were already bent up so bad, it looked like they'd been flying hard and put up wet. Circles of gold garland made the haloes for their heads. They all wore gowns made of white sheets, tied around the waist with gold swags.

With one exception.

Lee-Lee Walker had insisted at the last moment on wearing her ballerina costume. She put up such a fit that Francis finally stepped in and said, "Fine, tiny dancer. Go for it." He tried not to laugh, but was not successful when Lee-Lee also demanded to carry a small red purse, which dangled daintily from her wrist. She put on white gloves at the very last minute, and seemed to have trouble not staring at the sheer beauty of them.

Rosalyn, who had been sitting quietly in her mother's lap, squealed when she saw her best friend. "Lee-Lee!" she said aloud, and waved. Joanie whispered into her daughter's ear, and she quieted down, but she was thrilled to lay her eyes on Lee-Lee, the ballerina angel.

Turner's five-year-old, John Blaine, had agreed to be an angel on the condition that he be allowed to wear his bicycle helmet. Each Ya-Ya had tried to reason with him, but as Caro sagely observed: "Kid's smart. With this pageant gang he's running with, he's a helluva lot safer wearing protective gear."

When the singing began to lag or the angels forgot the words, their moms mouthed them for them or sang along from the audience to try to keep them in tune.

Next came the animals. A sheep led the parade. Crawling expertly on all fours, Virginia, Rose's daughter, wore a huge fluffy white bath towel around her neck. Necie had put her foot down when it came to having any animals that required two kids under one costume. "That is a recipe for disaster if I ever heard one," she declaimed. "Trust me."

One of Lissa's girls was a brown cow with white spots (compliments of Clorox spilled on the wrong load of towels), and she had been adamant about wearing her pink cowgirl hat. "So they'll know I'm a cow," as she had explained to Necie.

Everyone did their best not to laugh out loud, which meant lots of strange coughing and snorting noises from the adults in the audience.

There was a pause before the audience saw Mary and Joseph. But that did not mean they could not hear Caitlin berating Daniel, Turner's nine-year-old. "Walk right!" Caitlin was saying in the loudest stage whisper east of the Mississippi: "I thought I told you how to walk! You're a carpenter, from Nazareth. Act like it, stupid! You want them to think you're from Arkansas or something?"

The audience attempted to ignore this, but several of them gazed in Chick's direction, pointing to their glasses for a refill. Stealthily, he made his way to the bar.

When they finally made their entrance, Caitlin had erased all harshness and looked perfectly sweet and holy. In blue and white gowns compliments of Melissa's linen closet, Caitlin carried the Christ child, a doll, in her arms. She held the doll with utmost care and from time to time gazed down at the doll like it really was the Baby Jesus. Everything about Caitlin was perfectly holy, except for the "Riveting Red" carefully applied to her lips—and the heavy black mascara coating her eyelashes.

Next came the shepherds, each of them wearing different variations of bathrobes with ropes around their waists. Their heads were covered with long scarves anchored by yet other scarves, which were rolled up and tied. Jeff looked like a midget Arafat with a penchant for Hermes accessorizing. Just as Necie switched the music to "Away in a Manger," Jeff looked out into the audience and gave a big smile, revealing vampire fangs.

Baylor cracked up, slapping his thigh and ignoring the fact that Melissa was mouthing "NO" to their son.

George muttered, "Jesus, Mary, and Joseph, pray for us."

With the help of the audience, the children were now attempting to sing "Away in a Manger." Necie mouthed the words exaggeratedly as she sang along with them.

Then came Alise, the angel of the Lord, Bernard's five-year-old daughter. She was carrying a stick with a tinfoil star atop it. The only one with lines in the pageant, she played it to the hilt. She came skipping in, stopped, looked straight out into the audience, and yelled: "Unto yall a child is born!"

At this point, George accepted a drink from Chick, shaking his head the whole time.

"Just be thankful Louisiana is a far piece from the Vatican," Chick whispered.

"Amen," George said, and took a small sip.

Shifting into the intro for "Hark, the Herald Angels Sing," Necie could be seen to heave a sigh as the children began (at Jeff's insistence) to whistle, rather than sing, the carol. Jeff took out his fangs and began to whistle loudly. Of course half the kids couldn't really whistle, so there were a lot of air-blowing sounds. Big Shep, Shep, and Baylor—all expert whistlers—helped out, along with Chick and Bernard. And there could be heard from the doorway to the backstage area some pretty fancy whistling from Francis, who was working hard to keep this pageant afloat. Kane was the only mother in the audience who could whistle worth a damn, and so she did.

Stumbling over each other, the Three Wise Men entered, mischief in their eyes. Kurt and his two pals, Turner and Jack, wore brightly colored recut caftans that the Ya-Yas had last donned in the 1960s, and crowns made of glittered-up Quaker Oats boxes cut jagged at the top and covered with leftover caftan fabric. They presented one wild trio. The one distinct Louisiana touch was the duck calls they all wore on strings around their necks.

Bearing gifts for the Baby Jesus, they were followed by Vivi, Teensy, and Caro, each of whom wore tiaras. And more.

As head Queen of the Three Wise Women, Vivi had modeled herself entirely on Liz Taylor in *Cleopatra*. Complete with low-cut white gown, black wig, tons of black eyeliner, arms loaded with jewelry, and of course, wearing the violet contact lenses, Vivi had outdone herself. She had to hold hands with Teensy because without her trifocal eyeglasses, she was having a little trouble finding her way around. And she was clearly irritated. She'd be damned if people thought she'd been drinking too much. She'd only had one mimosa during the so-called run-through, and two tiny glasses of champagne.

It took folks a moment to realize that it was indeed Teensy with whom Vivi was holding hands. Topped with a long blond wig done up in a high ponytail, Teensy's tiny form was clad in a sequined bra and a pair of harem pants, with bells attached to her ankles.

"I should have known," George muttered. *"I should have known."*

"Mother!" Jacques howled and then clasped his hands over his mouth while his whole body shook with laughter.

Blaine and Richard let out wolf whistles, to which Teensy responded with a little shimmy.

"She always did love *I Dream of Jeannie*," Chick whispered loudly. "Isn't she something else?"

Caro, wearing a peacocklike blue and green bejeweled robe with a high collar, brought up the rear.

"Beyond regal!" Richard whispered, then gave himself a fake slap in the face when George shot him a look that could kill.

"And they marveled all," Blaine whispered, and winked at George.

The Three Wise Women took their places on chairs strategically placed to the side of the manger near the piano.

Before Vivi had had a chance to straighten her wig, the Three Wise Men began. They had been warned and warned and warned. It was the last warning that made them do it. The three boys broke into song:

> *"We three Kings of Oriadore*
> *Tried to smoke a rubber cigar*
> *It was loaded, it exploded . . ."*

Necie cleared her throat loudly and hit a particularly scary chord on the Steinway at the same time that Vivi said in a frightfully loud stage whisper: "Cut that out, or I'll demote yall from Wise Men to cows in a split second!" The boys switched to the original verses. By this time, Shep had called out, "Way to go, boys!" Baylor had taken out his starched white handkerchief and was laughing into it.

After they finished singing one verse, the Wise Men (or "wise asses," as Shep later proudly called them) laid their offerings down in front of the manger and went to stand as far away from the Ya-Yas as they could. Caro had a cane, and she'd threatened to poke them with it.

Francis, who had been keeping things organized backstage, had slipped into the audience to watch as unobtrusively as a six-foot-tall drummer boy can.

Softly playing "Silent Night" to accompany herself, Necie ended the official pageant.

"But Mary kept all these things, and pondered them in her heart. And the shepherds returned, glorifying and praising God for all the things that they had heard and seen, as it was told unto them."

When the song was finished, everyone started clapping and cheering. The three wise Ya-Yas all stood and performed deep, elaborate curtsies that would have been envied by Sarah Bernhardt. Necie gestured to the children, who all bowed, then ran offstage, tripping over their costumes and each other. Necie gave a brief nod of acknowledgment to the audience, then began to play "God Rest Ye, Merry Gentlemen" as all the angels, animals, shepherds, Mary and Joseph, and the Angel of the Lord came running back into the massive living room for a rehearsed curtain call. Jeff's fangs were back in, and prominently displayed with his big smile. John Blaine's bike helmet was askew, as were most of the angels' halos and the Wise Men's Quaker Oats crowns. Only Lee-Lee was in total command of her exit. At the door to the back of the house, she stopped and did a full pirouette.

Rosalyn could restrain herself no longer. She wiggled out of Joanie's arms and ran to Lee-Lee's side. "Me too!" she said. "Me too!" Lee-Lee took off her halo and put it on Rosalyn, and Rosalyn copied Lee-Lee's pirouette. Then she ran backstage with the rest of the children.

It all happened so fast that Joanie's arms forgot to ache. Joanie forgot to be afraid of blinking, lest something happen to her daughter. Baylor had been right: all eyes were on Rosalyn, and she was safe. Tears came to Joanie's eyes. And as if he could hear the tears, her father raised his head and witnessed the moment.

Yea, George thought, *a sword shall pierce through thy own soul also.* Then came other words to his mind: *To give light to them that sit in darkness.* He looked at his daughter until she felt his eyes on her, and she turned to look at him. The look that passed from father to daughter was so tender that the rest of the group could feel it. Then, before you could indeed blink, the cast of thousands was back on the stage. Necie stopped playing and joined hands with the other Ya-Yas, who joined hands with the children, who all joined hands with each other. Lee-Lee, and thus Rosalyn, managed to be front and center, and Joanie threw kisses like flowers at her daughter's feet.

All the little holy families, Baylor thought.

The children could not get enough of the clapping, but Francis was already leading them backstage, acutely aware that too much of a good thing can spoil a show. The Ya-Yas exited as well, this time Vivi holding on to Necie's arm. "Damnit," she muttered. "I'm jerking these contact lenses out! I don't know how Liz does it."

He should have known better, but he did it anyway. "Encore!" Baylor shouted, and the call was taken up by Shep and Big Shep.

To no one's surprise, Francis bounded back into the living room, doing a *grand jeté* in the process. Pulling it off was quite a feat—especially considering that he was wearing a toy drum around his neck. He hadn't rehearsed such a move since his sisters went to ballet class years ago, not that he hadn't wanted to.

"Thank you. Thank you. Thank you very much. We are delighted that you enjoyed our little trifle. As a matter of fact, we do have a couple of encore numbers lined up for your viewing pleasure. Please allow me to introduce"—and with this, he extended his arm dramatically in the direction of the door and began a drum roll—"the Très Petits Duck Call Caroling Chorus!"

At that, the Three Wise Men came center stage. They waited for the other children to come out and take their places in the audience. Then, with a look of seriousness on their faces, they took up their duck calls and began to honk out "God Rest Ye, Merry Gentlemen."

Necie pounded the piano keys as loudly as she could to make it sound like a melody was actually somewhere in the room, but the sound of the duck calls overpowered her efforts.

"All right!" Shep hollered out, lifting his hand to conduct.

"Way to go!" Big Shep said.

Watching her son's performance, Kane whispered, "I wish these duck callers were anonymous."

The crowd screamed with laughter. No one had ever heard a Christmas carol on duck calls before. Turner was standing up, holding his side with laughter. Jacques was saying, "Only in Louisiana."

The Duck Call Caroling Chorus finished to wild applause, which they took in stride, even though they betrayed themselves by slapping each other's hands and nodding their heads. "Cool, man. Way cool," Kurt said.

Francis leapt up again. "Boys, what you have done tonight is unforgettable."

"Unforgivable is what it is," George said, but not without a certain degree of wryness. Rosalyn had climbed into his lap, and he was aglow with happiness.

"Last, dear family and friends, but certainly not least, we have for your pleasure on this cold winter's night the Four Original Ya-Yas sharing the stage with a trio of young singers who will soon be breaking out of Thornton and heading out on their world tour of life. Ladies and Gentlemen, I give you the Deux Generational Ya-Ya Noël Songbirds!"

As he was speaking, the Ya-Yas were assembling center stage. Vivi and Teensy gestured for Necie to leave the piano and join them as Francis pulled Caro's chair up next to them and made sure she was settled, her oxygen tank by her side. Then all four Ya-Yas threw their arms out to welcome Caitlin, Dorey, and Alise. Each young girl had added a tiara to her costume, and Vivi, Teensy, and Caro were busy doing the same.

Necie blew on a small pitch pipe, and the seven of them began to sing. The voices of the four aging Ya-Yas melded with the high, pure little girl voices, and what resulted was a vocal gumbo of richness and texture that melted the hardest Christmas-hating heart. Together they sang:

"Have yourself a merry little Christmas,
Let your heart be light.
From now on our troubles will be out of sight.

Have yourself a merry little Christmas,
Make the yuletide gay.
From now on our troubles will be miles away.

Here we are as in olden days,
Happy golden days of yore.
Faithful friends who are dear to us,
Gather near to us, once more.

Through the years we all will be together,
If the fates allow.
Hang a shining star upon the highest bough.

And have yourself a merry little Christmas now."

Baylor smiled and clapped, and then smiled and clapped some more. The three little girls curtsied, then, in unison, gestured to the Ya-Yas, who majestically bowed and gave royal waves.

The pageant was over. And that holy thing which shall be born was coming closer.

Baylor watched Rosalyn as she sat in her grandfather George's lap. She gave him a big surprise kiss on the cheek, which knocked off the crown he had worn.

"Sorry!" she said.

He gazed with love at his granddaughter, whose arms were wrapped tightly around him, and said, "Who needs to be a wise man when you've got an angel in your lap?"

Then, squirming, Rosalyn looked puzzled. She patted her hand underneath her grandfather's arm and said, "Grump got bump!" A look of terror and sadness passed through George's face, but it happened so quickly that Baylor was the only one who caught it. George put Rosalyn down, upon which both Lee-Lee and Joanie took one of Rosalyn's hands.

Lee-Lee looked up at Joanie and said, "Excuse me, please, Miz Joanie, we want to play."

Joanie hesitated for a moment, then let go of her daughter's hand. She took a deep breath, then turned to help the others with bringing out the cornucopia of Louisiana food.

The children's tables were being set with macaroni and cheese, small slices of ham, and a few green beans. Also, there was blue Jell-O with small pieces of fruit in it—Kane's contribution. "I don't know why," she claimed, "but that color blue just wins them over. They stick their fingers in it, then eat it up."

Kurt opened the glass doors that led out to the patio, where the BBQ pit had been set up, and Big Shep called out, "Ta-daaa!" as he brought in the pork tenderloin, warm, sliced on a platter to be put in rolls. Shep followed his father with a smoked beef ribeye, cooked medium rare. The living room was filled with the good garlic smell the ribeye was cooked with, and people oohed and aahed at the progression of the men's cooking.

Melissa brought out mirlitons—vegetable pears—stuffed with shrimp dressing, and dirty rice with chicken livers and gizzards.

"Mais oui!" Chick called out, "the dirtier the better!"

Once the rest of the food had made its way from the kitchen to the dining room, the table groaned with the fruits of the Louisiana earth.

"Enough to feed 84,000 armies!" Vivi said as she surveyed the table. "Thank God I had the good sense to pop out those damn contact lenses and put on my trifocals. Now I can actually see what I'm eating."

The moms gathered the children to their tables, and the grown-ups began filling their plates and sitting on the sofas, love seats, and chairs that filled Baylor and Melissa's living room. The aroma of good cooking was everywhere.

"I love it," Melanie said. "Enough for all of us not to have to cook for days."

They looked around for George, who usually insisted on saying the blessing, but when no one saw him, Big Shep took over.

"Old Padnah, thank you for this good eating and these good friends and family. We bless this food and wish everyone had as much. Rubadubdub please pass the grub."

The children loved that a grown-up would say such a grace and giggled as they began picking on their food. The rest of the crowd ate happily, not missing a beat of conversation. It was one contented bunch.

On the ruse of getting something out of the kitchen, Baylor began searching for George. He stood in front of the kitchen sink and looked out at the sky. It was growing more and more gray. It could really snow, he thought to himself, not without some excitement.

George had not stepped outside. Where was he? Baylor walked in the direction of his large study. His perfectly designed study, with French doors opening to the long back patio. The custom-built bookshelves with glass doors. The perfect brown leather gentleman's chairs. His retreat, his inner sanctum. Everything in its place. The antique globe with the light angled just right on it. The kids were not allowed in there. It was his private place, where he came to think, to write, to call Sidda.

He knew he would find him there. George stood leaning over, bracing himself against Baylor's desk, his body shaking. For a moment, Baylor was afraid the older man was having a heart attack. He waited for a beat before stepping closer, then realized that George was sobbing. George the Judge was sobbing his heart out in Baylor's office.

Baylor stepped to the small wet bar in his study and got George a glass of water. He handed it to the older man, along with a fresh handkerchief, which he took out of one of the desk drawers. He stepped back and waited for George to pull himself together.

When George continued to sob, Baylor took him gently by the elbow and led him to one of the leather club chairs.

"Sit down, Judge," he said. "Take a load off."

Then Baylor turned on the switch for the gas fireplace. A rosy glow filled the room. "Have a few sips of water."

George sipped the water. Then he looked up at Baylor, tears still in his eyes. "Sorry, son. Sorry." Then he started to sob again.

"It's okay," Baylor said. "I've done some crying myself recently in this study."

George glanced around the study. So handsome. So organized. Almost compulsively so. "Fine study you've got here. Everything in its place."

"But it's hard to keep everything in its place, isn't it, Judge?"

George looked at him. "Please don't call me Judge anymore. I'm tired of being a judge."

"All right. Mister Ogden."

"No, call me George. I was a fool for making yall call me Mister Ogden when all the kids called everyone else by their first name or 'Uncle.' I wanted to be the big man. I wanted respect. I was the big man."

Baylor crossed to close the door of his study. It was down a long hall, so they had privacy. When Baylor had added on the study, he had it soundproofed so that no noise from other parts of the house could get in. The two men were, for the moment, insulated from the party.

"Got to tell you something, George," Baylor said, softly. He studied the man in front of him. He realized how much that generation had aged. He looked at George's eyes, red, scared, unspeakably sad. "You've got a firearm on your body. I noticed the bulge in your suit jacket when you arrived. Well disguised with that tailor-made suit, but I spotted it."

Baylor waited for a moment for this to sink in.

"George, I don't allow firearms in my home. You are either going to have to leave it out in your car or give it to me to put in the safe."

A sob came up from deep within George, but he stifled it. He looked out the windows. In a tired voice, he began to speak.

"I've been wearing this thing everywhere since Rosalyn got kidnapped. Necie and I fight about it. I had new suit jackets made so it wouldn't show. Somebody's got to protect these children."

"I know," Baylor said, softly. "I know."

"I can't take this thing off. I'd feel naked."

"Who've you been praying to, sir?"

"To Jesus, Mary, Saint Joseph, Saint Jude, all of them. I've been praying every minute since Rosalyn disappeared."

"And do you think that God doesn't protect Rosalyn? Do you think her guardian angel doesn't protect her? Or Saint Joseph? Or Saint Jude? Or Saint Rose? George, you've been a Catholic for what—"

"Almost seventy years. Since I was baptized when I was two weeks old."

"And you think your God doesn't look out for the little ones most of all?"

George was silent. His head hung down. He let out a painful-sounding sigh. "I used to believe. I don't know what happened."

"You got tired, George. You got pushed. But think about it. You know the Bible better than me. Man, I'm a half-ass agnostic, but I'll tell you this: If there is a God, then He's the one who takes care of them. He's the one who said, Let the little ones come unto me."

George's hands unconsciously assumed the position of prayer.

"I want you to hand me the gun, George."

George's hands went under his arms. He glared at Baylor. "Are you telling me what to do, son?"

"No sir, I am making a request. You hand me the gun, and I'll lock it in my safe. We'll go back into the party, and you drop a load that has been weighing you down. You go back in there with me and participate in our crazy families' crazy Christmas party. You give it up, George."

"I can't. You don't understand."

Baylor stood. "I am a father, too! You are not the only one who was scared shitless by that kidnapping."

Baylor pressed a hidden button, and a wooden panel slid open, revealing a high-tech safe. He punched in the code and opened the steel door.

"You see this safe? It has no gun in it. But it almost did. A thousand times I thought about buying a revolver, even though I've given every hunting rifle I've ever owned to my brother. Protecting my children was all I could think about."

Baylor was sounding angry, not so much at George, but at his own difficulty at containing his emotions.

"I almost lost my mind. I imagined over and over again shooting any son of a bitch who touched my children straight through the heart. I could have lost my family to my own fear. That is the thing, *that is the only thing*, when it comes to protecting children, sir: not to kill them with our own fear.

"George, you know the Saint Joseph Altar at Divine Compassion?"

"I know it well, Baylor."

"Well, not well enough. Saint Joseph is what masculine love is about. It is not about power. It is not about judging. It is about a quiet calm, a quiet love that is the only defense from loss. I don't want to be a knight. I don't want to ride on a white stallion with a spear and a shield. I want to hold my children in my arms. I want my hugs to be their protection. You do what you must, sir, but do not tell me I don't understand. I am not a boy anymore. I am a father. I'm a man. And your own son is a man, even if you don't like his leotards. If you don't hand me that gun in the next moment, I will have to ask you to leave."

Slowly George shifted positions in the chair. He reached into his suit coat, pulled a Glock semiautomatic out of a shoulder holster, and carefully handed it over.

"Shit," Baylor said, looking at the sleek state-of-the-art firearm. "You don't kid around. I couldn't get past a revolver. I guess I'm just a Buckaroo at heart."

"I didn't want a moment to lapse in between shots. I wanted to be able to shoot over and over and over again, no pauses."

"Well, you chose the right weapon. No, let me amend that: you chose the right firearm."

"You are right: I did not choose the right weapon," George said. "No, I didn't." He leaned back in the chair and closed his eyes. "Thank you, son. I want you to know you have my thanks."

Then Judge George Ogden took a deep breath and opened his eyes. He watched as Baylor put the Glock in the safe, reset the code, and pushed the button to slide the wooden panel in front of the safe.

A moment later, Big Shep flung the study door open and walked in, his red flannel bathrobe happily incongruous in the setting. He was carrying a drink in each hand.

"Hey, *Feliz Navidad*. What yall doing back here, talking law?"

George wiped his eyes.

"You okay, George?" Shep asked.

"Fine. Just got something in my eye."

Shep took a sip from his drink and glanced quickly at Baylor, who met his father's gaze head-on.

"What you got is love in your eye," Shep said.

He handed George a crystal glass of Glenlivet neat and said, "Here. Some of your Scotch. Don't know how you stand the stuff."

"Thank you," George said. The two men locked eyes. They had never been close; they could not have been more different. But because of their wives, they had developed a kind of tolerance for each other.

George accepted the glass. Shep saw how badly George's hands were shaking. In an uncharacteristic move, Shep stepped over to George and lightly put his hand on the other man's shoulder.

"It's Christmas, man. We all get shit in our eyes. I used to fight it. Now I just go head-on and let it get to me. Doctor says it's better for my heart. Think about that."

For one fleeting moment, George Ogden put his hand over Shep's, then lifted it.

"Thanks, Walker. I could use a sip or two." George took a small drink of Scotch, then looked from father to son. "You got one fine son here, Shep. I hope you know that."

Shep walked over to Baylor, who was leaning against the wall, where the safe was, watching the two old men. Shep put his arm around Baylor in that gruff Louisiana man way.

"As a matter of fact, I do know. In spite of his parents, he turned out pretty damn good."

"Okay," Baylor said. "This is a party. Let's get back to it."

"Damn well better," Shep said. "I hate to think of what those Ya-Yas could have cooked up while we were in here."

"They move fast, don't they?" George said.

"Hell, George, we've never been able to keep up with them and never will. Knew it when we married them, didn't we?"

George smiled. "I was dumber than you, Shep. I actually thought I would be the boss."

Shep laughed. "Boss a Ya-Ya? Man, you were one blind SOB!"

"In the land of the blind, the one-eyed man is king," George quoted. "Guess that makes you King Shep."

Shep laughed again. "George, you made a joke. You actually made a goddamn joke. I'm going to let the rest of them know it. Next thing I know you'll be a full-blown comedian. Shame Ed Sullivan croaked. You could be on his show."

George looked at Shep and shook his head.

"You bastard," he said.

"Finally. Finally! I got you to cuss," Shep said. "Wonders will never cease."

George looked at Shep. Then he broke into a smile.

"I don't know how I got mixed up with this gang," George said.

"I don't know how I did either," Shep said. "But there's no way out, George-o, no way I'm ready for yet, anyway."

"Hey, old man," Baylor said, "there is no way out, period. You think kicking the bucket lets you out of the Ya-Ya reach, you got it all wrong. This stuff goes beyond the grave, you know what I mean?"

"Yes," George and Shep said at the exact same time.

Just as they were turning to leave the study, Lee-Lee, Rosalyn, and Caitlin burst into the room.

"Hey, yall, it's snowing! Come on! It's really *snowing!*"

Back in the living room, Baylor watched as the French doors to his backyard were flung open. Every child who could run, walk, or toddle was outside, screaming with delight. Snow was actually falling on the Louisiana earth. The adults stood on the patio, watching while the kids went crazy. All except his big brother Shep. Shep was out there, running around, excited as any eight-year-old. The sun had gone down on the land and on the bayous and on the passionflower vine Baylor had covered in case of frost. He flicked on the outdoor lights, which illuminated the snowflakes, making it all the more magical. He took a moment to look at each person there. Every adult, every single child.

"Miz Necie," he heard his father say, "won't you play us a pretty Christmas carol?"

"I'd be happy to, Shep," she said. On her way to the piano, she gave her husband a kiss and squeezed his hand.

Then she sat at the baby grand and began to play "It Came upon a Midnight Clear."

The melody of the ancient song drifted out onto the patio as the grown-ups watched their children play. Can't believe it, Baylor thought. It's actually sticking. It had not snowed in Louisiana for he couldn't remember how long. He took in the sound of the kids yelling and playing and could believe in that moment that angels really were bending near the earth.

Abruptly, the portable phone just inside the patio rang. He'd left it on on purpose. He knew it would be her. After clicking it on, he said, "Hey, Big Sister."

"Hey yourself," Sidda said. "How yall doing? Everybody okay?"

"Sidd-o, we're so much more than okay. It's snowing, do you believe it?"

"You're kidding."

"No, I am not. Necie is playing 'It Came upon a Midnight Clear,' and all the kids are out in the yard going wild, including that overgrown kid, our brother."

"He didn't hit any sliding glass doors on the way outside, did he?" Sidda asked.

"No," Baylor laughed. "Lucked out this time. No trip to the ER."

"So everyone is safe," Sidda said.

"We're safer than we'll ever be, Sidda. The only thing we don't have is stars. But you can't have snow and stars at the same time. But you know what? You're the only one I could tell this to: it feels like there are stars inside each one of us. Like some clean light has come down through our heads and rubbed our hearts spotless so light is coming out of our heads and our feet. When I look out at the kids, it's like they are fireflies, each one of them giving off light. And when I close my eyes like I'm doing right now, for just one second, I can see a circle of light around all of us. Do I sound drunk?"

"You do sound intoxicated," Sidda said, "like a man who knows he's already in heaven."

"Hah!" Baylor laughed, crying at the same time. "I am in heaven. Right here in Thornton, Louisiana. Right here with my family and the crazy Ya-Ya tribe and the one hundred and fifty wild daffodil bulbs I planted, which are cozy underneath the earth, all safe till they bloom in spring."

"I love you, Baylor," Sidda said. "Merry Christmas."

"I love you, Sidd-o."

"I wish Connor and I were there."

"You're here. Right here in my heart."

When Baylor and Sidda signed off, he held the phone to him, as though he could embrace his sister long-distance.

Then he stepped out into the yard, gathered up a handful of snow, snuck up behind his brother, and put it down the back of his jacket.

Shep turned around. "Are you crazy, little brother?! You know what I could do to you?"

"Yeah," Baylor said. "I'm crazy. What you gonna do about it?"

Shep shook the snow out from under his clothes, then turned to his little brother and wrapped him in a huge bear hug.

From the patio, they could hear their mother's voice saying, "Hug him! Kiss him! Hug him! Kiss him! The Baby Jesus just loves hugs and kisses!"

It came to pass in December 1994, in Thornton, Louisiana, that the tribe of Ya-Yas and those they had begot felt a star shining inside them. Those who had feared for the safety of their children and their grandchildren, for the safety of their own souls and bodies, felt perfectly safe, held in the arms of love, divine love that knows no bounds, and human love with all its flaws. In Baylor's garden, which was asleep for the winter, new life sprang forth, and a gathering of fragile creatures knew without a doubt they were a flock being watched over by night.

ACKNOWLEDGMENTS

Heartfelt gratitude to:

Thomas Schworer, Jr., my co-creator in love and work.

Kim Witherspoon, my agent, whose deep wisdom, compassion, and intelligence has guided me through countless storms.

Neil Rabitoy and Barbara Connor, who helped me cross many thresholds.

Meaghan Dowling, my first-class editor and champion at HarperCollins.

Mary Helen Clarke, whose editorial eye with part of the book was of much assistance.

Wayne Richardson-Harp, Louisiana raconteur and the best friend a Southern writer could have.

Susan Ronn, my own best Ya-Ya, whose friendship is constant and whose astute reading of the manuscript was a great gift.

And to these essential ones:

My agent's fabulous associate, David Forrer, and the wonderful staff at Witherspoon Associates; Brenda Hafer, webmistress extraordinaire, and the Ya-Ya.com Sisterhood; T.O. Wells, Tom Sr. and Barbara Schworer, Wendy Best, Donna Lambdin, T. Gibson, Zelda Long and the memory of Cary Long, Toni Carmichael and Gary Larson, Kitty, Carl, (and Pierre) of Le Club Riff-Raff, Peg Maas, Corrie Moore, Leta Rose Scott, Mark Lawless, George Sheanshang, Miranda Ottewell, Rome Quezada, Mary Stien, the Rev. Lauren Artress and Veriditas, who introduced me to the power of walking the Labyrinth; Sue Bucy and her tribe of prayerful players, Bruce Hornbuckle, Steve Coenen, Ann New, Darrell Jaimeson, Nancy Chambers Richards, Sally and John Renn, Marta and David Maxwell, Nans and Bob Metts, D. Buscher, Bernard Fouke, Marian Wood, Ken Boynton, Julie and Bard Richmond, Jon Kabat-Zinn, whose work inspires me daily; Pat Conroy, Fannie Flagg, John O'Donohue, and Barbara Kingsolver, big-hearted writers who gave me counsel and kindness; Willie Mae Lowe and family; the mama and baby whales in the Maui waters, and the herons near my home on Puget Sound.

And, always: The Holy Lady and her band of tireless angels.

Virginia

Rosalyn Hammond

Rose Ogden

Melanie Ogden

Malissa Ogden

Annie Ogden

Joanie Ogden + Grove Hammond

Francis "Frank" Ogden

Denise "Necie" Rose Kelleher + George Ogden

Francis P. Kelleher + Rose Kelleher

Necie's Family
+ = Married
⊤ = Children

Illustrated

Jack Claiborne

Genevieve Claiborne

Jacques "Ruffin" Claiborne + Sophia

Genny Claiborne

Genevieve "Teensy" Whitman + Chick Claiborne

Jack Whitman

Newton S. Whitman III + Genevieve Aimee St. Clair Whitman

Teensy's Family
+ = Married
⁚ = Children

aura Hartman Maestro © 2004